LODESTAR

Also by Shannon Messenger

The KEEPER OF THE LOST CITIES Series
Keeper of the Lost Cities
Exile
Everblaze
Neverseen
Nightfall
Flashback

The SKY FALL Series
Let the Sky Fall
Let the Storm Break
Let the Wind Rise

KEEPER OF THE LOST CITIES

LODESTAR

SHANNON MESSENGER

Aladdin

New York   London   Toronto   Sydney   New Delhi

ALADDIN

An imprint of Simon & Schuster Children's Publishing Division
1230 Avenue of the Americas, New York, NY 10020
First Aladdin hardcover edition November 2016
Text copyright © 2016 by Shannon Messenger
Jacket illustration copyright © 2016 by Jason Chan
All rights reserved, including the right of reproduction in whole or in part in any form.
ALADDIN is a trademark of Simon & Schuster, Inc., and related logo
is a registered trademark of Simon & Schuster, Inc.
For information about special discounts for bulk purchases, please contact
Simon & Schuster Special Sales at 1-866-506-1949 or business@simonandschuster.com.
The Simon & Schuster Speakers Bureau can bring authors to your live event.
For more information or to book an event contact the Simon & Schuster Speakers Bureau
at 1-866-248-3049 or visit our website at www.simonspeakers.com.
Jacket designed by Karin Paprocki
Interior designed by Mike Rosamilia
The text of this book was set in Scala.
Manufactured in the United States of America 1020 FFG
8 10 9
This book has been cataloged with the Library of Congress.
ISBN 978-1-4814-7495-5 (hc)
ISBN 978-1-4814-7497-9 (eBook)

For Katie and Jo,
who bring new meaning to the words
"above and beyond"

LODESTAR

PREFACE

THIS IS WHAT THEY WANT.

The words tumbled through Sophie's mind as she raced up the spiral staircase, counting her steps, trying to guess which door to take.

The first handle she tried was locked.

Another opened into darkness.

A third revealed a path that glowed with eerie blue balefire sconces.

The floor shook as she hesitated and threads of dust slipped through the ceiling, scratching her throat and making it hurt to breathe.

She followed the flames.

Back and forth the halls snaked—a careful maze, designed to deceive. Swallow. Separate.

The tremors grew with every step, the shifting subtle but unmistakable.

And too far away.

No one else would feel the ripples swelling, like waves gathering speed.

They were too focused on their celebration.

Too caught up in their imagined victory.

Too trusting.

Too blind.

Too late.

The ground rattled harder, the first fissures crackling the stones.

This is what they want.

ONE

THIS IS A SECURITY NIGHTMARE!" Sandor grumbled, keeping his huge gray hand poised over his enormous black sword.

His squeaky voice reminded Sophie more of a talking mouse than a deadly bodyguard.

Several prodigies raced past, and Sandor pulled Sophie closer as the giggling group jumped to pop the candy-filled bubbles floating near the shimmering crystal trees. All around them, kids were running through the confetti-covered atrium in their amber-gold Level Three uniforms, capes flying as they caught snacks and bottles of lushberry juice and stuffed tinsel-wrapped gifts into the long white thinking caps dangling from everyone's lockers.

The Midterms Celebration was a Foxfire Academy tradition—hardly the impending doom Sandor was imagining. And yet, Sophie understood his concern.

Every parent roaming the streamer-lined halls.

Every face she didn't recognize.

Any of them could be a rebel.

A villain.

The enemy.

Sandor watched Sophie tug on her eyelashes—her nervous habit, back in full force. "Nothing is going to happen," he promised, tucking her blond hair behind her ear with a surprisingly gentle touch for a seven-foot-tall goblin warrior.

It definitely helped having Sandor back at her side—especially after almost losing him during the battle on Mount Everest. And Sandor wasn't the only goblin at Foxfire anymore. Each of the six wings in the main campus building had been assigned its own patrol, with two additional squadrons keeping watch over the sprawling grounds.

The Council had also added security throughout the Lost Cities.

They had to.

The ogres were still threatening war.

And in the three weeks since Sophie and her friends had returned from hiding with the Black Swan, the Neverseen had scorched the main gate of the Sanctuary *and* broken into the registry in Atlantis.

Sophie could guess what the rebels had hoped to gain from the elves' secret animal preserve—they obviously didn't know that she'd convinced the Council to set the precious alicorns free. But the registry attack remained a mystery. The Council-lors kept careful records on every elf ever born, and no one would tell her if any files had been altered or stolen.

A bubble popped on Sophie's head, and Sandor caught the box of Prattles that had been hovering inside.

"If you're going to eat these, I should check them first," he told her.

Sandor's wide, flat nose scented no toxins in the nutty candy, but he insisted on examining the pin before handing them over. Every box of Prattles came with a special collectible inside, and in the past, the Black Swan had used them to send Sophie messages.

He fished out the tiny velvet pouch and Sophie caught her-self clutching her allergy remedy necklace. She still kept the silver moonlark pin that Calla had given her attached to the cord—a reminder of the friend she'd lost, and a symbol of the role she needed to figure out how to play.

"Looks like we're good," Sandor said, handing her the small boobrie pin—a strange black bird with bright yellow tail feath-ers. "Can't imagine *that* means anything important."

Sophie couldn't either. Especially since the Black Swan had been annoyingly silent.

No notes. No clues. No answers during their brief meetings.

Apparently they were "regrouping." And it was taking forever.

At least the Council was doing *something*—setting up goblin patrols and trying to arrange an ogre Peace Summit. The Black Swan should at least be . . .

Actually, Sophie didn't know what they should be doing.

That was the problem with having her friend join the enemy.

"There you are!" a familiar voice said behind her. "I was starting to think you'd ditched us."

The deep, crisp accent was instantly recognizable. And yet, the teasing words made Sophie wish she'd turn and find a different boy.

Fitz looked as cute as ever in his red Level Five uniform, but his perfect smile didn't reach his trademark teal eyes. The recent revelations had been a huge blow for all of her friends, but Fitz had taken it the hardest.

Both his brother and his best friend had run off with the Neverseen.

Alvar's betrayal had made Fitz wary—made him doubt every memory.

But Keefe's?

He wouldn't talk about it—at *all*.

Not that Sophie had many chances to bring up the subject. Only a handful of people knew the truth. The rest believed the Black Swan's carefully crafted lie, and thought Keefe was taking time away to mourn his mother's disappearance. Even the

Council had no inkling, and Sophie hoped it would stay that way. The less everyone knew, the easier it would be for Keefe to come home.

If he came home.

"You okay?" Fitz asked, making her realize she'd forgotten to say hello. "I hope you're not worrying about your tests. There's no way you didn't pass."

"I don't know . . ."

Her photographic memory *helped*—but lately she'd struggled to concentrate during her school sessions. Honestly, though, she'd barely given her midterms a second thought. She wasn't the same girl she'd been the year before, who thought failing out of Foxfire would be the end of the world. Now she'd been kidnapped, presumed dead, banished from the Lost Cities, and helped stop a plague from killing off the entire gnomish species. She'd even snuck into the ogres' capital and helped destroy half the city—which happened to be why the Council was struggling to negotiate a new elvin-ogre treaty.

"Relax," Fitz said as her mind spun to nightmares of lumpy-faced ogres tearing through the elves' glittering streets. "We're supposed to be celebrating."

His cheer sounded forced. But she knew Fitz was trying.

That's what they did now.

Try.

Wait.

Hope.

"Just let me grab my thinking cap," she told him, heading for her locker. The long floppy hat was required during midterms, designed to restrict Telepaths and preserve the integrity of the tests—not that anything could block Sophie's enhanced abilities. But after the exams, the hats became present sacks, and everyone filled them with treats and trinkets and treasures.

"I'll need to inspect your presents before you open them," Sandor warned as he helped Sophie lift her overstuffed hat.

"That's perfect," Fitz said. "While he does that, you can open mine."

He pulled a small box from the pocket of his waist-length cape and handed it to Sophie. The opalescent wrapping paper had flecks of teal glitter dusted across it, and he'd tied it with a silky teal bow, making her wonder if he'd guessed her favorite color.

She really hoped he couldn't guess why. . . .

"Hopefully I did better this year," Fitz said. "Biana claimed the riddler was a total fail."

The riddle-writing pen he'd given her last time *had* been a disappointment, but . . .

"I'm sure I'll love it," Sophie promised. "Besides. My gift is boring."

Sandor had declared an Atlantis shopping trip to be far too risky, so Sophie had spent the previous day baking her friends' presents.

She handed Fitz a round silver tin and he popped the lid off immediately.

"Ripplefluffs?" he asked, smiling his first real smile in days.

The silver-wrapped treats were what might happen if a brownie and a cupcake had a fudgey, buttery baby, with a candy surprise sunken into the center. Sophie's adoptive mother, Edaline, had taught her the recipe and helped her invent two flavor combinations.

"How did you know that chocolate and mint is my favorite?" Fitz asked, peeling off the silver wrapper and devouring the whole fluff in one bite.

"I didn't," Sophie admitted. "If I had, I wouldn't have given you any of the butter toffee ones."

"Those look amazing too," he said, then frowned at his present. "Aren't you going to open it?"

"Shouldn't I wait until we're with the others?"

"Nah. It'll be better if it's just the two of us."

Something about the way he said it made her heart switch to flutter mode, even though she knew Fitz didn't think of her that way. Her mind raced through a dozen theories as she carefully tore the shimmering paper. But she still wasn't prepared to find . . .

"Rings?"

"They go on your thumbs," Fitz explained. "It's a Cognate thing."

She wasn't sure what thumb jewelry had to do with their

rare telepathic connection. But she noticed Fitz was wearing an identical set. Each ring had initials stamped into the verdigris metal. *SEF* on the right—Sophie Elizabeth Foster—and *FAV* on the left.

"Fitzroy Avery Vacker."

"Your full name is Fitzroy?" she asked.

"Yeah. No idea what my parents were thinking with that one. But watch this. Try opening your thoughts to mine, and then do this."

He held his hands palm-out, waiting for her to do the same.

As soon as she did, the rings turned warm against her skin and snapped their hands together like magnets.

"They're made from ruminel," Fitz said, "which reacts to mental energy. It doesn't change anything, but it'll show us when our minds are connected, and I thought it would help us concentrate and . . ." His voice trailed off. "You hate them, don't you?"

"Of course not!"

She liked them a little too much, actually.

She was just trying not to show it.

There were a lot of kids staring at them.

And whispering.

And giggling.

Fitz twisted his palms, breaking the rings' connection. "I guess I should've gone with the necklace Biana showed me. You just have so many necklaces—and the last one you got . . ."

He didn't finish the sentence.

It would've meant mentioning Keefe.

"I'm glad you got me these. Seriously. They're my fave." She pointed to the "FAV."

That earned her another smile, and Fitz brushed his dark hair off his forehead. "Come on, I'm sure Dex and Biana are getting sick of waiting for us."

"Where did Grizel go?" Sandor asked as they turned to leave. "She's supposed to stay by your side."

"I'm right here," a husky female voice said as a lithe gray goblin in a fitted black jumpsuit seemed to melt out of the shadows. Fitz's bodyguard was just as tall as Sandor, but far leaner—and what she lacked in bulk she made up for in stealth and grace.

"I swear," she said, tapping Sandor on the nose. "It's almost too easy to evade you."

"Anyone can hide in this chaos," Sandor huffed. "And now is not the time for games!"

"There's always time for games." Grizel tossed her long ponytail in a way that almost seemed . . . Was it flirty?

Sandor must've noticed too, because his gray skin tinted pink. He cleared his throat and turned to Sophie. "Weren't we heading to the cafeteria?"

She nodded and followed Fitz into the mazelike halls, where the colorful crystal walls shimmered in the afternoon sunlight. The cafeteria was on the second floor of the campus's five-story glass pyramid, which sat in the center of the courtyard framed by the U-shaped main building.

Sophie spent most of the walk wondering how long it would take Dex to notice her new accessories. The answer was three seconds—and another after that to notice the matching rings on Fitz's thumbs.

His periwinkle eyes narrowed, but he kept his voice cheerful as he said, "I guess we're all giving rings this year."

Biana held out her hand to show Sophie a ring that looked familiar—probably because Sophie had a less sparkly, slightly more crooked, definitely less pink version on her own finger.

"I also made one for you," Dex told Fitz. "It's in your thinking cap. And I have some for Tam and Linh, whenever we see them again. That way we'll all have panic switches—and I added stronger trackers, so I can home in on the signal even if you don't press your stone. Just in case anything weird happens."

"Your Technopath tricks aren't necessary," Sandor told him, pointing to their group of bodyguards—four goblins in all.

"But it's still good to have a backup plan, right?" Biana asked, admiring her ring from another angle. The pink stone matched the glittery shadow she'd brushed around her teal eyes, as well as the gloss on her heart-shaped lips. Biana reminded Sophie of the dolls her human parents had tried to get her to play with as a kid—too beautiful and stylish to be real.

"Thank you again," Biana told Dex. "I'm never taking it off!"

Dex's cheeks turned the same color as his strawberry-blond hair.

Sophie smiled, glad to see Dex and Biana getting along so well—especially after all the years Dex had spent resenting the Vackers. He used to call Fitz "Wonderboy" and claimed their legendary family was too snobby and perfect.

Nobody thought that anymore.

In fact, both Fitz's and Biana's thinking caps looked emptier than they'd been the previous year. Their parents had decided not to let the Black Swan cover for Alvar's disappearance like they'd done for Keefe. Alvar had lied for more than a decade and used his position in the nobility to spy on his father and the Council—and helped kidnap Sophie and Dex. He didn't deserve protection, even if it brought undeserved shame on the family.

Awkward silence settled over their table and Sophie tried not to look at the empty chairs. Not only was Keefe missing, but Jensi had chosen to sit with his old friends. He'd reconnected with them during the months that Sophie and the others had lived with the Black Swan, and he seemed reluctant to come back, like he was worried they'd abandon him again. Marella was avoiding them too—though she also wasn't at Stina Heks's table, like Sophie would've expected. Marella sat by herself in the farthest corner, while Stina sat with Biana's former best friend, Maruca.

Stina caught Sophie watching her and didn't return her

smile—but she didn't offer her usual glare either. Apparently that was as nice as Stina was going to get, now that her dad was working with the Black Swan.

"Here," Dex said, placing a white box into Sophie's hands. "Made this for you—and sorry it's not wrapped. Rex and Bex used up all the ribbon tying Lex to a chandelier."

Dex's younger triplet siblings were notorious troublemakers. Sophie had a feeling the loudest shouting on the other end of the cafeteria was coming from them. And she'd expected to open the box and find another Dex-ified gadget. But his gift reminded her that he was also an amazing alchemist.

"You made me Panakes perfume?" she asked, shaking the fragile crystal bottle and watching the pinkish-purplish-bluish petals swirl through the shimmering syrup.

She twisted open the top and closed her eyes as she inhaled the rich, sweet fragrance. Instantly she was back in the Havenfield pastures, standing under the swaying branches of Calla's tree. A Panakes only grew when a gnome willingly surrendered their life and shifted into their final tree form. Calla had made the sacrifice for her people, to let her healing blossoms end the deadly plague the ogres had unleashed.

"I'm sure you smell them all the time," Dex said, "but I know how much you miss her. And this way, when you wear the perfume, you're keeping a small part of her with you everywhere you go."

Sophie's voice failed her, so she grabbed Dex and hugged him as tight as she could—but she *might've* held on a bit too long. When she let go, Dex was redder than Fitz's school uniform.

They were saved from the awkwardness by the doors to the cafeteria bursting open.

Despite her earlier calm, Sophie's palms turned clammy as she searched the flood of parents for Grady and Edaline. She spotted Grady's tousled blond hair first, and as soon as his bright blue eyes met hers, his chiseled features curved with an enormous smile.

"Passed with flying colors," he and Edaline both shouted as Sophie raced across the room to meet them.

She threw her arms around both her parents. "Even linguistics?"

That had been her iffyest subject—by far. Being a Polyglot made her naturally understand languages, but after the trick Keefe had pulled, Sophie refused to practice mimicking voices. Plus, her relationship with her Mentor was . . . complicated. Lady Cadence had a special affinity for the ogres, and was *not* happy with Sophie for helping flood the ogre capital.

"That was your lowest score," Edaline admitted, shaking a piece of her wavy amber-colored hair out of her eyes. "But you were still well within passing range."

"And your highest score was inflicting," Grady added. "Councillor Bronte said you've been incredibly dedicated during your sessions. In fact, he said you've now reached his most advanced level of training."

"Is that bad?" Sophie asked, not missing his raised eyebrow. She didn't *like* inflicting pain—but the ability had saved her life. And training at least gave her *something* she could do to prepare for the next time she faced off with the Neverseen. "I just want to make sure I can defend myself—and I know I have Sandor. But it's not like he's invincible. Isn't it smart to plan for the worst-case scenario?"

"It *is* smart," Grady agreed. "But I also think you and I should talk later. Okay?"

Sophie gave him half a nod. The last thing she wanted was another "with great power comes great responsibility" lecture. But she was pretty sure it was unavoidable.

"Do you guys want to go?" she asked, knowing her parents weren't fans of crowds. Before she'd moved in with them, Grady and Edaline had spent sixteen years hiding away, mourning the death of their only daughter. Jolie had been killed in a fire they'd recently discovered was set by her fiancé, Brant—a secret Pyrokinetic, and a leader of the Neverseen.

"We're fine," Grady promised, squeezing Sophie's hand. "And we can't leave until Magnate Leto makes his final announcement."

He said the name so easily, without tripping over it the way Sophie tended to. Now that she knew his secret identity, her brain always wanted to call him *Mr. Forkle*.

Sophie scanned the room to check for her friends and found them smiling and celebrating. Even Alden and Della—Fitz and Biana's parents—looked happier than she'd seen them in weeks. She was on her way to say hi when the lights dimmed and Magnate Leto's face projected across the glass walls.

"You kids did an excellent job on your midterms!" he said, starting his speech with his two favorite words.

No matter how many times Sophie studied his slicked dark hair and sharp features, she still couldn't see the bloated, wrinkled face of the Black Swan leader behind them. But she'd watched Mr. Forkle's ruckleberry disguise fade right before her eyes.

"I realize this is usually the point where you're dismissed for a six-week break," Magnate Leto continued, "but in light of recent events, the Council has elected to do things a bit differently. I won't go into further details—the Council will be sending out official scrolls after the weekend. But I wanted to mention it now so you'd be prepared. In the meantime, enjoy the rest of the celebration. And remember, change can be a powerful, inspiring thing when we keep an open mind."

Murmurs turned to a roar as his projection flashed away, leaving everyone debating possibilities.

"Do you have any idea what he's talking about?" Grady asked Sophie.

She didn't—and that made it even more frustrating. After all the debates she'd had with the Black Swan, all her endless pleas for them to include her and trust her, they still insisted on keeping her at arm's length.

"Looks like everyone's heading home," Grady said, offering to gather up Sophie's gifts while she returned her thinking cap to her locker.

The atrium was empty when she arrived—just Sophie and Sandor and a few forgotten candy bubbles. She left her hat on the middle shelf of her locker and was about to walk away when she noticed a white envelope bearing a familiar curved black symbol on the top shelf.

"Finally," she whispered, ripping the thick paper right through the sign of the swan.

Inside she found a short note—and a gift.

She slipped the long necklace around her neck, not bothering to inspect the pendant's swan-neck shape, or the round piece of glass set in the center. The Black Swan had given her the same monocle when she swore fealty to their order, and she was glad to have a replacement for the one Brant had destroyed.

"What does the note say?" Sandor asked, reminding her that she would not be sneaking off for secret assignments without him.

She handed him the paper, which was more direct than the Black Swan's usual clues:

Principal's office.
Now.
Come alone.

"I don't like this," Sandor mumbled.

"You never do."

He followed her without further comment as she made her way back to the glass pyramid. Sophie kept her eyes down as she walked, relieved when she reached the apex without running into her friends. If they'd known about the note they would've *insisted* on joining her.

"You may come in, Miss Foster," Magnate Leto's deep voice called through the heavy door before Sophie could even knock. "But I'd like Sandor to keep watch outside. This conversation cannot tolerate eavesdroppers."

Sandor's sigh sounded like a snarl. "I'll be *right* outside—and if you leap away without me, there will be *consequences*."

"Close the door behind you," Magnate Leto told her as she entered, the words echoing around the glass office.

Afternoon sunlight streamed through the windows, turning the triangular room blindingly bright. The sloped glass walls had mirrors set into every other pane, remnants from the days when Councillor Alina—Sophie's least favorite Councillor—was principal of Foxfire.

"I'm glad you came," Magnate Leto said from the other side of his huge swiveling desk chair. He was turned toward the windows, hidden behind the stiff winged-back cushion. "Sorry my note was so hasty. Next time I'll make sure it rhymes."

The last few words sounded higher pitched, and Sophie was

trying to figure out why when the chair slowly spun around to face her.

Instead of the dark-haired elf she'd been expecting, she found a boy dressed all in black, with artfully styled blond hair and an infamous talent for mimicking voices.

"Keefe?" she whispered.

He smirked. "Did you miss me?"

TWO

WHOA, THAT IS AN EPIC wave of emotions you're hitting me with," Keefe said, fanning the air between them. "It feels like you either want to hug me or strangle me—and personally, I'm rooting for the hug."

He leaned back in the chair, stretching his arms wide open.

"You're really going to joke about this?" Sophie asked, trying to keep her voice low. She didn't want Sandor bursting in until she'd gotten some answers.

"Don't come any closer," she warned as Keefe stood to approach her. "I've been practicing inflicting. A *lot*."

One hand moved to her stomach, rubbing the knot of

emotions lodged under her ribs. Bronte was teaching her to tie them away, ready to unravel whenever she needed a burst of furious power.

Keefe's smile faded. "Are you *afraid* of me?"

"You're the Empath."

The words hung there for several seconds, turning heavier and heavier.

Keefe sank back into his chair. "Wow . . . I didn't expect that."

"What *did* you expect? You ran off with the Neverseen! You realize those are the people trying to kill me, right? The same people who killed Kenric and Jolie, and almost killed all of the gnomes and—"

"I *know*," Keefe interrupted. "But you know me, Foster."

"I thought I did."

"You *do*. I'm still the same guy. All I'm trying to do is end this nightmare. If I can figure out what they're planning—"

"Nope," Sophie jumped in. "Worst idea ever. Playing both sides never works. Sooner or later they're going to make you *commit*."

Keefe shifted in his seat. "I realize that what I'm doing is risky—"

"And stupid," Sophie added. "And dangerous. And—"

"I still have to do it. And it'll be fine. It's all about keeping the right balance."

"There's no *balance* when it comes to the bad guys, Keefe. They're bad. It's that simple."

"You and I both know it's *never* simple. In fact, I seem to remember you telling me that the villains are never *all* bad."

"I didn't say that because I wanted you to join them! I said that's what makes them so scary!"

"I know. But . . . I have a plan. I have to stick to it."

His ice-blue eyes met hers, pleading for understanding.

She shook her head. "We can beat them together. Team Foster-Keefe, remember?"

"And how many times will you almost die in the process?" he asked. "How many emergency physician visits will there be? And what if Elwin can't fix you?"

"What if Elwin can't fix *you?*"

"I . . . don't matter."

And there it was.

Keefe's *guilt.*

The most dangerous emotion an elf could feel.

Most were crippled by it. Alden's sanity had once shattered because of it. But for some people it made them *reckless.*

"It's not your job to protect me," she told him.

"Maybe not. But if something happens . . ."

She waited for him to say the rest—the real reason he felt so responsible. When he didn't, she said it for him.

"I know you blame yourself for what your mom's done—"

"This isn't about her!"

But it was.

Sophie knew him too well.

Keefe's family life had always been miserable, thanks to his stiff, insulting father. But he'd been on a downward spiral ever since he'd discovered that his mom was one of the leaders of the Neverseen. She'd even erased some of his childhood memories and hidden a tracker in his family crest pin so he'd lead the Neverseen straight to his friends. But that was all before the Neverseen left her to die in an ogre prison as punishment for allowing one of her cohorts to be captured.

Keefe kept claiming he didn't care. But Lady Gisela was still his mom—and he'd joined the Neverseen right after he found out they might be willing to help him rescue her.

"Please," Sophie begged. "We can do anything they can do. Just come home—before it's too late."

"It's already too late."

His voice was the same flat tone he'd used before, when he'd told her *I can't pretend I'm who you want me to be anymore.*

"So this is about the Lodestar Initiative, then?" she asked.

She'd only heard the mysterious project mentioned twice— once from the Neverseen and once in Keefe's mind, in a memory his mother had tried to erase. It seemed to be the Neverseen's grand plan. And Keefe believed he was a part of it.

Keefe stood to pace the small room, keeping a careful space between them.

"What *is* the Lodestar Initiative?" she pressed. "And what other lost memories did you recover? You said there were more."

"It doesn't matter."

"Obviously it does."

Keefe tilted his head toward the ceiling, his eyes focused on the highest point. "All you need to know is that I'm not like you, okay? The Neverseen aren't going to give me a choice."

Sophie was part of a project too—the Black Swan's Project Moonlark. They'd genetically enhanced her abilities and filled her mind with important secrets for reasons they'd still never fully explained. But Mr. Forkle had always made it clear that any further involvement was up to *her*.

"There's always a choice, Keefe."

"Yeah—I'm going to find a way to end this on *my* terms. *That's* my choice."

Silence swelled between them, and Sophie played with the monocle pendant he'd included with the note. "Was this the one that Brant ordered you to brand me with?"

Keefe cringed. "No. That one's mine. I stole it back."

"What happens when they notice it's gone?"

He shrugged.

She sighed. "This is never going to work, Keefe. Brant and Fintan are crazy—but they're not stupid. Neither is Alvar. One of them is going to figure out what you're doing, and then who knows how they'll punish you? Just quit now and we'll come up with a new plan together."

She offered him her hand.

Keefe stared at it for so long Sophie's arm muscles began to ache.

"That's it?" she asked when he turned away. "You'd rather keep hurting the people who care about you?"

"I'm helping you!"

"And hurting us. Do you know what Fitz did when I told him you left?"

Keefe ran his hands through his hair, wrecking his careful style. "I'm guessing yelling was involved."

"That's what I'd been hoping for. But he didn't even raise his voice. He just looked away so I wouldn't see him crying. So did Biana. Even Dex teared up."

Seconds ticked by. Maybe minutes. It felt like forever before Keefe whispered, "What about you?"

"I cried harder than any of them," she admitted. "And then I got angry. You stole Kenric's cache from me. You mimicked my voice!"

The marble-size gadget held seven Forgotten Secrets—information deemed too dangerous for even the Council to know. Each Councillor had their own cache, and Kenric had asked Oralie to entrust Sophie with his when he died. Sophie had vowed to protect the cache with her life, and if she didn't get it back before the Council discovered it was missing . . .

"I also helped you escape," Keefe reminded her.

"Yeah, but you only made me one special bead. So what happens the next time the Neverseen find me? Or Dex? Or Fitz? Or Biana?"

"I'll find another way. I'm already working on a few things. And I only rigged one bead because I knew the Neverseen wouldn't fall for the same trick twice."

"I love how you keep talking about them like you're not one of them now."

"I'm *not*."

"Are you sure?"

She pointed to the patch on the sleeves of his long black cloak, the same symbol that kept haunting her nightmares—a white eye set in a circle.

"This is just a costume," Keefe insisted.

"Even if it is, the things you're doing are *real*. That cache could destroy everything. And you handed it over like it was no big deal—"

"Because it wasn't! They can't open it. They've had all their Technopaths working on it, and they can't break through the security."

"And when they finally figure it out?"

"I'll steal it back long before that happens. I can handle this, Sophie. It's my *legacy*."

"What does that mean?"

"I'm still putting all the pieces together. But I know enough to know I have to do this. And my plan is already working. Every day they're trusting me a little bit more."

"Why is that?" she snapped. "What horrible things are they making you do to prove yourself?"

Keefe tried to pace again, but she blocked his path. "Did you help them break into the registry?"

"Of course not."

"Because they didn't ask you? Or because you told them 'no'?"

His fidgeting made her wish she didn't have to ask her next question.

"What about the Sanctuary?"

The Neverseen had spent months trying to break into the animal preserve to steal Silveny and Greyfell—the only known alicorns, who also happened to be Sophie and Keefe's friends.

"You were there, weren't you?" she asked when he moved away from her. "You helped the Neverseen burn the gate?"

"All I did was keep watch."

She shook her head. "How could you be a part of that?"

The Neverseen were willing to risk anything to steal Silveny. They'd even broken one of her wings. All because the elves believed that allowing a creature to go extinct would throw off the delicate balance of the entire planet. Whoever controlled the last two alicorns—and their unborn baby—could blackmail the Council. They'd also prove to the world how little the Council could do to protect something it cherished, and fuel the unrest threatening to boil over.

"I knew Silveny and Greyfell weren't there anymore," Keefe argued. "That's the only reason I agreed. And in case you're wondering, I haven't told the Neverseen *anything*."

"*Yet,*" Sophie corrected. "Even if you don't tell them, they can use a Telepath to fish out all of your secrets."

"They don't have a Telepath right now. Gethen was their only one, and the Council has him locked away—thanks to *us.* I'm telling you, I've thought this through. I just need you to trust me."

She wanted to.

She really did.

She'd even done her best to convince Fitz, Dex, and Biana to not give up on him.

But she could still hear the Neverseen telling Keefe: *Surely you've realized that switching sides means betraying your friends.*

"Please," Keefe begged. "I promise, I'm still me. And I can do this."

He took a cautious step toward her.

Then another.

And another.

Until he was right in front of her, his lips curling with the world's saddest smile.

"Back to nervous habits, huh?" he asked as he brushed a fallen eyelash off her cheek.

"It's been a rough few weeks," she whispered.

"Yeah. It really has."

He blew the eyelash away and she wondered if he'd made a wish—until she remembered that elves didn't have silly superstitions like that.

She probably shouldn't either, but she went ahead and sent a silent plea into the universe.

"You're not still afraid of me, are you?" he asked. "You trust me?"

She honestly didn't know. So she offered him a shaky hand. "You tell me."

Keefe's fingers curled around hers and his brow creased as he closed his eyes.

"Thank you," he whispered, his lips stretching into a glorious smile. "I knew I could count on you, Foster."

"Don't make me regret it."

"I won't. That's why I came here today—I had to find a way to warn you. The Neverseen are planning something big. I don't know any specifics yet, but I know it involves Grady and Edaline and—whoa, easy there." He steadied her when her knees wobbled. "It's going to be okay. See why I'm doing this? I can stop things *before* they get bad."

Sophie took a slow, deep breath, trying to remind herself that Grady's ability as a Mesmer gave him an incredible advantage. She'd seen him make all twelve Councillors smack themselves in the face. He'd even made Brant burn off his own hand.

But the Neverseen were ruthless.

And clever.

And always ahead of the game.

Which made her realize . . .

"You can't go back there, Keefe. Today was probably a test. I bet they gave you that information to see if you'd sneak away to warn me. They could be tracking you right now—what?" she asked when she noticed how hard he was biting his lip.

"It's not a test. They . . . *sent* me here."

"Why would they do that?"

Keefe's eyes returned to the ceiling. "Probably because I suggested it. I needed a way to warn you—and they needed me to prove my loyalty. This was the best solution I could come up with."

Cold chills washed through Sophie as he removed two items from his cloak pocket—a flat golden triangle and a blue pendant with a single facet.

"This next part is going to be rough," he whispered. "But if you cover your face, I promise you'll be safe. And just in case . . ." He unfastened his cloak and wrapped it around her shoulders, pulling the hood up over her head. "I'll tell them I lost this in the chaos."

"What chaos, Keefe? What are you doing?"

"I'm helping you. Sometimes things have to get worse before they get better."

Sophie tried to shout for Sandor, but Keefe covered her mouth with one hand and flung the golden triangle toward the ceiling with the other. One of the points stuck to the center of the apex and the gadget flashed green.

"That means we have ten seconds." Keefe said. "Just get down and cover your face—everything is going to be okay.

Sandor will be safe. Goblins have super-thick skin—just trust me, okay?"

He pulled his hand back, but Sophie was shaking too hard to scream. She dropped to her knees and pulled the hood against her head.

"Please don't hate me," Keefe begged as he held his blue crystal up to the light to make a path. "Tell everyone I'll be back as soon as I finish this. And remember—I'm on your side."

He glittered away right as the green gadget turned red and a high-pitched squeal blasted from the ceiling, sending a rippling sound wave rushing down the walls.

Shattering all of the glass.

THREE

I T'S NOT AS BAD AS IT SEEMS."

Magnate Leto had said the words a dozen times—and Sophie wanted to believe them. But all she could see were the slivers of glass glinting in his hair.

She was covered in them as well, but they were mostly stuck to Keefe's thick cloak. She'd been spared any cuts or scratches, just like he'd promised.

The glass pyramid hadn't been so fortunate. Magnate Leto's office was in shambles, its walls now empty metal frames. And while the rest of the pyramid had simply crackled and splintered, all of the glass would have to be replaced.

At least no one had been hurt—and the other buildings on

campus had been spared. But that didn't change the fact that the Neverseen had now attacked Foxfire.

And it had been Keefe's idea.

All twelve Councillors had visited the school to assess the damage, and questioned Sophie thoroughly. Then Magnate Leto had followed her home to get the *real* story.

The fading twilight glow seeped through Havenfield's glass walls, painting the elegant white décor of the main room in shades of purple, gray, and blue. Even with the soft shimmer from the twinkling chandeliers, Sophie felt like the whole world had been bruised.

"Truly, Miss Foster," Magnate Leto said as he plopped next to her on the plush sofa. "I've been meaning to redecorate my office since I took over as principal. I've never been a fan of my reflection—especially in this form."

Sophie shook her head. "You know this is about more than broken mirrors."

"She's right," Grady agreed, stalking down the curved staircase in the center of the room with Brielle—his svelte goblin bodyguard with tight curly hair—in tow. "This is about That Boy! I know he used to be your friend—"

"He *is* my friend," Sophie corrected.

And he was working with her enemies.

Grady crouched in front of her. "Whatever he is or isn't to you doesn't change the things he's doing." He plucked an especially jagged shard of glass off of her sleeve.

The razor-sharp edges would've shredded her skin if Keefe hadn't given her his cloak.

Then again, she wouldn't have needed it if he hadn't blown up the place.

She reached for Grady's hands. "I'm fine. And Keefe did this to warn us."

"That doesn't make destroying Foxfire okay!"

No, it didn't . . .

"Technically, he only destroyed my office," Magnate Leto argued. "And my own foolishness is partially to blame. I should've suspected something the moment I was called to the Level Five atrium to remove a pair of gremlins from the lockers. Causing havoc has always been one of Mr. Sencen's specialties. As is breaking into the principal's office."

"You're seriously going to equate this with one of his pranks?" Grady asked. "Like it's just another Great Gulon Incident?"

If the vein in Grady's forehead hadn't been so bulgy, Sophie would've asked someone to *finally* share the story of Keefe's legendary triumph.

"It's all a rather dark shade of gray," Magnate Leto admitted. "But that's a color all of us are familiar with, aren't we? Wouldn't you use it to describe your behavior when you confronted Brant about what he did to your daughter? Or Miss Foster, when you drugged your human family so you could be erased from their lives? And surely the Council would apply it to most of my actions. After all, I helped form an illegal organization. Experimented with the genetics of an innocent child. Secreted her away in the Forbidden Cities to be raised by humans. Erased two of her memories without her permission—"

"We have a bigger problem," Sophie interrupted, not needing any more reminders of how weird her life had been. "I'm sure Oralie knew I was lying when I said I didn't see who triggered the sound wave. I was way too emotional to fool an Empath."

"Councillor Oralie has always been your loyal supporter," Magnate Leto assured her.

"Okay, but Councillor Alina looked suspicious too—and she hates me. All it takes is one of them to figure out that it was Keefe, and he'll never be able to come back."

"Not necessarily," Magnate Leto said. "Questionable actions can be forgiven when they're done with good intentions. Think of the Ancient Councillors' reasons for not warning the gnomes that the ogres possessed the plague. With time, most have come to understand their complicated motivations."

The key word in that sentence was "most."

In Keefe's case there'd be many who'd see a notorious troublemaker graduating to a new level of mayhem. Or worse: a loyal son stepping into the role his mother designed for him.

Sophie sank back into the sofa's cushions, trying to disappear into the fluff—anything to avoid having to figure out what to do or think or—

"I know this is all very overwhelming," Magnate Leto said. "But that's only because you're trying to interpret Mr. Sencen's actions with your head. You have a very good head, Miss Foster. Very logical and clever and strong. But do you know what's even more powerful?"

He pointed to her heart.

"Which means what?" Grady asked. "We're relying on *teenage feelings*?"

"I wouldn't be so quick to dismiss them. Miss Foster understands Mr. Sencen in ways the rest of us simply cannot. I watched them most carefully during their time in Alluveterre. He opened up to her. Leaned on her. Trusted her. So"—his eyes met Sophie's—"what does your heart tell you?"

Sophie crossed her arms over her chest, wishing she could reach in and pluck out the answer. Instead, her head kept taking over, flooding her consciousness with memories:

Keefe crying on her shoulder the day she'd had to tell him that his mom might be dead.

The window slumber parties they'd held so they wouldn't have to face the tougher nights alone.

His room covered in notes and crumpled bits of paper as he desperately tried to piece together the truth hidden in his past.

A much younger Keefe, sitting and waiting in Atlantis for a family that didn't care enough to remember him.

Over and over the scenes replayed, until another image slowly replaced them.

Keefe, in the Healing Tent in Exillium, his humor and confidence stripped away, revealing the scared, angry boy he kept hidden underneath.

The memory didn't tell her anything. But it made her heart ache—made her wish she could wrap her arms around him and make everything okay.

Magnate Leto nodded, as if he'd been eavesdropping on her thoughts. Which made her wonder . . .

"When we were in Alluveterre, did you ever read his mind?"

Telepaths weren't supposed to invade anyone's privacy without permission—but Magnate Leto had never been one to follow rules.

"You're asking if I knew he was going to join the Neverseen?" he asked. "I knew he was considering it. But the idea was incredibly tentative. It didn't truly take shape until you were heading for Ravagog—and even then, he still seemed undecided. But I can tell you that he saw it as a necessary evil to right the wrongs his mother caused."

"'Evil' is right," Grady muttered. "And if That Boy comes anywhere near you again, I want you to drop him with the full weight of your inflicting."

"Grady!" Edaline gasped.

She'd been standing by the farthest wall next to Cadoc—her hulking new bodyguard, who almost made Sandor look skinny—staring so silently at the pastures of grazing dinosaurs and other crazy creatures that Sophie had forgotten she was there.

"Need I remind you that Keefe's doing the same thing our daughter tried to do?" Edaline asked him.

The words knocked Grady back a step.

They hit Sophie pretty hard too.

Jolie had tried to infiltrate the Neverseen, and the plan had been working—until they ordered her to destroy a human nuclear power plant to prove her loyalty. A few days after she refused, she was dead.

Grady moved to Edaline's side and wrapped his arm around her waist. "I'm sorry. I guess I have some trust issues, after Brant."

He said something else, but Sophie didn't catch it, her mind too stuck on the huge reality Keefe was facing.

As much as she'd worried and fretted and stressed, she'd never truly imagined the impossible choices he'd have to face—or the worst-case scenario:

A tall, lean tree with blond shaggy leaves and scattered ice-blue flowers growing on a grassy hill in the Wanderling Woods—the elves' version of a graveyard.

Each Wanderling's seed was wrapped with the DNA of the person it had been planted to commemorate, and it grew with their coloring and essence.

"He's going to get himself killed," Sophie mumbled as the knot of emotions under her ribs twisted a million times tighter. "We need to get him out."

"How do you propose we do that?" Magnate Leto asked.

Sophie wished she had suggestions. But she didn't even know where Keefe was. She'd been trying to track his thoughts for weeks, like she used to do when she played base quest. But all she could tell was that Keefe was very far away.

"He'll come home when he's ready," Magnate Leto told her. "In the meantime, I suggest we make use of the information he's gone to such lengths to bring us." He turned to Grady and Edaline. "I trust that you'll allow your new bodyguards to do their jobs?"

"Brielle and Cadoc are some of our regiment's best," Sandor added.

"Do you think the Neverseen will guess that Keefe warned us if Grady and Edaline suddenly have goblins following them around?" Sophie had to ask.

"I'm sure Mr. Sencen has a plan for that," Magnate Leto promised.

"Uh, we're talking about the same Keefe, right?" Sophie asked.

"It doesn't matter," Grady told her. "I don't need a bodyguard."

Brielle cleared her throat. "With all due respect, Mr. Ruewen, there's a reason the elves rely on goblin assistance. Are you truly prepared to kill if the need arises?"

Grady looked more than a little green as Brielle unsheathed her sword and slashed it with a deadly sort of grace. The elvin mind couldn't process violence. Their thoughts were too sensitive—their consciences too strong. It was why the Never-seen were so unstable—though Fintan held his sanity together far better than Brant.

"What if we stay here?" Edaline suggested. "The Council hasn't given Grady an assignment in weeks, and we have plenty to keep us busy with the animals. We can pass Cadoc and Brielle off like they're additional guards for Sophie—which shouldn't seem strange after what happened."

"*That,*" Magnate Leto said, "is a brilliant solution."

"Except it puts us on house arrest," Grady argued.

"Isn't it worth it to be safe?" Sophie countered.

"Hey—that works both ways, kiddo," Grady reminded her. "If I agree to this, I need you to agree that there will be no more one-on-one meetings with anyone associated with the Neverseen—especially That Boy."

Sophie groaned. "His name is Keefe!"

"Not right now, it isn't. He has to earn that back. And if he's really on our side, he won't mind you having your bodyguard around as backup. Understood?"

Sophie agreed, mostly because Sandor would clobber her if she didn't. "What do you think the Neverseen want with you guys?"

"I suspect this is primarily a power play," Magnate Leto said quietly. "Much like their attempts to capture the alicorns. If they possess something you love . . ."

"They can control me," Sophie finished.

Magnate Leto nodded. "I'm betting that they—like myself—assume Kenric would've known his cache is far more valuable to you if you have a way to access the information inside. This could be their plan to force you to open it for them."

"Oh good—so the thing That Boy stole is putting all of us in more danger," Grady muttered.

"If it weren't that, it would be something else," Magnate Leto assured him. "They've been after Miss Foster from the beginning. And honestly, the more valuable they see her as, the safer she is—relatively speaking."

"I don't even know how to open the cache," Sophie reminded everyone—though *technically* she'd never tried. She had enough crazy information stored in her head. The last thing she wanted was to fill it with secrets even the Council couldn't handle.

Still, Magnate Leto's theory raised other questions—the kind that made her voice get thick and squeaky.

"I know you don't want to tell me who my genetic parents are—"

"Wrong," Magnate Leto interrupted. "I *can't* tell you."

Sophie glanced at Grady and Edaline, trying to decide if she should leave the conversation at that. She rarely mentioned her genetic parents around them—or her human family. It was complicated enough having three different moms and dads—especially since one pair no longer remembered her, and another was a complete mystery.

But she needed to know.

"Was Kenric my father? He was a Telepath. And he was always so kind to me." Her throat closed off as she remembered his bright smiles.

The red-haired Councillor had been one of Sophie's strongest supporters, right up until the day she'd lost him to Fintan's inferno of Everblaze.

Magnate Leto reached for Sophie's hand, tracing a finger across the star-shaped scar he'd accidentally given her when he healed her abilities. "Kenric wasn't involved with Project Moonlark. And that's *all* I can tell you. Some secrets must remain hidden. Besides, we have much more pressing matters to discuss, like the other significant piece of information we learned from Mr. Sencen. Did he really say that Gethen was the Neverseen's only Telepath?"

"Why does that matter?" Sophie asked.

"Because telepathy is generally considered to be our most vital ability. We'd never have known the humans were plotting to betray us all those millennia ago if our Telepaths hadn't overheard their schemes. That's why there are more Telepaths in the nobility than any other talent. So either the Neverseen have failed to recruit any others—which could tell us something about their method of operating. Or there's a reason they're avoiding the talent. Either way, it means I should press the Council about allowing a visit to Gethen."

Sophie's eyes narrowed. "I've been saying that for weeks!"

"I know. And I've been stalling—partially because I promised to bring you with me, and I still believe Gethen intends to harm you if you try to search his mind. But mostly because I wanted to see exactly what role Mr. Sencen was going to play before choosing our next step."

"Well, now we know," Grady muttered, holding up the shard of glass again.

"I know you look at that and see violence and destruction," Magnate Leto told him. "But I see a boy willing to do anything to tear the Neverseen's organization apart. And I for one am going to believe in him—especially since he may have unwittingly given us another advantage. May I have that cloak, Miss Foster?"

"I'm sure there's a hidden tracker," Sandor warned as Sophie handed it over.

"That's what I'm hoping for. Perhaps if we move it somewhere *interesting*, we can lure them out of their little hiding places."

"You want to meet with them?" Grady asked.

"I want to send a message. Can I borrow a dagger?"

Brielle whipped a jagged silver knife from her boot and handed it to Magnate Leto. He sliced open the cloak's hem along the bottom edge, revealing two disks—one gold and one black—sewn between the folds of thick fabric.

Sandor frowned. "The gold one's the tracker—but I've never seen anything like the black. It's not even made of metal."

"Indeed it's not," Magnate Leto said, severing the threads securing the black disk to the lining. "And it's not magsidian, either."

The rare dwarven mineral changed properties depending on how someone carved it, and it was often used as a form of security authorization.

"Careful," Sophie warned as he held the disk up to the grayish light. "I'm sure that's covered in aromark."

The powerful ogre enzyme wouldn't hurt him. But it could only be removed through an *unpleasant* process.

"I've only seen aromark on metal," Magnate Leto murmured. "And this symbol . . ."

He traced his finger over the thin white etchings across the top—a line decorated with dashes, sandwiched between two different-size circles.

"Do you know what it means?" Sophie asked.

"Sadly, no," Magnate Leto admitted. "But I've seen it before—along with other similar markings—on a shard of memory I recently recovered."

"From who?" Sophie asked.

Magnate Leto sighed, letting several seconds crawl by before he told her, "From Prentice."

FOUR

RENTICE," SOPHIE REPEATED, NOT sure if she felt relieved or furious. "The same Prentice you've been telling me isn't strong enough to have me search his mind?"

"That would be him," Magnate Leto agreed, and with that, Sophie's fury won.

Prentice used to be a Keeper for the Black Swan, in charge of protecting their most crucial secrets. And he'd allowed his sanity to be broken to prevent the Council from discovering Sophie's existence. He'd spent years locked away in the elves' underground prison, needing her abilities to grow strong enough to heal him. But when Sophie was finally ready—and the Council had freed him from Exile—his consciousness disappeared, leaving him an empty shell.

Nothing had seemed capable of bringing him back—until a few weeks earlier, when Prentice woke up. Sophie had assumed the news meant he'd made a major recovery, but sadly, his mind was still badly broken. She'd been begging the Black Swan to let her heal him, and each time she'd been told that Prentice's mind was too weak, too fragile, too unstable.

"Why would you lie to me?" she snapped as Edaline placed a calming hand on her shoulder.

"I didn't," Magnate Leto promised. "I told you he wasn't ready to be *healed*—not *searched.*"

"And I thought my enhanced abilities made me the only one strong enough to search a broken mind," Sophie argued.

"You are. I paid dearly for my attempt. But I had to see if I could figure out why he called swan song."

The Black Swan used the words as a code, to warn each other when they were in extreme danger. Prentice had given the signal right before the Council arrested him, almost like he'd known it was coming.

"Why didn't you let me help you search his mind, then?" Sophie asked.

"Because . . . I didn't trust myself not to beg you to heal him. You have no idea how much it pains me to leave him in darkness. But his mind needs to grow stronger before we bring him back to full consciousness. He has far too much to bear—and if his sanity collapses again, I fear there won't be enough left for you to attempt another repair."

The crack in his voice deflated a bit of Sophie's anger.

The rest faded when she admitted she shared the same worries.

A lot had changed in Prentice's life since he'd sacrificed his sanity. His wife, Cyrah, had died in some sort of light leaping accident. And his son, Wylie, had grown up barely knowing his father. That was a tremendous amount of grief for a weakened mind to process.

"You could've at least told me what was going on," Sophie grumbled.

"I know. When it comes to Prentice, I never seem to follow the course of wisdom. I suppose I feel too responsible."

"How do you think I feel? He's broken because of me!"

"Careful, Sophie," Grady warned. "You saw what thoughts like that did to Alden."

Alden's guilt over his role in Prentice's capture—even though he hadn't known Prentice was one of the good guys at the time—had shattered his sanity. If Sophie hadn't found the strength to heal him, he'd still be lost to the madness.

She took a steadying breath and pointed to the black disk. "We need to find out what that symbol means. And the best way to do that is to take me to see Prentice—just to search his mind for additional memories. Not to heal him."

Magnate Leto's jaw set and Sophie braced for him to argue.

But when he spoke, he told her, "I suppose I can arrange to bring you tomorrow."

"Why not now?" Sophie pressed.

"Probably not a good day to sneak away," Grady reminded her, pointing to the crystal dangling from her choker-style registry necklace. The pendant monitored her location—and while a Technopath could cheat the signal, after what happened at Foxfire the Councillors would likely be watching her much too closely.

"Do you think it'll be safe to slip away tomorrow?" Edaline asked.

"It will with careful arrangements." Magnate Leto tucked the black disk into his cape pocket. "I'll test this for enzymes tonight, just to be safe. I'll also see if I can figure out what it's made of. And we should get rid of this."

He handed Keefe's cloak to Brielle.

"Do you want me to salvage the tracker?" she asked.

"No, I think it's best we avoid the Neverseen's attention until we better understand the significance of the disk. I'd prefer that they believe we destroyed the cloak without discovering its secret."

Brielle headed for the door, her curls bouncing with every step. "Will fire be enough?"

"As long as the tracker melts completely." He turned to Sophie. "I'll be back to pick you up at dawn, along with Mr. Vacker. I think it would be wise for you to have your Cognate on hand. He won't be able to enter Prentice's mind, but he can boost your mental energy."

Sophie's stomach soured. "Does Fitz know that Keefe was behind what happened today?"

"If he doesn't already, he will soon. His father hailed me before I left campus, and I promised to get back to him with details. I suspect he fears his eldest son was involved. Why? Is that a problem?"

"It might be. Fitz has been weird about Keefe. It's like he wants to pretend they were never best friends."

"Sometimes that's easier," Edaline said quietly. "Missing someone can hurt too much. It's safer to be angry."

Anger definitely was Fitz's default. But his reaction to Keefe felt different.

Less angry. More . . . afraid.

"Well, if there's one thing I have no doubt of," Magnate Leto said as he reached for his pathfinder—a slender wand with an adjustable leaping crystal on one end—"it's that you know how to help your friends through their struggles. Perhaps you can help Mr. Vacker tomorrow. In the meantime, try to get some rest. I'll need you in top form to face Prentice."

They watched him glitter away, leaving behind a silence that felt itchy.

"I think I'm going to shower and get in bed early," Sophie decided, kissing each of her parents' cheeks before heading upstairs, where her bedroom suite took up the entire third floor.

"Do you think you'll be able to sleep?" Edaline called after her.

"Probably not."

But no one offered her any sleeping aids. They knew how much Sophie hated sedatives, after all the times her enemies had drugged her. Even Sandor said nothing as he completed his nightly security sweep of her bedroom. But his check was more thorough than usual—inspecting every corner and closet and cranny—despite the fact that none of the petals in the flowered carpet showed even the slightest trace of a new footprint.

"All clear," he announced after peeking under her giant canopied bed. "And I'll be right outside if you need me."

As soon as he closed her door, Sophie jumped straight in the shower to let the warm, colored streams wash away the last flecks of glass. They looked insignificant as they swirled down the drain. But her brain wouldn't stop repeating what Keefe had told her.

Sometimes things have to get worse before they get better.

Emotions swelled with each reminder. Fear. Doubt. Dread.

She closed her eyes and imagined each as a solid thread—then twisted them into the knot under her ribs the way Councillor Bronte had taught her. The tangle burned as she worked, and she pressed her hands against her skin, taking deep breaths until the feelings cooled.

Worry can bring power, Bronte had told her. *Better to embrace it than ignore it.*

But as she crawled into bed and clung tightly to Ella—the bright blue stuffed elephant she couldn't sleep without—new threads of fear kept flaring up. Even when Iggy—her tiny pet imp—flitted to her pillow and snuggled his blue furry body up next to her, his squeaky purring couldn't make her relax. Only one thing might help—the thing she'd been too scared to try before.

Her enhanced telepathic abilities allowed her to stretch her consciousness impossibly far and transmit to people and creatures on the other side of the world. She mostly used the talent to communicate with Fitz—or for her regular check-ins with Silveny to make sure everything was going safely with the alicorn's pregnancy. But that night, there was someone she needed to talk to so much more.

Keefe?

She sent the thought spiraling through the deep black nothingness, shoving the call with her full mental strength. She'd never pushed her limits to communicate with someone who wasn't a Telepath—which was the excuse she'd been using for why she hadn't tried this before. But really, she'd been afraid she couldn't trust him.

Or that he would ignore her.

Keefe? she called again, repeating the word over and over. He wouldn't be able to transmit back to her, so she'd have to connect directly to his thoughts.

She pressed her consciousness lower, imagining she was

aiming for his mind like an arrow slicing through the night. A rush of warmth flooded her head when she finally hit the mark, along with a single, shaky thought.

Foster?

Yes! she transmitted—a bit too loudly. She lowered her mental voice before asking, *Can you still hear me?*

DUDE. This wins for freakiest mind trick ever!

Sorry! Did I scare you?

You think? How does Fitz not pee his pants every time you do this—or wait, DOES HE?

Don't be gross.

I'm not. I'm keeping it real. And, um . . . does this mean you're searching my memories right now?

She didn't actually know if she *could* from so far away—but it didn't matter. She'd paid the price for violating the rules of telepathy too many times.

Besides—if she was going to trust Keefe, she had to *trust* him.

I'm keeping my mind focused on what you're saying, she promised—though his loudest thoughts buzzed in the back of her consciousness like a TV in the background. So she could hear how relieved he was to know that she was safe—and even more so that she was still talking to him. He also sounded very worried that someone would catch them communicating.

Is this a bad time? she asked.

No. But I'm glad Ruy and Alvar are heavy sleepers. There was definite squealing and flailing when I first heard your voice.

The idea of him being so close to one of her kidnappers—and the Psionipath who'd attacked her and Biana—made Sophie shiver. *Can you go somewhere we can talk?*

I'm not allowed to leave my room without one of them with me. But I should be fine here, as long as I stay still. So . . . what's up? Did something happen?

Aside from you destroying part of Foxfire?

Hey, it was my turn to blow up the school. You've been hogging all the fun.

This isn't a joke, Keefe.

It can be if we make it one. We just have to commit!

Sophie sighed, letting her frustration ripple through her mind.

Nobody was hurt, right? he asked.

You got lucky this time, she agreed.

Luck had nothing to do with it. I planned it perfectly.

That's exactly the kind of overconfidence that's going to get you killed.

Not necessarily. I know you don't want to hear this—and believe me, I'm not happy about it either—but . . . I'm kind of important to their plans. At least, I think I am. I'm still working it all out. But I can tell they want me here. I just have to convince them they can trust me before they'll tell me why—and I made some serious progress today. Fintan totally looked ready to join Team Keefe when I met him at the rendezvous point so he could bring me to the hideout.

Every part of that made Sophie sick to her stomach. But she reminded herself that he was doing this for a reason—the same reason she'd reached out to him.

If you're really going to stay there, you need to let me help. You can't keep sneaking away—sooner or later they'll catch you. So I'll reach out to you like this every night and you can tell me anything you've learned.

That's actually not a bad idea, he admitted. *Though it does mean I won't get to use my brilliant plan for my next escape. It didn't have any explosions, either. Just a LOT of selkie skin.*

Sophie felt her lips smile, even if she probably shouldn't.

I'm not going to be able to tell you everything, though, his mind added quietly. *I can only leak so much without getting caught.*

I know. Sophie tried not to wonder how much he was already hiding. *Are nights safer to reach you? Or would mornings be better?*

Definitely nights. My training starts early—and I'm sure you're probably imagining all kinds of scary things, so just know the stuff they've been having me do isn't a big deal.

That'll change once they really trust you.

Yeah. Probably.

It was his cue to tell her he had a brilliant plan for that, too. But his mind had gone achingly silent.

I really hope you know what you're doing.

I do. I can't promise I won't have to be a part of some more shady things. But I know where the hard lines are, and I won't cross them.

She could feel the threads of his conviction, like roots digging deep. But whether they would hold him steady through the coming storms, she couldn't tell.

She'd have to keep an eye on him.

Is this the best time to reach out to you each night? she asked.

Yep—it's a date. Tell your boyfriends not to be jealous.

She wished she had a way to roll her eyes in a mental conversation. *I don't have any boyfriends.*

I dunno. I can think of a few dudes who might not be fans of all this Keefoster time.

Keefoster?

Sounds way cooler than Sophitz or Dophie, right? And don't even get me started on Bangs Boy. By the way—don't think I didn't notice those new rings on your thumbs today. The Fitzster has a matching set, doesn't he? I bet they look so cute when you guys are holding hands and staring deep into each other's eyes.

We don't stare into—why are we talking about this?

Would you rather hear about how loud Ruy snores? Or how this room smells like rotting toenails? Or Alvar's crazy theories for who the Forklenator is?

The last question reminded her that Keefe had already run off before the Magnate Leto–Mr. Forkle reveal happened.

You found out another one of his identities, didn't you? Keefe guessed.

I did. But I don't think it'd be good to tell you. You already have enough secrets to protect.

There you go, ruining all the fun with your logic.

I guess that's my job.

That doesn't mean you have to be so good at it—though it is kinda nice having someone look out for me.

You don't make it easy.

Another thing you and I have in common.

His floating thoughts made it clear how determined he was to protect her. It made her heart somehow both light and heavy at the same time.

Have you learned anything else I should know? she asked.

I wish. They haven't let me meet any of the other members of their order yet. And this run-down shack I'm in is where they bring all new recruits because there's nothing worth finding. They won't give me my own crystal or pathfinder—and the ones they let me borrow always leap to neutral meeting places.

They trusted you enough to let you help at the Sanctuary, she reminded him.

Only because that mission was about causing chaos. They knew they wouldn't get inside the preserve. They just wanted to make the Council look bad and keep people on edge.

Is that what the registry was about too?

No, they were super secretive about that, so I'm betting there was more to it. It's on my list of things I'm trying to find out.

What else is on that list?

Not gonna lie—it's a LOT. But I'm trying to focus on details that will tell me how to shut them down.

Well . . . I know one thing that might be worth looking into. Her mind filled with the symbol from the black disk they'd found in his cloak.

Am I supposed to know what that is? Keefe asked.

You've never seen it before?

Nope. Why, where did you find it?

If you don't know, I don't think I should tell you. It might be something they're trying to keep hidden from you. Just keep an eye out for it, okay?

Done. Anything else?

That's all I can think of for now.

Awesome. Then it's my turn to ask you a question. He paused, like he was gearing up for something incredibly important. *How'd Dizznee react to your new rings?*

Sophie shook her head, refusing to dignify the question with a response.

You can ignore it all you want, Foster, but sooner or later you're going to have to solve the triangle. Or should we get real and call it a square?

I have no idea what you mean.

I'm pretty sure you do. I bet if I were there I could feel your mood shifting.

Right, because I'm trying to figure out if it's possible to strangle you with my thoughts!

There you go, rocking the whole adorable-when-you're-angry thing. I think that's what I've missed about you the most.

She knew he was only teasing—but she still found herself transmitting, *I miss you, too.*

His thoughts went quiet for a second. And when he came back, his mental voice sounded heavier.

Well, he told her, *I should probably get some sleep. Gotta rest up for another day of playing nice with the bad guys—and no need to tell me to be careful. I've got that one down.*

She doubted that. "Careful" wasn't a word that described Keefe Sencen.

Fine, she said. *But before I go, I need you to promise me something.*

Yes, I will call you Lady Lectures-a-Lot every time you transmit to me.

That's definitely not what I meant.

What about Little Miss Heartbreaker?

Keefe!

Okay, fine, we'll stick with the Mysterious Miss F. Deal?

Deal, she agreed. *And can you focus for one second?*

I suppose I can try. . . .

I need you to promise that if this gets too tough, you'll walk away. No matter how close you are to what you're trying to learn.

Edaline had once made Sophie give her a similar promise, after admitting she should've said the same thing to Jolie.

It's not going to come down to that.

Then promise me anyway.

Endless seconds slipped by before he told her, *Okay, fine, I promise. Now get out of my head, Miss F. I need my beauty sleep.*

FIVE

YOU KIDS WOULD SLEEP THE DAY away if I'd let you," a wheezy voice grumbled, dragging Sophie out of her tangled dreams.

She rubbed the crustiness from her eyes and waited for her vision to adjust to her still-very-dark bedroom. "I thought you said dawn—and whoa. You're back to the Forkle disguise?"

She hadn't seen the heavyset figure standing in her doorway since the day he'd revealed his other identity. But there he was, looking wrinkled and puffy and reeking with the dirty-feet scent of ruckleberries.

Strangely, Sophie liked him better that way.

This was the face she'd known her whole life. The nosy

next-door neighbor who'd kept watch over her while she'd lived among humans. The elf who'd healed her abilities after they'd been damaged by a failed light leap, and fought at her side on Mount Everest. The elf who'd driven her crazy with his riddles and secrets—but who seemed to know her better than anyone.

"As I told you before," Mr. Forkle said, "it's easier for me to compartmentalize my life. When I'm in the Lost Cities, I rely on my established identities. But today we're going to the Stone House."

The name launched sparks through Sophie's nerves.

She'd only been to the isolated cottage twice, and neither were happy memories. One was the day they'd first brought Prentice home—when they'd discovered how severely his condition had deteriorated. And the other was when Calla had brought her there to deliver devastating news about the gnomish plague.

"You know, the last time I was there, you weren't in Forkle mode," she reminded him.

She probably should've figured out his secret identity right then. But Magnate Leto had given her some story about how the Black Swan had brought him along to help cover for Tiergan and Wylie's visit.

Sometimes it was better if she didn't think about how good he was at lying.

"That was for young Mr. Endal's benefit," Mr. Forkle told her. "He's unaware of my other identities—and I'd prefer it stay that way for the time being."

"Will Wylie be there today?"

"Are you hoping to avoid him?"

Seeing Wylie tended to be unpleasant—he'd spent the majority of their conversations blaming her for every horrible thing that had happened to his dad.

But their last talk hadn't been *as* awkward.

"I just want to be prepared," she said. "I'm sure he's wondering why I haven't healed Prentice yet."

"Actually, Wylie came to us after his father woke, begging us not to perform the healing until we understand why Prentice slipped away. He's terrified of undoing what little progress his father has made. So remember: You and Mr. Vacker are going there to retrieve, not heal."

"Wait—Fitz is here?"

She scrambled to cover her frumpy pajamas and accidentally launched poor Iggy off the bed. He flapped his black batlike wings and shook his tiny blue arms as he flew to the top of her canopy and glared down at her.

"Mr. Vacker's waiting downstairs," Mr. Forkle said, snapping his fingers to turn on her lights, "and your imp looks like he's plotting revenge. So I'll leave you to get ready. But do try to hurry. I'd prefer to get out of here before sunrise."

Sophie tried not to think about how early that meant it was—or how little she'd slept—as she stumbled out of bed and threw on a simple tunic and pants.

"You might want to consider using a hairbrush," Sandor

warned as she passed him on her way to the stairs.

Sophie rarely gave much thought to her appearance, but Sandor's twitching smile sent her rushing to the nearest mirror.

A tiny face appeared in the corner and immediately burst into laughter.

"What'd you do—get zapped by a Charger?" Vertina asked, swishing her silky dark hair.

Sophie glared at the spectral mirror, wishing she could tell Grady and Edaline to get rid of the obnoxious piece of technology. But the mirror had once belonged to Jolie. And Vertina had occasionally proven herself useful.

Plus, her hair *did* look like the top part of a pineapple.

"You're making it worse," Vertina said as Sophie tried brushing out the tangles. "Go grab a box of hair pins and let me save you from this impending disaster."

Sophie was tempted to ignore her—Vertina would disappear the second she stepped out of the mirror's range—but she let Vertina walk her through pulling her hair into some sort of sleek, twisty ponytail.

"Aren't I a genius?" Vertina asked as Sophie tucked the final strand.

"You actually are," Sophie begrudgingly admitted.

"Okay! Now for your makeup. Go get—"

Sophie stepped out of range, done with primping.

"Whoa," Fitz said as she made her way down the stairs. "I didn't recognize you for a second."

"Bad hair day," she mumbled, fidgeting with the end of the ponytail.

"No—it looks good," he promised. "It really draws attention to your eyes."

She knew Fitz probably meant it as a compliment. But she'd never gotten used to being the only brown-eyed elf.

Why couldn't the side effect of her tweaked genes have been green eyes?

Or purple?

"You should do that more often," Grizel said, emerging from her hiding spot in the shadows. "It'll drive the boys wild."

"Um, maybe."

Attention made Sophie sweaty and fidgety. Especially attention from Fitz.

He was studying her so closely she finally had to ask, "What?"

"Just . . . checking for cuts or scratches. Making sure he didn't hurt you."

"You mean Keefe?"

Fitz cringed at the name. His hands also curled into fists—the knuckles turning white from the pressure.

Sophie turned to Mr. Forkle. "Can we have a minute?"

Mr. Forkle nodded and led Sandor and Grizel to the other side of the room.

Sophie motioned for Fitz to take a seat next to her on the sofa and decided it'd be easiest to talk telepathically. She gave him permission to enter her mind—he and Mr. Forkle were the only ones who could—and he effortlessly slipped past her mental blocking. Apparently she had a point of trust, and if someone transmitted the right thing, it worked kind of like a mental password. But it all happened subconsciously, so she had no idea what they said.

Okay, Sophie thought, sitting on her hands so she couldn't tug on her eyelashes. *We have to talk about Keefe. I know you don't want to. But the more we ignore it, the more it's going to affect our ability to work as Cognates.*

All of their training focused on being open with each other. Their ultimate goal was supposed to be *no secrets at all.*

Are you sure it's a good idea? Fitz asked. *We both know I say stupid stuff when I'm angry.*

Are you angry? she asked. *I know you are at Alvar—and I'm with you on that. But are you sure that's what you're feeling toward Keefe?*

Uh—did he or did he not destroy part of Foxfire yesterday?

Yeah, but it wasn't like how you're picturing.

In his mind, Keefe looked like a proper villain, laughing as the glass rained down.

Just watch, okay? She rallied her concentration and replayed what actually happened, from the moment she stepped into Magnate Leto's office, to the final shattering seconds. Her photographic memory painted the scenes in perfect detail, and she left nothing out.

Okay, so maybe it's not as bad as I thought, Fitz reluctantly admitted. *But I still think you should've Sucker Punched him as soon as he spun around in that chair.*

I thought about it, Sophie admitted, tracing her finger across the wide bracelet Dex had given her to make her punches stronger. *But I'm glad I heard him out.*

Fitz sighed. *I guess that's why he went to you instead of me.*

Does that bother you?

No.

There was a strange prickliness about the thought, though.

What would you have done if he'd left the note for you instead of me? Sophie asked.

Fitz flopped back against the pillows and stared at the cascading crystal chandelier. *I have no idea.*

Are you sure? Sophie pressed. *I can feel the words bubbling in the back of your mind. Just let them out—I can take it.*

Fitz chewed his lower lip. *Fine. I . . . don't trust Keefe. I know you want me to—and I know I probably should, since he's my best friend and he's been through a ton of hard stuff. But he also has a LOT in common with my brother. Shoot—he used to call Alvar his hero.*

Keefe didn't know Alvar was with the Neverseen when he said that.

Maybe not. But it still makes me sick. Did you know that Alvar went to your planting in the Wanderling Woods? After he'd drugged you and tied you up and staged the cave to make everyone think you'd drowned? Then he stood there with his hand on my shoulder and offered to let me borrow his stupid handkerchief. And later that night, he snuck back to the Neverseen's hideout and helped them torture you.

The skin on her wrists stung, phantom pain left from the interrogation.

Brant was the one who questioned me, she reminded him quietly.

Yeah, but Alvar let it happen. He knew what they were doing. Probably heard you screaming.

He punched one of the fluffy pillows so hard, bits of feather swirled through the air.

You're right, Sophie said as the fluff slowly settled. *But that was Alvar. You can't keep lumping him together with Keefe. Your brother is . . . I don't even know. I don't understand why he would turn his back on his family, or do such unimaginably awful things. But Keefe really is trying to help us. He's in over his head, and his plan is probably full of holes, and I'm betting we're going to have to save him before this is over—but . . . his heart is still in the right place. I have to believe that.*

Fitz shook his head. *How do you stay so trusting after all you've been through?*

It's not always easy. Her hand moved to rub the emotions tangled under her ribs. *Did I ever tell you what happened with Councillor Bronte? Remember how much he used to hate me?*

Yeah, I used to hear my mom and dad whispering about what they'd do if Bronte got you expelled or banished.

He tried really hard. And when the Council made him my inflicting Mentor, I was pretty sure that would do it. It got so bad that Kenric had to be there to make sure Bronte wasn't hurting me during the lessons. But then, Bronte made me teach him how I inflict positive emotions. And the happiness I blasted into his mind caused this weird mental shutdown. I still don't know how to explain it. But I had to pull his consciousness back, and his head was seriously one of the scariest places I've ever been.

She shuddered just thinking about it.

After that, I figured things would get way worse between us, she continued. *But somehow Bronte ended up becoming one of my only supporters on the Council. I didn't know what caused the change until after the whole ability restrictor nightmare. Bronte sent me a message through Magnate Leto. He told me, "It takes a special person to see darkness inside of someone and not condemn them." But the funny thing was, I had condemned him. I'd decided he was a traitor. I'd even asked Keefe to go all Empath-lie-detector on him to see if we could find proof that he was leaking confidential information from the Council. So . . . now I try to be the person Bronte thinks I am. Which is why I'm not ready to give up on Keefe. Not yet.*

I guess that makes sense. But—

I'm not trying to change how you feel. In fact, maybe it's better this way. I'll be the believer and you can be the skeptic and we'll keep each other in check—but that only works if you're honest with me and actually talk about stuff.

He sighed. *There you go being all practical and wise.*

Hey, one of us has to be.

He laughed at that—and reached over to give her ponytail a playful tug.

She moved to block him and their rings snapped their hands together—which would've been startling enough without Mr. Forkle asking, "I take it the hand-holding means you've worked things out?"

"I think so," Sophie mumbled, not looking at Fitz as she pulled her palm free.

"Very good, because we really do need to get going. The window of time that we can be away is closing by the minute."

"And you have your Imparter in case you need me?" Grady asked Sophie as he strode in from the kitchen.

Sophie showed him the square silver gadget she'd tucked safely in her pocket. Imparters were the elves' much sleeker voice-commanded version of a videophone.

"All will be fine," Mr. Forkle assured Grady. "We're going to a secure location."

Grady strangled Sophie with a hug anyway. "I keep thinking it's going to get easier, sitting back and letting you take risks," he told her. "But every time, I want to drag you back upstairs and barricade you in your room."

"That makes two of us," Sandor said. "But I'll keep an eye on her."

"And *I'll* keep an eye on both of them," Grizel said. "Show them how it's done."

Grizel tossed her long hair—which she'd let hang loose that day—as Mr. Forkle pulled a pink pathfinder out of his cloak, making Sophie wonder how many types of leaping crystals the elves actually used. Blue went to the Forbidden Cities. Green went to the ogres. Pale yellow to the Neutral Territories. And clear to the Lost Cities. She'd also seen the Black Swan use purple crystals. But this was the first time she'd seen pale pink—and its hundreds of facets sparkled with different colors, like a diamond.

"Please tell me this isn't going to be like leaping with the unmapped stars," Sophie begged. She'd experienced that particular misery several times, and really didn't have the energy to endure it again.

"No, the hint of opalescence is simply an added security measure," Mr. Forkle assured her. "Now everyone lock hands."

Their group formed quite a chain, with Sophie, Fitz, Mr. Forkle, Sandor, and Grizel.

"You ready for this?" Fitz asked.

"Of course she is," Mr. Forkle answered for her. "This is what she was made for."

SIX

PRENTICE'S NORMALLY RICH BROWN skin had a grayish tint, and shiny streams of sweat trickled down his forehead and soaked his tangled dreadlocks.

But he was awake.

His cloudy blue eyes kept darting blankly around the room.

Even his mumble-gurgle sounds were a huge improvement from his previous deathly silence.

Still, Sophie understood Mr. Forkle's reasons for keeping her away.

Watching the string of drool hanging from Prentice's lips made her want to dive into his mind and call him back to reality. He deserved to be *truly* awake—not strapped to a bed so that his flailing limbs wouldn't send him crashing to the cold silver floor.

All in good time, Mr. Forkle transmitted. *And I'm not reading your mind, in case you're worried. I know you well enough to know that your thoughts echo mine. But we must be strong.*

"Everything okay?" Fitz asked as Sophie gave Mr. Forkle a reluctant nod.

She forced a smile and tried to look anywhere but at Prentice.

The house was exactly as she remembered it. Sleek and sterile and sparse—and small. Sandor and Grizel chose to patrol the moorish grounds to escape the low ceilings.

The only pieces of furniture were the neatly tucked cot Prentice was resting on and a medicine-strewn table next to it. The rest of the space was floor-to-ceiling apothecary shelves and one narrow counter under the room's only window, covered in an elaborate alchemy setup.

"Isn't someone watching him?" Sophie asked, studying the beakers on the burners, which were bubbling with some sort of smoky magenta liquid.

"Of course," a ghostly voice said from the loft hidden above.

Seconds later, Wraith's silver cloak came swishing down the narrow corner staircase. *Just* his cloak—though his invisible body was clearly moving underneath the slinky fabric. He used a trick called partial vanishing—hiding his body, but not his clothes—to keep his true identity secret.

All five members of the Black Swan's Collective had crazy nicknames to match their even-crazier disguises. So far Sophie and her friends had only learned who two of them actually were. They knew Mr. Forkle was both Magnate Leto and Sir Astin—though he'd admitted that he still had other identities they'd yet to uncover. And they knew . . .

"Granite!" Sophie said as a bizarre figure struggled up the narrow staircase from the cramped basement below. He looked like a cracked, unfinished statue come to life, thanks to the chalky indurite powder he ingested for his disguise. Sophie knew him better as Tiergan, her telepathy mentor at Foxfire—and she still couldn't believe she'd trained with him for more than a year and never guessed he was secretly involved with the Black Swan.

"Squall already left," Granite told Mr. Forkle. "And she won't be able to return for our evening meeting."

Mr. Forkle nodded. "I'd suspected that might occur."

Squall used her ability as a Froster to crust herself with ice and obscure her identity—and whoever she was in real life seemed to make it very difficult for her to sneak away from the Lost Cities for long.

"Blur should be here momentarily," Granite added.

Almost on cue, a smudged-looking figure passed through the solid wood of the cottage's front door. As a Phaser, Blur could break down his body and walk through anything—but he only let himself partially re-form, in order to hide what he looked like. All Sophie could see were splotches of color and shadow in a vaguely elflike shape as he turned back to open the door for two familiar figures.

"You know, you could use the door like a normal person," Tam said as he stalked into the room.

"Where's the fun in that?" Linh asked, trailing behind her brother.

She'd opened her mouth to say something else when she spotted Sophie and Fitz. Then there was a whole lot of hugging—while Tam settled for a nod-shrug-wave from the doorway.

The twins looked a lot alike—especially with their silver-blue eyes, and the silver tips they'd added to their jet-black hair. But personality-wise, they were night and day.

"I wish I'd known you'd be here," Linh mumbled. "I was so happy to leave the house, I didn't bother changing out of my training clothes." She fussed with the sleeves of her simple blue tunic, which were wet along the edges. She must've been practicing hydrokinesis.

"You look beautiful," Sophie promised.

Linh always did.

All elves were inherently gorgeous, but Linh was especially striking with her soft pink cheeks and lips contrasted against her dramatic eyes and hair. Tam was just as handsome, but with more edge to his style, thanks to his jagged bangs and ultra-intense stare.

"Why aren't you letting Tam and Linh leave Alluveterre?" Sophie asked Mr. Forkle.

"The same reason we haven't let you visit," he told her. "Far too many people would love to find that hideout."

Tam and Linh lived in the same tree houses that Sophie and her friends had stayed in while they were banished from the Lost Cities, hidden deep under the earth in a subterranean forest only the Black Swan knew how to access. They could've returned home when their banishment was lifted, but they chose to stay away from their family—not surprising, considering their parents let them spend more than three years scrounging for food and living in tattered tents instead of standing by Linh's side as she adjusted to the strength of her ability.

"Does that mean you're not going to Exillium anymore?" Fitz asked the twins.

"No, they let us out for that," Tam told him, "but only with our dwarven stalkers."

"Bodyguards," Blur corrected. "And they'll only surface if they hear trouble."

"King Enki assigned four of his royal brigade to Tam and Linh's charge," Granite clarified as he made his way over to check on Prentice, who seemed completely unaware of the noise around him. "The goblins have been spread a bit thin, between the forces they've stationed outside Ravagog and the patrols in the Lost Cities. And honestly, it's better for Tam and Linh to have a discreet form of cover at Exillium."

"How's it going there, by the way?" Sophie asked.

Linh smiled. "It keeps getting better—thanks to you."

Sophie shrugged, not sure she should be given credit for the changes. All she'd done was tell Councillor Oralie what life was truly like at the neglected school. Oralie had arranged the improvements herself.

"I never thought I'd miss that place," Fitz said. "But some of the skills they taught were pretty awesome."

"We miss you guys even more," Sophie added. "Dex and Biana are going to be so jealous that we got to see you."

"Seriously," Fitz said, "Biana was already super sulky that she couldn't come with us this morning, so when I tell her we saw you guys she's going to flip."

"All four of them have been nagging me to let them visit you two for weeks," Mr. Forkle added. "I'd wager they've broken Mr. Sencen's record for Most Visits to the Principal's Office to plead their case."

The name drop might as well have dragged a giant woolly mammoth into the room.

Tam cleared his throat. "So . . . have you heard from him?"

"You could say that," Fitz said, glancing at Sophie.

"I saw him yesterday." She hoped Tam would leave it at that. But of course he didn't.

"I'm guessing there was drama?"

"Mr. Sencen has chosen a very challenging path," Mr. Forkle said carefully. "But we're still hoping for the best. And I want you all to know that we are not trying to keep you separated from each other. But we have to protect Alluveterre. The Council is watching your pendant feeds *very* closely, and while they may not be actively working against our order, we also cannot truly count them on our side."

"I'm sure Dex could cover us sneaking away for a few hours," Sophie argued.

"Mr. Dizznee's talents are especially creative," Wraith agreed. "But the Council's new measures are cleverer than you might expect. It took our Technopath most of last night to set up the false feed we're using right now. And it's only for a limited time."

"Besides, we need Dex concentrating on other things," Blur added.

"Like what?" Sophie asked, surprised that Dex hadn't mentioned anything.

Mr. Forkle shot Blur a look that seemed to say, *That was top secret information!* before his voice filled her head.

We've given Mr. Dizznee access to all of the eldest Mr. Vacker's registry records, hoping he'll be able to determine why the Neverseen went to such lengths to destroy the files.

Is that why they broke in to the registry? Sophie asked.

In part. The investigators were unable to determine if any additional files were accessed. But all of Brant's, Fintan's, Ruy's, and Mr. Vacker's records were erased. It's quite fortunate we'd made our own copies before the break-in. And I'm sure you can understand why we asked Mr. Dizznee to keep this project quiet.

"I know you're talking about me," Fitz said when Sophie's eyes darted his way. "And you know I can eavesdrop on what you guys are saying, right?"

"But you won't," Granite told him. "Because you respect Sophie too much to violate the rules of telepathy."

Tam snorted. "Telepaths are weird."

"Said the guy who won't trust anyone until he's read their shadowvapor," Linh teased.

Tam was a Shade, which meant he could manipulate shadows—including the inner darkness everyone hid in their minds. He claimed he could tell whether someone was trustworthy simply by sensing how much shadowvapor he felt when he took a reading—and it seemed to be true. Tam had doubted both Alvar and Keefe because they'd refused to submit to the test. Sophie was still waiting for the *I told you so.*

"Just tell me what's going on," Fitz said, and Sophie could hear the desperation hidden in his voice.

She sighed. "Dex is investigating your brother, trying to see if he can learn anything about the Neverseen. And they didn't tell us because . . ."

She pointed to his hands, which were fisted so tightly, his thumb rings were cutting into his skin.

It took Fitz six painful seconds to relax his grip, and when he did, he turned to Mr. Forkle. "I want to know what he's found."

"Nothing at the moment—another reason we've waited to

tell you. If you don't believe me, you're welcome to speak to Mr. Dizznee directly."

"I will," Fitz assured him—and Sophie made a mental note to be there in case the conversation turned into an epic disaster.

"Now, can we focus on the reason we're all here?" Mr. Forkle asked. "Mr. Song—"

"I've told you I don't want to be connected with my parents' name," Tam interrupted.

"Right. My apologies. Mr. *Tam*. Did Blur explain the plan?"

"He said something about having me lift another veil. And I've been hoping I misunderstood. You remember what happened last time."

"I do," Mr. Forkle said. "Prentice finally woke up."

"Right—but after that," Tam pressed. "I'm never going to forget those screams."

"Why was Prentice screaming?" Sophie asked as Linh reached for her brother's hand.

"It only lasted a few minutes," Mr. Forkle assured her—which was hardly reassuring. "And I suspect it was from the influx of jagged memories released by the veil."

"Anyone else confused?" Fitz asked.

"Very," Sophie said. In all the times she'd been in people's minds, she'd never felt any veils.

"Shadowvapor forms in layers," Tam explained. "Only Shades can sense them. And I like to think of them as veils, since they usually feel thin and wispy—and they're always covering the things we're trying to hide. That's why I can learn so much from reading someone's shadowvapor. The more you have, the more secrets you have. But the veils of darkness in Prentice's mind felt like they were made of solid metal. It took all my energy to lift one, and when I did, his consciousness surged back as it released the memories hidden underneath."

"All the years of Exile and madness must've buried him in darkness," Granite said quietly. "I just wish I understood what caused the final avalanche."

"We'll figure it out," Mr. Forkle promised. "But today, we need to focus on peeling back another veil—which should be lighter now that we've lifted the layer that smothered him. The piece of memory I recovered was tethered to something else—something weighed down by darkness. Hopefully if we remove the veil, Miss Foster can find it."

"But what if this makes Prentice worse?" Sophie whispered.

"Believe me, I've asked that question a thousand times," Granite told her. "But last time, the process made him significantly better. So it stands to reason that lifting another veil might actually help him."

Out of everyone in the room, Granite had the strongest connection to Prentice. He'd resigned from Foxfire after Prentice's Memory break, and despised the Vacker family for years because of Alden's involvement with what had happened. He'd also adopted Wylie and raised him as his own son.

So if Granite thought it was worth the risk, it had to be a good sign.

"Have you told Wylie we're doing this?" Sophie asked.

Mr. Forkle nodded. "He gave us his blessing."

"Then why isn't he here?" Fitz asked.

"Knowing something is the right decision doesn't make watching it any easier," Granite reminded him. "But he trusts me to protect his father—and I *will*."

"As will I," Mr. Forkle said. "As I'm sure you will as well, Miss Foster. And you, Mr. Tam. We all have the same goal."

Tam sighed. "What memory are we even trying to find?"

"The remaining portion of a symbol. I found one piece during my ill-advised search, and we've now found part of it etched onto a disk connected with the Neverseen—which, by the way, tested negative for any enzymes, in case you were worrying," he told Sophie. "It's made of a stone called duskitine, which is neither rare nor valuable. But it does react to starlight, which may be a clue to its purpose—though at the moment, I'm still at a loss for what it could be. Perhaps once we have the rest of the symbol all will become clearer."

"Can I see the full piece of memory you already found?" Sophie asked.

He shuffled to her side and placed two fingers on each of her temples, sending a scrap of jagged darkness surging into Sophie's mind. The chill made her shiver as the memory emerged from the shadows: white symbols glowing through the dark—three diagonal lines, each decorated with different patterns of dashes before they ended in open circles. The line in the center matched the disk from Keefe's cloak.

"It's possible we're missing more than one piece," Mr. Forkle warned.

"How will I know if I've found them all?"

"Send anything you find to me," Fitz offered. "I'll piece them together and let you know when you're done. And if you need an energy boost, just squeeze my fingers."

He offered her his hand, and after all their months of working together, relying on Fitz felt like putting on a pair of comfy running shoes.

"Are we ready?" Mr. Forkle asked.

Everyone turned to Tam.

He shook his bangs out of his eyes and let go of his sister. "I really hope we don't regret this."

"As do we all," Granite whispered.

Tam's shadow sprang to life, crawling slowly across the room until it fell across Prentice's face and sank into his mind.

SEVEN

TAM HAD BEEN RIGHT ABOUT Prentice's screams.

Sophie would never forget his eerie wails—the sound of someone caught between pure terror and overwhelming despair.

Each second was an eternity.

Each breath a knife in her throat.

And then, as quickly as it started, it was over.

Prentice's mouth snapped shut and his head lolled to the side as Tam stumbled back, his shaky legs collapsing underneath him. Linh lunged to catch him, easing Tam's trembling body to the cold floor as she gathered the moisture in the air into some sort of floating forehead compress.

"Wow," Fitz breathed, the same way he always did when he saw Linh's Hydrokinetic tricks.

Sophie was impressed too—especially with Linh's control. Linh had come a long way since her days of being the Girl of Many Floods and causing so many catastrophes that she'd ended up banished.

"I'm fine," Tam managed to mumble. "How's Prentice?"

"Strong," Mr. Forkle promised.

Sophie turned to check for herself, relieved to see how clear Prentice's eyes looked. The cloudiness she'd noticed earlier had lifted, and his gaze was focused and steady. Even his thrashing had calmed, and his mumbles had dulled to whispers.

"What happened?" Linh asked her brother, shifting his water compress with him as he sat up. "You weren't this affected last time."

"Yeah, well, last time the veil wasn't that heavy." Tam turned to Mr. Forkle. "Your theory about the next layer being lighter was *way* off. It was like trying to lift a big, blubbery whale."

"That's quite the mental picture," Mr. Forkle noted. "And that should give you extra pride for the strength and skill it took to lift it."

"Yeah . . . about that." Tam curled his arms around his knees. "It felt like he helped me."

All four members of the Collective crouched around him.

"What does that mean?" Granite asked.

"It's hard to explain," Tam mumbled, reaching though

Linh's water compress to tug on his bangs. "But I was running out of strength, and I thought . . . maybe it'd help if Prentice knew I was on his side. So I used my shadow to send a message—which won't mess with his consciousness at all, I swear," he added quickly.

Tam had used the same trick when he was first getting to know Sophie. Exillium had strict rules about Waywards communicating with each other, so their first conversations had happened entirely in her head. Whenever his shadow crossed hers, it opened a channel between them, allowing him to whisper directly inside her mind.

"Anyway," Tam continued, "I told him I was working with the Black Swan, and that I needed to move the darkness so that Sophie could search his memories. And as soon as I said her name, the resistance lessened and the veil started budging."

Granite whispered something Sophie didn't catch as he rushed back to the cot and grabbed both of Prentice's hands. "Prentice—can you hear me?"

Everyone stopped breathing.

Waiting.

Wondering.

And . . . nothing.

"It's for the best," Mr. Forkle said quietly, before turning to Sophie. "If Prentice responds to your name, I'd be wary of using it when you're in his mind. And speed must be of the essence. In fact, I think we should set a timer."

He fumbled in his cape pocket and pulled out a shimmering crystal hourglass.

"Do you always carry that around?" Sophie asked.

"A wise leader is always prepared. You'll have ten minutes. I don't think you should be in his mind any longer than that."

The lump in her throat blocked Sophie's voice. But she did her best to look confident as she approached Prentice's bed. Fitz moved behind her, taking her hand to help steady her nerves.

"Squeeze my fingers if you need me," he told her. "I'll also randomly send a few bursts of energy just in case."

Sophie nodded, taking one last look at each of the worried faces of her friends before she focused on the only one that mattered.

"I'm not going to hurt you," she promised Prentice.

Then she pressed her consciousness into his mind.

Down, down, down she sank—through darkness and shards of memory that battered against her mental barriers. Her stomach plummeted with the rush, even though she knew her body wasn't actually moving.

The farther she fell, the more the blackness faded.

First to gray.

Then to white.

Then to something . . . else.

A color too bright for her mind to name.

It was all colors in one—blindingly perfect in its purity. And as her consciousness slowly adjusted, other images took shape.

Fractal patterns.

Flecks of rainbows.

Everything opalescent and swirly.

And standing amid all of that beauty was a figure.

A young woman in a pale purple gown, with long blond hair and a dazzling smile.

"Hello, Sophie," Jolie whispered. "I knew you'd come back to see me."

EIGHT

SOPHIE KNEW JOLIE WASN'T ACTUALLY there—but that didn't make the vision any less real.

Prentice had conjured up Grady and Edaline's daughter in perfect vibrant detail, right down to the wispy, frilly gown in Jolie's favorite color. He'd used the same projection once before, to guide Sophie out of his madness when she'd first tried reading his mind. But this time, instead of a meadow, they were nestled in a pocket of space among all the shimmer and sparkle.

"I'd thought your mind would feel more familiar," Jolie said. "But it's different somehow. Stronger."

You remember me? Sophie transmitted.

"Sometimes I do, and sometimes I don't. Reality is relative."

Jolie's turquoise eyes focused on her slender fingers, wiggling them, like she was checking to see if they really belonged to her. "Am I right? Has something changed?"

Last time my powers were broken, Sophie told her. *They had to fix me before I could come back. And then you were gone.*

"I had to go away," Jolie whispered. "I don't remember why. But I'm here again—and it's so much brighter this time!"

She raised her arms and twirled, her featherlight skirt floating around her.

Why do you use Jolie to communicate with me? Sophie had to ask. *Did she mean something to you?*

"You're still looking for reason. The mind is a funny thing. Logic doesn't always run things the way it should. So often it's feelings." Jolie reached out and caught a green fractal pattern floating by, and it turned blue and swelled large enough to surround them.

"I make you feel safe, don't I?"

Yes.

Sophie had never met Jolie, but she knew that if she had, she would've liked her. Everyone who knew her had loved her. Even the person who'd killed her.

"You remind me of her," Jolie said, flipping the ends of her golden hair. "And it's easier this way. I've lost such track of myself, I don't know how to be me."

But I am talking to Prentice right now? Sophie asked, needing to be sure.

Jolie's smile faded. "Prentice is everywhere and nowhere. *He* can't help you. Though rumor has it, you can help him."

I can, Sophie said, her heart thundering so loud, she wondered if the whole room could hear it. *But it might not be safe yet. He—or, I guess I should say* you—*need to get stronger.*

The fractals shifted again, flickering through so many colors it felt like standing in a disco ball. Jolie's image flickered too, her features growing vague and smudged. "It's strange. Sometimes I feel so sane. And other times . . ."

The light shattered.

Icy splinters jabbed Sophie's consciousness, screeching like nails on a chalkboard as she plummeted. She tried to squeeze Fitz's hand for help, but her body felt disconnected.

No strength.

No power of her own.

Blackness crashed around her, so thick it felt tangible—and then it *was* tangible as the shadows twisted into—

A swan?

"Sorry," Jolie said from somewhere behind her as Sophie struggled to get a firmer grip on the soaring bird's slender neck.

Jolie's arms wrapped around her waist and the touch felt warm and soft—despite the blizzard they were flying through. A storm of blurry fragments that seemed determined to send them careening again.

"I'm trying to hold it together," Jolie told her. "Black Swans always keep me centered."

I wasn't supposed to talk to you, Sophie admitted. *They're afraid I'll make you worse.*

"Nothing could be worse than where I've been."

I'm so sorry.

The words were never enough—but Sophie didn't have anything else to offer.

Where are we going? she asked, trying to figure out if they were flying forward or backward or sideways.

"Somewhere. Nowhere. Everywhere. It's all the same here. Always now but never then. Always then but never now."

That doesn't make a whole lot of sense.

"Welcome to my world. I'd love to say you get used to it, but . . ."

The swan started spinning loop-di-loops, tossing Sophie's stomach around with it. She wondered if she could throw up in someone else's head.

"You're looking for something, aren't you?" Jolie asked. "That's what the voice in the shadows told me before you came."

That was Tam. He's a friend.

"I'm glad I didn't drag him under, then."

You do that?

"Sometimes. Not always by choice."

So . . . sometimes you do it on purpose?

"If I did, would that scare you?"

A little. But I trust you.

"Does that mean you'll come back?"

Of course I will, Sophie promised. *But right now, I'm only allowed to stay for a few more minutes. Can you help me find the memory I need before I have to go?*

"I can try," Jolie said as the swan tucked its wings and plunged. "But the memories here aren't what they used to be."

On and on they sank, until they reached a fog of glowing shards all scrambled up and flipped around and crashing into each other. Some had images painted across them. Others moved like fragments torn from a movie. And others held only a cacophony of noises.

"Everything that once was, is gone," Jolie said sadly. "All that's left is fractured and fragmented."

I'm only looking for a piece—or maybe a few pieces.

Sophie projected the image Mr. Forkle had sent her and it flared in front of them like a hologram.

"That doesn't look familiar," Jolie murmured.

Mr. Forkle found it the last time he was in here.

Jolie's arms tensed. "Someone else visited?"

You don't remember?

"I hear voices sometimes. But I can never tell if they're echoes. I hope I didn't hurt him."

He was able to get out—but only barely. That's why he sent me.

"You're the moonlark," Jolie whispered. Her arms clung so tightly that Sophie had to fight to breathe.

Or maybe the pain in her chest came from Jolie's next question.

"How long has it been since I was me?"

I'm probably not supposed to tell you.

"But you're old now, aren't you? Far older than my son was when . . ."

Don't think about it, Sophie said. *There's a lot that needs to be explained—but we have to wait until you're strong enough to handle it.*

"That doesn't sound like good news."

It is and it isn't. There are a million reasons to keep fighting. But it's probably not going to be easy.

The shards trembled and tightened.

"I think I'm slipping away," Jolie warned.

A burst of energy flooded Sophie's senses—probably Fitz sending backup—and Sophie wrapped it around Jolie's fading form.

Please—if you can't stay for me, do it for Wylie.

"Wylie," Jolie repeated. She kept murmuring the name as she waved her arms and made another glowing bubble around them, spinning the shards like leaves in a windstorm. "I still don't see what you're looking for."

It has to be there. I'm pretty sure this is one of the memories you were protecting. Maybe even the reason you called swan song.

The bubble burst at the words.

"I don't know what that means," Jolie said as they sank

into the glittering oblivion. "But the phrase has a pull, like an anchor dragging me toward . . . I don't know."

Down they went again—so far that Sophie wasn't sure she'd ever be able to claw her way back up. But it was worth the fall when Jolie whispered, "There."

She waved her arms and the fragments parted, revealing three blindingly bright pieces. "Those are what you need. I . . ."

Jolie's image vanished into the dark.

Sophie had just enough strength left to wrap her mind around the gleaming shards and transmit a call for Fitz's help.

He sent a tidal wave of heat, launching everything up, up, up—through softness and sludginess and pain and relief until she was back in her body, shivering in a pair of warm arms that held her close and careful and wouldn't let her fall.

"Shhhh," Fitz whispered. "You're back. You're safe."

"How's Prentice?" she asked as Mr. Forkle pressed two fingers against her temples to check her memories.

"Same as before," Fitz promised. "Why? What happened in there?"

"Incredible things," Mr. Forkle whispered. Tears streamed down his wrinkly cheeks as he cleared his throat and added, "I'll explain later. Right now we must focus. Mr. Vacker—perhaps you could ensure I'm assembling these memories properly?"

Fitz slipped into Sophie's mind and she watched as the bits of symbol snapped together. The three diagonal lines from the original image converged with other lines bearing similar circles and dashes, all meeting in a central point and fanning out like rays from the sun.

The symbol was abstract, of course, but it reminded Sophie of an asterisk.

Or a star.

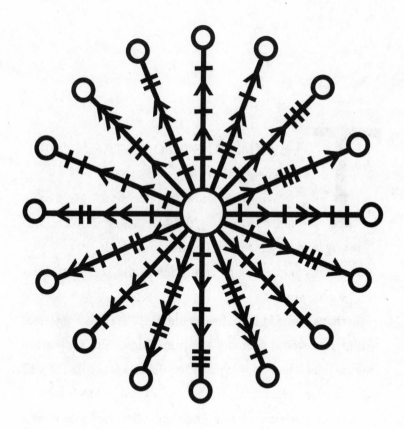

NINE

THE SYMBOL IS A LODESTAR," SOPHIE whispered. "Isn't it?"

"We don't know that for sure," Mr. Forkle said. "Technically, the word 'lodestar' refers simply to any kind of star that can be used as a guide."

"But this could easily be connected to the Lodestar Initiative," Sophie argued.

"Perhaps it would help if we could see?" Granite suggested.

Blur retrieved a memory log from one of the apothecary drawers, and when Sophie projected the image across the stiff pages, everyone had to admit the symbol looked like a star.

"Even if the symbol *is* a Lodestar," Granite said after a moment, "we're still a long way away from understanding what it means. All those dashes and circles have to be signifi-cant. I'm assuming you saw nothing that could help us trans-late while you were in Prentice's mind?"

"I wish. It seemed like Prentice didn't even remember that he'd seen the symbol before. But . . . he only found it after I mentioned swan song. So the two must be connected."

They all tilted their heads and squinted at the star from dif-ferent angles, as if the explanation would pop out at them if they just stared hard enough.

"Soooooo," Tam eventually said, "anyone want to explain why lodestars are so important? Or are you going to keep act-ing like Linh and I aren't here?"

"Didn't they tell you?" Fitz asked, glancing at the members of the Collective.

"I told them Keefe joined the Neverseen," Blur said. "I didn't get into why."

"Care to clue us in now?" Tam asked, not sounding happy to have been kept in the dark.

Mr. Forkle explained what little they knew about the Lode-star Initiative and how Keefe's mom seemed to have created it.

"And the Initiative had something to do with what hap-pened to the gnomes?" Linh whispered, tugging nervously on the silver ends of her hair.

"*That* is unclear," Mr. Forkle emphasized. "Fintan implied a connection when he first threatened the Council with the plague. And he made the Initiative sound as though it's the

Neverseen's grand plan. But he also admitted to eliminating Mr. Sencen's mother so he could take over the project, so it's highly possible he's made his own amendments."

"Does Keefe know what the plan is?" Tam asked.

"He says he's still piecing it together—but I know there's something he isn't telling me," Sophie said quietly. "Maybe he'll be more willing to share when I show him the whole symbol."

"I assume that means you've found a way to transmit to him?" Mr. Forkle asked.

Sophie nodded. "We're going to check in every night."

"You are?" The tightness in Fitz's voice made Sophie realize she'd forgotten to mention that detail when they talked.

"It'll be safer this way," she explained. "He can update me on anything he's learned without having to sneak away."

"Or feed you a bunch of lies," Tam pointed out. "Hey—don't look at me like that. You have to admit it's possible."

"*Anything* is possible," Sophie argued. "All I know is that if I'd been brave enough to try transmitting to Keefe sooner, he wouldn't have had to destroy part of Foxfire to warn me."

"Whoa—back up," Tam said. "*He destroyed part of Foxfire?!* Okay, seriously, am I really the only one who thinks trusting this guy is a bad idea?"

"No," Wraith said, folding his invisible arms under his cloak. "Some of us are a bit more reluctant."

"I'm not," Blur jumped in.

"Well, Squall is just as torn as I am," Wraith said. "So is Granite."

"You are?" Sophie asked.

Granite had seemed so supportive when he first heard about Keefe. He'd even decided to reveal his true identity to help reassure her that she shouldn't be afraid to trust people. But now he shifted his hefty weight, filling the small space with the crunch of his crystallized joints. "I don't doubt that Mr. Sencen left with good intentions—but we can't ignore the possibility that he might become corrupted. He's immersed in the Neverseen's world—training in their methods, being exposed to their teachings and theories. There's no telling how that might influence him."

"Exactly," Tam agreed. "You're with me on this, right?" he asked Linh.

Linh shook her head. "Remember how people have doubted us? Their murmurs and snipes about the strength of our powers. Their outrage when you left with me after I was banished. Not to mention the mistrust because we're twins. They had reasons for their feelings. Did that make them right?"

"No—but their reasons are stupid," Tam argued.

Multiple births were rare in the elvin world, and for some reason that bred judgment and scorn. Sophie would never understand how the elves could be so brilliant and sophisticated and still have so many strange prejudices. They didn't care about skin color or money or appearance. But they condemned anyone without a special ability, or anyone with unusual genetics.

"And you think that's the same as joining the enemy?" Tam asked.

"No, I think it means we shouldn't pass judgment until we see how things play out. Actions never tell the whole story. Good can be done for the wrong reason. And bad can be misunderstood."

"Fine," Tam grumbled. "But if he comes anywhere near me, I'm siccing the dwarves on him until he lets me take a reading. And you guys should be keeping us way better updated about this stuff," he told the Collective.

"The incident at Foxfire was only yesterday," Mr. Forkle explained. "But I realize you're both feeling very separated—and that's because you are."

"Maybe it would be easier if we returned to the Lost Cities," Linh told her brother.

"You really want to go back to Choralmere?" he asked. "You want to deal with Mom panicking that you're going to flood the house every time you gaze at the ocean? You want to hear Dad constantly lying about us, like our very existence brings him shame?"

"Of course not," Linh told him. "I just—"

"I might have a solution for you," Mr. Forkle interrupted. "I've been in talks with the Council about a new arrangement that would allow you to visit the Lost Cities regularly. But nothing is official yet, so I'm going to need you—"

"Let me guess," Tam jumped in, "You want us to be patient?"

Mr. Forkle smiled. "I know I ask for that a lot. I also demand it of myself. I've often said that it seems we're attempting to drain the ocean with a leaking spoon. But even if that's the case, we can either give up, or we can continue taking it one dripping spoonful at a time. And *this*"—he pointed to the symbol Sophie had projected—"is a pretty important spoonful. We need to find out what it means."

"I can ask Keefe," Sophie offered. "Though he didn't recognize the black disk or the symbol when I showed it to him last night, so I doubt he'll be much help."

"I can think of someone who might know more about the symbol," Fitz mumbled. "But . . . you're not going to like it."

Sophie was about to ask who when she figured it out on her own.

She groaned. "Please tell me you're not asking us to trust Lord Cassius."

TEN

WOW," LINH WHISPERED, staring at the stark crystal sky-scraper looming over them. "*This* is where Keefe grew up?"

"It explains a lot, doesn't it?" Sophie mumbled.

Mr. Forkle hadn't been sure if it would be wise to bring the twins on this excursion—but Sophie had insisted. Maybe it would help Tam understand where Keefe was coming from.

Their feet crunched on the gravelly ground as they crossed under an intricate arch with the word CANDLESHADE woven into the iron. Lord Cassius answered the golden door before Mr. Forkle finished knocking, looking pristine in his intricately embroidered blue cape. He reminded Sophie far too much of his son—same blond hair and ice-blue eyes. Same handsome features. But he was the version where all the fun had been squeezed out and only the sour was left.

Even his smile was creepy—oily and insincere as he said, "Why, Miss Foster. I almost didn't recognize you with your hair back. But it's always a pleasure to see you. And you as well, Mr. Forkle. And Mr. Vacker." His eyes flicked past Sandor and Grizel without acknowledging them and settled on Tam and Linh. "And who might our surprise guests be?"

"This is Tam and Linh Song," Mr. Forkle told him, ignoring Tam's scowl at the use of his last name.

"Song?" Lord Cassius repeated. "You're Quan and Mai's children?"

"Their *twins*," Tam corrected.

Tam's father had tried to convince people that Tam and Linh were a year apart in age, but they refused to play along.

"I see the resemblance now," Lord Cassius said, studying the twins more closely. "I know your father well. He was a Level ahead of me at Foxfire, but we often studied together. We still meet for drinks in Atlantis sometimes."

Tam glanced sidelong at Sophie. "I suppose I shouldn't be surprised to hear that."

"Do your parents know you've joined the Black Swan?" Lord Cassius asked.

"I don't see why they would," Tam told him. "And for the record, we haven't sworn fealty."

"*Yet,*" Linh added quickly.

"I know the feeling." Lord Cassius had volunteered to join the Black Swan himself—which made Sophie want to vomit on his jewel-encrusted shoes. She didn't care that he'd been searching his wife's possessions for clues to her Neverseen activities. Finding a bunch of maps and a leaping crystal kit would never make up for the way he'd treated his son.

"Oh my," Lord Cassius said, fanning his face, "I always forget how intense your emotions are, Miss Foster. It's such a strange sensation to feel them wafting through the air. A bit like static electricity, only pricklier."

Most Empaths needed physical contact to take a reading, but for some reason Keefe and his father were different—at least when it came to Sophie.

"Well," she said, hoping he could feel the massive waves of disgust she was sending his way, "some things give me a stronger reaction than others."

Abuse came in all forms—and while Lord Cassius had never hit his son, his constant belittling criticism had done plenty of damage.

Not surprisingly, he didn't bother asking for an update on Keefe as he stepped aside to let them in. The sparse foyer felt as cold and welcoming as a morgue—black floor, sleek walls glinting with sparks of blue balefire, and a silver staircase that spiraled all the way up to the two hundredth floor.

"You said you needed my help with something when you hailed," Lord Cassius prompted.

"Indeed. We're looking for any information you might be able to provide us about this symbol." Mr. Forkle removed the memory log from his cape pocket and handed it over.

Lord Cassius's eyes widened. "Lodestar."

"So that *is* what the symbol means?" Sophie asked.

Lord Cassius frowned, turning the memory log to study the symbol from different angles. "It's strange. The word clicked when I looked at the image, but I have no idea why."

Memories could do that sometimes—especially memories that had been erased. Some triggers only dragged certain details back. Others unleashed the entire scene in a dizzying rush. Sophie knew the feeling well, thanks to the secrets the Black Swan had planted in her brain. It was also why she wasn't allowed to ever visit her human family, in case seeing her made them remember.

"I feel like there's something I'm missing," Lord Cassius said, scratching his head and messing up his immaculate hairstyle.

"The mind is a tricky thing," Mr. Forkle told him, taking the memory log back. "If you remember anything else, you know how to reach me."

"Of course. Though I don't see why you need *me*. Surely you realize there's someone who could be infinitely more helpful."

Sophie was about to ask who when realization dawned, spreading goose bumps across her skin. "You . . . want us to ask your *wife* about the Lodestar Initiative?"

"Why not?" Lord Cassius asked. "Isn't this whole thing her mess? Who better to solve the problem than the one who created it in the first place?"

"Uh, maybe someone who's not locked away in an ogre prison?" Fitz suggested.

For the briefest glimmer of a moment, Lord Cassius's expression faltered and he looked like a grieving husband and a crushed father, standing all alone in his cold, empty tower.

Then he blinked and it was gone, replaced with his dripping smile. "Where there's a will, there's a way."

"Not in this instance," Mr. Forkle told him. "If we express interest in Lady Gisela, we turn her into an ogre bargaining chip—one that would come at far too high a cost."

"Diplomacy so rarely yields results," Lord Cassius agreed. "But that's why I've grown so passionate for your order. Rumor has it, the Black Swan staged a rather successful raid on Exile a few months back. Why not pull the same trick again?"

"Because we've gained wisdom," Mr. Forkle told him. "And experience."

Their adventures in Exile hadn't exactly gone as planned, between Fitz nearly dying and the Council almost arresting everyone. And yet, Sophie couldn't help finding Lord

Cassius's suggestion *tempting*. Not only could Lady Gisela teach them all the things Keefe was so determined to learn from the Neverseen, but Keefe also wouldn't need Fintan to rescue his mom.

No, Mr. Forkle interrupted. *A jailbreak in an uncharted prison run by a particularly violent species will never be a worthwhile risk—especially considering that Lady Gisela may no longer be alive.*

Dread hit her stomach with a thud. *But Fintan told Keefe—*

Yes, I know what he promised. I also know he gave Mr. Sencen that information when he was trying to lure him into joining their order. And even if the report was accurate, it's been weeks since then—and Lady Gisela was badly wounded at her arrest. Or if she is alive, it's also incredibly likely that they erased her mind before they sent her away.

You've put a lot of thought into this, Sophie noted.

Of course. The Collective and I have discussed it at length. I never mentioned it because I know how you struggle to ignore possibilities.

Or maybe it was because your first instinct is to say no to everything. You realize that ninety percent of the time, you give me a big speech on all the reasons why an idea is too dangerous, and then a few weeks later we end up doing it anyway?

A rueful smile curved his lips. *And in each of those instances, it was only because the situation grew especially desperate. Thankfully, we're not there yet. There are avenues we haven't yet explored—like showing the symbol to Gethen when we meet with him and seeing if we can trick some answers out of him.*

I guess that's true, Sophie hated to admit.

She'd been expecting him to offer his usual less-than-helpful solutions, like "read a bunch of really long books" or "practice telepathy with Fitz."

Gethen . . . might actually work.

Good—it's settled, Mr. Forkle told her as he turned to their group. "Forgive our moment of distraction."

Lord Cassius nodded. "I'm sure we're all used to Telepaths. Have you at least come to a decision?"

"Only that we'll be focusing on alternate plans. But thank you for the suggestion. I wonder if I could trouble you with one further request. I'd love to take a look around before I leave. Perhaps my fresh eyes might turn up a clue your wife left behind."

"Where would you like to search?" Lord Cassius asked. "There are *quite* a few places."

Talk about an understatement.

Sophie doubted an army of gnomes would be able to search the massive estate in less than a week—and gnomes were the most efficient, industrious creatures she'd ever met. Still, Keefe had stayed at Candleshade the night before he ran off with the Neverseen. And while he was there, *something* must have changed.

When he'd left Sophie's house he'd seemed upset—but nothing like the mess he'd been the next day.

Something had triggered new memories—memories that made him believe he was part of the Lodestar Initiative.

So maybe if she searched his room, she could find what made him remember.

ELEVEN

UH," FITZ SAID. "SO THIS IS KEEFE'S room."

Sophie blinked. "That's right—you've never been here."

"Uh, have *you*?"

"I'd like to know that answer as well," Tam said.

She shook her head. "Keefe told me he didn't like to have friends over to his house. But I've seen it in a few of his memories."

The memories weren't happy memories, though, so she hadn't paid much attention to the scenery. The room took up three stories, and was one of the fanciest places Sophie had seen—sparkling crystal walls, swirling chandeliers, and tons of ornate furniture in shades of black, white, and gray.

"This place reminds me of our old room," Linh mumbled. "We weren't allowed to decorate it either."

"You guys shared a room?" Fitz asked.

"It was our punishment for telling people we were twins." Tam rolled his eyes.

Linh hooked her arm around him. "Too bad I liked sharing a room better."

"And yet you ditched me the first second we got to Alluve-terre."

"Hey, what girl is going to pass up her own private tree house?" Linh asked.

"Definitely not me," Sophie said, trying to figure out where to start their search. Everything seemed so un-Keefe, it was hard to imagine him touching any of it.

"What exactly are we looking for?" Tam asked. "Keefe doesn't hit me as the Dear Diary type—though if we find one, I call dibs."

"No you don't," Sophie told him. "We're not here to *snoop*. I just figured we should look around and make sure there's nothing important."

"Well, this place is huge," Fitz said. "So maybe we should split up—some of us upstairs and some of us downstairs and meet in the middle?"

"New game!" Grizel jumped in. "Girls versus boys. Losers owe the others a favor. GO!"

"Bring it on!" Fitz said, sprinting for the stairs.

Grizel beat him there and bolted downstairs, so Fitz raced up.

"Looks like we have closet and bathroom duty, guys!" he shouted.

"I'm going on record right now and saying I'm not getting within ten feet of Keefe's underwear!" Tam shouted back.

Sandor heaved a sigh as he turned to follow the boys. "If you care about me at all, Miss Foster, *lose* this silly game. Do whatever you have to do."

Sophie and Linh shared a look before they made their way downstairs, where Grizel was already busy flipping though one of the notebooks piled on an enormous gilded desk. "Either of you want to give me a hand with these?"

Linh grabbed one. "Wow. The whole first page is just *'bored bored bored'* written over and over."

"He also makes some rather entertaining notes about his Mentors in the margins," Grizel said. "But none of that is particularly useful, so we'd better get moving. We're winning this thing! And when we do, Sandor is taking me dancing."

"Dancing?" Sophie repeated, trying to picture that.

Nope.

Her brain couldn't compute.

"Does dancing mean something else to goblins?" Linh asked.

"I don't know—does it mean this?" Grizel hummed a silky beat and shook her hips in a move that reminded Sophie of belly dancing, only with less arm waving and more head bopping.

"You really think Sandor's going to do *that*?" Sophie asked.

"He will if you help me force him. Think of the favor you could demand from that pretty boy up there. And I bet our little Linh would love to force her brother to do something especially embarrassing."

Linh grinned. "How do we win? You never explained the rules."

"Of course I didn't. How else can I change them? Now get to work!" Grizel pointed across the room—which seemed to be some sort of study, complete with oversize armchairs and walls of bookshelves. From a distance, anyone would think a model student lived there—or maybe a snooty professor. But as Sophie looked closer, she could spot glimmers of Keefe in the details. Like the subtitles he'd scrawled on the spines of the books:

688 pages that don't actually tell you anything.

Does anyone honestly care this much about fungus?

I tore a page out of the middle somewhere—good luck trying to find it!

"Think this is significant?" Grizel asked, pulling a silver Imparter from one of the desk drawers.

"I'm betting he left that so no one could track him down," Sophie said "But you're welcome to compare it to mine to see if there's something unique."

She handed over her Imparter, and Grizel studied them from every angle. "Ugh, I guess you're right. These look identical—oh, what's that?"

Linh showed them the notebook she'd been flipping through, where Keefe had drawn a detailed map of Foxfire and marked several places with "Hide gulon here."

Grizel snorted. "I'll give the boy this—he's definitely creative."

"That's true," Sophie realized, trying to see the room through Keefe's eyes. "We need to search beyond the obvious places. He'd want to be clever—hiding stuff in plain sight where no one would suspect. He'd also enjoy damaging things his father cared about, like the walls or the floor or . . ."

Sophie squatted to find the *S* section on the bookshelf. Specifically: *The Heart of the Matter* by Lord Cassius Sencen.

Keefe's father had published his theory that elves generated emotions in both their minds and their hearts, and believed the heart was where the purer emotions lived. Sophie actually found the idea fascinating—and it synced with certain things she'd experienced during her inflicting training. But Keefe's subtitle was: *I'd rather gouge my eyes out with a Prattles pin.*

She flipped back the cover and found that Keefe had glued all the pages together, then cut out their center, creating a hollow space he'd packed with vials of elixirs.

"Victory is ours!" Grizel shouted, handing Sophie back her Imparter.

"It's not about who finds something first—it's about who finds the most!" Sandor snapped back. But Sophie could hear him yelling at Fitz and Tam to work faster.

"I'm not sure this stuff is actually important," Sophie warned, holding up two of the vials—Burp Blaster and Pus Powder. "I think it's Keefe's pranking supplies."

"Maybe some of it," Grizel said, fishing out a silver forklike gadget from the bottom. "But this is an effluxer—also known as an ogre repeller. One of my favorite inventions you guys make, by the way."

"Yeah, but Keefe uses those for pranks," Sophie argued. "One time he tried hiding them in the grounds at Foxfire, so they'd go off right as the principal walked by."

"No wonder he and my brother don't get along," Linh said. "They're basically the same person."

Practically on cue, Tam shouted from the bathroom above, "Dude—this guy uses more hair products than I do!"

"Well," Grizel said, tucking the effluxer next to her sword, "I'm still counting this as a find. The rules never said it had to be related to the Neverseen."

She winked.

"But we're not done searching yet," she added. "I don't just want to win. I want to crush them like a sanguillisk."

"Do I want to know what that is?" Sophie asked as she followed Grizel back upstairs.

"Depends on how you feel about bugs," Linh told her.

"Imagine a roach and a mosquito having a ten-pound flying baby."

"And . . . now I'm never going to sleep again."

Grizel laughed as she and Linh got busy searching under the bed and between the mattresses.

Sophie studied the space, trying to think like Keefe again. "Where's Mrs. Stinkbottom?"

"Am I going to regret asking what that is?" Grizel asked.

"She's a green gulon stuffed animal that Elwin and I gave Keefe to help him sleep. He didn't have a satchel when he left, so she should be here."

They checked under the bed again, and under the decorative pillows piled on top, before making their way upstairs.

"This is our territory," Sandor growled, blocking them from entering the humongous bathroom, complete with mirror-lined walls and a swimming pool–size bathtub.

Grizel stroked his cheek. "Are we making you nervous?"

Sandor flinched out of the way, not saying a word as Sophie and Linh made their way into the closet. They found Fitz and Tam sorting through the racks of clothes—*so* many clothes. Enough to last Keefe a decade or two.

"Anyone see any stuffed animals?" Sophie asked. "I can't find Mrs. Stinkbottom."

Tam snickered.

"Hey, all the cool kids are sleeping with stuffed animals these days," Fitz informed him.

"I take it that means you have a Mrs. Stinkbottom of your own?" Linh asked.

"*I* have a Mr. Snuggles."

"Wow." Tam said. "Just . . . wow."

Grizel clapped her hands. "Enough about stuffed animals. Did you boys find anything?"

Sandor's smile was undeniably smug when he showed her the two stashes of pranking elixirs they'd found in Keefe's shoes—plus a rather terrifying container labeled MIXED FECES that had been hidden behind a rack of tunics.

"We also found my favorite bramble jersey," Fitz added. "I *knew* he stole it."

"That doesn't count," Grizel told him.

Sandor shrugged. "Either way, we're still winning. And I already decided on my favor."

"Yeah, well, don't go counting on it yet," Grizel warned. "Girls—help the boys with this closet. I'm sure they've missed something."

Sandor was busy assuring her they hadn't when Linh noticed the edge of a silver chest in the shadows of the highest shelf.

Sophie floated the trunk down using her telekinesis. "Looks like more pranking supplies—another effluxer, a few empty medicine vials, and a bottle of Drooly Dew."

The bottle was wrapped in crumpled green paper, and when she spotted an opened card underneath it, Sophie realized she was looking at the gift she'd given Keefe for midterms the year before. He'd teased her mercilessly about the detention dance lesson she'd been forced to share with Valin—nicknamed one of the "drooly boys" by Marella—so she'd decided to get back at him. In the card she'd written, "Now you can be drooly too!"

She couldn't believe he'd kept it.

"All right, back to searching," Grizel said. "I'm not settling for a tie. You boys found three stashes, and we found two, and learned that Mrs. Fartbottom is missing."

"Stinkbottom," Sophie corrected. "And honestly, I'm starting to think we're wasting our time. If Keefe left something for us, he probably would've asked me if I found it. And if he had something to hide, he probably would've taken it with him."

Grizel shrugged. "Either way, we still need a winner. Did you boys already check all of the cape pockets?"

"Some of them," Fitz said.

Grizel clicked her tongue and rushed over to a rack of cloaks. "Clearly I need to teach you some dedication. But we'll do that *after* I destroy your lazy butts with the find of the night. Come on, Sophie and Linh, let's crush these boys!"

"Not if we crush you first!" Sandor shouted, charging into the cape-pocket showdown.

"Are all goblins this competitive?" Sophie asked, deciding to watch from the sidelines as Sandor and Grizel tried to shove their meaty hands into the narrow pockets.

"It's just *her*," Sandor squeak-growled.

"Nothing wrong with a girl who goes after what she wants,"

Grizel argued. "And what I want is a whole night of you wearing those silver pants I know you still have and sashaying around the dance floor."

Sophie giggled. "Can I be there?"

Sandor tore through the capes even faster. "No, because it's not happening!"

"Oh, sweetie, I hate to break it to you—but BAM!" Grizel pumped one fist while she used the other to wave a sealed envelope under Sandor's nose. "Would you like do the honors, Sophie—even if you don't deserve it, after you chose to be Too Cool for the Cape Hunt?"

Sophie caught herself holding her breath as she took the envelope from Grizel, slid her finger under the flap, and removed a folded, crumpled paper.

"Did Keefe draw that?" Fitz asked, peeking over Sophie's shoulder at the photo-real sketch of Lady Gisela looking elegant and aloof—but with a hint of her son's smirk.

"I think so," Sophie said.

She'd seen the same sketch in a memory Keefe had shown her, of his father screaming at him for drawing during his Foxfire sessions. Lord Cassius had torn all the pages out of Keefe's notebook and stormed off. But after he was gone, Keefe's mom had retrieved one drawing.

Sure enough, when Sophie turned the portrait of Lady Gisela over, she found a note in loopy writing.

Signed: *Love, Mom.*

TWELVE

T HE ENVELOPE WAS STILL SEALED,"
Fitz said, taking the drawing from Sophie to study
it closer. "So that means Keefe never saw this."

"But why would Lady Gisela hide it somewhere Keefe wouldn't look for it?" Sophie asked.

The note gave them the answer.

Dear Keefe,
   You may think you understand what you
saw today on the mountain. But there's so
much more that needs to be explained.
   I think you're ready for the truth. But
it's going to be confusing.

I need you to trust me.

I've left a way for you to find me.

And I know you're smart enough to figure it out.

This is your legacy. All it takes is a leap of faith.

I'll see you soon.

Love, mom.

81 / 34 / 197

"Lady Gisela must've written this right after the battle on Mount Everest," Sophie mumbled, rubbing her knot of tangled emotions. "After she phase-shifted off the cliff, she must've come here and left it for him."

"But Keefe didn't come home," Fitz added. "We all went to my house—and then we left to find the Black Swan. So he never found it."

"I wonder what he would've done if he had," Sophie whispered.

Would it have stopped him from joining the Neverseen?

Or would it have made him run away sooner?

More important: What had Lady Gisela planned to tell him?

"It sounds like there are a bunch of stories you haven't shared," Tam said, reading the letter over Fitz's shoulder. "But I guess that's how it goes for the new kids in the group."

"We'll try to catch you up," Fitz promised.

Linh pointed to the digits under Lady Gisela's signature. "Do you guys know what those numbers mean?"

"I'm guessing that's what she meant about leaving Keefe a way to find her," Sophie said. "But I have no idea how three numbers would help."

The only theory she could come up with was latitude and longitude coordinates. But those were always in pairs, and they usually had decimal points.

"What's the sparkly stuff?" Linh asked, pointing to the glints on the edge of the paper.

Sophie had been wondering the same thing. They were too small to be temporary leaping crystals, and there were more inside the envelope, like Lady Gisela had added in a pinch of microglitter before she sealed the letter.

But why would she bother—especially since it seemed like she'd been in a rush? Her writing looked much sloppier than the other time Sophie had seen it.

"Well," Grizel said, "while you guys ponder all of that, let's not forget that girls win!"

"Forget it!" Sandor snapped. "It's not happening."

"What isn't?" Mr. Forkle asked from the top of the stairs. Lord Cassius loomed behind him.

Grizel grinned and shook her hips. "Dancing. Sandor's going to be doing a *lot* of it."

"I . . . think I've missed something." Mr. Forkle's eyes were on Sophie, and she was pretty sure his piercing stare meant he'd noticed the not-so-subtle way Fitz had flailed to hide the note behind his back.

Lord Cassius must've noticed too.

"I'm assuming you found something," he said.

Before Sophie could figure out a good lie, Tam grabbed the jar of feces from Keefe's stash and tossed it to him. "We did. Isn't it awesome?"

Lord Cassius grimaced and stalked over to one of the bathroom sinks to wash his hands, even though he'd only touched the container. "We both know that's not what I was referring to."

"We also know that anything Keefe hid in here was because he didn't want *you* finding it," Tam said. "So do you really think we're going to tell you about it?"

Lord Cassius raised one eyebrow. "I see why your father struggles."

All the shadows in the room seemed to stretch.

Lord Cassius let out a sigh. "No need for dramatics. Keep your secrets. I'm done trying to control willful teenagers."

Sophie breathed a sigh of relief, even as Mr. Forkle's voice filled her head.

As soon as we get back to Havenfield, you're showing me that letter.

Out loud he said, "Can someone at least explain why Grizel keeps dancing?"

"Because it's *happening*," Grizel told him.

Sophie explained the specifics of their game.

"And let's not forget that Pretty Boy owes you a favor too," Grizel reminded her. "And Twinny is at his sister's mercy."

"I'm betting this means we're getting a pet," Tam mumbled.

Linh nodded. "As soon as we're able to leave the house more, you're taking me to Claws, Wings, Horns, and Things."

Lord Cassius whistled. "Either your control has improved significantly or you enjoy flooding Atlantis."

Linh didn't reply, but she formed a small bird out of water, letting it soar around the room before splashing Lord Cassius's shoes.

"Whoa," Fitz breathed, blinking several times before turning to Sophie. "What about me? What's my punishment?"

"I'm . . . still narrowing it down," she hedged, her mind screaming with too many possibilities.

"That's fine," he said. "But I think we need to set a time limit so you can't hold this over me forever. Let's say: If you don't call in the favor within a month, it becomes mine."

Sophie agreed, not sure why the deal made her nervous. Worst-case scenario, she'd just rattle off whatever lame idea she came up with off the top of her head.

"Anyway," Mr. Forkle said, "we shouldn't impose on Lord Cassius's hospitality any longer."

"One thing before you go," Lord Cassius said as Mr. Forkle reached for his pathfinder. "I know you saw my son yesterday," he told Sophie. "And that he was behind the damage at Foxfire.

I wanted to thank you for keeping that information private."

"I didn't do it for you," she said.

"That doesn't stop me from appreciating it. I've always valued your friendship with my son. If anyone can guide him along this challenging path he's chosen, it's you. I also assume he'll be contacting you again—and if so, I hope you'd be willing to give him a message."

Sophie steeled herself for some sort of cruel threat. Instead, Lord Cassius told her, "Please let him know that no matter what happens, he will always have a room here at Candleshade. I realize my son and I do not get along. I'll even own that it's primarily my fault. But regardless of our differences . . . Keefe and I will always be family. And no matter where he goes or what he does, he can *always* choose to come back home."

It definitely wasn't the kind of speech that left Sophie feeling warm and snuggly. But Lord Cassius was offering his son more than Tam and Linh's parents had done for their children.

"I'll let him know," she promised.

Lord Cassius nodded. And with that, they leaped back to Havenfield.

Mr. Forkle gave them ten seconds after their group arrived in the creature-filled pastures before he held out his pudgy hand. "Show me the letter."

Fitz obediently passed it over.

"Well," Mr. Forkle said when he'd finished reading, flipping the note over to study the drawing. "Mr. Sencen is a remarkable artist."

"That's it?" Sophie asked as Tam groaned. "What about the note? And the numbers?"

"And the sparkles," Linh added.

"Excuse me for wanting to give proper praise to Mr. Sencen's talent. Look at those details! Do we know how old he was when he drew this?"

"He was a Level Three at Foxfire," Sophie said. "And now you're stalling,"

"I am," Mr. Forkle agreed. "But only because I know you're all going to start shouting at me in a few seconds—even Sandor and Grizel."

"Why would we do that?" Fitz asked.

"Because . . . I know what the numbers mean."

"YOU DO?" six voices shouted in unison.

Mr. Forkle rubbed his temples. "Just as I expected. And now . . ."

He pointed to the path that led to the T. rex pasture, where Grady came sprinting toward them covered in neon green dinosaur feathers.

"Is everything okay?" Grady asked. "I heard shouting while I was bathing Verdi."

"We're fine," Mr. Forkle said. "But by all means, please join this conversation. It'll save me from having to explain a second time."

Mr. Forkle handed Grady the note from Keefe's mother and pointed to the line under the signature. "Eighty-one, thirty-four, one hundred and ninety-seven. I'm surprised none of them could guess after seeing the crystal powder."

Grady sighed. "Path angles."

Mr. Forkle nodded. "For those who've never made a temporary leaping crystal before, the beam is made by three facets that converge to a single point, and then collapse in on each other once the leap is done. In this case, the crystal that Lady Gisela is instructing her son to carve has an eighty-one-degree angle, a thirty-four-degree angle, and a one-hundred-and-ninety-seven-degree angle. She also provided the crystalline powder he'd need in order to form it, so he could take the leap of faith and meet her."

"So we can do the same thing, right?" Sophie asked, hoping she hadn't lost any of the powder when she opened the letter.

"I assumed that would be your next question," Mr. Forkle said. "And I'm sure all of you are now imagining rather dramatic scenarios that involve storming a secret Neverseen hideout and solving everything with an epic showdown."

"That'd be nice," Tam said.

"Though I'd be even happier if they surrendered without a fight," Fitz admitted. He rubbed the spot on his chest where he'd been impaled during their Exile prison break.

"*We* are the only ones who will be storming anything," Sandor assured him, pointing to himself and Grizel.

"That won't be necessary," Mr. Forkle interrupted. "And no, Miss Foster, I'm *not* saying that because my first instinct is to deny things. I happen to know where this particular crystal will lead, and it's nowhere we need to be visiting. I used the same angles the day I came to rescue you and Mr. Dizznee from the Neverseen."

THIRTEEN

THE FLASHBACKS HIT SOPHIE HARD.

No visuals. Only sounds.

Ghostly laughter. Haunting threats. Questions with no answers.

"Are you okay?" Fitz asked as Sophie dug her fist under her ribs, trying to keep the tangled emotions from unraveling.

"I'm fine," she promised—then cleared her throat and tried again without the definitely not-fine squeak. "I just don't have good memories of that place."

"Neither do I," Mr. Forkle mumbled. "Seeing you blistered and drugged and strapped to a chair . . ."

Everyone shuddered.

Sophie didn't have the same memories. Her blindfold had prevented her from seeing the hideout. And the cloyingly sweet-scented drugs had dulled the rest.

All she remembered was pain.

And panic.

And scattered random details, like the weight of her bonds, the rush of the elevator they'd used during their escape, and the endless minutes as Mr. Forkle had carried her and Dex through the halls. Then she'd woken up on the streets of Paris with new abilities and three vague clues to help them find their way back to the Lost Cities.

"Just so I'm understanding this right," Tam said, "you guys actually know where one of the Neverseen's hideouts is?"

"An abandoned one, yes," Mr. Forkle said. "They managed to destroy the entrance in the brief time it took me to treat Miss Foster's and Mr. Dizznee's wounds—and by the time I found a new way in, they'd removed all trace of themselves. Which is probably why Lady Gisela chose it for her rendezvous point. If the note fell into the wrong hands, all anyone would find are a few empty underground rooms—and even then, only if they knew exactly how to find them."

"Does that mean the numbers in the note are a dead end?" Fitz asked.

"Unfortunately, yes. I'm sure any lookout Lady Gisela posted there is long gone now that she's in prison. And we monitor the area. No unusual activity has ever been reported."

Fitz's shoulders slumped. "Just when I thought we were getting somewhere."

"We *are* getting somewhere," Mr. Forkle said. "This note is not the only discovery we made today. All we need—"

"I'd like to see it," Sophie interrupted. "The hideout, I mean."

"That would be very unwise, Miss Foster. Reliving all the trauma—"

"I can relive the trauma anytime," Sophie interrupted. "I'm doing it right now."

Grady pulled her close.

"Really, I'm fine," she promised, glad her voice matched the words. "All I'm trying to say is that it's not like I'll ever forget what happened to me."

"Maybe not." Grady kissed her forehead. "But you could trigger additional flashbacks."

"That could be a good thing," Sophie argued. "We might learn something important."

"I can assure you, Miss Foster, that whatever miniscule truths you might glean from those dark flashbacks won't be worth the additional stress they'll cause. Your mind and sanity are far too precious to take such a risk."

"I can handle it," she insisted.

It'd been months since her kidnapping, and she'd never once considered going back. But to stand in a Neverseen hideout—even just the shell of it . . .

Maybe it would help her get inside their heads.

"We know way more about the Neverseen now than we did when I was taken," Sophie reminded them. "Back then, we didn't know the name of their organization, and we hadn't seen the creepy white eye symbol on their cloaks. We'd also never heard anyone mention the Lodestar Initiative. So it *is* possible you missed something when you were there. We have to at least check. I promise it won't be too hard for me, and you already said it won't be dangerous—"

"Funny, I don't remember saying that," Mr. Forkle interrupted.

"You said there's been no unusual activity," she reminded him. "Same difference."

"Just because we've seen no sign of the Neverseen doesn't mean it's safe to go sneaking off to a Forbidden City—especially with the Council watching your registry feed so closely."

"We're following an important lead," Sophie argued. "I'm sure the Council realizes that finding the Neverseen is going to require us bending a few rules—and if they don't, who cares? We've never let that stop us before."

Mr. Forkle sighed so hard it made his pudgy cheeks flap. "Can we at least let this idea sit for a few days?"

"What will that accomplish?" Sophie asked. "Besides wasting time we can't afford to lose? If we have a shot at learning something, why not learn it *now*?"

"I'm with Sophie on this one," Tam jumped in.

"Me too," Linh said.

"You kids are getting too smart for your own good," Mr. Forkle muttered. "Fine. Let me reach out to Blur."

He stepped away to whisper into his Imparter, and Grady shifted so Sophie was facing him. "Are you sure this is a good idea, kiddo?"

"I'm never sure of anything," Sophie told him. "But I've been back to the cave they grabbed me from, and it didn't cause a breakdown."

"This will be much harder," Grady warned. "And you've already had a long, tough day. You've been up since before dawn."

"I know." Sophie yawned just thinking about it. "But we both know I'm never going to sleep until this is done."

"I doubt you will afterward either," he said sadly. "Just . . . promise you won't be afraid to admit if it gets too hard and you need to leave. There's no shame in saying *I can't*."

Sophie promised as Mr. Forkle returned looking equal parts determined and resigned.

"Blur sent two of our gnomes to inspect the area," he said. "As long as they give the all clear, I'll take you for a quick look—but the emphasis must be on 'quick.' Understood?"

"And you mean all of us, right?" Fitz jumped in.

"I leave that up to Miss Foster. She may well prefer to keep this a private moment."

The idea of bringing an audience to her torture chamber felt *strange*.

But facing it alone sounded worse.

"Just . . . don't freak out if I start bawling, okay?" Sophie asked.

Tam and Linh nodded, and Fitz patted his shoulder. "Ready to cry on if you need it."

"What about Dex?" Grady asked.

The question had a weight to it, pressing on Sophie's heart as she imagined how furious Dex would be if she left him out.

But could she watch him relive the horrors—knowing they happened because of *her*?

"I think the smaller the group, the better," she whispered.

"I agree," Sandor said. "It will be easier for me to protect you."

"*You're* going?" Tam asked.

"I go where Sophie goes."

"And I go where he goes," Grizel said, grabbing Fitz's arm.

"But you guys are seven feet tall and gray," Tam argued.

Sandor was unmoved. "I went with Sophie to visit her former home."

"Yeah, but that street's almost always empty," Sophie reminded him. "Paris is one of the humans' most popular cities. There will be people everywhere, taking pictures and videos. And hilarious as your old-lady disguise was, it was *not* convincing."

"Hang on—old-lady disguise?" Grizel asked, cracking up when Sandor flushed.

Even Mr. Forkle was smiling as he said, "No disguises should be necessary. We'll be mostly underground. And I always keep one of these with me for emergencies."

He showed them the obscurer hidden in his pocket—a small silver orb that bent light and sound to hide their presence.

"Some of us won't need your gadgets," Grizel said as she moved into the shadow of a nearby tree. She pressed herself against the trunk and held so still, Sophie lost sight of her.

Sandor coughed something that sounded a whole lot like "show-off" as Mr. Forkle's Imparter flashed with what must've been the equivalent of a text message.

"The gnomes feel the hideout is empty," he said. "And they've agreed to stay nearby in case we need them. So I suppose this is happening."

He pulled a handful of crystals from his pocket and chose one that was pale blue and pear shaped. "I had a permanent crystal cut once I knew the hideout existed."

"You don't think you should change into human clothes before you go?" Grady asked.

"The gnomes are reporting rain in the city," Mr. Forkle said. "Which will clear the streets and make our capes appear far more normal should someone somehow spot us beyond the protection of the obscurer. This mission may seem hasty, but I assure you, I would *not* make it if I foresaw any dangers—no matter how grumpy it might make your daughter."

Grady cracked a smile at that, strangling Sophie with a hug

before Mr. Forkle removed the hourglass from his pocket and handed it to him.

"That will last twenty-five minutes," Mr. Forkle explained.

"I thought it was ten," Sophie said.

"It lasts however long I need it to. Is everyone ready?" He offered Sophie his hand, and she tried not to tremble as Fitz took her other hand and the rest of their group formed a tight circle.

"I'll be waiting," Grady said, holding the hourglass ready to flip.

Mr. Forkle nodded. "We'll be back by the final grain of sand."

FOURTEEN

THE DWARVES WERE RIGHT ABOUT the rain. In fact, "downpour" would've been a better word. The fat, sloshy drops fell so fast they blurred the scenery, bouncing off the gravelly ground and soaking Sophie's group from both above and below.

She could feel the dirty water seeping through her boots when Linh waved one arm back and forth, twisting the rain into thin, gurgling streams and weaving a weblike bubble around them. She pulled her other arm into her chest, drawing the moisture out of their hair and clothes.

"Seriously," Fitz told her. "You're amazing."

Linh's cheeks flushed a deeper pink. "My ability makes it easy."

"I wouldn't sell yourself short," Mr. Forkle corrected. "This is remarkable control."

"He's right," Fitz said, unable to take his eyes off Linh.

"Shouldn't we keep moving?" Sophie asked, sounding grumpier than she meant to.

"We should," Mr. Forkle said. "Just let me get my bearings."

They'd leaped to the edge of some sort of garden, where neat rows of trees led toward an extravagant palace surrounded by flowers and benches and statues and a lake-size fountain. The place was probably a huge tourist trap on a clear day, but for the moment it was empty, save for one couple clinging to their cheap umbrellas as they scurried around looking for better shelter.

"Relax," Mr. Forkle said as Sandor and Grizel clutched the handles of their swords. "The obscurer will do its job."

Linh kept the rain away as they headed toward a narrow gate in the iron-and-gold fence, but her legs were shaking from the strain by the time they reached a main street.

"It's fine," Tam told her. "Getting wet isn't going to kill us."

"But the water smells like pollution. Besides. If I could hold back a tidal wave in Ravagog, I can hold back a little rain."

"I seem to remember us having to carry you while you did that," Tam reminded her.

"Well, this time I've got it covered." But she nearly tripped as they ran through the puddled crosswalk.

"How much longer until we're there?" Sophie asked as Fitz wrapped his arm around Linh's waist to keep her steady.

The city looked familiar—narrow streets, stone buildings with iron balconies, charming cafés with bright awnings, and tiny cars that looked more like toys than actual transportation. But she didn't recognize anything. No sign of the Eiffel Tower. Or Pont Alexandre III, with its fancy lanterns. She couldn't even see the Seine.

"We're close," Mr. Forkle promised, ducking down a street that felt more like an alley. Cars were parked right on the sidewalk.

"I've always wondered what it would be like to drive around in these things," Fitz said.

"Did you ever ride in one?" Tam asked Sophie.

"Pretty much every day," she said.

"Wow—was it scary?" Linh asked.

Mr. Forkle said "yes" at the same time Sophie said "no."

"*You* drove?" Sophie asked.

"Of course not. But occasionally I was unable to avoid being a passenger—and there is nothing quite so terrifying as putting your life in the hands of a distracted human who's operating a piece of deadly machinery they only marginally understand and can hardly control. It's a wonder any of them survive the process."

A siren blared in the distance, making a different wail than the police cars Sophie was used to hearing, followed by screeching tires and a whole lot of honking.

"Case in point," Mr. Forkle told them, turning down an even narrower alley lined with trash cans.

"Lovely place the Neverseen chose," Tam grumbled as Mr. Forkle dropped to his knees in front of a gunk-encrusted manhole cover.

"It gets worse," Mr. Forkle warned.

"Is that their symbol?" Fitz pointed to the curved markings etched along the grimy circle of metal—and he was right. The whole pattern was made of the Neverseen's round eyes.

"See?" she told Mr. Forkle. "Bet you didn't notice that last time."

"I did not," Mr. Forkle admitted as he twisted the cover and lifted it free.

Dread clawed around Sophie's stomach as she stared at the ladder descending into the darkness. "Wasn't there an elevator?"

"They collapsed that tunnel to stop me from coming back. Took me a whole day to find this back entrance—and it's not a direct access point. We still have a journey underground."

"I'll go first," Sandor said, already lowering himself onto the ladder. "And I'll scout the path ahead."

"You might want to duck when you're down there," Mr. Forkle warned. "I remember the ceilings being rather low. You'll also need this."

He removed a long necklace and breathed on the crystal pendant, letting the heat reignite the blue balefire dormant inside.

"Got any more of those?" Fitz asked as Sandor disappeared into the darkness.

"Unfortunately, no," Mr. Forkle said. "So hopefully you remember your Exillium training. You covered night vision, right?"

"Yeah, but I wasn't good at it," Fitz mumbled.

"You were probably overthinking it," Linh told him. "There's always *some* light present. If you make your mind believe that, it will amplify it for you."

"Precisely. Trust your mind, not your eyes. And if all else fails, remember that you have other valuable senses to guide you. I'll see you at the bottom." Mr. Forkle's hefty girth barely squeezed into the cramped tunnel as he shuffled down the ladder.

"I'll go next," Tam said, already crouching to reach for the top rung. "Maybe I can thin some of the shadows and make it brighter for you guys."

"I should go last," Grizel decided. "To make sure no one follows."

"Then I'll go next to last, to keep the rain away," Linh said.

Which meant it was Sophie or Fitz's turn.

"What would be easier for you?" Fitz asked. "I can be a few steps ahead, or right behind you. Either way, I'll be close."

"I'll go first."

She gave herself five deep breaths—wishing they didn't taste like putrid, rotting trash—before she lowered herself onto the ladder. The metal felt cold and scratchy under her fingers, and she cursed the ruined elevator as she climbed down into the stale darkness.

Her mind was racing way too fast to focus on her night vision, so all she could see were smudges and vague outlines. But she could hear shaky breaths and scraping shoes and feel the vibration in the ladder, proving she wasn't alone. She counted the rungs to keep calm, and had just reached number one hundred and thirty-four when her foot touched solid ground.

"Over here," Tam said, taking her hand. "The floor's uneven, so be careful."

She still managed to trip. Several times.

Sandor returned from his sweep of the passage, and his balefire pendant cast a murky blue glow around the cavern, bouncing off the low ceiling and rough stone walls.

"Where are we?" Fitz asked as he climbed down behind her.

"I believe the humans call it the Catacombs," Mr. Forkle told him.

"I was really hoping you weren't going to say that," Sophie mumbled. "You know there are dead bodies down here, right?"

Linh froze on the ladder. "There are?"

"Yes, Miss Linh—I stumbled through several of the mass graves the day I found this passage. But they're quite far away."

"Still. Mass *graves*?" Linh shuffled up a couple of rungs. "Why would humans have something like that?"

"It's what happens when you have a species with a very short lifespan," Mr. Forkle explained. "As I understand it, they ran out of space to bury all of their bodies. So they moved them down to these old mine tunnels. Some of the bones were even arranged into patterns and decoration. Incredibly morbid, but I suppose some would see it as a tribute."

"So, how many bodies are we talking about?" Grizel asked as she forced Linh to finally climb down. Linh walked on her tiptoes, like she was afraid of stepping on bones.

"I remember reading that there were about six million," Sophie said.

"SIX MILLION?" Tam's too-loud voice echoed off the walls. "Sorry. That's just a *lot*."

"And that's only the dead from one city, right?" Fitz asked.

"Also from a specific time period," Mr. Forkle agreed. "Humans have buried billions of their species throughout the centuries. Their population size was one of the reasons the Ancient Councillors chose to leave the bulk of the world to them—if only they put it to better use. But we can lament their missed opportunities another time."

Sandor used the balefire crystal to illuminate a narrow gap in the far wall and motioned for everyone to follow him. They had to walk single file, so they stuck with their same order, and Fitz kept one hand on Sophie's shoulder in case she tripped.

She counted her steps, trying to keep her mind distracted. But the memories made her wrists burn with every pulse.

"Okay," Mr. Forkle called as she took step one hundred and sixty-four. "Ahead is a series of sharp curves, which will lead to what your eyes will tell you is a dead end. It's an illusion. There's a weak spot in the stones for us to slip through."

"What do you mean by 'weak spot'?" Sophie asked, imagining cave-ins.

"They must've had a Fluctuator alter the stones' density. You'll understand once you feel them. And try to hurry. This is all taking much longer than I wanted."

Sophie's knotted emotions pulsed with every step as she followed the zigzagging path to what looked like a very solid wall of rock. Tam ran his hands over the stones until he found the right spot—then pushed his arm straight through the wall. Sophie flinched, waiting for the stones to crumble, but somehow everything held strong.

"You ready for this?" Fitz asked Sophie as Tam shoved the rest of his body through. "If not, I'll turn back with you."

"I'll go too," Linh offered.

"I'm not a fan of this place either," Grizel said. "I could bring you back to the surface while the others search."

Sophie was tempted to take them up on it.

Very tempted.

But . . . she had to face this.

Before she could change her mind, she aimed for the same patch in the wall she'd seen Tam use and shoved her shoulder through the rocks.

FIFTEEN

SOPHIE COULD FEEL THE STONES ROLL across her skin—kind of like walking through one of those ball enclosures she used to play in as a kid. And when she emerged on the other side, it felt like she'd stepped into another world.

Gone were the rough walls and low ceilings. The hallway was sleek and metal and bright, lit by thousands of tiny flames of balefire glowing in the glass walls. Fitz stepped through the stones behind her, and Linh and Grizel followed right after.

"This is the hall you carried us through, isn't it?" Sophie whispered.

Mr. Forkle nodded. "Mr. Dizznee was kept over here."

His steps echoed off the metal floor as he led them down

the hall. Fitz held Sophie's hand, tightening his grip when Mr. Forkle slid a panel in the wall aside, revealing a small, dusty room.

A line of thick black bars divided the space in half, but otherwise the room was empty.

Mr. Forkle pointed to the cage's far corner, where a black scorch mark on the floor made Sophie shudder. "They'd left him tied up over there. He was lying so painfully still when I saw him, I feared he might be . . ."

"They burned him when he moved," Sophie whispered, tears brimming in her eyes. "I can't believe I had to *force* you to take him with us."

"I wasn't going to leave him," Mr. Forkle promised. "I simply thought it would be faster to carry you one at a time. And it would've let me hold you a gentler way. You both had raw burns—I was trying to make you as comfortable as possible."

When she turned away, his voice filled her mind.

I can see the doubt in your eyes—and I suppose I deserve it after the times I've failed to protect you. But you have to know that I would sooner die than allow harm come to any of you.

"Everything okay?" Fitz asked.

Sophie nodded and walked away from Dex's grim little cell. "Where did you find me?"

Mr. Forkle sounded like the world's most depressing tour guide as he asked her to follow him to a room on the opposite side of the hall with no bars, no furniture—just silver walls and a pile of splintered wood. Sweetness swam through the air, or maybe it was Sophie's mind playing tricks on her as her thoughts fuzzed and her eyes glazed over.

"I've got you," Fitz said, holding her steady.

Tam and Linh took her hands. Even Sandor huddled close, resting a meaty palm on her shoulder.

"This is it?" Sophie asked. "I wasn't in a cell?"

"They had you restrained to a chair." Mr. Forkle kicked a piece of the jagged wood, revealing thick black cords in the pile.

Sophie bent to touch the rope, remembering the feel of its thick fibers against her skin. The pieces of wood were heavy and solid. Unrelenting.

She picked up a piece that looked like the arm of the chair, gasping as she turned it over.

"Scorch marks," she whispered.

The wood slipped from her hand as the nightmares took over.

You're safe, Fitz transmitted, filling her mind with a soft thread of warmth. Their thumb rings snapped together as he pulled her gently away from the pile of wood.

"I told you this would be a bad idea," Mr. Forkle said, kicking a broken board into the wall.

"I'm fine," Sophie promised. "I just . . . need to get out of this room."

Fitz helped her wobble back to the hall and she sank to the floor, putting her head between her knees to stop the spinning.

Want me to carry you out? Fitz offered.

NO!

The thought was so loud he jumped.

Sorry. I . . . I don't want to be carried out of here again, like some helpless little girl.

No one would ever call you helpless. But I get what you mean. Is there anything I can do?

You're here.

He tightened his hold on her hands.

"Are we ready to go?" Mr. Forkle asked.

Sophie closed her eyes, focusing on tying the threads of panic away with her other emotions. The knot in her chest swelled so huge, it felt like it was pressing on her heart. But after a few slow breaths, she could bear it.

"There's still more to the hideout, isn't there?" she asked.

"Only the old entrance," Mr. Forkle said. "But it's nothing worth seeing. Just an empty room with a collapsed tunnel."

"I still think we should check it. We've come this far."

Fitz helped her to her feet and Sophie was glad to walk on her own. But she was grateful for the hand to hold on to.

"Okay, so I have a question," Tam said, breaking the silence. "And this might be one of those stories you need to catch us up on. But . . . how did you get past the Neverseen while you were here? I haven't seen a single hiding place."

"They must've let down their guard after they learned of the plantings in the Wanderling Woods, thinking no one would come searching for two children who'd been declared dead," Mr. Forkle told him. "So when I triggered my distraction, *all* of them left their posts to investigate."

"Why didn't you stage an ambush?" Fitz asked. "You could've captured the Neverseen and ended this."

"We considered it," Mr. Forkle said. "But there were too many unknown variables, and we couldn't risk that our ambush would lead to further harm to Miss Foster or Mr. Dizznee. I honestly wasn't sure if a rescue was even possible—that's why I didn't have a fully formed plan for returning them to the Lost Cities, and why I had to trigger Miss Foster's abilities and leave the two of them to find their own way back. I tried to comfort myself with the knowledge that Miss Foster was well prepared for such adventures, but . . . not a day goes by that I don't regret the decision. I'm very aware of how lucky we are that you had the strength and foresight to call for aid," he told Sophie, "and that Mr. Vacker found you before you'd completely faded away. This whole nightmare was a huge wake-up call for our order. None of us ever imagined our enemies would dare be so bold."

The saddest part was, their kidnapping seemed rather tame compared to the awful things the Neverseen had done since.

But Sophie was trying not to think about that.

She was trying not to think at all.

Trying to focus on breathing.

And walking.

One foot in front of the other. Until the hall ended in a round, empty room.

Half the curved wall had shattered, leaving a pile of jagged glass and twisted metal that looked ready to slice off the legs of anyone who dared to climb it.

"I take it that was the elevator?" Fitz asked.

Mr. Forkle nodded. "They were very thorough in their efforts to leave no trace."

Even the ceiling was crackled in the center, like they'd ripped out a chandelier.

"I can't believe there's *nothing* useful here," Sophie whispered.

"The Neverseen aren't fools," Mr. Forkle told her.

"Maybe not," Tam said. "But I don't think they understand how shadowprints work either. See this?" He kicked a dusty shard out of the center of the floor and pointed to what looked like a smudge underneath. "If the same light hits the same crystal in the same place enough times, it casts a shadow inside the facets. Most people would never notice them. But if you darken them up . . ."

He waved his hands, grabbing every shadow in the room and pulling them to the center of the floor, the smudges turning blacker and blacker as a shape slowly formed.

"Whoa," Fitz breathed as everyone stepped back to study the pattern. "Is that . . . ?"

Sophie nodded. "It's the Lodestar."

SIXTEEN

EVERYONE ELSE SEES THE SYMBOL, right?" Sophie whispered. "I'm not imagining it?"

"Oh, it's definitely there," Fitz said. "Though I don't remember this."

He pointed to one of the rays, where the open circle at the end had thin lines running through the center.

Linh circled the symbol, moving to the part closest to the rubble. "This is the angle they would've seen it from when they first entered from the elevator, right? If you look at it from here, that new mark looks like two runes that spell out . . . Alabestrine."

"The star?" Sophie asked.

Fitz grinned. "I keep forgetting you have the stars memorized."

"You do?" Tam and Linh asked, their jaws falling in unison when Sophie nodded.

"Wow, what must it be like to live in your head?" Tam asked.

"It's very complicated." Sophie squinted at the rune. "So does this mean the symbol is some sort of constellation?"

"If it is, it's none that I've heard of," Mr. Forkle told her. "My memory is far inferior to yours, but as I recall, Alabestrine is what we call a solo star—one that's not connected to anything else."

"Are there a lot of those?" Sophie asked.

"Millions. No idea why this one would be special." Mr. Forkle wandered the symbol several times, turning his head this way and that. "The problem is, even if this *is* a constellation they've created, we'd need to know more of the stars before we'd be able to match it up. And if we did . . . I'm not certain what that would tell us."

Sophie didn't know either.

But it had to mean *something*.

"Just to be sure that I'm understanding this correctly," Mr. Forkle said, turning to Tam, "you were able to create this mark because the symbol was projected here?"

Tam pointed to the damaged ceiling. "I'm betting there used to be a gadget right there that flashed the symbol across the foyer."

Mr. Forkle scratched his chin. "I don't understand why I didn't see it during the rescue. Mind you, I had a lot to consider in that moment—but I can't believe that I would overlook a glowing mark projected across the floor."

"Maybe they didn't keep it lit up all the time," Linh suggested.

"But it would've had to be on a *lot* in order to leave this strong of a shadow impression," Tam reminded her.

Sophie had a much bigger, much more terrifying question.

"Do you think this means that my kidnapping was part of the Lodestar Initiative?"

She knew the Neverseen had taken her, but she'd thought it was because they wanted to learn why the Black Swan created her. She'd never considered it might've been part of some sort of bigger *plan*.

Mr. Forkle sighed. "I figured you might be worrying about that—and before you panic, remember that it's possible this hideout was chosen for its convenience or availability. In fact, that could explain why the symbol wasn't illuminated while I was here."

"Maybe," Sophie said. "But those bars in Dex's cell were permanently installed, weren't they? So even if it wasn't built for me, it was built to hold *someone*."

"And therein lies the problem of only having pieces of information," Mr. Forkle told her. "It raises more questions than it answers. Which means we need to focus our efforts on learning as much about this symbol as possible—and *try* not to worry about the possibilities in the meantime. Have you memorized the details of this shadowprint? I'll need you to project it for me when we return to Havenfield. And speaking of which, I believe we're already past the timeline I gave your father."

They were.

And Grady was *not* happy.

"I was five minutes from hailing the Council and begging them to track your pendants!" he told them as Sophie made her way over and squished him with a hug. "Missed you too, kiddo. Everything all right?"

It wasn't.

But it felt better knowing she was home.

"Did you find anything?" Grady asked.

Mr. Forkle explained about the symbol.

"Wow," Grady whispered, hugging Sophie tighter. "I guess it's a good thing you went."

"It appears so," Mr. Forkle said, handing Sophie the memory log.

She projected the shadowy symbol on the opposite page from where she'd recorded Prentice's memory. The marks were the same except for the runes.

The design had sixteen rays with sixteen circles—so if each one was linked to a star, that meant they had a *lot* of secrets to discover.

"Speaking to Gethen has taken on a new level of priority,"

Mr. Forkle told her, "so use this time to start working on a plan for how to trick him into cooperating. We'll need something clever to get his attention, beyond showing him this symbol. It's always a game with him, and we cannot face him until we know how to win."

Sophie handed him back the memory log. "How long do you think it'll be before the Council lets us meet with him?"

"I'm on my way to Eternalia right now to find out. Mr. Ruewen, do you have any gnomes who might be willing to bring Mr. Tam and Miss Linh to the Alluveterre for me?"

"Lur and Mitya live here now," Grady suggested.

"Perfect. In fact, it might be wise to see if they know anything about the symbol," Mr. Forkle said.

Lur and Mitya had been the ones to discover the hideout in Paris. If it weren't for them, Sophie and Dex wouldn't be alive.

"So that's it?" Tam asked. "You're sending us home to wait?"

"Only because the next step falls squarely on my shoulders," Mr. Forkle told him. "I'll have more specific assignments once I secure the meeting with Gethen."

"Are you going to see the Council looking like that?" Grady asked, pointing to his Forkle disguise.

"Of course. This is the only identity the Councillors are allowed to know. And, if I'm being honest, it also makes the whole process of haggling with them much more entertaining. Councillor Emery looks so delightfully frustrated as he tries to push past my mental blocking. And Councillor Alina loves to pretend like she *almost* recognizes me. I'm certain she'll fall out of her chair when she realizes they nearly elected me instead of her."

"I've been wondering about that," Grady said. "What would you have done if you'd been voted in?"

"I truly had no idea. In all my years with the order, it never crossed my mind that any of my identities might be considered for the Council. It stirred *quite* the controversy among the Collective. Personally, I didn't fret too much, since I assumed I'd never win. But if I'd been wrong, I would've accepted the position. The same means that allowed me to live among humans for twelve years would surely have allowed me to be both Black Swan *and* Councillor."

"And you still won't tell us how you pulled that off?" Sophie asked.

"Perhaps someday. Now, if you'll excuse me, I must be off. And while I'm away, I trust that you four"—he pointed to Fitz, Sophie, Tam, and Linh—"will be responsible members of the order and await further guidance before doing any of your own investigating?"

"Linh and I aren't members of the order," Tam reminded him.

"Yes, and that's something you might want to reconsider. I'm not trying to rush you, of course. But you do push rather hard to be included in all of our happenings."

Tam tugged on his bangs. "I'm sure I'll take the oath soon. I just have . . ."

"Trust issues," Mr. Forkle finished for him. "Not something I blame you for. But keep in mind that there may also be times when something needs to be restricted to those who are officially in our order."

"Do we have to swear fealty together?" Linh asked.

"Of course not. You're each welcome to make your own decision. And speaking of decisions"—he turned to Sophie—"are you planning on telling Mr. Sencen about our discoveries today?"

Her eyelashes turned itchy. "Should I?"

"I . . . would be careful with the specifics," he said. "As I remember, the last time he found a note from his mother, he took the news quite hard."

"Hard" was putting it mildly.

Keefe had tried to run away to Ravagog to take on King Dimitar all by himself. But part of the reason for his recklessness had been that Sophie kept the note secret.

"Let me know how it goes," Mr. Forkle said before he leaped away.

Tam and Linh left with Lur and Mitya a few minutes later.

"Need me to stay while you talk to him?" Fitz asked.

Sophie shook her head. "I'm sure it'll be okay."

It wasn't.

Keefe's mind exploded with angry flashbacks, and he seemed especially fixated on the word "legacy."

Should I not have told you? she asked.

No—it's . . . whatever. I should be used to it by now.

Do you have any idea what she wanted to tell you?

I wish I did.

He also didn't recognize the Lodestar symbol.

You're sure? Sophie pressed. *Look at it really carefully.*

I am. The only part that's familiar is the piece you already showed me. And I have no idea why my idiot dad would think it's connected to the Lodestar Initiative.

Doesn't that scare you? Sophie asked.

A little, he admitted. *But I learned something super important today. Did you know Fintan has a cache—and not the one I stole from you and gave to him? He has one from back when he was a Councillor. Alvar told me. He asked me how I'm holding up after the Foxfire incident, making sure it wasn't affecting my sanity and getting all big-brothery about it—*

Gross, Sophie interrupted.

I know. But I was able to ask him how Fintan's mind didn't shatter after what he did to Kenric. He told me Fintan knows how to wipe his own memories, and locks anything dark-but-crucial away in his cache before he purges it from his mind so he doesn't have to live with it.

Do you think that's why he hasn't recruited any other Telepaths? Sophie asked. *Because he doesn't need them?*

Maybe—I don't know. But don't you realize what that means? His cache is probably filled with everything we need to know about the Neverseen.

Only if we can open it, Sophie reminded him. *Plus, it can't hold any of their current plans. Otherwise how could he work on them if he doesn't remember them?*

Either way, Keefe said. *That cache is my new target. I'm betting he keeps it with the other one. And I'm going to find a way to steal them both.*

SEVENTEEN

YOU'RE ALIVE!" SOPHIE SAID AS Sandor helped her shove through the crowd to where Dex stood with his lanky female bodyguard—Lovise—in the purple grass of Foxfire's expansive main field. "I'd started to worry."

A gleaming silver stage had been set up in the center of the field, awaiting the arrival of the Council for some sort of official announcement. Scrolls had been sent out that morning, instructing at least one representative of every family to gather.

"Sorry," Dex mumbled. "I know I haven't been around much."

"Much? I haven't seen you since midterms!" Sophie's eyes strayed to the damaged pyramid in the background, hidden under a bright orange tarp bearing the Foxfire seal.

A week had passed since Keefe set off the sound wave, and, other than that first day—when Sophie had gone to see Prentice and the Neverseen's hideout—it'd been an endless week of nothing, nothing, and more nothing. All Sophie had heard about Gethen was "We're waiting for an answer from the Council." And Alden and Della had asked Fitz and Biana to stay at Everglen for "family time." Even Keefe's nightly check-ins had been unhelpful. He was still trying to figure out if Fintan hid his cache the same way the Councillors did—tucked away in the void of nothingness that only Conjurers and Teleporters knew how to access. If it was—and Keefe could figure out Fintan's secret verbal command—he could steal it the same way he'd stolen Kenric's cache from Sophie. But so far, Fintan and Alvar weren't giving him any clues.

So Sophie had spent the week distracting herself by having lots of telepathic conversations with Silveny, making sure the alicorns were safe and happy and keeping themselves hidden. Silveny was still in the first trimester of her eleven-month pregnancy, and was happy to share more details than Sophie really wanted to know about preggers life—especially the morning sickness.

Spoiler alert: Apparently, alicorn vomit was just as sparkly as their poop.

Silveny's maternal instincts also seemed to be kicking in, and she kept making Sophie promise that she'd call for her if she ever found herself in danger. It was nice to know that

Silveny cared—but Sophie would never do anything to risk the safety of the baby alicorn, no matter how many times Silveny assured her she wasn't as fragile as Sophie feared.

The rest of the time, Sophie spent trying to learn whatever she could about Alabestrine—but she didn't find much in the library of Grady's office. The only slightly interesting detail was that Alabestrine was isolated from other stars, so its white glow was considered "pure" because no other light ever touched it.

But lots of stars were "pure." And pure light didn't seem to do anything special—though reading up on it did remind Sophie that there was a mirror called the Lodestar. The Silver Tower for the elite levels had a round room called the Hall of Illumination, lined with mirrors that were unique—each meant to teach the prodigies a different lesson about themselves.

The Lodestar mirror reflected pure light, and Sophie kept thinking that had to mean *something*. But . . . the mirror was centuries old.

She'd still asked Mr. Forkle about it, and he'd reminded her that the Neverseen didn't invent the word "lodestar." It still seemed like a strange coincidence, though.

"So what have you been up to?" Sophie asked Dex. "I tried hailing you a bunch of times but you didn't answer."

Dex patted his cape pockets and frowned. "I must've left my Imparter at Slurps and Burps. But I've had it with me every day and it never gave me any alerts. I've been trying to help my dad keep up with all the orders at the store. Everybody's been stocking up on medicines. I think people are worried that the next time the Neverseen attack, someone's going to get hurt."

Sophie was worried about that too—and even more worried that Keefe would somehow be involved.

"What about your *other* project?" she asked, keeping her voice low—though no one seemed to be paying them any attention. "The one the Black Swan told you to keep secret?"

Dex's ears turned red. "You know about that?"

"Blur mentioned it. And don't worry, I'm not mad. I know how hard it is to have a secret assignment from the Black Swan. But now it's my turn to be the one saying: *I want to help.*"

"So do I," Biana said, appearing in the space between them.

As a Vanisher, Biana had a special gift for sneaking up on people. It made her goblin bodyguard Woltzer's job a million times harder.

Sophie could see him now, using his skinny-for-a-goblin arms to shove his way over from the opposite end of the crowd. As soon as he made it, Sandor launched into an epic lecture about keeping track of his charge.

Biana gave Woltzer an apologetic smile before turning back to Sophie and Dex and leaning in to whisper. "Whatever you're planning, count me in—and don't even think about visiting any more secret hideouts without me."

Dex straightened. "What is she talking about?"

"I don't think—"

"Sophie went with Fitz, Tam, and Linh to the abandoned hideout where Mr. Forkle rescued you guys," Biana interrupted, not letting Sophie change the subject.

The color drained from Dex's face.

"Please don't be mad," Sophie begged. "It was just a weird, long day where one thing kept leading to the next."

"If it makes you feel any better," Biana told him, "they left me out too. Maybe we should start our own group. Team Bianex!"

Dex sighed. "That's . . . not the best name."

"It isn't," Biana agreed. "What about Dizznacker? Or Vackiznee?"

"I don't know what you guys are talking about," Fitz said as he and Grizel joined their group. "But I vote for Dizznacker."

"Traitors don't get a vote," Biana informed her brother.

"You're still on that?" Fitz asked. "Seriously—aren't you forgetting that you and Sophie snuck off with Calla and had a big showdown with the Neverseen's Psionipath without the rest of us? How was that any different?"

"Because you guys went to the place where *I* was held prisoner without me." Dex kept his voice low, but Sophie could see a few people glancing their way.

You're right, she transmitted, making Dex jump. *I made a selfish decision. I'm sorry. I didn't want to see the hurt in your eyes as you walked those hallways, knowing that every flashback you had was my fault. But it wasn't fair to leave you out. Please don't hate me.*

Dex bit his lip. "Is there anything else you haven't told me?"

Sophie nodded and transmitted a quick explanation about the Lodestar symbol, the note from Keefe's mom, the shadow on the floor of the abandoned hideout, the rune for Alabestrine, and Keefe's new plan to steal Fintan's cache.

"I was going to tell you everything," she promised. "That's why I kept hailing you."

"Stupid Imparter," Dex grumbled. "I bet it has a loose wire."

"Does that mean I'm forgiven?" Sophie asked.

"Only if you promise that from now on, you'll include me no matter what."

"Hey, that works both ways," Fitz whispered, glancing over his shoulder at the crowd, who'd thankfully gone back to ignoring them. "I want to know what you've learned from my brother's records."

"Me too," Biana said. "And I want to help."

"But you realize what I'm trying to do, right?" Dex asked. "The Black Swan are hoping I'll find a way to track your brother's movements and find him. And if that happens, best-case scenario is he gets sentenced to Exile. Or there could be way worse punishments."

Fitz shrugged, his eyes like teal ice. "No one forced him to do what he's doing."

"That won't make it any easier when it all goes down," Dex said quietly. "I know you're mad, but . . . he's still your brother. Are you sure you're up for it?"

"If I start to feel sorry for Alvar, I'll just think about how many times I've found my parents sobbing these last few weeks," Biana mumbled. "That's why they're not here now. They weren't up for all the stares and whispers—especially if the announcement has to do with the Neverseen."

"And I'll think about what he did to you and Sophie," Fitz added. "I saw the scorch marks on the floor of your cell, and the burned chair Sophie had been strapped to."

Dex rubbed his side, where Sophie knew he hid a thumb-size scar from the ordeal.

"I've tried to understand my brother," Biana whispered. "I've spent weeks researching my family history, hoping I'd figure out what he meant about the Vacker legacy. But so far I don't see anything wrong—or any reason why he thought *I* would understand and not Fitz. And I've decided it doesn't matter. I know our world isn't as perfect as I used to think it was—so I won't be surprised if my family turns out to be the same way. But nothing justifies doing the kinds of horrible things Alvar's doing. Someone has to stop him. I know it's not going to be easy, but . . . please let us help?"

"I guess you can try," Dex said. "But all the records are in tech code, so I doubt you'll be able to read them."

"Then *you* read them, and I'll help find the best dates to look," Biana suggested. "I can think of lots of times I saw Alvar sneaking away and never thought to ask where he was going."

"Same here," Fitz said.

"If that's what you guys want," Dex said. "Just warning—it's *beyond* boring. I thought nothing could be worse than searching that Lumenaria database, but at least with that I got to build the Twiggler to help sort the records. This is literally just reading scroll after scroll of dates and times and tiny coded numbers. I'm going cross-eyed."

"It's on paper?" Sophie asked.

"Yeah—it's easier to spot glitches that way."

"Well, that still sounds better than all the awkward family time I've been having with my parents," Biana told him.

"You guys okay?" Sophie asked.

"We're fine," Fitz said. "My parents definitely have their bad days. But they kept us home because they seem to want to know *everything* about us. It's like they're doubting themselves after not seeing what Alvar was up to."

"My dad even had the world's most awkward conversation with me about boys," Biana said with a shudder.

"Actually, *that* was pretty awesome," Fitz teased.

Biana rolled her eyes. "No, what was awesome was when they asked *you* about girls. You should've seen him squirm," she told Sophie. "They went through this long interrogation about which girls he might be interested in—way worse than the one they put me through. And then they took him to see the matchmakers."

EIGHTEEN

WAIT—WHAT?" SOPHIE ASKED, wishing she hadn't sounded *quite* so horrified.

But seriously . . . *what?*

"You went to see the *matchmakers?*" she asked

Fitz glared at his sister. "It's not like I got my first list or anything. All I did was pick up my packet—which every Level Five does after midterms, so we'll have time to fill it out by the end of the school year."

"It's a huge packet," Biana said, miming several inches of thickness. "Honestly, I had no idea it was that in-depth. And the questions are *crazy.*"

"How would you know?" Fitz asked.

"Um, I can turn invisible. Did you really think I wouldn't sneak into your room and read it? Your answers so far have been *adorable*."

"I hate you so much right now," Fitz said.

It took all of Sophie's willpower not to press for details. "I still can't believe you have your packet already. It seems so . . . early."

"It's really not," Biana said. "By Level Five, everyone knows if they're going to get a special ability or not, which is the most important detail for the match. And once they turn the packets in, the matchmakers take a whole year to work through all the information. Your first list isn't ready until you finish Level Six."

"That still feels very soon," Sophie mumbled—though she probably should've realized that was how the process worked. Edaline had told her that Jolie received her matches before she signed up for the elite levels.

Sophie had just never really thought about how young Jolie would've been.

The elite levels started at seventeen.

"It's not like anyone gets married right then," Biana told her. "Well, I guess a few people might. But most only get their lists so they can start considering their options. It takes a while to get to know everybody, you know? There are a hundred names—and that's only one list. It's kind of daunting when you think about it."

"Not everyone picks up their list right away, either," Fitz added. "I know I'm planning on waiting for a bit."

"You are?" Sophie and Dex asked at the same time.

"Yeah. I figure I'll wait at least a year or two."

"Why?" Biana asked. "Aren't you dying to see who's on it?"

"A little. But the thing is . . . you can only get five lists."

"Don't most people find someone on their first list?" Sophie asked.

"Not always. Sometimes it takes a while for the matchmakers to figure out who you're really compatible with. Plus, the longer you wait, the more people have registered, so . . . I want to make sure I have the best selection."

Dex and Biana looked stunned. Sophie, meanwhile, was trying to work out the math.

If she was a Level Three, and couldn't register until she was a Level Five . . .

"Oh, don't act so surprised," Fitz told his sister. "Look at what happened with Dad. You heard that story, right?" he asked Sophie.

"I don't think so." Sophie knew that Councillor Alina tried to break up Alden and Della's wedding, but that was about it.

"My dad is about a hundred years older than my mom, so she definitely wasn't on his first list. In fact, I don't think he actually dated any of his first matches. And after he finished the elite levels, he got super busy with his career. So he didn't ask for his second list for years."

Sophie remembered Edaline explaining that Jolie had been forced to wait at least a month between requesting each of her additional lists. But she'd never considered that people might choose to wait longer.

"And *that* was the list that had Councillor Alina on it," Biana jumped in. "Which was how they ended up dating. But she was too smothering, so they broke up, and after a little while, my dad asked for a new list—and that time, my mom was his number one match."

"So if my dad hadn't waited," Fitz finished, "Biana and I wouldn't exist."

"Wow." Sophie couldn't imagine Alden and Della *not* being together. They were one of the sweetest couples she'd ever known.

But it was hard to wrap her mind around the timeline Fitz and Biana were describing. It was *so* different from the things she'd seen growing up. Most humans married people who were within a few years of their own age, since a thirty-year-old and a ninety-year-old were practically a different species. But it didn't seem to be that way for elves.

In fact, Edaline had once explained that *that* was why the elves did matchmaking. Their indefinite lifespan—and ageless appearance—made courting extra tricky. If they weren't careful, someone could end up marrying a distant relative without realizing and . . . ewwwwwwwww.

Still, the matchmaking thing felt like a mountain of awkward looming on the horizon. The whole process sounded arbitrary and unromantic—especially since the matchmakers focused on things like *ideal genetic diversity*. And it was a *big* deal. If you married someone who wasn't on your list, the relationship was branded a bad match and the scorn would follow you—and your children—for the rest of your lives.

Sophie had seen the kind of hurt and problems the system caused, and it gave her a sour stomach.

"Well," Biana told her brother, "you're welcome to be boring if you want. But I know *I'm* getting my list the first second I can—right, Sophie?"

The best answer Sophie could give was a shrug.

She was torn between hoping the elves would see the flaws in their system and decide they were done with the whole matchmaking thing before she ever had to face it, and *really* wanting to know who would be on her lists.

"What about you?" Biana asked Dex.

He took a deep breath. "I'm still deciding if I'm going to register."

Biana's eyebrows shot up so fast they practically launched off of her face. "But . . . that would guarantee you'd be a bad match."

"So? It worked out fine for my parents."

Kesler and Juline did seem very happy—but they'd had to deal with a lot of drama over the years. Edaline had told Sophie that they'd even been nervous to have children, since they knew their kids would face a ton of judgment. And Sophie had heard some of the teasing Dex had endured—and it had to be a million times worse for the triplets.

"It's just . . . look at the mess matchmaking has made," Dex mumbled. "Brant wouldn't have joined the Neverseen if he and Jolie hadn't been ruled a bad match. If they want to give recommendations, that's one thing. But it shouldn't be mandatory."

"I guess I get where you're coming from," Biana said. "But you can always choose to ignore your lists if you don't like the names on them, right? So why not at least give it a chance? You might find the perfect person is part of your match and save all the hassle."

Dex stared at his hands. "Maybe. It just feels like . . . if I register, I'm saying it's okay. That everything that's happened to my family was fair—and it wasn't. I guess the good news is, I don't have to decide for a few more years."

"Right," Sophie said, deciding to change the subject to something that didn't make every part of her feel twitchy. "So what time should we come over to go through Alvar's records?"

"Oh, you want to come to my house?" Dex asked.

"Isn't that where all the stuff is? Why? Is that bad?" Now that Sophie was thinking about it, he'd never invited her over. Not even when they were practicing alchemy all the time—though that could've been because he was afraid she'd burn down his room.

"Would you rather come to my house?" she offered.

"No, my house is fine. But the triplets will be there." He pointed through the crowd, to where his mom was fighting to keep two boys who looked like mini-Dexes and a red-haired girl from tackling each other. "That's them on good behavior."

Biana giggled. "What are their names again?"

"Rex, Bex, and Lex. My dad's not nearly as funny as he thinks he is."

"Aw, I think it's cute that you guys rhyme," Biana said.

"That's because you don't have to be named Bitz," Dex told her.

"Ohhh, I should start calling you that!" Fitz said, grinning at his sister.

"If you do, I'll start calling you Fiana."

Sophie laughed. "Be glad Keefe's not here or those would be your names from now on."

The teasing screeched to a halt.

For one awkward second, they all just stared at each other. Then Biana whispered, "I miss him."

"Me too," Dex agreed.

"Maybe that's his real plan," Fitz told them. "Make us forget how annoying he can be so we let him be twice as obnoxious when he comes home. Though Sophie's still stuck with him. How are the check-ins going, by the way?" he asked her. "Learn anything useful?"

"Not yet. I'll tell you his plan once we're at Dex's house. Should we head over after we're done here?"

"Actually, I can't today," Dex said. "I promised my dad I'd help at the store as soon as I could. But we could meet up tomorrow morning. Not sure how you guys will get there, though. Rimeshire isn't on a lot of Leapmasters. And the Vackers and the Dizznees don't exactly run in the same circles."

"Well . . . they should." Biana pointed to the ring he gave her. "Go Team Vackiznee!"

"I should've known I'd find you arranging some sort of scheme," a whispery voice said behind them.

They all did a double take when they turned to find Sir Astin with his long blond hair and nearly translucent skin.

"How come you're here as him?" Sophie whispered. "Won't the Council be expecting to see Magnate Leto today?"

"Actually, Magnate Leto is off doing a favor for them. But I wasn't about to miss the big announcement."

"Does that mean you know what's coming?" Fitz asked.

"Most of it. Lately the Council has been full of surprises."

"Is the rest of the Collective here too?" Biana asked, turning to study the crowd.

"You're wasting your time trying to find them," Sir Astin warned. "If you haven't guessed their identities already, I daresay you never will."

"So that means we know them," Sophie said.

"Some of them, yes. Now please act normal—we do not need to create a spectacle. And dare I ask what you all were planning as I approached?"

He seemed relieved to hear they were only making plans to study Alvar's records together—though that didn't stop him from giving a lecture on how anything they uncovered was not to be investigated without checking in first.

"Any update on Gethen?" Sophie whispered.

"Not the news I was hoping for," he admitted. "They're saying Lumenaria is closed for visits of any kind, which is . . . surprising. I'm in the process of seeing if they'll reconsider."

"Is the Council late?" Fitz asked, pointing to the still-empty stage. "It feels like we've been standing here for a really long time."

Sir Astin glanced at the sky. "I was expecting them a few minutes ago. But I'm sure they'll be here any second."

"Did you guys notice that the scrolls the Council sent out said sending one representative from each family today was *mandatory*?" Biana asked. "I've never seen that before."

"Neither have I," Fitz said. "I asked my dad about it, and he said the last time was when the Council canceled the human assistance program."

"Seriously?" Sophie asked, turning to survey the crowd. It did seem larger than normal—easily several thousand people. But could it really represent *every* elvin family?

Sir Astin must've known what she was thinking. "The first wave of the announcement applies to those with family members attending Foxfire," he explained. "From there, it will ripple through the rest of our society as the new program progresses."

"So this is a big change," Sophie confirmed.

"It is. The Council is taking a very brave step. But, as Magnate Leto reminded you, change can be a powerful, inspiring thing."

He'd made his voice sound like his alter ego, and Sophie was still trying to wrap her head around the weirdness of hearing Sir Astin sound like Magnate Leto when two lines of heavily armed goblins marched through the crowd and formed a perimeter of swords and muscle.

"Brace yourselves," Sir Astin said as fanfare rang across the field and all twelve Councillors glittered onto the stage. "This should be very interesting."

NINETEEN

SEVEN DAYS AGO, OUR WORLD SUF-
fered an attack," Councillor Emery said as he
strode to the center of the silver stage. "Though
I suppose it would be more accurate for us to say
'*another* attack.' Such events are supposed to be unheard of.
And yet this was the third incident in as many weeks. And it
comes on the heels of the disgusting plague unleashed upon
the innocent gnomes. Surely you also remember the inferno
of Everblaze that stole the life of our beloved Councillor Kenric
and destroyed much of our beautiful capital. In fact, over the
last year, our world has experienced evils we can hardly begin
to process. And as a result, we've been forced to add goblin
police to our cities and armed guards to our schools."

He paused there, his sapphire blue eyes shining against his dark skin while he studied the crowd shuffling nervously around him.

Councillor Emery served as the spokesperson for the Council primarily because of his ability as a Telepath. He mentally mediated all of the other Councillors' internal discussions to ensure that—out loud—they always presented a united front. But there was also something in the way he carried himself that demanded attention. Maybe it was the rigid line of his posture. Or the dramatic sweep of his shoulder-length black hair. Whatever it was, the longer Sophie watched him, the more she found herself holding her breath.

Eventually she glanced away, focusing her attention on the other Councillors, who'd formed two neat lines on either side of the stage. They each wore a different color, with matching jewels glinting across their capes and circlets. Their posture was stiff and regal—heads held high. Shoulders squared.

But there were thin creases in their brows and cheeks, and their lips were pressed tightly together. Sophie had faced the Council many times—more than she ever would've chosen—and it was rare to see them looking so nervous.

She concentrated on her three most loyal supporters—Bronte, Oralie, and Terik—searching their faces for clues to what news might be coming. But Bronte was his usual scowling, pointy-eared, ancient self. Oralie was equally hard to read.

Her pink cheeks and soft blond ringlets always gave her a serene, ethereal air about her. And Terik was . . .

. . . staring right at Sophie.

His cobalt blue eyes held hers, almost like he was taking another stab at her reading. He was the elves' only Descryer, which meant he could sense people's potential. He'd tried to read Sophie once already, and had been unable to understand what he was feeling. The best he could tell her was that he'd felt "something strong."

"Our world has changed," Councillor Emery continued. "The safety and peace we've enjoyed for millennia is fading. But we will not let it disappear! The rebels' strength is an illusion. Soon all of this will be nothing more than a brief chapter in our long history—a chapter that will testify to our adaptability and reinvention—but we'll get to that in a moment. First, we want to assure you that anything damaged during these growing pains will be rebuilt. Councillor Darek, if you please . . ."

One of the Councillors Sophie didn't know moved toward the back of the stage. His skin had a warm brown tone and his shiny black hair curled at the ends. He reminded Sophie of a bullfighter, probably because of his bright red cape, which made a dramatic swish as he raised his arms toward the pyramid.

Sophie thought he might be a Guster as the tarp fluttered and rippled—but the air remained perfectly still as the thick fabric slowly rose from the center, almost as though a giant invisible hand were lifting it like a handkerchief.

The tarp hovered above the pyramid, casting the structure in deep shadow—which was why it took Sophie a second to notice the more important reveal.

The glass pyramid had been repaired.

Each pane had an opalescent sheen, reflecting swirls of color across the courtyard. And when Darek dropped the tarp and let the sunlight hit the glass, it shimmered and twinkled in every color of the spectrum, as though the pyramid were built from fireworks.

"Yes," Councillor Emery said as the crowd erupted with applause. "Thanks to the tireless—and generous—efforts of our gnomish and dwarven allies, we have brought our illustrious academy to a new level of magnificence. Even the interior of the pyramid has been completely redone with remarkable improvements."

"You'd think they might have consulted the principal before redecorating his office," Sir Astin muttered under his breath.

"Did you not know the pyramid had been fixed?" Sophie whispered.

"I knew they were working on it. Not that they were finished. And I'd heard nothing of the interior being altered."

"Let this be a lesson to those afraid," Councillor Emery said, "as well as to those who might view our world as vulnerable. Any efforts to make us weak will only make us stronger. Our resilience and resourcefulness are what have made our kind what we are. We are elves. We live to dream and inspire. And when we need to, we regroup. We rebuild. At times, we even change—but only when such changes are for the better of our people. And the time has come for one of those changes. Perhaps you've already noticed."

He paused, and the crowd started calling out suggestions.

"Yes, Timkin," Councillor Emery said, pointing to his left. "That's exactly it."

All heads swiveled toward the Heks family, who stood several inches taller than the other families around them. Stina and her mother were practically glowing as Councillor Emery asked Timkin, "Can you repeat that for everyone to hear?"

Timkin's puffed-out chest made Sophie wish she could tell everyone that when he helped the Black Swan, he spent his days as Coiffe, swathed in head-to-toe white curls like a giant two-legged poodle.

"Councillor Darek raised the tarp using telekinesis," Timkin shouted.

Emery nodded. "I suppose I shouldn't be surprised that you were the one to notice, given your background. And yes, Darek moved the tarp with his mind. It turns out, he has the greatest telekinetic strength out of all of us on the Council. We had our own Splotching match of sorts to test it out before we came here today—but that's a story for another time. The point is: Instead of having Councillor Liora snap her fingers and conjure the tarp away, or having Councillor Zarina disintegrate it with one of her electric charges, or even having Councillor

Clarette call a flock of birds to carry it away in their talons—we chose to let Councillor Darek use telekinesis—a skill, not an ability. And we did so to remind you of the underutilized arsenal that each and every one of us possesses. That's the beauty of skills. There are no *haves* and *have-nots*."

"Are you trying to tell us that skills are better than abilities?" someone in the crowd shouted.

"It's not a matter of *better*. It's a matter of missed opportunities," Emery told them. "We've been neglecting our skills for far too long. Somehow we've let ourselves become complacent about such opportunities and limited our focus to academics and abilities."

"But you just told us they could've done the same thing with their abilities," another voice yelled.

"Yes, but what would an Empath or a Telepath or a Vanisher do?" Emery asked. "I do not mean to devalue any talent—we all know the vital role that each special ability plays. But they also are limited to only a specific purpose, whereas our skills cast a much wider advantage—far wider than I suspect any of you realize. We brush on some of them in our physical education sessions at Foxfire, but it's a far cry from the proper training such gifts should be given. So from now on, we'll be correcting this—and before any of you protest"—he raised his arms to silence the fresh wave of murmurs—"keep in mind the precarious position we're currently in. It's no secret that elves are not warriors. Our minds shatter from the violence and gore. And that has led some to the mistaken conclusion that we're also defenseless. There are even those who believe that if we were to be separated from our goblin protectors, our world would crumble—and while that's obviously not the case, it does still raise a concern. How many of us could truly protect ourselves if the need ever arose? I'd wager only a small portion, which is unacceptable! And fortunately, we already have a system in place to help us train."

"Oh," Sophie breathed.

Sir Astin smiled. "I believe you're beginning to guess the shift that's coming."

That didn't make Councillor Emery's next words any less shocking.

"All of this is why, starting next week, the Exillium campus will be stationing itself right where we're standing, and we'll all begin a program of specialized skill training with their Coaches."

TWENTY

THEY'RE SENDING EVERYONE TO Exillium?" Sophie asked, turning to the rest of her friends. "As in *everyone*?"

The crowd around them seemed to be shouting the same question.

"Yes, I do mean all of us," Councillor Emery called over the din. "Young, old, and Ancient—*all* will participate in this new program, because *all* of us possess these vital skills. We're in the process of designing a schedule to accommodate this rather large undertaking. But those of you here—and your families—will be the first wave. We'll be dividing you into groups that will then be assigned to a specific day and time for training each week. The schedules will be finished by the weekend and sent out to each household. Training will begin on Monday."

Biana grinned. "I wonder if they'll make everyone wear the crazy uniforms."

"Or go through a dividing," Dex added.

When Sophie and her friends had first arrived at the Exillium campus they'd found themselves snared by thick ropes and left dangling upside down from a high metal arch while all the other Waywards watched. The method they found to escape was analyzed to determine which of the three Exillium Hemispheres they belonged to—the Left Hemisphere for those who favored logic and reason, the Right Hemisphere for those who were impulsive and creative, and the Ambi Hemisphere for those who used elements of both approaches.

"Let's just hope no one starts any fires," Biana said. "Right, Sophie?"

"Hey, if I hadn't started that fire, we might not have become friends with Tam and Linh," Sophie reminded her.

"Plus, a school isn't a school until Sophie tries to destroy it," Fitz teased.

"Uh, I think Keefe has taken over that role," Biana whispered. "I can't decide if that means she's the bad influence—or he is."

"I think they're mutually troublesome." Sir Astin gave Sophie a papery smile. "And much as it would delight me to see some of our particularly sheltered elves endure the kind of creative initiations Exillium specializes in, the Coaches have arranged a much faster, much less invasive dividing process. Everyone will also be provided with simple capes to wear with their tunics, pants, and boots. And in case you're wondering, you will be participating as well. So will all of the Exillium Waywards."

"Is this what you meant when you told Tam and Linh that you were working on something to keep them less isolated?" Sophie asked.

Sir Astin nodded. "They will now be coming to Foxfire twice a week—and should the experiment go well, I've been in talks with the Council about establishing a permanent connection between the schools. I envision an exchange program once a week, to allow both schools to interact and benefit from the other. But the first focus will be on self-defense training."

Dex pointed toward the grumbling crowd. "Doesn't sound like everyone's excited by the idea."

Sophie wasn't surprised. Most of the elves were snobs about Exillium—believing the school existed only for the *hopeless cases*. All the Waywards had been banished from the Lost Cities, and very few had done what Timkin Heks did and earned their way back.

Councillor Emery held out his hands, demanding silence. "Clearly this idea will take some getting used to," he told them. "But it is a *necessary* change."

A fresh round of shouts disagreed, and Bronte stepped from his place at Emery's side.

"Would you honestly rather risk your lives than train to use your skills?" he shouted.

"No, we'd rather you do your job and exile these black-robed idiots," someone yelled back, triggering an eruption of cheers.

Sophie couldn't hear what Bronte said in response, but the set of his jaw was pure disgust.

"If you don't calm yourselves," Councillor Emery shouted, "I will let Noland call for silence. And you all know the head-ache a Vociferator can trigger."

Most of the crowd obeyed—though Sophie caught a few grumblings about the hypocrisy of threatening them with someone's special ability.

"Regardless of how you may feel about this decision," Emery told them, "keep in mind that this arrangement is not optional. Anyone who refuses training will face a number of consequences."

"Like what?" Sophie whispered to Sir Astin. "They wouldn't exile people, would they?"

"Honestly, I'm not certain," he admitted. "But there is never a shortage of manure to shovel at the Sanctuary."

"And what about the ogres?" a female shouted from some-where off to the side.

Sophie recognized the voice even before the crowd parted to let her linguistics Mentor march toward the stage. Lady Cadence's dark gray gown looked as tight as the twisted bun in her dark hair and paired well with her stormy glare.

"Why am I not surprised you've decided to interrupt these proceedings?" Emery asked.

"Probably because you've ignored all my requests for a private meeting," Lady Cadence said smoothly. "And I'm hardly the only dissenter. I'd wager you could hear the shouting all the way in the Forbidden Cities. And while most of their arguments are weak and biased, that doesn't change the fact that your plan is deeply flawed. Improving our skills won't do a drop of good in the face of an ogre warrior—and we cannot afford to make them our enemy. When it comes to pure, brute strength, nothing can best them."

Every goblin in the audience snorted.

"Laugh all you want," she told them. "Goblins are powerful in your own way—and you have held your own in many battles. But you survive primarily because of clever battle tactics—tactics that can't rival the ruthless rage I've seen ogres manifest in the heat of a fight."

"The ogres are formidable adversaries," Councillor Emery agreed. "But King Dimitar is wise enough to avoid starting a war that he knows he would lose."

"Are you certain of that?" Lady Cadence asked. "Hasn't he ignored all of your requests for a Peace Summit?"

Councillor Emery glanced at the rest of the Councillors. Several seconds passed as he rubbed his temples, before he nodded and raised his eyes to the crowd.

"We'd been planning to deliver this announcement through

coordinated scrolls, that way everyone would be notified at once. But . . . in light of these apprehensions, it seems prudent to set your minds at ease now, and we'll notify the rest of the populace this evening. King Dimitar *has* agreed to meet for a Peace Summit. We're in the process of arranging the gathering in Lumenaria now. The exact date will not be shared—for obvious security reasons. But we expect to reach a satisfying resolution in the very near future."

The cheer that followed sounded mostly like a collective sigh of relief.

"Did you know about that?" Sophie whispered to Sir Astin.

"No," he admitted. "But it explains why I've received such pushback for our visit to Gethen. I'm not sure if we'll be able to get anywhere near Lumenaria until the summit is over. They'll have everything on lockdown to prepare their security."

"And there's no way to sneak in?" Fitz asked.

"Definitely not. Lumenaria—in many ways—is more secure than Exile."

"So then . . . it probably would've been good if we'd met with Gethen before the ogres agreed to the summit," Sophie said.

"Yes, Miss Foster. The power of hindsight strikes again. Though in all fairness, we wouldn't have known to ask him about the symbol, so there's no telling how useful that meeting would've been."

"I still wish we'd done it," Sophie mumbled.

"As do I. But I wish for many things. . . ." He stared into the distance, tempting her to violate the rules of telepathy and see what he was thinking.

"Does that satisfy your concern?" Councillor Emery asked Lady Cadence, snapping Sophie back to the present.

"Actually, I find it even more concerning," Lady Cadence told him. "King Dimitar is many things—but a fool is not one of them. He will not enter into a treaty lightly. I have no doubt he's monitoring our world very closely. And when he hears that every elf is being given special combat training? He'll assume we're forming an army."

"An army with children?" Councillor Alina asked, not bothering to wait for Councillor Emery to speak for her.

"Ogres begin military training from the moment their children can walk," Lady Cadence explained. "Their entire culture is built around defense and strategy. And I guarantee that if King Dimitar believes we're preparing for battle, it will alter any plans for a peaceful resolution."

"And how is it safer for them to see us as an easy target?" Alina countered.

"When dealing with a daunting opponent, it's far better to be underestimated than overestimated," Lady Cadence retorted. "The more the ogres doubt our strength, the less prepared they'll be should they choose the foolish course in the end."

"Valid as your concerns may be," Councillor Emery said, "they can't justify leaving our people defenseless. The ogres are not the only threat we're facing."

"Then why not focus our efforts on making it easier for people to flee?" Lady Cadence suggested. "I've long wondered why we don't wear emergency rings—crystals we'd always have easily on hand that leap to the same designated safe house at an undisclosed location. I'm sure the dwarves could help you set something up in a matter of days."

"That . . . is something we will take under consideration," Councillor Emery said. "But we must also ensure that we do not become a people ruled by fear. Our authority is being threatened from both without and within—and it's imperative that we prove our strength to everyone daring to challenge us. Spending a few years living with ogres doesn't prepare you for the complexities of ruling this world."

"No—but I know far more about our so-called enemies than you ever will," Lady Cadence argued. "Either you ignored the reports I sent, or that traitor you trusted made sure they never saw the light of day."

Fitz and Biana slouched as grumblings about their brother washed through the crowd.

"The insights I've gained could've prevented many of our current problems," Lady Cadence added. "So you would be wise to heed my counsel now if you want any hope of a successful treaty negotiation."

"Any information you see fit to provide we'd be happy to hear," Councillor Emery told her. "But in a proper, scheduled meeting. And just to be clear"—he turned to the crowd—"*nothing* is going to halt our plans for this program of skill training. We do not bow to fear and speculation or flee to avoid confrontation."

"We have in the past," Lady Cadence reminded him. "Our Ancient Councillors opted to sink Atlantis in order to convince the humans that we had died—and turned our species into a bunch of silly myths and legends—because they knew that was the smarter alternative to involving ourselves in a war."

"Those were different times," Councillor Bronte told her. "We were a small, scattered race, still getting a handle on the different worlds we'd unwittingly become responsible for. I would know. I was there." He tapped the points of his ears as proof of his Ancient standing. "We made the best decision we could—but it has also proven to be our most controversial. In fact, one of the ogres' greatest grievances with us is that we've allowed humans to continue living in relative freedom—and I've heard some in this very audience make the same complaint. I'm not saying it was the wrong decision. But times have also changed, and now is the time for strength. And confidence. And providing a ready reminder of why we found ourselves in charge of this planet in the first place. We didn't choose to rule the world. The world chose us, because our abilities and skills make us uniquely qualified—and yes, I *am* putting both on the same level. I don't know how we, as a race, became so shortsighted about the value of our skills. I myself have even been guilty of such judgments. But it's time we open our minds and start accepting their value."

Lady Cadence stalked closer to argue, then stopped and dipped an especially stiff curtsy.

"Very well," she said. "You've clearly made up your minds. I hope, for all of our sake, that these skills are as powerful as you say. We'll need them when we're dragged into war."

TWENTY-ONE

DO YOU THINK SHE'S RIGHT?" SOPHIE asked Grady and Edaline after she'd caught them up on the afternoon's drama. "Do you think the Council should've listened to Lady Cadence's warning?"

"I think there are degrees of rightness," Grady said, arranging a dozen empty silver buckets into a row. "Our days of easy answers are long past us."

"Did those ever exist?" Edaline asked. "I remember my elvin history sessions teaching about quite a few averted catastrophes."

"You may be right," Grady said. "Though I don't remember

having to worry this much when *I* was a kid—or even when Jolie was Sophie's age."

They both fell silent, lost in their own memories as Edaline snapped her fingers and conjured up a waist-high pile of swizzlespice. It was feeding time in the Havenfield pastures, which could be quite an adventurous process. The animals that Grady and Edaline cared for were transitioning to a vegetarian diet.

Part of the elves' conservation efforts included relocating any species that humans thought were "extinct" or "mythical" to their special animal preserve to ensure the creatures' continued survival. But the process only made sense if there were no predators in the Sanctuary. So they'd developed methods to quell the animals' hunting instincts and fed them a diet of gnomish produce, since the gnomes grew many things that tasted like meat.

"I will say," Grady added, dropping handfuls of shriveled tubers into each of the buckets, "I'm sure Lady Cadence is right about the ogres keeping tabs on what we're doing. And I wouldn't be surprised if the training did add tension to the treaty negotiations. But I can't imagine it'll lead to a violent retaliation. The ogres have never attacked the elves directly."

"What about the plague?" Sophie asked.

The ogres had tried to force the gnomes into servitude in Ravagog, knowing the Lost Cities would fall apart without them. The elves and gnomes had a uniquely symbiotic relationship, with each species relying heavily on the other. Gnomes were too defenseless to hold their own among the fiercer species that inhabited the planet. They also craved work and loved to garden, and were much more plantlike than animal, requiring very little food or sleep because they absorbed their energy from the sun. So in exchange for protection and shelter among the elves, the gnomes shared their excess produce and helped with any tasks that interested them. Sophie hadn't realized just how vital the gnomes were until she'd seen the withering plants and overall disorganization in the Lost Cities when the gnomes were sick.

"That was definitely the boldest move the ogres have made," Grady told her. "But I doubt they would've made it without the Neverseen's urging. They sat on the plague for millennia, and only acted when Fintan suggested it. And let's not forget that making that threat didn't exactly work out well for them."

"Thanks to you," a female gnome with plaited hair and a dress woven from straw said to Sophie as she hauled over more empty buckets. The stack was twice as tall as her child-size body. "I wish I could've been there to see the flood that you and your friends caused. I hope it washed all the filth out of Serenvale."

Most gnomes still referred to Ravagog by its original name, since it had been their homeland before the ogres ran them out, tore down all the trees, and contaminated the water and ground.

"Here are the cravettels," another gnome said—a male this

time, in a shirt sewn from leaves the same earthy tone as his skin. He dragged a huge bag of what looked like bright blue peanuts, flashing a green-toothed smile as he left it at Grady's feet. "There's plenty more where that came from if you need it—and I bet you will. I've never seen a T. rex who didn't gobble these up by the ton."

"Well, you've never met Verdi," Grady said. "Her picky eating is a big part of why we call her our permanent resident. But I can't wait to test them out."

The gnome waved and trotted away, and Sophie realized she didn't know his name. Just like she didn't know the female gnome helping Edaline fill the buckets with swizzlespice.

It wasn't *totally* her fault—they'd had dozens and dozens of gnomes move to Havenfield to be close to the Panakes tree. But ever since she'd lost Calla, Sophie found it too painful to get to know any of them. Staring into their huge gray eyes felt like opening a fresh wound.

"Personally, I'm proud of the Council for making this stand," Edaline said. "It's nice to see them focused on protecting *everyone*—especially the Talentless. And it'll be interesting to see how powerful our skills can truly become when we train ourselves properly."

"That might be a problem," Cadoc said from the shadows. "If either of you leave this house, Brielle and I will have to go with you, and everyone will know we're your bodyguards."

"But the Council said the training is mandatory," Sophie

reminded them. "So if they stay home, that could tip the Neverseen off too."

"Easy solution," Grady said. "You trust that we can take care of ourselves."

"Imagine what you would say if your daughter tried that argument," Brielle told him.

"Right, but she can't do this." Grady narrowed his eyes at Edaline, and her arms shot up on each side and started flailing about like an angry octopus.

"What have I told you about using your power on me?" Edaline snapped, smacking him with her thrashing appendages.

"I know—I'm sorry! I just figured you'd rather I proved the point with you instead of with Sophie."

He calmed Edaline's flailing and she snapped her fingers, conjuring a pile of dinosaur fluff above him and showering him in bright orange feathers. "Now we're even."

"I suppose we are," he said. "And I'm glad you went with feathers and not manure."

"Next time," Edaline warned.

"See," Grady told Sophie. "Strong abilities have consequences. Which reminds me—you and I still need to have that talk about your inflicting. So why don't you come with me to test these cravettels on Verdi and we'll chat as we work?"

"Verdi drool *and* a lecture?" Sophie whined. "Are you trying to punish me?"

"Far from it. I could really use your help. Maybe if you

transmit to Verdi, you can convince her how much she's going to like these new seeds."

Easier said than done. The fluffy green T. rex took one whiff of the cravettels and made a gag-snort-snarl. Then she spun around and knocked her trough over with her tail.

"Aw, come on," Grady said as he righted the silver basin and filled it with more of the seeds. "At least give them a try."

I hear all the other T. rexes love them, Sophie transmitted, adding images of happy dinosaurs gobbling them up.

The snort that Verdi gave them practically dripped with disgust.

"You know how this works," Grady warned. "If you won't try it, I'm going to have to make you."

Verdi threw back her enormous head and let out a defiant *ROOOOOOOOOOOOAAAAAAAAR.*

"All right then, you brought this on yourself." Grady unhooked one of the silver lassoes strapped to his belt, whipping the shimmering rope in wide circles over his head before letting it fly in one swift motion.

ROOOOOOOOOOOOOOOOOOAAAAAAAAAAAAAAAR!

"That's not hurting her, right?" Sophie asked as Verdi tried to claw at the cord around her neck with her tiny T. rex arms.

"Her feathers are so thick I doubt she even feels it," Grady promised, digging in his heels to keep his footing. "And don't worry—animals always fight what's good for them."

He had a point. Sophie once helped her human mom give

medicine to their cat, and the amount of yowling that followed made it sound like they were force-feeding him boiling poison.

Grady dragged Verdi toward her trough. "Okay, girl—time to try something new."

ROOOOOOOOOOOOOOOOOOOAAAAAAAAAAAAAAAR!

He took advantage of Verdi's open mouth and jerked the lasso hard, face-planting her into the seeds. Cravettels scattered everywhere—but some must've hit their mark because the next second Verdi was crunching.

"See?" Grady asked. "I hear they taste like pterodactyl."

Verdi crunched some more.

And . . .

SPIT!

"Wonderful," Grady said, shaking off the slimy blue bits he'd been sprayed with. "Can you give me a hand?" he asked Brielle as Verdi tried to drag him into her pasture.

Brielle grabbed him around his waist and together they pulled Verdi back to the trough.

ROOOOOOOOOOOOOOOOOOOAAAAAAAAAAAAAAAR!
Crunch.
SPIT!

And so the feeding went.

But somewhere around bite number ten—paired with a head full of Sophie's calming transmissions—Verdi swallowed and . . .

. . . licked her chops.

"If you would've trusted me from the beginning, you wouldn't have wasted half your dinner!" Grady grumbled as Verdi wolfed down the remaining blue seeds. "But let's hope this means we've found something she *loves*—and that it quells her urge to hunt. A flock of seagulls flew a little too close to her enclosure last week and a couple of them became Verdi snacks."

Sophie shuddered. "I bet you wish you could Mesmer her."

"That would be nice—and what a perfect transition for our important conversation!"

"Ugh, I already know what you're going to say."

"And what's that?" Grady asked, wrapping the lasso around his palm and elbow to coil it back up.

"You're going to tell me that inflicting is a dark power and that I have to be careful about how much I use it because it'll make people afraid of me, just like people were afraid of you after you manifested. And then I'll assure you that I'm just trying to fix a few weak spots. Biana and I had a run-in with the Neverseen's Psionipath a few months back, and my abilities wouldn't work through his force field. He was right there in front of us—and there was nothing I could do. I can't let that happen again. Fitz thinks our telepathy would've been strong enough if we'd worked together as Cognates. But inflicting comes down to me—and if I'd trained harder, I might've been able to stop Ruy from getting away. So see? As Alden would say: *There's no reason to worry.*"

"Actually, that's not what I was going to say—though I appreciate the Alden quote. And I get where you're coming from. I remember testing my ability against a Psionipath once, and it was incredibly unsettling. But you have to understand that there's a cost to training. I learned that the hard way—and almost let my power ruin me."

"Ruin?" *Now* he had her attention.

"You've seen how Fintan was led astray by his craving for flame," Grady said quietly. "I . . . let myself get just as out of control. I didn't kill anyone—but I started using my ability for any passing whim. If someone was slowing me down when I was in a hurry? I'd *motivate* them to clear out of my way. Or if I needed something and didn't have time to go get it? I'd *motivate* someone to bring it to me. The real low point was when the Council refused to grant my request to investigate an issue with the trolls. They didn't think I had enough evidence to justify the drastic measures I was proposing, and I was positive I'd find more than enough if they'd allow me to conduct the search. So I mesmerized Bronte into signing the scroll."

"Did he catch you?" Sophie asked.

"Of course. And if he'd wanted to, he could've had me exiled. At the very least, he could've hit me with the full force of his inflicting. Instead he sat me down and shared how he almost fell into the same trap with his ability. He told me that after years and years of training, he reached a point where the slightest aggravation or annoyance would flare his temper, and he'd unleash his rage. His low point was when he lashed out at his mother."

"So . . . what are you saying?" she asked. "I can't use my ability? Why would the Council order me to train in it, then?"

"Because the only thing worse than overusing an intense power is not learning how to control it. It comes down to moderation. Inflicting is an incredibly valuable ability—and I'm glad you have it. But don't let it take over your life. Bronte said he built up so much anger and frustration that he has to keep it all tangled up in a knot deep inside of him—a constant pressure he fights every day to keep from unraveling. And he told me he's had to teach you the same technique because of all the emotions you're battling."

"Aren't I allowed to be angry about the things that have happened?"

"Of course. And I know you want to protect yourself and your friends. I also know that you feel a tremendous responsibility to be the moonlark—whatever that even is. And those are much more noble reasons to push yourself than anything that motivated me. But that doesn't mean the training isn't eating away at you. Don't think I don't know what you're doing there."

He pointed to her hand, which was massaging the spot under her ribs.

"It's not just a knot of emotions," she told him. "It's power I can draw on when I need it."

Grady sighed and pulled her close. "I know. Just promise

me you'll try to let at least *some* of it go. If you hold on to every-thing, it'll tear you apart."

Sophie nodded, telling herself it wasn't a lie.

She *would* try to let it go.

But not until she felt ready.

Right now, she had too many enemies—too many questions—too many worries.

Keefe gave her another huge one that night when she stretched out her consciousness for their nightly check-in.

FINALLY! his mind screamed. *I was about an hour away from switching to my emergency plan.*

Why? What's happening?

I don't fully know. Something huge is going down tomorrow. No one will tell me any specifics—but based on what I overheard, I'm pretty sure they're going to Havenfield to snatch Grady and Edaline.

TWENTY-TWO

NO ONE SLEPT THAT NIGHT.

Havenfield was a blur of activity as the goblins and gnomes snuck around to prepare.

Everything needed to *look* normal, so that it wouldn't give away that Keefe had leaked the warning. But they still found plenty of ways to increase their security.

Booby traps were set. The Black Swan sent dwarven reinforcements to hide deep underground, ready to pop out at the first sign of trouble. And Grady and Edaline were each given melders—elvin weapons that caused temporary paralysis—and were planning to station themselves outside in the pastures that housed the most dangerous animals.

Sandor had originally suggested they stay inside, but the

last thing anyone wanted was to give Brant a chance to start another deadly house fire.

As for Sophie . . .

"No way!" she said, adding a foot stamp for emphasis. "You're not sending me away like a little kid!"

"Age has nothing to do with this," Grady told her, pulling her in for a hug. "It's about protecting the things that matter."

"I don't need protection."

"*Everyone* needs protection—why do you think we're taking so many precautions? But we have everything covered. You don't have to worry."

"Actually, that's exactly why I *should* be worrying," Sophie argued. "We thought we had everything planned out for the ambush on Mount Everest, and the Neverseen somehow knew we'd be there and showed up with ogres and dwarves."

She'd never forget the feel of those beefy ogre arms grabbing her through the ceiling of their cave and dragging her through ice and stone. If Sandor hadn't come after her, she never would've gotten away—and Sandor had ended up tossed off a cliff for his efforts.

"And we didn't have to deal with the two Pyrokinetics," she reminded him. "Brant and Fintan will try to burn this place to the ground."

Grady brushed her hair off her forehead. "That's why I've been keeping a supply of quicksnuff on hand. Alden also got us some frissyn, after my battle with Brant. So we're ready to extinguish any flames—even Everblaze."

The news *helped*.

But it still didn't feel like enough.

Frustration and anger bubbled up and she knotted them under her ribs, adding to her arsenal. "If you won't let me stay—come *with* me."

Grady shook his head. "I'm not letting them chase me out of my home. And I'm not going to pass up a chance to see if we can catch one of them. That's how you tackle problems like this. You take the organization down one person at a time."

"Then let me help," Sophie begged.

"You've risked your life enough times. Now it's my turn."

"That's stupid."

"It might be. But I'm willing to be stupid if it keeps you safe."

"And *we'll* keep *him* safe," Brielle promised, raising her sword and slashing it with a whip-fast spin that sent her curls flying. "Your father is my charge. No harm will come to him."

"Your mother will be safe with me," Cadoc added. "And Sandor is planning to stay as well."

"You are?" Sophie asked, turning to face her bodyguard.

"I assumed it's where you'd prefer that I be," Sandor told her. "But I'm only willing to separate *if* you stick to your original plan and go to Mr. Dizznee's house. Lovise will protect you there. She's an excellent warrior."

"But—"

"Think of the larger picture," Grady interrupted. "Where can you do the most good? Here? Wasting the day waiting for someone to pop out of the shadows? Or with your friends, working on one of your projects?"

"All we were planning to do is sort through a bunch of registry records," Sophie grumbled.

"Those records still need to be checked," Grady told her. "And I wouldn't be surprised if you guys learn something crucial. Think about all the problems you've solved together."

"We've also survived plenty of battles," Sophie reminded him.

He kissed her forehead again. "I know. But this one isn't your fight. So go pack an overnight bag. You're not coming home until this threat is over."

"Already got you packed," Edaline said, rushing down the stairs with Iggy's cage in one hand and Sophie's purple backpack in the other. Sophie had used the same bag to leave her human life behind—and again when she'd had to flee to the Black Swan's hideout.

She despised using it again to hide.

"Kesler and Juline know you'll be staying the night," Edaline told her. "I also hailed the Vackers and it sounded like Alden and Della were heading over here. I explained the risks, but they're not missing a chance to speak to Alvar. They'll be sending Fitz and Biana to stay the night at Dex's."

"Oh sure, send the kids off for a slumber party," Sophie grumbled.

Edaline smiled. "You can be mad at me if you want. But I'm always going to take any chance to keep you safe. Mother's prerogative."

"*Parents'* prerogative," Grady corrected. "I can survive a lot of things. But if something happened to you . . . ?"

He hugged Sophie again, and Edaline joined in.

"Please don't fight this," Edaline begged, kissing Sophie's cheek. "Let us protect you the way we couldn't protect . . ."

She didn't finish the sentence, but Sophie knew how it ended—and playing the Jolie card was a dirty trick.

"Fine," she said through a sigh. "But only if you promise that if it gets too intense here, you'll leap to safety."

"Deal." Grady tightened his hug before he finally let her go. "And thank you."

Sophie planned to give her best death glare as she slung her backpack over her shoulder and picked up Iggy's cage. But it hit her then that—if something went wrong—this *could* be the last time she ever saw her parents.

"I love you guys," she whispered.

"We love you too," they both said.

"Stay safe," she begged.

Grady wiped his teary eyes. "We'll see you soon."

TWENTY-THREE

SOPHIE COULD HEAR THE SCREAMING and shouting the second she glittered into the otherwise quiet valley, where puffy white clouds hung low around the snow-capped mountains.

"THAT'S MY BOX OF PRATTLES!"

"NOT ANYMORE!"

"MOOOOOOOOOOOOOOOOOOOOOM—REX STOLE MY CANDY!"

"DAAAAAAAAAAAAAAAAAAAAD—BEX SMELLS LIKE DRAGON POOP!"

"SO DOES REX!" another voice added.

"STAY OUT OF THIS, LEX!"

"NO WAY—THOSE PRATTLES ARE MINE!"

A whole lot of squealing and crashing—plus a "KNOCK IT OFF!" from Dex—followed the declaration.

"Welcome to Rimeshire," Kesler said, and Sophie spun around to find him standing next to Juline on a wide silver-stoned path. The smile he flashed looked exactly like his son's.

Kesler and Dex both shared the same dimples and strawberry-blond hair and periwinkle eyes. The only difference was time—and several inches of height.

"You'll get used to the noise," he promised as another shriek echoed across the valley.

"No you won't," Juline warned.

Juline was Edaline's sister—which technically made Sophie and Dex cousins by adoption—and they both had the same turquoise eyes and amber-toned hair. But Juline always looked rumpled and exhausted.

"Don't worry," she told Sophie, wrapping a flyaway hair back into her messy bun and securing it with a chewed-on pencil. "I have a trick to keep them under control this afternoon."

"We say that every day," Kesler teased. "I'm still waiting for it to be true."

Lots more squealing and stomping filled the air, along with an "OW—THAT'S MY ARM, YOU JERK!"

"It's okay," Sophie told them. Growing up a Telepath around humans had given her a high tolerance for noise. Plus, her main plans for the day involved obsessively check-ing her Imparter as she waited for news from her family.

She could do that with or without screaming kids in the background.

"Bet you're glad you're wearing long sleeves, huh?" Juline asked as an icy breeze whipped through Sophie's hair.

Rimeshire was definitely the chilliest place Sophie had visited in the Lost Cities—aside from the entrance to the Sanctuary in the Himalayas. Even the architecture of the Dizznee's house reminded Sophie of an ice castle. All the walls were built from blue cut glass and fitted together into sharp, dramatic angles. And the five swirling towers looked like upside-down icicles. But there was still something inherently warm about the place. Maybe it was the bright light glowing through the walls. Or the curls of white smoke coming from the spiral chimneys.

The house was also massive—probably bigger than Everglen. And the grounds were just as expansive. The landscaping was simpler, but it matched the stark valley: twisted evergreen trees lining each of the silver-stoned paths, and wide plains of jade green grass leading into the rolling foothills.

"You can say it," Kesler told her. "I'm guessing this isn't what you'd been imagining?"

"Well . . . no," she admitted.

She'd been in the Lost Cities long enough to know that social standing didn't affect wealth. Everyone was given the exact same birth fund—which contained more than enough money to live lavishly for the whole of their long existence. But she'd pictured Dex's house looking like Slurps and Burps, with topsy-turvy architecture and colorful walls that belonged in a Dr. Seuss book.

Rimeshire was . . . understated.

Elegant.

Impressive.

"We're only quirky in public," Kesler told her, "because it's fun to mess with the snobby nobles. Deep down, we're disappointingly normal."

"Not disappointing at all," Sophie insisted.

Juline beamed. "I'm so glad you like it. Dex was terrified to have everyone come over. He's in there right now, desperately cleaning his room, even though you'll be camping out in the solarium tonight."

"And don't worry," Kesler said. "The triplets have offered up their sleeping bags—and the gnomes already gave them a good wash."

"Sounds perfect," Sophie told him, even though she'd never considered that Dex, Fitz, and Biana might all be sleeping in the same room. Talk about potential for awkward . . .

But sleep was probably going to be a lost cause anyway.

She checked her Imparter for news from her family.

Nothing.

Not surprising—but it didn't help her antsy-ness.

"Are Fitz and Biana already here?" she asked, having to raise her voice over the triplets' latest shouting match. It sounded like Bex had stolen Rex's favorite jackalope toy and was threatening to tear off its antlers.

"No," Kesler said. "So you're welcome to wait in the house if you want."

Inside, something crashed and shattered into a million pieces.

"Waiting out here sounds good," Sophie decided.

Kesler laughed. "Probably a good call. And let's hope that sound means they finally destroyed the horrendous crystal yeti statue my brother gave us for a wedding present. I moved it to the entryway a few years ago, since the triplets love tearing through there like a pack of dire wolves. But I swear they spare it just to spite me."

"You have a brother?" Sophie asked.

"Actually, I have three. And two sisters."

"Wow, your mom had *six* children?"

Even for humans that was a ton of kids—and for elves it was practically unheard of.

"I see my son talks about his family a lot," Kesler said.

"No he—"

"I'm just kidding," he promised. "You guys have had way more important things to talk about than Dex's estranged relatives."

They definitely had. But Sophie still felt like the world's worst best friend. Sometimes she didn't pay as much attention to Dex as she should.

"Anyway," Kesler said, "my parents were definitely not concerned about the whole 'optimal genetic purity' nonsense."

"That's another recommendation from the matchmakers," Juline explained. "They believe our strongest, purest genetics go to our first child, and after that, our genes grow increasingly diluted. That's why so many families stop after one kid."

"That *can't* be true, can it?" Sophie asked.

"It's hard to say for certain," Kesler said. "I know some pretty incredible second and third children—though my existence tends to verify it. I'm the youngest, and the only one in my family who didn't manifest."

Juline reached for his hand. "I still married the best Dizznee."

"Ha—that's not what your match lists said!"

Sophie wondered if that meant that Juline had been matched with one of Kesler's brothers. She was tempted to ask, but didn't know if that would be rude.

Before she could decide, Fitz and Biana leaped into the valley.

"Wow," Biana breathed as she took in the scenery. "I can't believe Dex lives here."

"And why is that?" Kesler's voice had sharpened along the edges.

Biana didn't seem to notice as she made her way over and flashed her brilliant smile. "I can't believe you live in the Gloaming Valley! My mom told me this is where the Alenon

River connects to the ocean. That's where the wild kelpies live, right? I've always wanted to see them."

Kesler's shoulders relaxed slightly. "Well . . . we're actually on the other side of the mountains. But I'm impressed that your mother knows so much about this place. It's not an area many pay attention to."

"They should," Biana told him. "I hear there's nothing quite like watching the kelpies come ashore."

"There isn't," Juline agreed. "If you visit again, we'll have to make a trip over to the beach. I'd take you today, but Dex's bodyguard is insisting we all stay close to the house so he can keep a better eye on you."

"How you holding up?" Fitz asked Sophie as she checked her blank Imparter again.

"Oh . . . you know. People I care about are in danger, and none of the adults want my help. Same old, same old."

"Right there with you," he mumbled.

"So your parents did go to Havenfield?" she asked. "Is that why Grizel and Woltzer aren't with you?"

Fitz nodded. "Woltzer didn't want to leave us, but Grizel talked him into it when she found out Sandor was at Havenfield. I tried to convince them to let me go too, but my mom gave me a long speech about how she didn't want us getting hurt."

"The nerve of parents these days," Juline said, "trying to keep their kids safe."

"I'm not saying I don't get it," Fitz said. "But, come on. We took on an army of ogres—I think I can handle my *brother*."

"We don't know that Alvar will be there," Biana said, swallowing hard, like there was a lump in her throat. "And if he is . . . Dad deserves to be the one to face him. Besides—we were planning to come here today anyway, right? Is it really so bad?"

Fitz sighed and turned to Kesler and Juline. "No, it's not bad at all—sorry if that sounded rude. Thank you for letting us stay here. My dad wanted me to tell you that Everglen is always available if you ever need him to return the favor."

"Does that offer include babysitting the triplets?" Kesler asked. "Because I'd be happy to drop them off anytime. But somehow I don't think he'd enjoy having them tearing through his historic halls."

Biana shrugged. "We could put them in Alvar's room and let them break all his stuff. And wait—is that Iggy?" she asked as Sophie shifted the cage she was holding.

Iggy greeted Biana with a cage-shaking fart.

Biana coughed. "Whoa, smells like someone ate too many sludgers last night. Clearly we need to work on your diet."

"Yeah, good luck with that," Sophie told her. "The last vegetables I gave him ended up plastered all over my ceiling."

"Aw, he'll eat some for me—won't you, boy?" Biana asked. "I'll give you an extra-long tummy rub—and save you the softest spot on my pillow."

"*You're* going to sleep with the imp?" Kesler asked.

"Of course! We shared a pillow every night at Alluveterre. I still miss his rumbly snore."

Biana nuzzled Iggy's nose through the bars and Sophie noticed Kesler studying her like he was seeing her for the first time. She might look like a pampered princess, but that definitely didn't make her a delicate flower—despite the fact that she'd packed *two* overnight satchels.

"Can I help you with your bags?" Kesler offered. "They look heavy."

"They are," Fitz said, holding up his own half-full bag as a comparison. "I think Biana packed enough for twenty people."

"He teases me now," Biana said. "But when it's time to do his hair in the morning he'll totally be sneaking a bit of my LovelyLocks."

An earsplitting howl cut off Fitz's retort, followed by what sounded like a pack of galloping brontosaurs as the door to Rimeshire burst open and the triplets sprinted down the path.

Bex was in the lead, her red hair flapping against her cheeks as she waved a stuffed bunny with antlers.

"GIVE IT BACK!" one of the boys shouted as he lunged to grab her arm.

Bex pivoted out of his grasp. "NOT UNTIL HARRY GETS A MUD BATH."

"DO IT! DO IT! DO IT!" the other boy chanted.

"IF YOU RUIN HARRY I'LL—"

All three of them screeched to a halt when they noticed Sophie, Fitz, and Biana.

"HEY, DEX," Bex shouted toward the house. "YOUR GIRL-FRIENDS ARE HERE—AND THAT GUY WHO'S WAY COOLER THAN YOU ARE!"

"You'll have to excuse our daughter," Kesler said, glaring at Bex. "She's developed a gift for figuring out the most embarrassing thing she can possibly say and then saying it. We're working on it."

"If she bothers you," one of the boys told Biana, "let me know and I'll take care of it."

"Dude, she just saw you crying over your stuffed Jackalope!" the other boy snorted.

"I WASN'T CRYING!"

"That's because Harry hasn't gone mud-diving yet!" Bex waved the Jackalope under his nose and took off toward the trees.

"So," the other boy said as his brother chased after Bex. "Now we can all see who the cool one is."

He winked at Sophie and Biana.

"You guys are *the worst*," Dex groaned as he stomped outside to join them, shadowed by his bodyguard. "Can't I have Lovise tie them up somewhere?"

"I don't think I have strong enough rope," Lovise warned.

"He's just jealous," the boy told Biana. "He knows the ladies like me better."

"Okay," Kesler said, grabbing the boy's arm before he could wrap it around Biana's waist. "Looks like we need to have another talk about appropriate behavior around girls, Lex. Rule number one—we do not touch them without their permission."

"And by the way," Dex told his brother, "she's way too good for you."

"YEAH WELL THEY'RE BOTH TOO GOOD FOR YOU!" Bex and Rex shouted as they circled back.

Dex turned pleading eyes to his mom. "You *promised* you'd keep them away."

"I will," Juline said. "I was just waiting until everyone was here." She closed her eyes and raised her arms, sweeping her hands back and forth in broad, graceful motions.

"Are you a Froster?" Biana asked as tiny flecks of white formed all around them.

It felt like they were standing in the middle of a shaken snow globe, and the flakes swirled in the same pattern as Juline's wispy movements.

The triplets stopped fighting to watch as their mom gathered the bits of ice into a cloud that grew and stretched until their whole property was covered. Then, with a whoosh of breath, Juline dropped her arms and let the snow fall, turning their yard into a winter wonderland.

"Amazing," Sophie whispered.

But something about it felt wrong.

"Didn't you tell me that being a Froster is a stupid talent?" she whispered to Dex. "After the day they made you test for it in ability detecting?"

"I probably did," Dex mumbled. "And it's *not* my favorite talent. But . . . I think I was grumpy because I didn't manifest. I'd figured that was my best shot, y'know?"

Biana seemed to be asking herself much bigger questions. She glanced between Juline and the snow—back and forth. Then her eyes widened. "It's you, isn't it?"

"I don't know what you mean," Juline said—but there was a tightness to her voice that said otherwise.

"No one else sees it?" Biana asked, turning to Sophie, Fitz, and Dex. "Try really looking at her—and think about her voice."

"Really, I think you have me confused with someone else," Juline insisted. "And maybe we should—"

"Wait," Fitz interrupted. "I think I see it."

"See what?" Dex asked.

"Nothing," Juline said quickly.

"You're really not going to tell him?" Biana asked.

"Tell me *what?*" Dex snapped, his eyes narrowing at everyone.

"I don't know what's going on," Kesler jumped in, "but if you're accusing my wife of something—"

"I'm not *accusing*," Biana interrupted, focusing on Juline. "If you don't want me to say anything I won't."

Juline smiled sadly. "I think we're well past that."

Her fingers scratched nervously at her neck as she watched the triplets disappear into the trees, lobbing snowballs at each other the whole way. "And I suppose it's overdue. I've been putting this off, hoping I'd find a perfect moment."

"What are you talking about?" Kesler asked.

"It's . . . probably easier if I show you."

Juline took a slow breath and held up her arms, letting the snow gather around her again. But instead of whipping into a storm, she pulled the flakes in close and let the frost coat her skin.

Layer by layer, the ice grew thicker, until her whole body was encased in a frozen shell.

"See?" Biana said as Sophie sucked in a breath.

Dex's jaw dropped as far as his lips could stretch.

"Will someone please tell me what's going on?" Kesler asked.

It took Dex a few seconds to mumble, "She's . . . Squall."

TWENTY-FOUR

SQUALL?" KESLER REPEATED, GRAB-
bing Juline's frozen hands. "Who is Squall?
Wait—you're one of *them*? Like the guy who eats
all the ruckleberries?"

"The Black Swan," Juline corrected, keeping her voice low
as she glanced over her shoulder to check for triplets. They
were still among the trees, screaming and shouting through
their snowball fight. "I'll have to figure out how much I can
trust them to know. I should've prepared better for this—I just
didn't expect anyone to notice. It's not like I'm the only Froster
in our world!"

"Sorry," Biana mumbled. "The whole time I've been here,
I kept thinking your voice sounded familiar. So when I saw

the snow, it clicked. I think it's because Squall—or I should probably say 'you'—was the member of the Collective I was the most curious about. I actually thought you were someone on the Council who was secretly a Froster, because you were always having to race back to the Lost Cities."

"That would've been a more interesting anecdote," Juline said, twirling a few times to shed her icy disguise. "Really I'm just the only member of the Collective with a family living at home who would notice my absence. Wraith was also concerned that Dex would recognize me."

Dex laughed—dark and thick and definitely not because he found anything funny. "Guess he was wrong. Apparently I'm an idiot."

"No, you're not," Sophie promised.

"She's right," Kesler said. "There's nothing idiotic about trusting your mother not to lie to you."

"I haven't *lied*," Juline said quietly. "But yes, I have kept secrets. I had to—those who know the truth have to be involved, and that required risks and sacrifices that I wasn't about to let any of you suffer."

"What if I wanted to be involved?" Kesler asked. "You know I have no warm feelings toward the Council."

"I know." She reached for his hand, and for a second it looked like he might pull away. But he sighed and let Juline twine her fingers with his. "If both of us were part of an illegal rebellion, it would've put our whole family at risk. Who would've cared for our children if we'd been discovered and captured?"

"Okay, but what about me?" Dex asked. "I'm *part* of the Black Swan. How could you stand there in Alluveterre after I swore fealty and not tell me?"

"It was the Collective's decision—though I did support it." She reached for him, but unlike his father, Dex *did* pull away. "I'm so sorry, sweetheart. I know how huge this must feel. But I had to protect our organization. We'd never planned to let any of you join—"

"Not even me?" Sophie interrupted.

"Not this early, no. But if we've learned anything over the years, it's that we have to adapt in order to survive. So we let the five of you swear fealty—but we also took measures to minimize our risk. And one of those measures was to keep our identities anonymous until each of you had proven that you could protect our secrets. As it turned out, that was a wise decision, given what Keefe has done."

The frustration in her voice reminded Sophie that Wraith had included Squall in the not-trusting-Keefe camp.

"Okay, fine," Dex said. "But Forkle and Granite showed us who they are a few weeks ago—you could've come clean then!"

Juline stared at the ground, where tiny crystals of ice swirled around her feet. "I could give you a thousand excuses, but none of them will change the fact that I handled this wrong. I should've told you before your friends caught me."

Biana slouched lower. "Sorry again."

"It's not your fault," Juline told her. "If anything, it's a valuable reminder of why none of us should ever underestimate the four of you."

"You mean the three of us." Dex said, kicking the snow. "I'm the jerk who didn't recognize my own mom."

"Hey, my brother was spying on my family for most of my life, and I never noticed," Fitz reminded him. "At least your mom is one of the good guys."

Dex shrugged. "I dunno. The Black Swan have done some pretty shady stuff—don't even try to deny it."

"I won't," Juline said. "It's yet another reason I didn't want to involve my family. I've never done anything I didn't believe in—but that doesn't mean I haven't crossed hard lines."

Sophie remembered the nightmares she'd had after she'd learned that Squall would be freezing off Gethen's fingernails to remove whatever enzyme kept allowing the Neverseen to track him. Squall had assured her the process was painless, but . . .

"See?" Dex said when she shuddered. "Sophie gets it."

"I do," Sophie said. "But I also think we *all* know the hard choices we have to face for this cause. You don't defeat a group of murderers with rainbows and candy."

"I know," Dex mumbled. "It's just . . . weird."

"Aren't you always telling people you like weird?" Juline asked.

She reached for Dex again and this time he stayed put. He didn't even flinch when she brushed the back of her fingers against his cheek.

But he didn't stop scowling, either.

"Am I allowed to know how long you've been with the Black Swan?" Sophie asked.

"Not as long as you're probably thinking. Project Moonlark was well under way by the time I swore fealty. In fact, you'd already been born."

"So when was it?" Kesler pressed.

Juline bit her lip. "A few months after I had the triplets."

"The *triplets*?" Kesler and Dex repeated.

"Are you talking about us?" Bex shouted from somewhere among the trees.

"I'm sharing stories about when you were babies. Want to join us?"

Juline's answer was perfect—not a lie, but all three shouted, "NO WAY!"

Kesler kept his voice low as he said, "You've been with the Black Swan for *eleven years*?"

"Closer to ten," Juline corrected. "But yes, it's been a long time. And it wasn't something I planned. I was at the birthing center, and I kept holding my three innocent, adorable babies and thinking about how horribly our world was going to treat them. I could already see it happening. My physicians kept ending every sentence with 'for triplets,' like they automatically had low expectations. *The babies are healthy 'for triplets.' Their speaking skills are normal 'for triplets.' Their intelligence is strong 'for triplets.'* It broke my heart and made me want to cry and punch people in the throat and pack up our lives and leave the Lost Cities."

Kesler closed the space between them, wrapping his arm around her shoulders. "Why didn't you tell me that was happening?"

"Because I didn't want you to blame yourself. Sometimes you act like you ruined my life by marrying me—and I hate that. I *love* you. I've never regretted my decision for one second. But it's also helped me to see that our world is deeply flawed. That's why I was so grateful to find Physic."

"*Physic* recruited you?" Sophie asked, sharing a look with Fitz.

Physic was the physician who came to Alluveterre to save Fitz's life after he'd been injured in Exile.

Juline nodded. "When I left the birthing center, I asked Elwin for a list of pediatric physicians who would be more . . . open-minded."

"Does that mean Elwin knows who Physic is?" Biana asked.

"Knowing and realizing are two different things. But I'm sure Physic will reveal herself soon. She's not a fan of subterfuge. In fact, she never made any attempt to hide what she was from me. When she came to the house for the first checkup, she asked why I wasn't at the birthing center, and when I gave a vague answer, she flat-out asked if I ever worried that the Council was blind to our world's prejudices. After that, whenever she'd come for a checkup, she wouldn't stop pushing until I'd admitted any callous things people had said or done. A few months later, she asked me, 'If you could change our world, would you?' And when I said yes, she asked if my answer would be different if the only way to change the world involved breaking rules. I was surprised to admit that it wouldn't matter. That's when she told me about the Black Swan and asked me to join. I swore fealty a few weeks later and started out as a simple information channel. But over time, they trusted me more. Eventually, when Physic stepped down from the Collective, she suggested me as her replacement—and I accepted the position."

"Physic was part of the *Collective*?" Fitz asked. "Why did she step down?"

Juline glanced at Sophie.

"It was because of my allergy, wasn't it?" Sophie guessed.

One of the memories the Black Swan had stolen from her— the one they hadn't yet given back—was from when she was nine and woke up in the hospital after a severe allergic reaction. Her human doctors couldn't figure out what had triggered it, but once she moved to the Lost Cities, she discovered she was allergic to limbium—an *elvin* substance. So an *elf* must've given her something that made her sick. But the who and the how and the why were all a big blank.

"I'm guessing you're not going to tell me what happened?" Sophie asked.

"I think we've unearthed enough secrets today," Juline said. "And honestly, Forkle and Physic never told us the whole story. But it did make her decide to focus on medicine again. So she nominated me to take her place in the Collective, and by that time the triplets were in their daily tutoring sessions, and Dex was helping at the store, so I had a few extra hours to devote to the cause."

"And you couldn't have told me *then?*" Kesler asked.

"I thought about it. But I was terrified. I couldn't bear the thought of you hating me."

"I could never *hate* you," Kesler promised.

"But you're still mad at me."

"Well, I think I'm allowed to be a little upset that my wife lied to me for ten years."

"I didn't lie," Juline insisted. "I was very careful about it. If I said I was going somewhere, I really did go. I just . . . took a detour along the way. It's not ideal, I know. But I don't want you thinking you can't trust me. Everything about the life we've shared is real."

"Is it?" Dex asked. "What about when Sophie first showed up at Slurps and Burps and I told you about meeting her? You acted surprised."

"I *was* surprised! I'd had no idea she'd be living with Grady and Edaline. The last I'd heard, she was supposed to live with

Alden and Della. But things were changing minute by minute. We'd planned for a much longer timeline before we brought Sophie into our world. But the Neverseen sparked the white fires and we had to get her somewhere safe." Juline turned to Sophie. "I can't imagine how confusing those days must've been for you. And I'm so sorry we had to uproot you that way. But I'll always be grateful that you ended up with my sister."

"Me too." Sophie's eyes burned with the words, and she had to check her Imparter again.

Still no hails from anyone.

"Are you going to tell your parents about me?" Juline asked.

"Do you not want me to?"

"I think . . . it would be better if I tell them. I'm sure they'll have lots of questions."

"So do I," Dex jumped in. "'Cause I see a lot of things that don't add up. Like, what happened when I was kidnapped? Why would you do a planting in the Wanderling Woods if you knew the Black Swan were still searching for me? And why was Forkle the one who came to rescue us?"

"The days after you were taken were the worst days of my life," Juline whispered. "None of us could piece together what happened, and there were too many conflicting reports for me to feel any hope. I also had a family that needed closure—and a world that expected me to grieve a certain way. So I went along with the planting. I didn't know what else to do. And Forkle went to save you because his mental blocking is stronger than mine, and we weren't sure if he'd have to confront your kid-nappers. But if I'd known he was going to leave you both alone in Paris, I never would've let him go without me. When he came back empty-handed, I slapped him so hard he had my handprint on his cheek for three days."

It wasn't the right moment to smile—but Sophie felt her lips twitch anyway.

"This . . . is a lot to take in," Kesler said quietly.

"I know," Juline told him. "This is why Councillors aren't allowed to have families. And the Black Swan used to follow the same policy. They amended their rule for Tiergan—but he was already a member of the Collective when he adopted Wylie. The real reason they agreed to appoint me was because they believed our family could handle it. And we can. I just need you to trust me."

"I need to know something first," Dex said, not quite meeting her eyes. "Did you bring me to Havenfield that first day because you wanted me to spy on Sophie? Like Keefe's mom did with him and Fitz?"

Juline took him by his shoulders. "I promise, Dex. I brought you there because you asked. That's it. And honestly, I was reluctant to do it. I could feel my worlds colliding. But you were so excited to meet Sophie, and I wanted so badly for you to have a friend. I didn't want you spending another year eating lunch in your alchemy session."

"You ate in your alchemy session?" Biana asked.

Shame burned Dex's cheeks as he nodded.

Biana's blush looked even brighter as she whispered, "Sorry. I was really stupid back then."

"Me too," Fitz said.

Juline smiled sadly. "We all make mistakes. The only thing we can do is try to move past them. Can we do that?"

She seemed to hold her breath as Kesler and Dex looked at each other.

"I think we can," Kesler decided.

Dex nodded.

Juline pulled them close, kissing Dex's cheek before she kissed Kesler a whole lot longer.

"EWWWWWWWWWW," the triplets shouted as they raced out of the tree line. "YOU GUYS AREN'T SUPPOSED TO DO THAT WHERE WE CAN SEE YOU."

"Deal with it," Kesler said, kissing Juline again before scooping up an armful of snow and flinging it at his kids.

"Well," Juline said as the triplets retaliated, sending slushy balls of ice whizzing past everyone's heads. "I think that's our cue to get out of the battle zone."

She took Iggy's cage from Sophie and grabbed one of Biana's bags before she marched toward Rimeshire.

Fitz and Biana followed, but Sophie noticed Dex lagging behind.

"You okay?" she asked him.

He kicked more snow. "Would you be?"

"I don't know. It's a lot to get used to. But . . . I keep thinking about the oath we made when we swore fealty. Do you remember it?"

"*I will do everything in my power to help my world,*" Dex said quietly. "It wasn't nearly as fancy as I'd been expecting."

"Same here. But it's actually kinda perfect for what we're all trying to do. Sometimes we hide things. And sometimes it hurts. And sometimes the adults send us away instead of letting us fight alongside them. But . . . we're all just trying to do everything we can to help people."

Dex's sigh lasted several seconds.

"If it helps, I wouldn't have cared why you came to Havenfield that day," she added. "I'm just glad you did. I needed a friend too. And I got the best friend ever."

"GROSS—ARE YOU GUYS GOING TO KISS?" Bex shouted.

"IGNORE HER," Kesler called, scooping up another huge armful of snow and dropping it over the triplets' heads. They squealed and ran into the trees with Kesler right behind.

Dex's face looked so red it was basically purple. "Siblings are the worst."

"They can be," Sophie agreed.

She still missed the human sister she'd grown up with, though. They'd fought all the time. But that's what sisters did.

"Anyway, don't worry," she said. "I know she's giving you a hard time. It's not like . . ."

"Yeah." Dex's brow scrunched, and he opened his mouth like he wanted to say something else. Then he shook his head and his lips shifted to a different word. "Come on, let's go inside. I'm losing feeling in my toes."

Fitz and Biana were waiting by the door, ready with generous amounts of encouragement and support. And amazingly enough, Dex seemed like he was actually glad they were there. They'd come a long way as a group—and had some crazy, impossible, scary, frustrating things happen.

But they also had each other. And *that* was something special.

TWENTY-FIVE

EX'S HOUSE WAS EVEN MORE beautiful on the inside. Everything looked blue and gray and shimmery, with swirls of white like waves in the ocean.

Kesler was right, though—the crystal yeti in the entryway definitely needed to be destroyed. Its jaggedly carved fur looked like some sort of demented, oversize porcupine. And once again, the triplets seemed to have spared its life. Instead, they'd shattered what must've been a vase filled with glass marbles. The white stone floor was covered in the clear glass orbs.

"Walk very carefully," Juline warned.

Sophie made it about ten steps before her foot rolled on a

marble and sent her flying backward like a cartoon character slipping on a banana peel. She would've been in for some killer bruises if Fitz hadn't caught her.

"Maybe I should carry you," he said when she slipped again on her next step.

His teasing smile made it extra hilarious when he fell a second later, landing on his butt with a loud "Oof!"

Biana laughed so hard she nearly fell over too—but Dex was able to catch her by her shoulders.

"Perhaps I should carry all of you," Lovise offered, making it look easy as she helped them back on their feet. "The trick is to slide your steps, so nothing gets underneath you."

She was right—though they all looked like the world's most uncoordinated ice skaters.

"You okay?" Sophie asked when she noticed Fitz rubbing his tailbone.

"He's fine," Biana answered for him. "I knock him down way harder than that in tackle bramble all the time. And by the way—he told me about the favor he owes you. If you need ideas for how to torture him, I have *lots* of suggestions."

"See, Dex?" Fitz asked. "You're not the only one with annoying siblings."

"Trade you!" Dex offered.

"Only if you take Alvar as part of the deal."

The name killed everyone's smiles and had Sophie checking her Imparter again.

"Do you think it's a bad sign that we haven't heard anything?" she whispered.

"We've barely been gone an hour," Biana reminded her.

"Ugh—is that really all?" Sophie asked. "This day is going to take forever."

"I know." Biana twisted the panic switch on her finger. "I think we need to stay busy so we don't go crazy."

They'd made it to the main room by then, where the plush gray carpet was blissfully marble-free, and the clear ceiling let in warm rays of sunlight. Five curved staircases broke up the space, each leading to one of the towers. And all the gray-blue furniture had been arranged around a giant glass cloche in the center. Silver flames tipped with blue flickered under the dome, shimmering with each spark and crackle. Sophie had seen many types of fire since she'd moved to the Lost Cities, but she'd never seen any that were quite so beautiful.

"You okay?" Fitz asked her. "I know you don't like to be around flames."

"I don't," Sophie agreed. "But for some reason these don't bother me."

"Probably because they're a hologram." Juline snapped her fingers and the glowing flames morphed into a black orb of the night sky filled with twinkling stars. "This is one of Dex's inventions."

"That's amazing," Biana said, snapping again and creating a sphere of sunset. "You seriously made this?"

Dex shrugged. "It wasn't hard. All I did was tweak a fire emulator."

Biana shook her head. "You don't give yourself enough credit."

"Sophie's just as bad with compliments," Fitz said. "Look at how red they're both turning right now."

"They really are adorable, aren't they?" Biana asked.

Sophie sighed. "Who invited the Vackers?"

"That one's on you," Dex said. "But at least we have someone to prank now. As soon as they fall asleep—"

"Sleep?" Biana interrupted. "Only lame people sleep during slumber parties. Besides, we all know Sophie's going to keep us up sending telepathic messages to Keefe. Or wait—you don't think he'll go to Havenfield, do you?"

"I . . . don't know if they'll give him a choice," Sophie mumbled. "But Keefe would *never* hurt our families."

"What happens if they tell him he has to?" Fitz asked.

"We hope he has a plan to get out of it," Sophie said. "Like how he had a plan to save me with that bead."

"And if he doesn't?" Fitz pressed.

Sophie didn't have an answer.

"Come on," Juline said, breaking the suffocating silence. "The solarium is this way."

She led them toward the back of the house, into a giant glass bubble of a room that made it feel like they were standing in a life-size fishbowl. A thin row of plants lined the round space, and Sophie noticed that their emerald green leaves shimmered with a thin layer of hoarfrost. The rest of the room was mostly empty—just a few topiaries scattered around and a pile of four rolled-up sleeping bags.

The real focus was the view: a wide stretch of garden filled with flowering vines, gleaming silver fountains, and the most lifelike ice sculptures that Sophie had ever seen—a mix of spring and winter only a Froster could have at the same time.

The woolly mammoth had been carved to scale, and somehow its icy fur looked soft and silky. And the saber-toothed tiger's eyes gave Sophie chills.

"They're amazing," Biana whispered.

Juline's cheeks reddened at the praise. "Thank you. Our lives are too chaotic for pets, so this is my compromise with the triplets. They get to decide which creatures I carve every week. And speaking of pets, is your imp going to need a bathroom spot? We can set up some sort of box if you don't want him out in the cold."

"Or we could give him a way fluffier fur coat!" Biana jumped in. "Maybe change his color, too! Do you have any elixirs, Dex? I'm thinking purple this time—or maybe green."

"I'll check my room," he told her.

Biana clapped. "Yay—first makeover of the night!"

"You mean the *only* makeover," Fitz corrected.

"Aw, come on—you and Keefe let me do it once before!" Biana whined.

"Seriously?" Sophie asked. "Now *that's* a story I have to hear."

Dex snorted. "Me too."

"Aren't we supposed to be searching Alvar's records?" Fitz asked.

Biana shrugged off her satchel. "I can't imagine that's going to take *all* night."

"It might," Dex warned. "There are a *lot* of scrolls. I'll need help carrying them down."

Fitz volunteered, and Biana pouted as the boys headed for the stairs.

Juline handed Biana her other bag and gave Sophie Iggy's cage. "For the record, I hope you guys have a little fun tonight. I know you're worried about your parents. And I know how hard you all work trying to solve everything. But I speak for all of us when I say that we want you to enjoy being normal teenagers."

"But we *aren't* normal teenagers," Sophie reminded her. "Or I'm not, at least."

Juline took her hand. "Yes, you are. Even after everything you've been through. Even with everything you have ahead. You're still a fourteen-year-old girl who deserves to relax and have fun with her friends."

"So what you're saying," Biana said, "is I have your permission to give Dex a makeover?"

Juline laughed. "I'll leave that up to Dex."

She winked and left them alone, and they got to work setting up the sleeping bags—which turned out to be a much trickier job than it should've been. The all-in-a-straight-row concept felt super awkward. But the round room made it impossible to go to separate corners. Eventually they settled on an X shape. That way their heads would be close enough to talk to each other, but they'd each still have as much space as possible.

"Keefe is going to pout so hard when he finds out he missed this," Biana said, claiming the sleeping bag closest to the room's entrance. "We could've all scooted over and put his sleeping bag right here."

Sophie tried not to notice that the arrangement would've looked like a star.

"You know what I hate?" she said, moving her backpack to the sleeping bag on the left of Biana's. "If the Neverseen really do attack Havenfield today—and everyone stays safe—they'll probably know that Keefe warned us. We tried to make it look like all the security was stuff they'd have set up in order to protect me. But *I'm* not there."

"Right, but it's not like you never leave the house," Biana reminded her. "And Keefe's a quick thinker."

"Also a good liar," Sophie mumbled.

But talk didn't mean much to the Neverseen.

If they got suspicious, Keefe would have to do something to prove himself again. And it would have to be even bigger than what he already did at Foxfire. . . .

"You know what *I* hate?" Biana asked, pulling a tab on the

side of her sleeping bag and making it plump up like a pillow.

Sophie copied her, and when she sat down, it felt like sinking into a giant stretched-out marshmallow.

"I hate wondering how many times I should've figured out what my brother was doing," Biana whispered.

"That's why Edaline told me hindsight is a dangerous game," Sophie reminded her.

"I know. But it feels so *obvious*. Like, I remember after my dad's mind broke, Alvar decided to stay the night at Everglen because my mom had a super-rough day. And I couldn't sleep, so I got up to wander the halls. I heard him in my dad's office, talking to someone on his Imparter—but I figured he was trying to help finish one of my dad's projects."

"Do you remember anything he said?"

"Bits and pieces. I should've paid better attention. I heard him say something about changing the timeline. And he asked about test subjects. I also remember him using the word 'criterion' a couple of times. But I don't know what any of that means."

Sophie pulled Ella from her backpack and leaned her cheek on the elephant's pillowy belly. "You know what I miss? Back when I first moved to the Lost Cities—and the Black Swan were running my life from the shadows—I'd know I was on the right track because I'd hear a word and it would trigger new memories. Now it seems like everything we learn is stuff that even the Black Swan don't know."

"Do you think that means they were preparing you for the wrong thing?" Biana asked.

"Ugh—I do now!"

Just when Sophie thought she'd reached maximum worrying capacity.

What if the role she'd been designed to play wasn't even the right one?

Could Project Moonlark be . . . a fail?

TWENTY-SIX

U H-OH, DID SOMETHING HAPPEN?" Fitz asked as he stumbled into the solarium carrying a black trunk that looked like it weighed as much as he did. "You haven't heard from Grady and Edaline, right?"

Sophie double-checked her Imparter. "Nope. Still nothing."

Fitz set the trunk down in the center of the X and took the empty sleeping bag closest to Sophie. "Then why do you look like you want to tug on your eyelashes?"

Sophie sighed. "Biana told me about a conversation she overheard Alvar having. I'm trying to figure out what it could mean."

"What conversation?" Dex asked as he brought an equally enormous trunk and set it down next to the one Fitz brought.

Biana repeated the story while Dex sank onto the only empty sleeping bag, between the two Vackers.

"So . . . you're worried that Project Moonlark is a bust?" Fitz guessed.

Sophie couldn't look at him as she nodded.

"Okay, but even if it is," Fitz said, "haven't you hated feeling like you're some sort of puppet?"

"Yeah, but it's way scarier thinking there's no safety net," Sophie mumbled. "I didn't like feeling controlled—but I *did* like thinking the good guys had a plan."

"I don't know, wouldn't it be kinda weird if the Black Swan knew all these horrible things were going to happen and didn't do anything to stop them?" Fitz asked.

"And just because parts of their plans have changed doesn't mean all of them have," Biana added. "You still have crazy powerful abilities. *And* you have us. We've got this!"

"I guess," Sophie said. "I just wish we had *any* idea what the Neverseen are planning, or what the Lodestar Initiative actually is. I mean, why would your brother be talking about 'test subjects' and 'criterion'? That sounds like some sort of experiment."

Dex sucked in a breath. "Okay—this is going to sound crazy—but hear me out. What if the Lodestar Initiative is the Neverseen's version of Project Moonlark?"

"I'm not sure I know what that means," Biana told him.

"I do," Fitz said. "And please tell me you don't actually think they're trying to build another Sophie."

"Why not?" Dex asked. "They've known she exists for a while. Don't you think they'd try to do something to counter her?"

"They did," Fitz argued. "They tried to find her. And capture her. And now they're trying to control her."

"Maybe," Dex said. "But they could do all of that *and* try to re-create her."

"Can everyone stop talking about me like I'm Dr. Frankenstein's monster?" Sophie grumbled.

"Is that a human thing?" Biana asked.

"Yeah, it's this big scary guy with bolts in his neck, who's pieced together from dead things," Fitz said. "I remember seeing pictures of it one of the times I visited the Forbidden Cities. I think it was a movie?"

"And a book," Sophie mumbled.

"Sorry," Dex said. "I didn't mean it like that. But . . . it would explain what Alvar meant by 'test subjects.' I've also heard the word 'criterion' used with DNA and genetics and stuff."

Sophie hugged Ella so tight all the stuffing bulged in the elephant's head.

"Hey," Biana said, patting Sophie's shoulder. "Even if he's right, it doesn't change anything about *you*—or Keefe."

"I don't think he's right," Fitz added. "Keefe's mom helped create the Lodestar Initiative, and she's definitely not a scientist. And don't even try to convince me Keefe's their version of Sophie. He's older than she is. And he wasn't raised by humans. And he only has one ability. And he's not nearly as awesome."

He grinned at Sophie, but she was too busy panicking to return it.

"He does have a photographic memory, though," Biana said—which did *not* help. "And his empathy is more powerful than other Empaths. Do you think his mom could've had his genes tweaked somehow after he was born?"

"I guess we could ask Forkle about it," Dex said.

"And he'll tell us we're being ridiculous," Fitz assured him.

"Maybe. But they did for sure mess with Keefe's memories," Dex argued. "So maybe all they did was plant secrets in his head, like the Black Swan did with Sophie. You have to admit it's at least possible."

Sophie wasn't going to admit anything.

It was too weird.

Too wrong.

Too . . . no.

Just *no.*

She tried to bury the theory deep—lock it away with all the other Things She Didn't Want to Think About.

But the idea had already dug its claws in deep.

So had the bigger, scarier question it raised, echoing around her head on autorepeat.

If Dex was right, and the Lodestar Initiative was the Never-seen's version of Project Moonlark . . . did that mean Keefe was meant to be her nemesis?

TWENTY-SEVEN

"YOU WERE MADE TO BE THE HERO,"
Sophie mumbled. "I was raised to be something . . . else."

"What?" Fitz, Biana, and Dex all asked.

"That's what Keefe told me. At the Lake of Blood. When he ran off with the Neverseen. Do you think he meant . . . ?"

She couldn't finish the question.

"Hey," Fitz said, scooting next to her on her sleeping bag. "I don't think it means what you're thinking it means. Brant and Fintan were there—and Keefe needed to convince them he was joining for real. He had to sound like a guy trying to explain to his friend why he was betraying her—and remember, I'm saying that as someone who still has trust issues with Keefe."

"I guess," she said quietly. "But *you* think it proves your theory, don't you, Dex?"

"I don't know," Dex said. "I mean . . . it could. But I *am* also just guessing."

"Exactly," Biana jumped in. "All we really know is that we *don't* know anything."

Somehow, that was the most depressing thought of all.

Sophie flopped onto her back, rubbing the knot under her ribs and trying to tie all the complicated things she was feeling into it. She stared at the sky through the curved glass ceiling, wishing she could stretch out her consciousness to Keefe and pummel him with questions. But it was still early in the day—way too soon for their check-in. And she probably didn't want to know what he was doing anyway.

"Okay," Fitz said. "I think we need a subject change before Sophie's brain explodes."

"He's right," Biana agreed. "Maybe if we figure out where Alvar used to sneak off to, it'll help us understand what that conversation *actually* meant."

Dex scooted over to the trunks and popped both lids open, revealing so many tightly coiled scrolls that Sophie wondered if there was any paper left in the world.

"I told you this is going to be boring," Dex reminded them as Biana unrolled a scroll and gaped at the thousands of tiny black numbers printed across it. "This part you'll probably be able to read"—he pointed to the narrowest column on the left of the scroll—"that's the time stamp, telling you the date, year, and time in hours, minutes, and seconds. But the rest is all code. Some of it has obviously been altered, and I've been trying to figure out which parts, but so far I haven't been able to find a pattern."

"Have you checked the days you were kidnapped?" Biana asked. "That's the one time we know that Alvar wasn't where his records said he was—*and* we know exactly where he was."

"I haven't," Dex admitted. "The triplets got in my room and got into the trunks and . . . let's just say I'm currently brewing a very special elixir for payback."

Fitz sighed. "So all of these are in random order? That's going to take forever."

"Maybe not," Biana said. "Now we have four of us working on it. Okay, so Sophie and Fitz—you guys work on putting the scrolls back in order while Dex and I focus on trying to find the dates from the kidnapping. And once we find one, Dex will switch to checking the tech code part to see if he can find the pattern we need."

"You're assuming they altered Alvar's feed the same way every time," Dex reminded her.

"I know—but isn't that what you'd do?" she asked. "If you knew something was working, wouldn't you keep doing it?"

"I suppose."

"All right then," Biana said. "We have a plan!"

They did.

But the process was *sloooooooooooooooooooooow*. It took them hours before Biana found the first scroll from the time frame they needed.

"I think I'll need at least three to really be able to compare," Dex warned as he squinted at the numbers.

Hours later, Sophie found scroll number two.

"So we only need one more, right?" Biana asked.

"Assuming I can find the pattern," Dex said. "And assuming the pattern actually applies to the other days he snuck away. And assuming I can figure out what the pattern even means."

"That's a lot of assumptions," Fitz noted.

"It is," Biana agreed. "But Dex found secret information about the plague by digging through a database that spanned *centuries*. I'm sure we can find what we're looking for in a couple of trunks of scrolls."

When she put it that way, it didn't sound so daunting. But they still hadn't found the third scroll by the time Juline brought them dinner—which looked like blue french fries and tasted like nachos with extra cheese.

"Still at it?" Juline asked. "And I'm assuming you haven't heard from anyone at Havenfield?"

Sophie shook her head. "I've been checking my Imparter every few minutes. It's driving me nuts."

"Your Imparter *is* working, right?" Biana asked. "Weren't you having a problem with it?"

"I thought the problem was Dex's Imparter," Sophie said.

Dex pulled the silver gadget out of his pocket. "I ran every test I could think of, and they all came back normal. Have you tried hailing me again?"

Sophie held her Imparter to her mouth and told it, "Show me Dex Dizznee."

Dex's Imparter stayed blank.

"That doesn't make sense," Dex said. "Fitz—can you try hailing me?"

Fitz did, and Dex's screen immediately flashed with Fitz's face.

"Hmm. Maybe yours is the one with the loose wire," Dex said. "Give me a sec."

He ran upstairs to get tools, and Sophie stared at her finicky gadget.

"Do you think I should check on my family with your Imparter?" she asked Fitz. "What if they've been trying to hail me?"

"My parents are there too," Fitz reminded her, "and they haven't tried to reach me."

Dex raced back into the room with a kit of the world's tiniest screwdrivers. Within minutes he had the whole Imparter disassembled and hundreds of paper-thin gears scattered across his sleeping bag.

"See anything weird?" Sophie asked as he picked up an especially tiny gear.

Dex shook his head. "Everything was exactly where it should be. I just don't . . ."

His voice trailed off and he leaned closer, squinting at one of the cog's teeth.

"Is that grease?" Biana asked, peering over his shoulder.

Dex said nothing as he fished his monocle pendant out from underneath his tunic and used the magnifying glass to examine a speck of black.

"Whoa," he whispered—then covered his mouth.

"What is it?" Fitz, Biana, Sophie, and Juline all asked at once.

"I . . . think some dirt got into the mechanism and clogged it," he said. "Can someone get me a pen and paper so I can make a note of which cog needs to be replaced?"

Juline pulled the pencil from her hair and Biana flipped one of the scrolls over for Dex to write on the back.

"So it's just a normal malfunction?" Sophie asked.

"Should be."

But Dex's note told a different story.

His left hand shook as he held it to his lips and made the universal *Shhh* sign before he showed them what he'd written.

Someone might be listening.

TWENTY-EIGHT

T HE GOOD NEWS IS, YOUR IMPARTER still works," Dex said, adding another sentence to his note.

We need to act normal.

"Once I put it back together, it should connect to everything except my Imparter," he added. "I forgot that I added a safety protocol to mine, blocking it from communicating with any abnormal tech."

He amended his sign again.

Can we talk telepathically?

Juline grabbed the note and added:

ALL of us!

Lovise snatched the scroll and wrote: *I expect updates as well.*

Sophie nodded and turned to Fitz, who offered her his hand. Their thumb rings snapped together as the mental energy hummed between them and they opened their minds to Dex, Biana, and Juline.

Okay, Sophie transmitted while their mental voices flooded her head. *I think we're doing what Councillor Emery does when he mediates the other Councillors—and wow, it's LOUD.*

Yeah it is, Fitz said, rubbing the sides of his forehead.

Sophie tried to think around the questions being shouted at her, but it was too much too fast.

Okay, so here's how this needs to work, Fitz said. *Sophie and I can hear all of you guys, but you can't hear each other. So you need to take turns, and then we'll transmit what you said to the rest of the group so everyone can hear it.*

Dex first, Sophie said. *What do you mean someone might be listening? And why aren't we smashing that gear to stop them?*

Because, if they don't know that we've found it, they won't destroy their end of the signal. And that might give me a chance to trace it back to the source. But first I have to get the Imparter reassembled.

His hands were already busy fitting all the tiny cogs back together.

Fitz relayed the information to the others—even jotted down a brief update for Lovise—and transmitted Biana's question: *Who else would it be besides the Neverseen?*

It could be the Council, Fitz told her. *Mr. Forkle said they're keeping close tabs on us.*

Can they hear everything we say? Sophie asked. *Or only when the Imparter's in use?*

I can't tell yet, Dex said. *That's why I don't want us talking, just in case.*

But won't they get suspicious of all this silence? Fitz asked. *Especially since they would've heard that we were disassembling the Imparter?*

That's actually a good point, Dex admitted.

I need you guys to start talking again, Fitz told Juline and Biana.

Biana rustled some of the scrolls. "I think I need a break, guys. All the numbers are turning into a big black blur."

I need to update the rest of the Collective, Juline thought as she told them, "I'm going to make you guys some mugs of cinnacreme. It's always my favorite thing on a cold night."

"Ohhhh, that sounds amazing!" Biana launched into a long explanation of what it tasted like—and it *did* sound delicious. But Sophie was more focused on Dex.

How long do you think they've been listening? she asked.

I'm guessing it's pretty recent. I've had that safety protocol on my Imparter for a while, and it never used to block you. That's why I didn't think of it at first. But now it makes total sense. My Imparter shuts out any signals that aren't secure.

So someone must've tampered with yours, Fitz said to Sophie.

But when? It's always with me. Or it's in my room, and if someone had been in there, Sandor would've known—wouldn't he?

Hasn't Brant fooled Sandor's senses before? Dex thought. *Using ash or something?*

But wouldn't he still have left footprints in the flowered carpet? Sophie asked.

Unless he levitated, Fitz said.

She hated him for being right—hated even more what the possibility meant.

I had my Imparter with me the day Keefe visited Foxfire, she transmitted. *If it was broadcasting, that means the Neverseen might know Keefe's betraying them.*

Her mind flashed through visions of Keefe being dragged to the ogres' prison, bleeding and begging for mercy like his mom.

Hey, Fitz said, tightening his hold on her hand. *Try not to think about that stuff until we know what we're dealing with, okay?*

I'm close to tracking the signal, Dex told them. *But I think we've gotten too quiet again.*

Fitz told Biana to start talking again, and she fumbled for something to say.

Wait—I know! she thought. "Makeover time! Who wants to go first?"

"I think it should be Dex," Sophie told her.

Uh, I'm a little busy here, Dex argued.

I know—but if they think you're getting a makeover, they'll be less suspicious about what you're doing to the Imparter.

Dex sighed. "Fine—but *no* makeup!"

"Duh," Biana told him. "All I'm going to do is fix your hair."

"What's wrong with my hair?"

"Let me show you the many things." Biana dug through one of her overnight bags and pulled out a pink sparkly pouch filled with pots of different colored gels. She chose a yellowish concoction and unscrewed the lid.

"That better not have pee in it," Dex told her.

"Don't be gross. And don't be such a baby."

Fitz snickered. "Now you see what I live with."

How's it going? Sophie transmitted to Dex.

Good. I'm just setting up some aliases to shield my search signals and—

"Ahh! What are you doing?" he shouted.

Biana had scooted closer and was running her fingers through his hair.

"Relax—I'm just making it so your hair isn't plastered to your forehead anymore. Hold still." She dipped her fingers in the yellow goop and reached for him again.

Sophie had never seen Dex so red.

"This style will draw way more attention to your eyes," Biana said. "And the flecks of gold in the gel will bring out the blond undertones in your hair."

She handed him a mirror from her bag. "See? It's awesome, right?"

Dex's grin was so huge it practically caved in his cheeks.

Sophie shifted to get a better look. "Wow. That's . . . *wow.*"

Who knew a new hairstyle could make such a difference?

Not that Dex hadn't been cute before—he was an elf, after all. But there'd been something about him that always felt *young*.

Not anymore.

Aren't we supposed to be dealing with the fact that someone might be eavesdropping on us right now? Fitz transmitted. *Or are you trying to bore them to death with all this hair talk?*

Biana smirked. "I think Fitz should be my next makeover. His style has gotten a little helmety lately."

"It has not!" Fitz said. But Sophie noticed he reached up and mussed his hair a bit.

Okay, Dex thought. *I'm ready to track the signal—we have to make sure we keep talking.*

Out loud, he added, "If Fitz is being a baby, how about we give Iggy a new look?"

Biana squealed happily as he handed her a vial filled with a cloudy liquid, and she scooted over to Iggy's cage, waving the elixir near his furry lips. Iggy sniffed the milky serum once before downing it in one giant slurp. He'd barely finished licking his chops when he sneezed and his fur poofed out in every direction, turning him into a ball of blue fluff with only the tips of his ears, hands, wings, and nose sticking through.

"Isn't he going to change color?" Sophie asked.

"Give it a second," Dex said, and sure enough, Iggy's fur started to shimmer as it shifted to a bright purple.

"Awwww, just when I thought he couldn't get more adorable!" Biana cooed.

Iggy bounced up and down and flapped his fluff-buried wings.

"Who's ready for cinnacreme?" Juline asked, sweeping into the room with a tray of four steaming mugs. She froze midstep when she spotted Dex's hair.

"Like it?" Biana asked.

Juline looked a little misty-eyed.

"Ugh, why are parents so embarrassing?" Dex grumbled.

"It's our job." Juline handed everyone mugs of cinnacreme— which tasted like melted snickerdoodles.

What did the Collective say? Sophie asked her.

I was only able to reach Wraith. He's tracking down the others as we speak.

Do you think—

Sophie's question was cut short by a white light flashing from her Imparter.

Dex frowned and tapped the screen a few times.

Something wrong? Sophie asked.

Not necessarily. It looks like I have good news, bad news, and weird news. The good news is: I'm pretty sure no one's listening to us right now. The signal doesn't seem to be reaching anything— which is the bad news. I can't track where it's going. The receiver's either been turned off or destroyed.

So what's the weird news? Fitz asked.

Dex handed the gadget to Sophie. *This isn't your Imparter.*

TWENTY-NINE

WHAT DO YOU MEAN IT'S NOT *my Imparter?* Sophie asked. *I brought it from home.*

I know, Dex told her. *But I just checked the activity log. And unless you hailed yourself a ton of times—which I don't even think is possible—it has to be someone else's. Someone who also hailed Fitz a lot, and made a few very brief hails to Lord Cassius.*

Sophie's eyes widened. *This is Keefe's Imparter?*

Dex nodded.

Why would you have Keefe's Imparter? Fitz asked. *Did he slip it to you the day he blew up Foxfire?*

Wouldn't I have two, then? Sophie asked.

Unless he swiped yours, Fitz said. *Maybe when he put his cloak around you?*

Sophie replayed the moment, but all she remembered were Keefe's hands near her shoulders.

I guess it's possible, she admitted. *But I don't see why he would do that. And I don't think he would've been able to hide that from me during our check-ins. I can see enough of his fleeting thoughts to know what stuff he's worrying about.*

Then where else would you get his Imparter? Dex asked.

No clue. Actually, wait. Grizel found an Imparter in Keefe's desk when we were searching his room, and I gave her mine so she could compare the two. She might've accidentally mixed them up before she gave it back.

I guess that makes sense, Fitz said. *And you know what? I bet this Imparter is how the Neverseen knew about our ambush on Mount Everest. Keefe's mom probably rigged it so she could eavesdrop on Keefe's conversations, and heard us arranging the trap.*

Sophie cringed. *As if hiding a tracker in his family crest pin wasn't disgusting enough.*

HEY GUYS—REMEMBER ME? Biana thought, waving her arms to get their attention. *I'd like to know what's going on too!*

Fitz caught her up on the newest discoveries, then updated Juline and Lovise.

Does that mean it's safe for us to talk? Biana asked.

Dex squinted at the Imparter. *I think we should still be careful—unless you want me to disassemble it again.*

I hate to do that, Juline said after Sophie relayed the info. *Every time we tamper with it, we risk undoing whatever they did, and we might still be able to learn something from it.*

Guess that means we're in for more makeover talk, Sophie transmitted as Juline left to see if Wraith had made contact with the rest of the Collective.

"We could play truth or dare," Biana suggested with an evil smile.

"No way—that got *weird* last time," Fitz told her.

Biana tossed her hair. "I don't know what you're talking about."

"Yes you do—just like you totally knew what you were doing when you turned your head at the last second."

Sophie was about to ask for details, when she remembered Keefe admitting that he'd kissed Biana once on a dare. He'd described it as "mostly on the cheek."

"How about we work on the scrolls again?" she said, deciding that games were too risky. Truth or dare was definitely out, and the only other game she could think of was spin the bottle—which would be a *very* bad idea.

Biana pouted. "I suppose that's the smart thing to do."

And so the hours went, filled with lots of squinting at tiny black numbers on endless scrolls. Their only breaks were for quick checks of their still-silent Imparters.

"Brought you a refill," Juline said, carrying a fresh tray of cinnacreme mugs into the solarium. *And I finally heard from Mr. Forkle. He was over at Havenfield.*

HE WAS? Sophie and Fitz both transmitted together.

Did something happen? Sophie asked.

No—it's still quiet. And it's after midnight, so technically the day is over.

Do you really think the Neverseen care about technicalities? Sophie asked.

I don't know what the Neverseen care about, Juline admitted. *All I know is, for the moment, everyone is safe and I'm going to be grateful. They'll stay on alert for the rest of the night, of course. But we're all cautiously optimistic that the threat has passed. And Mr. Forkle agreed that we should keep avoiding important conversations around the Imparter until he can retrieve it in the morning. So why don't you four try getting some rest?*

"We're getting so close," Biana said after Sophie passed along the message. "We might as well finish."

And they did. And Dex scowled at the final scroll. "I don't know who their Technopath is—but they're *good*. I can't figure out the point of these numbers."

Any chance you're just saying that for the benefit of the Imparter? Fitz asked him.

I wish. This is the code I found hidden in Alvar's records from the days we were kidnapped. He scribbled on the back of the nearest scroll:

0-11-<<-1-1-1-0*

Sophie studied it from a few angles. *Okay, yeah, that doesn't make any sense.*

It really doesn't, Dex agreed. *The most basic digital code—the kind that's so basic, even humans use it—is made of ones and zeroes. But I have no idea what those other symbols are supposed to mean, or how they work.*

Well . . . I'm guessing the asterisk is for Lodestar, right? Fitz asked.

Maybe. But some of the normal registry codes use asterisks too. Plus, the asterisk switches sides sometimes on the other codes I found hidden in Alvar's records. Like this, which I'm pretty sure is from the day Sophie saw The Boy Who Disappeared.

*0-1->-1->-111-0

And I found these during the days that Alden's mind was broken:

*0->-111->>>-1-0
0-<<-1-1-11-<-0*

I'm assuming the sequences are different because each one stands for a different place Alvar went, Dex said. *But no matter how long I stare at it, I still don't understand how to read the numbers and symbols and AARRGGGRRHHH!*

He made the same noise out loud and collapsed backward onto his sleeping bag.

Biana flopped back too, and Sophie and Fitz did the same.

It's still progress, Sophie transmitted. *Remember, this is how it always goes. It's always piece by piece, and it feels like we're never going to figure it out—and then we find another clue and it all comes together.*

I just wish we could skip to the it-all-comes-together part, don't you? Fitz asked as he yawned.

Biana yawned too. "I can't believe I'm about to say this, but I'm exhausted. So I propose a truce. No one pranks anyone, and we all get to sleep. Is that proof that I'm becoming lame?"

"It's proof that we have a lot going on," Fitz told her. "And we'll handle it better if our brains are actually working in the morning. So how about this—if anyone breaks the pact, we make them brush their teeth with reekrod."

"Deal," Dex said. "I'd rather save my prank elixirs for the triplets anyway."

"I'm in," Sophie agreed.

Biana called Iggy to her pillow, and within seconds his squeaky purr filled the room. Dex's soft snores followed, and everyone seemed to still.

Are you trying to reach out to Keefe? Fitz transmitted, nearly making Sophie yelp. *Sorry—didn't mean to startle you.*

It's fine. And . . . I think I'm going to skip tonight's check-in.

Because you're afraid of putting him in danger? Or because you're afraid he's doing something you don't want to know about?

Both, she admitted, hugging Ella tighter.

I wish I knew what to say to help.

I don't think those words exist.

What Keefe was doing was a complicated, impossible mess.

If it makes you feel any better, Fitz told her, *I'm keeping my Imparter right by my head. That way, if my parents hail me I'll be sure to hear it.*

You'll wake me up if they do?

You really think you're going to be able to sleep?

No idea.

Well, you can borrow Mr. Snuggles if you want.

Sophie smiled. *Nah, I couldn't bear to keep you two apart. But thanks.*

Anytime.

His mind went quiet, and Sophie figured he'd dozed off with the others. But right as her mind started to drift, he added, *I'll always be here if you need me.*

THIRTY

SOFT CONVERSATION FLOATED THROUGH Sophie's mind, the words blurring with her dreams—until one question caught her attention.

Aren't they cute?

The voices sharpened into focus and she realized there were a *lot* of sappy adults watching her sleep. But she was too relieved to be annoyed about it.

"Mom?" she asked, scooting out of her sleeping bag and waiting for her eyes to focus. "Dad?"

"We're here," Edaline said as both her parents smothered her with a hug.

"Sorry we woke you, kiddo," Grady said. "Juline told us you

guys were up half the night, after a pretty eventful day. You must be exhausted."

She was. Somehow getting only a little sleep always felt worse than getting no sleep—but she didn't care about that right now. "You guys are safe?"

"For now," Edaline said, squeezing her tighter. "And don't worry, we'll be back on house arrest this afternoon. I just needed to talk with my sister in person. She's been filling me in on . . . everything."

Sophie followed Edaline's gaze to a fidgety Juline—who stood with Wraith, Blur, and Mr. Forkle, clearly making no attempt to hide her involvement with the Collective.

Alden and Della were there too—and Sandor and Brielle and Cadoc and Woltzer and Grizel and Lovise and Kesler. Everyone except Granite and the triplets.

"Wow," Biana mumbled from her sleeping bag. "That's a lot of faces to wake up to."

"It is," Della said, blinking in and out of sight as she crossed the room to hug her daughter. "Did you forget to pack pajamas?"

Biana looked down and blushed when she saw she was still in yesterday's clothes. "No, we forgot to get changed. Ugh, and I forgot to brush my teeth."

She covered her mouth, trying to spare the world from her morning breath.

"So what happened yesterday?" Sophie asked. "Did the Neverseen really not show up?"

"Not at Havenfield," Grady said. "We spent the whole day jumping at shadows—unlike you guys. Why am I not surprised that you had a way more productive day than we did?"

Are we still supposed to be quiet around the listening device? Fitz transmitted as he sat up and stretched.

Mr. Forkle held up a thin black box. "Mr. Sencen's Imparter is in here for the moment. Our Technopath put a small speaker inside to broadcast the sound of normal conversation until she can take a closer look and check for anything Mr. Dizznee could've missed."

"Speaking of Dex," Biana said, pointing to where he lay twisted up in his sleeping bag. "Shouldn't we wake him?"

"Be my guest," Kesler told her. "And good luck. Waking Dex is like waking a hibernating bear. The only thing worse is waking the triplets, who are thankfully still conked out upstairs."

Biana tried nudging Dex's shoulder. And flicking his ear. And kicking his leg. Nothing worked—until she put Iggy on Dex's pillow. One good Iggy burp in the face and Dex was sputtering and coughing and looking very disoriented.

"Hey," Biana told him. "Thought you might not want to miss this."

She pointed to the crowd of adults—who were trying very hard not to laugh.

"Thanks," Dex told her, sitting up and rubbing his eyes. "So . . . what's the bad news?"

"What makes you think there's bad news?" Juline asked.

"Please—there's no way you'd all be here if you didn't have something bad to tell us."

The adults shared a look.

"Why don't we wait until you've all had some breakfast?" Kesler suggested. "The Vackers brought over these amazing pastries. They're like eating a sweet, buttery cloud."

"Uh-uh," Sophie said, ignoring the gurgle in her stomach. "Tell us what's going on."

Mr. Forkle opened his mouth, but his voice didn't seem to cooperate.

"At the moment, we're still piecing the details together," Alden said quietly. "But . . . it appears the Neverseen did have a mission yesterday, like Keefe suspected—but the target wasn't Grady and Edaline. It was—"

His voice caught and he turned away.

Sophie's mind ran through worst-case scenarios, but none felt as shocking—or heartbreaking—as when Della told them, "The Neverseen attacked Wylie."

THIRTY-ONE

WYLIE?" BIANA REPEATED. "Prentice's son?"

Shadows darkened Mr. Forkle's eyes as he nodded. "He suffered an extensive interrogation."

Sophie rubbed her wrists as the ghosts of old wounds haunted her again. "Will he . . . ?"

"Physic is treating him as we speak," Juline promised. "But he'll need to remain sedated for several days."

"Days," Sophie repeated.

She'd only needed *days* of treatment when she'd almost died.

Red rimmed her vision and the knot in her chest begged to

unravel as she sucked in deep breaths, trying to calm the rage bubbling under her skin.

"It's okay," Grady whispered, tightening his hug. "Don't give them this power."

Sophie gritted her teeth, using the anger to bind everything back together.

"Does Physic think Wylie will recover?" Fitz asked.

"She seemed pretty confident," Blur said. "She thinks we caught the injuries early enough that he won't have any scars—physically at least. Psychologically is anyone's guess."

"Granite's with him now, searching his mind to piece together the details of what happened," Mr. Forkle added. "Then we'll decide how many memories to erase."

Normally Sophie wasn't a fan of altering people's memories. But she could see how it might be for the best in this case.

"How's Granite holding up?" Biana asked.

"No one can prepare for such evil to happen to their family," Wraith told her.

"He's barely said ten words since we found Wylie in a crumpled heap on the Stone House's porch," Blur added. "Wylie must've crawled for the door with the last of his strength, after whatever desperate measures he used to escape."

"He still had bonds on his feet—and partial bonds on his wrists—and he reeked of sedatives," Wraith finished sadly.

"Do you know where he escaped from?" Sophie asked.

Mr. Forkle cleared the thickness from his throat. "Unfortunately, no. At the moment, all we know is that he was taken from his room in the Silver Tower."

"How?" Fitz asked. "Aren't there goblins patrolling the campus?"

"Not as many as there should've been," Mr. Forkle admitted. "We're between terms, so most of the fleets have been reassigned to Lumenaria to prepare for the Peace Summit. And the one remaining patrol has been focusing its efforts on securing the newly arrived Exillium tents."

"But even if they got past the patrol, how did they get into the tower?" Dex asked. "The security in the elite towers is supposed to be legendary. My technopathy mentor went on and on about how it was designed the same way they did the insane security at Lumenaria, with a team of anonymous Technopaths each building only one small piece. That way no one would know the full scope, or how all the levels of security actually fit together."

"Truthfully?" Mr. Forkle said, "I have no idea how they got in. I've already accessed the security logs, and there were no unauthorized visitors. In fact, the records show that Wylie is the only prodigy who remained in the tower for the break—with no evidence that the files were altered. And since I'm sure you're going to ask about the Lodestar mirror"—he paused to let everyone react to the name—"let me assure you that it was the first place I checked. Nothing in the Hall of Illumination had been disturbed. There was no trace of a fingerprint or a footprint. No way to remove the mirror from the wall and access behind it. The mirror is just a mirror, designed to teach the elite prodigies to see that the purest version of themselves comes from power, not appearance."

"Could a Phaser have walked through the walls to get in?" Biana asked.

"The tower is impervious," Blur said. "Trust me. I've tried."

"Then they must have someone who has access to the tower who let them in," Fitz said.

"That was my thought as well," Mr. Forkle told him. "But as I said, all the logs show Wylie being alone. I also watched the prodigies quite closely during my time as the tower's Beacon, and none of them ever did anything to suggest a connection to the Neverseen."

"Neither did Alvar," Della said quietly.

The name hung heavy in the air.

"If he was a part of this," Alden whispered. "If he . . ."

Sophie had been thinking the same thing about Keefe. He'd said he wouldn't cross the hard lines—but would he count Wylie as one of them? Or would it be one of those "shady things" he was willing to do in order to keep playing the game?

Wraith's sleeves moved toward Alden, reaching for him with invisible hands. "*You* are not responsible for your son's actions."

"But if we'd noticed—"

"Please don't go down that path," Edaline begged. "We cared for Brant for sixteen years and never suspected either."

"It's one of the biggest regrets of my life," Grady said. "But I'm learning to divide the blame. Yes, I should've paid closer attention and asked more questions. But everything else was Brant's choice. Brant's actions. Brant's wickedness. And the same goes for Alvar."

"I'll try to remember that," Alden told him.

"Try to *believe* it," Grady insisted.

"So where is Wylie now?" Dex asked. "Still at the Stone House?"

"No, we had Physic move him to Alluveterre once he was stable enough for a leap, since we're assuming they'll come after him," Blur said. "The fact that he escaped probably means they hadn't gotten everything they wanted from him."

"What *do* they want?" Kesler asked. "Does anyone know?"

"I can't even hazard a guess," Mr. Forkle mumbled. "And so far, his mind has been too clouded by the trauma for us to recover much."

"He's not broken, right?" Sophie asked.

"Thankfully, no. The Neverseen not having a Telepath worked in our favor—though I suspect that's also why Wylie's injuries were so extreme. Their only means of interrogation was torture."

Everyone shuddered, and Mr. Forkle handed the packaged Imparter to Blur. "I trust you'll take care of getting that to our Technopath? I should get back to Alluveterre."

"I want to go with you."

Sophie didn't realize she'd said the words out loud until everyone turned to her.

"No one will be able to search Wylie's memories better than I will," she argued.

She left out her other reason—it was too terrible to admit. But she needed to see Wylie's memories for herself and make sure Keefe wasn't there.

She could forgive him for shattering glass and burning gates—but standing by while someone was tortured?

She had to be *sure*.

"You really think you can handle it?" Edaline asked her. "Wylie probably looks awful."

"'Awful' is not a strong enough word," Wraith warned.

Sophie swallowed hard. "I handled Paris, right?"

"Not the same, even in the slightest," Mr. Forkle told her.

"Doesn't matter," Sophie said. "Wylie needs my help."

"For what it's worth," Blur chimed in, "I think she's right. I think you should take her."

"Take *us*," Fitz corrected. "This has Cognates written all over it."

"If they go—Dex and I are going too," Biana added.

Mr. Forkle rubbed his temples. "Wylie is not up for visitors."

"Then we'll wait outside," Biana pressed. "But we should be there. You might learn something we need to know. Or Sophie and Fitz might need moral support."

The members of the Collective turned to each other, probably conferring telepathically.

"Very well," Mr. Forkle eventually said through a sigh. "But I have a favor to ask." His focus shifted to Sandor. "I need you to separate from your charge for the day. Miss Foster will be well protected by the fleet of dwarves stationed at Alluveterre. We have need of your exceptional senses in the Silver Tower. Perhaps you'll catch something we've overlooked."

"If you're looking for powerful senses," Grizel jumped in, "You should have me go with him. Sandor lacks a certain . . . shall we say, sensitivity?"

"If you feel comfortable separating from Mr. Vacker, we'd be happy to have your assistance," Mr. Forkle told her. "The more thorough we are, the greater our chances of solving this mystery."

"One condition," Sandor said, fixing a stern gaze on Sophie. "*Swear* you will go nowhere beyond Alluveterre and home."

"Are we even sure Havenfield is safe?" Sophie asked. "The Neverseen may still be planning something."

"We've left most of yesterday's precautions intact," Brielle assured her. "And Cadoc and I will not leave their side. You can trust us to protect your family the same way you trust Sandor with your life."

That seemed to settle things, and Sophie and her friends rushed to get dressed in fresh clothes, none of them saying a word as they hugged their parents and locked hands for the leap.

"Brace yourselves," Mr. Forkle said as he created a path to Alluveterre. "Nothing I say can properly prepare you for what you're about to see."

THIRTY-TWO

SOPHIE HADN'T SET FOOT IN Alluveterre's subterranean forest since the day she and her friends left for their mission to Ravagog. And the scenery was as lush and beautiful as ever. But her memories blanketed everything in shadow.

Everywhere she looked, she could see signs of Calla's former presence. Earth Calla had walked. Trees she'd touched. Roots she'd called to transport everyone underground for their various adventures. Even the air seemed to carry the faintest whispers of Calla's songs—though Sophie knew she was probably imagining it.

"This way," Mr. Forkle said, leading them up a winding stairway that wrapped around and around a massive tree, bringing them to one of the mansion-size tree houses. Each step felt like swallowing lemon juice mixed with something spicy, and it coated Sophie's insides with a sour kind of burn.

Mr. Forkle had chosen the western tree house, where the boys lived during their months there, and the inside looked exactly the same as they'd left it. Same hammocks swinging from the ceiling. Same flickering fire pit in the center. But this time the boy reading on one of the boulder-shaped beanbag chairs had silver-tipped bangs.

"Hey," Tam said as he glanced up from his book. "They moved Wylie to the other house. I guess one of the bedrooms has some special plant growing in it that might keep him calm?"

"The reveriebells," Sophie whispered.

Calla had hybridized the flowering vine especially for her, training it to grow across the canopy of her former bed. The blossom's sweet scent had given her some of her most peaceful nights of sleep ever.

"Has he gotten worse?" Mr. Forkle asked.

"Not *worse*," Tam told him. "But I don't think he's getting better as quickly as Physic wants. And Granite—or Tiergan—or whatever I'm supposed to call him, is worried that Wylie's mind is getting darker. He asked me to try lifting a veil—but Wylie's shadowvapor is fine. He had less than I would've expected, given all the awful things he's been through."

Mr. Forkle closed his eyes. "Sounds like you were right to insist on coming, Miss Foster. I suppose we should head over."

"You might want to stay here," Tam warned Dex and Biana. "Physic's being super strict about who she's letting in the room. And at least over here you don't have to stay quiet."

"I guess that makes sense," Biana said. "Plus, I haven't seen you in forever."

Tam's lips twisted into a shy smile. "I hear we'll be seeing more of each other soon."

Sophie had forgotten all about the Exillium training. She wondered if Wylie's attack would delay things.

"Aren't you coming?" Mr. Forkle asked from the doorway.

Sophie and Fitz hurried to follow, but Dex stayed put. She figured that meant he wanted to stay with Biana and Tam, but as they reached the arched bridge connecting the two tree houses, Dex came racing up.

"I know I'm not a Telepath," he mumbled, "but I've been through what Wylie's been through. Maybe I can help."

Sophie reached for his hand, holding on to Fitz with her other as they made their way across the creaky bridge connecting the two houses. Sophie swore she could smell Calla's starkflower stew when they passed through the gazebo in the center. The dish had been Calla's specialty, and even though she'd taught Sophie the recipe, it never tasted the same without Calla.

"Wow," Dex and Fitz breathed as they entered what used to be the girls' tree house.

"Linh's been busy," Sophie mumbled.

The waterfall in the center—which used to be only a misty

trickle—now thundered with torrents of cascading water. The falls splashed hard into the shallow basin, but instead of spilling over and soaking the floor, the water ricocheted up and split into individual streams that arced toward the glass ceiling and fanned out before crashing back down into pots of flowers.

"Wait here," Mr. Forkle told them, pointing to the shrubbery-shaped chairs, which were speckled with glittering dew. "I'm going to let Physic know I've brought you."

The room felt way too quiet after he left.

"Where's Linh?" Dex whispered.

Sophie ducked under a stream of water as she looked down the empty hallway. "She must be in with Wylie."

"How bad do you think he's going to look?" Fitz asked. "Like . . . worse than I looked after Exile?"

The black barb jutting from Fitz's chest—and the swirls of black venom under his skin—had definitely been one of the most gruesome sights Sophie had ever seen. But she had a horrible feeling it had nothing on the pain and suffering Brant and Fintan would be willing to cause in order to get what they wanted.

"I think we need to prepare ourselves for something pretty awful," she said.

She'd flicked three loose lashes away before a familiar woman strode into the room, followed by an ashen Mr. Forkle. Physic's Mardi-Gras-style mask was red this time, with a rim of gold glitter that had showered bits of sparkle across her dark skin.

"You're still wearing your disguise?" Sophie asked.

"I didn't want the focus to be on me." Physic twisted one of her skinny braids around her finger, making the red beads woven through shimmer. "I'm glad you guys are here. Wylie's vitals are improving, but Tiergan's afraid his mind is deteriorating. I don't see any physical proof of that, but I want you two to make a *very* thorough check. And when we go in there, *try* to keep in mind that healing starts on a cellular level. Right now, most of the change is something only I can see—and only with special light and special lenses. But he's honestly recovering faster than I could've hoped for, in large part thanks to Linh. She has him wrapped in a cold-water cocoon to draw out any latent heat while I brew a fresh batch of my burn ointment."

"Do you need help?" Dex asked. "Or need me to get any supplies?"

"I'm low on a few things," Physic admitted, "but they're not the kind of ingredients you'd be able to get from your dad's store."

"Try me," Dex said.

She raised an eyebrow. "Okay, how about jaculus venom?"

"Clear or cloudy? We keep both in my dad's 'extreme collection.'"

"Interesting," Physic said. "Nice hair, by the way."

Dex's cheeks turned the same color as Physic's mask.

"Aren't jaculuses those flying, blood-sucking snake things?" Sophie asked, remembering the first day she'd met Grady, when she'd watched him pull one out of Verdi's feathers.

"They are," Physic agreed. "And their venom has a powerful anticoagulant, which turns into an even more powerful tissue regenerator when I mix it with a few drops of Phoenix sweat."

"We have that, too," Dex said. "And Bennu tears. I'm guessing you also need Pooka pus? If so, we have solid and liquid."

"Okay, now I'm legitimately impressed," Physic said.

"Meanwhile I'm pretty sure I'm going to throw up," Fitz told them.

Physic shrugged. "It's either this or yeti pee—and trust me, yeti pee is way harder to wash off."

Sadly, Sophie knew that firsthand.

"All right," Physic told Dex, "I'll give you my recipe and we'll see what you can find at Slurps and Burps. Take Forkle with you, so you'll have a way to leap back—and so I won't have to watch him wring his hands anymore. He's going to disjoint all his fingers, and I really don't need another patient."

Sophie had almost forgotten that Mr. Forkle was there. He hadn't said a word, and his skin had a sweaty sheen.

"If you think he looks bad," Physic said, "wait till you see Tiergan. I can't get him to let go of Wylie's hand. Even when Linh started with the water stuff, he stood there and got soaked. It might be the saddest thing I've ever seen. But somehow the sweetest, too. You guys ready?"

Sophie didn't trust her voice not to crack. So she nodded, letting Fitz take her hand as they followed Physic down the hall to her old room.

"Remember, he's on some crazy pain medicine *and* a sedative," Physic warned. "So if you can't make sense of his thoughts, don't be afraid that it means anything's permanently wrong. He's just drugged up."

Fitz tightened his grip on Sophie's hand as Physic pulled open the door and the three of them made their way into the bedroom. Sophie inhaled the calming scent of Calla's reverie-bells as she studied her surroundings, avoiding the figure on the bed as long as she could.

Tiergan stood with his back to them—though parts of him were still Granitized, like he'd been standing so long at Wylie's side that his indurite powder was slowly wearing off. His left shoulder was jagged and rocky, and his neck was white-gray instead of its usual olive tone. Even his pale blond hair had bits of dust and gravel tangled in it.

On the other side of the bed, Linh leaned against the edge with her eyes closed, lips parted as she whispered softly to herself. Her hands were raised over the bed, and Sophie forced herself to look down, and . . .

. . . gagged.

Fitz choked too, and they clung to each other.

Sophie had thought she was prepared—thought the water Linh had swirling around him would muffle the gore. But the giant welts and blisters marring Wylie's arms and legs were too huge and red and violent to be ignored.

And they were shaped like hands.

I'm so sorry they did this to you, Sophie transmitted, digging her fist under her ribs to keep control of her emotions. *I wish I knew how to stop them. I wish I knew what they want.*

Let's find out, Fitz transmitted back, and their thumb rings snapped together as the mental energy rushed between them.

They moved closer to the bed and Sophie put her hand on Tiergan's rocky shoulder. "You can take a break. We're here to help now."

Tiergan didn't seem to hear her.

"You need to let go," she whispered. "Let me try for a minute."

Eight endless seconds passed. Then Tiergan blinked and turned her way.

"He won't talk to me," he whispered. "His mind only gives me cold darkness."

"Should we wait, then?" Sophie asked. "I don't want to force Wylie if he's not ready."

"I . . ." Tiergan spun back to the bed and pressed the fingers of his free hand against Wylie's temples.

"Is everything okay?" Fitz asked.

"I don't know." Tiergan's expression was the strangest mix of relief, disappointment, and fear as he turned to Sophie and told her, "He's asking to talk to you."

THIRTY-THREE

I'M ON MY WAY, SOPHIE TRANSMITTED TO Wylie as she pressed two fingers against his right temple. Fitz did the same on his left, and Linh's water shell splashed their hands as they pressed their consciousness into Wylie's mind.

The blackness felt almost solid—like it had hardened into a wall. But when Sophie transmitted *It's me,* the barrier liquefied, letting them drop down deep into the shadows.

Wylie's mind grew colder as they fell, his thoughts an icy blur, until they landed in a pool of warm light hovering in the nothing. A form emerged from the shadows, growing arms and legs and features and slowly morphing into a boy.

"Hello," he said, offering a shy wave.

His twitching hands fiddled with the pin clasped through his light blue cape—a jeweled sun with rays in yellow and orange and red. His face was rounder than Wylie's, his dark hair longer, crowning his head in a neat Afro. But she could recognize him through the features.

How old are you right now? Sophie transmitted.

Wylie scratched his chin. "Six."

Why is he talking to us as his six-year-old self? Fitz transmitted to Sophie.

I think it's a defense mechanism. I'm pretty sure he was seven or eight when his dad's mind broke, so I bet he's reverting to a safer, happier time.

"I knew you'd understand," six-year-old Wylie told her. "You know how it feels to have a before. And an after."

He shuddered with the words, and the tremors triggered a growth spurt, stretching his body taller and broadening his shoulders as his chin squared and his hair shrank to a short crop.

He looked like a surly teenager—but his eyes looked far older. This was the Wylie who'd lost his father *and* his mother.

I doubt I'll ever understand everything you've been through, Sophie told him. *But I'm here to help.*

"*Can* you help?" he asked.

I'll try. Will you tell me what happened?

Wylie's hands shook so hard, his pin ripped off his cape, vanishing into the darkness.

If you're not ready, we can—

"No," he interrupted. "It's never going to be easier."

He buried his face in his hands, and Sophie noticed red blotches forming.

What are you thinking about? Fitz asked him.

"All the things I shouldn't." Wylie scratched at his arms until they streamed with red.

I think we're going too fast, Sophie said as he morphed into the present-day Wylie she'd seen lying unconscious on her old bed—bloody and blistered and thrashing with the agony of his wounds. *Is there a way to bring back the six-year-old-you?*

Wylie took a shaky breath and closed his eyes, humming a song that sounded like a lullaby as his wounds closed, his body shrank, and his face rounded out.

"Is this better?" six-year-old Wylie asked.

You tell me, Sophie said. *Does it hurt right now?*

"It feels funny. But not, like, 'ha-ha' funny. More like an itchy tingle. I think I can live with that."

I know this is hard to believe, Sophie told him as he stared at his arms. *But the pain only exists in your memories. When you wake up, everything will be healed, and you'll look exactly the same as before.*

"I won't *be* the same, though. Will I?"

She couldn't lie. *Part of the pain will never go away. But you're a survivor, right?*

"Not by choice."

It never is, Fitz told him. *But that only proves how strong you are.*

"I should've been stronger," Wylie whispered. "I shouldn't have let them take me."

You couldn't have stopped them, Sophie promised. *I tried my hardest, and I couldn't.*

Wylie nodded slowly. "I didn't give them what they wanted, either."

What did they want? Fitz asked.

"If I talk about it . . . the other me's will take over."

We can handle them, Sophie promised.

And we can help you hold on, Fitz added as their pocket of space grew brighter and warmer. *I just gave you some extra energy to boost your strength. See how strong you are now?*

Wylie flexed his skinny six-year-old arms, patting the small curve of biceps that shifted. "Okay. I'll try."

"You'll do great," Sophie told him. "Think of it like you're telling us a story. Start at the beginning. How did they find you?"

"I don't know. I was reading in bed when the door burst open and my room swelled with a tornado."

So one of them was a Guster? Fitz asked.

"Must've been. The wind pinned me to the floor. And then I heard people rush in."

Did you see them? Sophie asked. *Or recognize their voices?*

"I couldn't hear much over the wind. And the one who

jumped on me must've been a Vanisher, because I couldn't see him as he ripped off my registry pendant."

Fitz's whole body shook as he transmitted. *That was my brother.*

Sophie tightened her hold on his hand, wishing she had time to properly comfort him. But they had to focus. *What else do you remember?* she asked Wylie.

"I remember kicking and punching and clawing and scratching. But then this white light wrapped around me, and I couldn't move anymore."

That means Ruy was there, Fitz transmitted. *He's a Psionipath. He must've wrapped you in a force field.*

"It shocked me if I touched it," Wylie said. "And it trapped me with the drugs. When I breathed, everything went blurry."

So it was just the three of them? Sophie asked. *No one else?*

"Actually, I think there were four. They said someone was keeping the path open."

Could they have meant the Guster? she asked.

"I don't think so. They made it sound like the path was somewhere else. But everything was far away at that point. I remember someone grabbing my feet and dragging me. I don't know how long or how far. Then warmth pulled me away. After that I couldn't see. My ears were ringing. Everything smelled too sweet. I wanted to throw up, but I couldn't tell if I was actually awake. Is that how it was for you?"

Sort of, Sophie thought quietly. *I was gone for a lot longer than you.*

"How long was I missing?"

We're not totally sure, Fitz said. *But it was less than a day. Do you know what time they grabbed you?*

"No. But I hadn't had breakfast yet." He clutched his middle as his stomach growled.

Do you want Physic to wake you up so you can eat? Fitz asked.

Wylie shook his head. *Awake sounds . . . hard.*

It will be at first, Sophie told him. *But it'll get easier every day. Take the time you need to recover. You'll wake up when you're ready.*

Is there anything else you remember that might help us? Fitz asked.

"Just the interrogations. And my head stayed mushy for those. The only thought I could hold on to was *wait.* I knew they'd make a mistake, and when they did, I'd have to move. It took hours and hours—but they finally burned one of my bonds. It didn't sear all the way through, but it let me shift my hands just enough that I could wiggle my fingers into the secret pocket in my sleeve where I keep the crystal that takes me to see my dad. I think I broke my thumb trying to grab it—I heard a snap." He held his hand up, frowning as the thumb seemed to work perfectly. "But it was worth the pain because as soon as I had the crystal in my hand I sparked a ball of light and leaped out of there."

Sparked? Sophie thought. *Are you a Flasher?*

"Yeah. Same as . . ."

Who? Sophie asked when he started trembling. *Same as who?*

Wylie scratched hard at his neck. "They kept asking the same question over and over, no matter how many times I told them I didn't know. Everything was about her."

Sophie was about to ask, *Her who?* when she figured it out on her own.

Your mom?

Wylie shifted back to surly teenager form.

What did they want to know about her? she asked.

"They thought I was with her when she made her last leap. I kept telling them I wasn't, but they kept burning me over and over and telling me it would stop when I stopped lying. They didn't get it. She died because I found her too late."

Tears streamed down his cheeks as he shifted to the present-day Wylie, screaming through the pain as his wounds reappeared.

Fitz tried sending more warmth and energy, but it didn't help, so Sophie tried inflicting. She couldn't find any happiness, but she gave him a soft wave of hope, and Wylie's breathing slowed to raspy breaths.

"Sorry," he told her. "I guess I'm not as strong as you thought."

You're stronger, Sophie promised. *You've been through so much.*

"Too much," Wylie said. "I don't know if I can take any more."

Maybe you won't have to. Mr. Forkle and Granite are planning to erase the worst memories—

"NO! They can't!"

I know it's weird to imagine them rooting around in your head— but why live with the nightmares?

"Because there might be something important! You can't let them erase anything, Sophie. Promise me you'll stop them."

Okay, she said when he kept repeating the plea. *I promise.*

"You have to stick to that," Wylie begged as he shifted back to six-year-old form. "You owe me."

I know, Sophie said. *And maybe you should rest now. I think your mind could use the break.*

He faded into the shadows. "I'll try. But I need you to do something for me. I need you to look into my mom's death. I don't think it was an accident anymore."

THIRTY-FOUR

THIS HAS EVERYTHING WE KNOW about the day Cyrah faded away," Mr. Forkle said, holding up a golden orb the size of a gumball. "All the evidence we gathered suggested her death was nothing more than an unexpected tragedy."

He spun the top and bottom in opposite directions until they clicked like a combination lock, then handed it to Dex.

Sophie and Fitz had brought everyone back to the boys' old tree house to make sure their conversation wouldn't disturb Wylie—and so Biana and Tam wouldn't miss the update. Only Physic had stayed behind, wanting to run additional tests to triple-check that the pain they'd seen Wylie battling truly lived only in his memories.

"Do you always carry that with you?" Sophie asked Mr. Forkle, wondering how he fit so much in his pockets—and why she'd never noticed him carrying so many weird things before.

"Of course," he said. "It's similar to the Councillors' caches, except it holds the things I need to remember, not the secrets I want to forget."

"So then, there's probably all kinds of info about Sophie on here, right?" Dex asked.

"There are files on all of you—and before anyone gets any ideas, let me assure you that I'm the only one capable of accessing that information. So can we focus on the fact that young Mr. Endal has given us an urgent project?"

"Right," Dex said, squeezing the top and bottom of the sphere to make a hologram flash from the center.

Everyone scooted closer to squint at the projection, which started with a family picture.

Prentice looked like he'd been midlaugh, his eyes focused on his wife—whose auburn hair glowed wild and red where it caught the sun. Between them was the same six-year-old boy Sophie had spoken to in Wylie's memories, and now she could see what an even mix he was of both of his parents. He had his mom's smile and a dash of her creaminess to his skin, and his dad's hair and eyes and nose.

"They were so happy," she whispered.

"They were," Tiergan said, wiping his eyes.

Dex twisted the gadget again, revealing a single document. "This isn't much to go on."

"I know," Mr. Forkle said. "Cyrah was alone for her final leap. Wylie found her sometime after, and it was impossible to tell how long she'd been there. She was unconscious. Barely breathing. Wylie hailed Elwin for help, but the damage was beyond anyone's skills. By the time Elwin called Alden to search Cyrah's memories, her mind had grown too weak to recover anything. The last of her form faded not long after. All they could do was watch."

Sophie blinked back tears as she imagined it.

In order to light leap, their bodies had to break down into particles small enough to be carried by the light. And the only way to re-form was to hold the pieces together, either with a bracelet-style gadget called a nexus—which all younger elves were required to wear until their mental strength reached a proven level—or with the power of their own concentration. If you lost too much of yourself . . .

There were worse ways to die, of course. In fact, out of all of Sophie's brushes with death, fading had been the most pleasant. It started with shocking pain—but the agony soon eased, replaced with an irresistible rushing warmth that pulled like a gentle breeze, begging her to follow it to a world of shimmer and sparkle and color and freedom.

But it was a death all the same.

"Wylie tried to reach me after it happened," Tiergan said,

turning to stare out the windows. "He hailed me four times before he gave up and let Elwin hail Alden. Maybe if I'd answered, we could've recovered something from Cyrah's mind."

"Do we know where Cyrah leaped from?" Sophie asked.

"She told Wylie that she was going back to Mysterium—which matched what her registry pendant recorded," Mr. Forkle said. "She went to take inventory of her stall."

"Cyrah had a small sidewalk booth where she sold custom hair ribbons," Tiergan explained. "It wasn't as fancy as the boutique she'd had before Prentice was arrested. But very few nobles wanted to support the wife of a criminal, so she'd moved to a working-class city."

"I went to that stall," Biana said. "My dad took me when I was little—I still have the combs he bought. And I remember being surprised we went to Mysterium instead of Atlantis."

"Alden was always trying to find small ways to assist Cyrah," Tiergan muttered. "As if buying hair clips could make up for destroying her family!"

The words sliced through the room, too dull to draw any blood. But Fitz and Biana winced all the same.

"I'm sorry," Tiergan told them. "I just hate having to think about this again. Wylie's been through so much—and I keep *trying* to make it up to him. But no matter what I do . . ."

He pounded his fist against the window.

Sophie crossed the room and rested a hand on his arm. Tiergan wasn't a touchy-feely kind of person, but . . .

He placed his hand over hers.

She wished she could guarantee that everything would be okay—that they'd find a way to solve all of this. Instead she told him, "Wylie's strong."

"He is. He has to be. Just like you." He squeezed her hand tighter before slowly pulling away. "I suppose the one small relief is that Prentice is unconscious through all of this."

"I've been thinking the same thing," Mr. Forkle said. "We cannot bring him back to a life where his son is in danger and his wife's murder unsolved. He'd never survive it."

"Am I the only one who doesn't understand how murder by light leap is possible?" Tam asked. "An accident, I get. But aren't we the ones in control of our consciousness?"

"That's what I thought too," Sophie admitted. "Otherwise, wouldn't we wear nexuses our whole lives?"

"We remove our nexuses because technology should never replace the natural power of our mind," Mr. Forkle told them. "And because we're supposed to belong to a society where people would never violate the safety of another. But the sad truth is, if someone were to cause Cyrah severe pain right as she was leaping, it could've broken her concentration during the crucial transformation."

"Or if someone shined a secondary light in her path," Tiergan added, "her consciousness would've divided without her realizing. Part of her would've followed one beam—the rest, the other. And she wouldn't have had enough of herself left in either place."

Linh curled her arms around herself. "That's really scary."

"It is," Mr. Forkle agreed. "Safety is an illusion. It exists only when we, as a society, agree to enforce it. But theoretically, any situation could turn violent if someone decided to treat it that way. During my time with humans, I witnessed many horrors that were the result of one individual—or a small group—choosing to violate the trust we all put in each other. The time is coming when we as a species will have to decide if we're going to stray down the same dark path. But I think I've gotten off track. My point is that, yes, sadly, murder by light leap—and many other unimaginable means—is possible."

"Okay, but . . . the streets in Mysterium are always crammed with people," Dex reminded them. "Wouldn't someone have noticed something weird going on when Cyrah leaped?"

"People rarely notice things they don't expect to see," Tiergan told him. "They're too distracted by their own perception of reality."

"Did anyone see her final leap happen?" Sophie asked.

"Not that I could find," Mr. Forkle said.

"So then she could've wandered to a more isolated place before she leaped away," Sophie pointed out. "Maybe she had a secret meeting in the area where the Council stores my human family's old things. It seemed pretty deserted when Councillor Terik took me."

"Or she wasn't in Mysterium at all," Fitz added. "We all know registry feeds can be altered. Did anyone actually see her there?"

"They did," Mr. Forkle said. "Several people saw her sorting stock in her stall."

"This list at the end here," Dex jumped in. "Is that the people who saw her?"

"Yes," Mr. Forkle said. "Why?"

"Marella's mom is on it." He pointed to the name *Caprise Redek*, glowing among a dozen other names.

"Caprise was one of my more memorable interviews," Mr. Forkle said quietly. "She seemed to be struggling quite a bit that day."

Marella's mother had suffered a traumatic brain injury a few years earlier, and despite Elwin's best efforts, she'd battled unstable emotions ever since. She took elixirs to manage the condition, but sometimes they weren't enough.

"What did she say?" Sophie asked.

"Mostly she kept mumbling that Cyrah should've been more careful. I assumed she meant careful during leaping."

That *did* make sense, but . . .

"Now that we know her death might not have been an accident, do you think she could've meant something else?" Sophie asked.

"If it were anyone other than Caprise Redek, I might be ready to wander down that path," Tiergan told her. "But I've seen Caprise on her bad days. It's not her fault—and she tries her best. But reason and rationality abandon her. And when you consider that she would've been saying these things after hearing the devastating news about Cyrah, I think it needs to be taken with an especially potent grain of salt."

"I still wonder if Cyrah went somewhere after Mysterium and her feed was altered," Fitz mumbled. "It just seems too random that she went to count hair ribbons and ended up dead."

"But who would've altered the feed?" Tiergan asked. "We know it wasn't us. And Cyrah was a Flasher, not a Technopath. And if the Neverseen were involved with her death, why would they need to interrogate Wylie?"

"Maybe she was working on something important for them, and they were hoping she might've shared certain key information with him before she died," Tam suggested.

"But then why go after him *now*?" Dex asked. "Why not interrogate him right after it happened?"

"They might not have wanted anyone to know that Cyrah's death wasn't an accident," Linh said.

"Or, it could have something to do with whatever they're planning through the Lodestar Initiative," Biana mumbled.

"We can debate theories all day," Mr. Forkle told them, "But it won't bring us any closer to the truth."

"So what's your plan?" Sophie asked.

"I . . . have no idea." He sounded more tired than Sophie had ever heard.

"Gethen might know something about all of this, right?" Fitz asked.

"That's true!" Sophie realized. "And after Wylie's attack, I'm sure the Council is going to be *very* motivated to find out what happened, so—"

"We're not going to tell the Council about this," Mr. Forkle interrupted. "They do not make wise decisions when they're frightened. And learning that one of their citizens was captured and brutalized—from one of our world's most secure buildings—will send them into a frenzy. The last time that happened, they declared *us* their number one enemy, instead of focusing on the Neverseen. And let's not forget about the ability-restricting circlet they ordered Miss Foster to wear."

Dex winced. The circlet had been his invention—but he'd never thought the Council would use it on Sophie.

"Working against the Council hasn't gone well for us either," Sophie reminded him. "And if Gethen—"

"Gethen is not the grand solution you believe him to be!" Mr. Forkle snapped. He turned away, tearing his hands through his grayed hair. "I know you want to believe—"

"*You* said he was a priority," Sophie interrupted.

"I did. But circumstances have changed. Now our priority must be protecting Wylie—and that includes sparing him the stress of becoming a public spectacle. Surely you remember what it felt like to be The Girl Who Was Taken. Would you wish that on him? After everything he's been through?"

"I'm sure the Council would keep this quiet if we asked," Biana said quietly.

"All we can be *sure* of, Miss Vacker, is that we *can't* be sure of how the Council will respond. So we must err on the side of caution. We must regroup and strategize. And we must wait to act until we have a plan that is in Wylie's best interest."

Sophie glanced at Tiergan. "You really think we should waste time sitting around, lying and hiding things?"

Tiergan turned to the windows, staring at the gently swaying trees. "I think our next course should be up to Wylie. He's the one who will endure the consequences."

Sophie headed for the door. "Okay, I'll ask him."

Mr. Forkle blocked her. "We will *not* be troubling him with these questions until he's fully recovered."

"But that could be *days*."

"In the grand scheme of things, that is a very small amount of time." His tone left no room for arguing.

"We have to do *something*," Sophie insisted.

Sneaking into Lumenaria without the Council's permission sounded impossible—especially with how little they knew about the security in the fortress. And she couldn't imagine she'd be able to communicate telepathically with Lady Gisela in the ogre prison—or that Lady Gisela would actually tell her anything if she could.

So where did that leave them?

"Keefe's trying to steal Fintan's cache," she said after a few seconds. "Do you think it might have any information on it about Cyrah?"

"If it does, why would they need to go after Wylie?" Fitz asked.

"And while we're talking about Keefe," Tam jumped in, his silver eyes focusing on Sophie, "I know you're going to get mad at me for saying this. But before we keep trusting him, we need to find out what he knows—and I don't just mean the little bits he tells you during your nightly flirt sessions."

"That's *not* what they are," Sophie snapped.

"Maybe not for you. But I doubt the guy who calls himself the president of the Foster Fan Club is going to have a bunch of private convos with you and not use that chance to try to keep winning you over."

"Winning me—what?" Sophie asked. "That's not—I— what?"

"Not important," Tam said. "But you know what is? Making sure he's not involved with horrors like this. Can you honestly tell me you're not worried he was somehow part of what they did to Wylie? Or that his whole 'warning' about the danger to your family was actually a lie to keep everyone distracted from what was really happening?"

Sophie rubbed the knot under her ribs. "I know you don't trust Keefe—"

"And I know you do," Tam interrupted. "I get that you two are really, really close—"

"They're not *that* close," Fitz mumbled.

"Uh . . . sure . . . ," Tam said. "All I'm saying is, we need to know exactly who we're dealing with—and not just what he says. We need to know what he's thinking, and hiding, and planning."

"You want me to search his mind," Sophie guessed.

Tam nodded. "I know Telepaths have rules, but Wylie deserves protection *way* more than Keefe deserves privacy."

"But I don't actually know if I can search his mind from far away," Sophie argued. "Having a telepathic conversation is different from probing memories. For that, I usually need physical contact."

She *had* been able to search Prentice's memories through the walls of his cell in Exile—but there was a big difference between stretching her mind to someone a few feet away and searching someone who was probably on the other side of the planet.

"You'd have a better chance if I help," Fitz reminded her.

"Can I be there too?" Biana asked.

"I'm pretty sure all of us want to be there," Tam told her. "You're all welcome to crash here tonight, if that makes it easier."

"Unfortunately, that's not an option," Mr. Forkle informed them. "Those with registry pendants need to get back to the Lost Cities quite soon. I've had our Technopath scrambling our feeds, but it's a slapdash cover at best, and if we stay too much longer, the Council might be able to track us to this hideout. Besides, if you decide to follow this plan, Miss Foster and Mr. Vacker are going to need the full weight of their concentration to have even the slightest chance of achieving this rather impossible task. I'm sure they'll be happy to provide a full report when they're finished."

"I don't have an Imparter," Sophie reminded him.

"I'll get you another," Mr. Forkle said.

And with that, the matter seemed to be decided.

All that was left to do was head home.

And wait.

And hope Keefe didn't let them down.

THIRTY-FIVE

ITZ WENT WITH SOPHIE BACK TO Havenfield, so they could work through Cognate exercises to prepare, while Biana and Dex went to Rimeshire to see if Dex could hack the registry for Cyrah's records. They knew it was a long shot, but they wanted to see if her feed had been altered the day she faded.

"Do you think this is a mistake?" Sophie asked Fitz when they leaped into the surprisingly quiet, empty pastures. Cadoc and Brielle must've made Grady and Edaline stay inside.

"Checking on Keefe?" he asked.

Part of her wanted to say yes—she still felt scrambled up about their plan. But she had bigger worries at the moment.

"It feels like we're wasting time on the wrong things.

Especially since we don't have any actual plans. I mean . . . what is the Collective doing right now—besides shutting down all our ideas and telling us to wait?"

"I know. I think what happened to Wylie really shook them up."

"It shook me up too—but that doesn't mean it's a good idea to sit around doing nothing. I know I'm not as close to him as the Collective is—but maybe that's a good thing. Maybe that makes me able to see what really needs to be done."

"Which is what?" Fitz asked.

Sophie looked away, tugging out an itchy eyelash before she asked, "Do you have a pathfinder?"

"Not with me," Fitz said, "Why? Where do you want to go?"

Somewhere she didn't want anyone knowing—and she needed to do it now, before she changed her mind. They had no bodyguards for the moment. No one even knew they were home. If they were going to sneak away, this was the time.

But how?

Making it up to the fourth-floor Leapmaster without Grady and Edaline spotting them was probably impossible. And teleporting created quite the spectacle, between the whole jumping-off-the-cliff thing, and the booming thunder as they slipped in and out of the void.

They needed something subtler, like maybe . . .

She ran toward Calla's Panakes, hoping to find Lur or Mitya

tending to the majestic tree. But the only gnome she found was the plaited-haired female she'd seen helping Edaline when they tested the cravettels on Verdi.

"Did you need something?" the gnome asked, setting down the garland she'd been weaving from the fallen pink, purple, and blue flowers.

Sophie bit her lip. "Never mind."

"Are you sure?" the gnome pressed. "I'm here to help. Especially *you*, Miss Foster."

Sophie's cheeks burned. "But . . . I don't even know your name."

"Well, there's an easy way to fix that, isn't there?" She flashed a green-toothed smile. "I'm Flori. What can I do for you?"

"Don't look at me," Fitz told Flori when Sophie hesitated. "I'm just as confused as you are."

Flori tilted her head to study Sophie. "Perhaps that means you've come to me as the moonlark?"

Sophie sucked in a breath.

"And if that's the case," Flori continued, "I'm *happy* to help. No questions asked. No need to be shy. Please let me assist you, Miss Foster. It would be my honor."

Sophie closed her eyes, inhaling the sweet scent of Calla's blossoms to fuel her courage as she whispered, "If I needed to go somewhere right now, would you take me?"

"Anywhere," Flori promised.

Sophie nodded, mentally running through her plan one

more time before she turned to Fitz. "You're going to think I'm crazy."

He grinned. "I usually do. But I *also* think you're brilliant—and have solved way more problems than anyone else has. So I'm in."

He offered his hand and she took it, turning back to Flori. "I need you to take us to Eternalia."

THIRTY-SIX

FLORI USED THE ROOTS FROM THE Panakes to carry them to the elvin capital city, and somehow that made it feel like they had Calla urging them along their journey.

Sophie closed her eyes, listening to the fragile sound of Flori's voice as she sang to the roots, pushing them faster and faster through the narrow, musty tunnel in the earth.

"I'll be waiting right here," Flori promised when they'd come to a stop and she'd opened a hole for them to climb to the surface.

"Actually, I have my home crystal," Sophie told her, squinting as her eyes adjusted to the sunlight streaming in. "That way you won't have to worry about being gone too long."

"I'm not worried," Flori said. "And either way, I'll still stay here, keeping an ear to the ground until I know you've leaped safely away."

Sophie's voice sounded thick as she thanked her and turned to climb out of the tunnel. Before she reached the top, she spun back and met Flori's soft gray eyes. "I'm sorry it took me so long to talk to you."

Flori smiled. "Time is a relative thing, especially when grief is involved." She patted the roots at her feet. "Someday we can share stories about my aunt. But only when you're ready."

"Wait—you're Calla's niece?"

"I think the proper term is great-great-grandniece. But she always told me the greats meant I was the best."

"She was right," Sophie told her. "And . . . I'd like that."

"Me too," Flori whispered. "Now go, be the brave moonlark you were born to be."

"So are you going to clue me in to what you're planning?" Fitz asked as they emerged from the root-lined tunnel and faced the twelve crystal castles glittering in the afternoon light.

Sophie led him behind one of the towering, palmlike trees that purified the air with enormous fan-shaped leaves.

"It's called *I'm sick of being patient*," she whispered. "So I'm going to talk to Oralie."

She'd expected him to freak out. But all he said was, "Do you know which castle's hers?"

"I wish. The only castle I've been in was Councillor Terik's." She pointed to a castle toward the center of the row. That left them with eleven other choices.

Fitz shielded his eyes, squinting into the distance. "Well, that one near the end over there has pink flowers lining the path to the door. Think that might mean it's hers?"

Oralie *did* love the color pink—and Sophie couldn't come up with a better guess.

"What are we going to say if I'm wrong?" Fitz asked as they bolted down the golden path. "Especially if Councillor Alina opens the door?"

"I'm *really* hoping that won't happen," Sophie admitted. "And that I'll come up with a brilliant excuse if it does. I guess we'll know soon enough."

She knocked the moment she reached the door, not giving herself a chance to wimp out. Each second felt like fifty lifetimes before the door swung open and Oralie's bright eyes widened.

"Sophie?" she whispered, her blond ringlets brushing her cheeks as she pulled Sophie and Fitz into the twinkling foyer and shut the door behind them, latching it with five heavy silver bolts. "Let's hope Alina didn't see you. She's in the castle next door."

"Ugh. Worst. Neighbor. Ever," Fitz grumbled.

"Yes. She is."

The sadness laced through the words made Sophie realize . . .

Councillor Alina had probably moved into Kenric's old castle. And Sophie had long suspected that Kenric and Oralie had secretly been in love, but couldn't act on it because they would've had to step down as Councillors.

So imagining them living side by side—and knowing Oralie was now alone—choked off Sophie's voice as she said, "Well, I'm guessing Alina would be banging on the door by now if she'd noticed us."

"I'm sure she would," Oralie said, checking the bolts again. "And I'm assuming the fact that you're here unannounced, without bodyguards, and with soil in your hair means that no one knows you're here."

Sophie bit her lip. "The gnome who brought us here does."

"Hmm" was all Oralie said to that as she reached for Sophie's cheek.

Sophie assumed Oralie was going to brush dirt off her face. But Oralie's fingers lingered, and she closed her eyes, her forehead crinkling as she read Sophie's emotions.

"Looks like it would be wise for me to sit down," she said when she let go. She led them down a crystal hall without another word and into a diamond-shaped sitting room with overstuffed pearl-trimmed pink armchairs, pink chandeliers, and pink crystals cut into the walls in floral patterns.

"This is pretty much Biana's dream room," Fitz said as he sank into one of the throne-size chairs and propped his feet on the jeweled footstool.

"She's welcome to visit anytime," Oralie told him, taking the chair across from Sophie.

"Wow, really?" Fitz asked.

"Why not?"

"Because . . . you're a Councillor. I didn't think you guys were open for visitors."

"Most of us aren't. I've gotten many lectures about my lack of constant security, and how I leave myself too vulnerable. But I think it's important that we make ourselves available to our people. After all, we never know what we're going to learn."

She raised one eyebrow in Sophie's direction and Sophie took the cue, choosing her words carefully.

"We . . . need you to set up a meeting with Gethen. And I know he's in Lumenaria, and that it's on lockdown because you're prepping for the Peace Summit. But we *need* to talk to him."

Oralie frowned. "You weren't hoping to meet with him *today*?"

"Is that possible?" Fitz asked.

"No, definitely not."

"What about soon, then?" Sophie pressed.

"I . . . don't know." Oralie's jeweled heels clicked across the crystal floor as she moved to the room's furthest corner and stood silhouetted by the sunlight, looking so elegant and regal in her pink ruffled gown that it made Sophie wish she'd shaken the dirt out of her hair before she'd come inside.

"I assume you won't tell me why there's such urgency?" Oralie asked.

Sophie glanced at Fitz.

"Your call," he said.

"You . . . might want to sit down again," Sophie mumbled.

Oralie lowered herself onto the arm of the nearest chair and nodded for her to continue. So Sophie did—telling Oralie the whole story, right down to the ogres searching the Silver Tower, Wylie's fears about his mother, and Mr. Forkle's decision not to tell the Council.

"Please don't make me regret telling you," she begged when she'd finished.

Oralie cleared her throat. "I won't. And . . . I'm so deeply sorry to hear about Wylie. Does he need anything?"

"Yeah," Fitz said. "He needs us to find out what happened."

Oralie smoothed the ruffles on her gown. "I fear you're over-estimating my power. I'm only one vote of many—and hardly a popular one at that."

"You were the one who fixed Exillium," Sophie reminded her. "And you did that without getting the support of the other Councillors."

"Yes, but that was a problem I could solve with money. *This* is something else entirely."

"I know," Sophie said. "But there has to be a way."

"Not without my telling the rest of the Council—and I do not believe that would be wise. I'm sure some of my fellow

Councillors would call for my circlet for saying so, but fear has inspired some of our worst decisions. And there are some who feel drastic measures are the only solution."

"Drastic how?" Fitz asked.

"You've already seen the beginning of it. Policing in our cities. Defense training for our citizens. I'm not saying those are bad things. Sadly, they're incredibly necessary. But where do they lead? Stricter crystal restrictions to further regulate where and when people can leap. Curfews. Much more invasive monitoring of our registry pendants. When rulers stop trusting their citizens, freedom is always the cost. And I can think of several Councillors who will see what happened to Wylie as proof that control is the answer."

"And what do *you* see as the answer?" Sophie asked.

Oralie sighed. "I honestly don't know. But . . . I think it starts with people like you. People asking hard questions and taking risks and never letting anything stop them—not because they want power or glory. Because they know it's the right thing to do."

It was a prickly sort of compliment. The kind that made Sophie want to throw her arms around Oralie to thank her— or run away screaming, *I don't need that kind of pressure.*

She settled for staying focused. "Does that mean you'll help us?"

"It means I'll *try*. But it's going to take time. I understand your haste—but this is not something I can snap my fingers and make happen overnight. Please don't let the passing days convince you that I've changed my mind. You have my word that I'll do all I can to help Wylie. His life—and the nightmares he's endured—is proof of my many failings. He deserves a much safer world than the one I've given him."

"It's not your fault," Sophie told her.

"No. But I'm not blameless, either."

Oralie's eyes met Sophie's, so bright and blue it took Sophie a second to realize they were welling with tears.

"I also need you to promise me you'll notify me if Wylie has any further problems."

"That may be tricky," Sophie said. "The Imparter you gave me before we fled to the Black Swan was conveniently missing from my bag when they sent home my things."

"That sounds like them," Oralie said, half a smile curving her lips. "But I can authorize any Imparter. Do you have yours with you?"

"Can we use mine?" Fitz jumped in, pulling the silver gadget from his pocket. "Sophie's is . . . well, it's kind of a long story."

Oralie took the Imparter and held her finger in the center of the underside. "I suspect you both have quite a few long stories that never make it to the ears of the Council."

A green light flashed and she held the gadget close to her lips, whispering, "Permission granted," and making the Imparter flash blue.

She handed it back to Fitz. "Perhaps this will allow us to keep each other better updated on many things. I'm not asking for all of your secrets. But there is one thing I need to know." She turned to Sophie, taking one of her hands as she whispered, "Where's Keefe?"

Sophie's mouth went dry and Oralie must've felt the fear seeping out of her skin.

She nodded, tightening her hold. "I can't tell you if you should go with your doubt or your faith, Sophie. But either way, don't let him make Kenric's mistake."

"What mistake was that?" Sophie managed to whisper.

Oralie let her go and turned away. "He underestimated Fintan. We all did. Don't let Keefe pay the same price we paid."

THIRTY-SEVEN

EVERYTHING OKAY?" GRADY ASKED as Sophie and Fitz tried—and failed—to sneak upstairs before anyone noticed they were back at Havenfield. They'd barely made it five steps into the living room before everyone spotted them.

Sophie was still grasping for the best lie when Fitz proved he was way ahead of her and told both of her parents the revelations about Cyrah to keep them distracted.

"Did you know her?" Sophie asked when Grady turned as white as the couch.

"Not as well as we should have," Edaline said, sinking down on a cushion beside him. "We'd crossed paths over the years, but never spent much time together until Prentice's memory break.

She reached out to us afterward, despite how antisocial we'd become. Said it was hard to find others who understood loss."

"We didn't see her much," Grady added quietly. "But she'd come to visit from time to time. Until she was gone."

"The Council actually asked us if we'd be willing to adopt Wylie," Edaline whispered. "But it was too soon. That's why we didn't go to her planting. I knew I'd never get through having to face Wylie after turning him down. I don't know if he realizes. But . . ."

"Tiergan was a far better guardian than we could've ever been back then," Grady reminded her.

"Wow," Fitz said as Sophie wrapped them both in a hug. "I don't think I realized any of that."

"I doubt your father knew, given his complicated relationship with the Endals," Grady told him. "It's strange, though, isn't it? How small our world truly is? There are always so many subtle connections between everyone and everything."

"I know—try keeping up with it all as the new kid in town," Sophie mumbled.

No matter how much she learned, how many stories people shared, it felt like she'd never actually catch up.

Grady hugged her tighter. "You're doing great, kiddo. Plus, I think it's *good* that all of this is new for you. Fresh eyes hold incredible value. In fact, I think I'll hail Alden and see if he can send me his notes on the day Cyrah died. Maybe I'll notice something he didn't."

Grady headed upstairs to his office and Edaline frowned as she turned back to Sophie. "Is there dirt in your hair?"

Sophie almost smacked herself as she fumbled to remove it. Fitz did the same.

Edaline's frown deepened. "I thought you went to Alluveterre."

"Yeah," Sophie mumbled. "But you know how muddy underground forests can be."

It might've been the lamest excuse in the entirety of elvin history. But Edaline let it go.

"Well," she said, "I'm assuming the odds of me convincing the two of you to relax for the rest of the afternoon are fairly slim. So I won't waste my time. But I *will* make a fresh batch of ripplefluffs. And I'm going to *insist* you take a break and eat them."

"You won't have to tell me twice," Fitz said, flashing his famous grin. "And I'll make sure Sophie takes a break too."

"If anyone can, it's you." Edaline's teasing tone seemed to add meaning to the words, but Sophie didn't feel like riddling out what she was implying.

"So," Fitz said, breaking the silence as they headed up the stairs to her room. "You're still up for some trust exercises, right?"

"I guess."

Fitz laughed. "You know, you'd dread them a lot less if you'd just tell me that secret you were going to share that time Keefe interrupted our training. Don't think I've forgotten."

Sophie kept her face forward, hoping it hid her blush. For one very brief lapse in judgment, she'd almost told Fitz about her silly crush on him. Thankfully, she'd been spared the humiliation.

"I wonder if I could guess," he said as they passed the second floor.

"I doubt it."

His obliviousness was both reliable *and* annoying.

"Oh really?" He scooted past her, blocking her from the next step up. "Want me to try?"

"I . . ." It was the only word she could get out before her voice dried up and crumbled away.

Fitz grinned. "Maybe it would make it easier. That way you wouldn't have to *say* it—assuming I guess right."

Easier.

Harder.

Possibly one huge disaster . . .

Sophie swallowed, trying to choke down the lump that had wedged itself in her throat—but her voice still refused to rise past it.

Maybe he saw the panic in her eyes.

Or maybe he really did guess her secret.

Either way, he backed up a step. "Sorry. It's not fair to rush you—especially after everything we've been through today."

"Yeah," she mumbled, nudging her way past him and trying not to wonder if she'd just been rejected—now was not the time for such petty distractions.

But her eyes still stung and her chest had a heavy, stretched-out feeling.

"Hey," Fitz said, catching up with her at the doorway to her room. "Did I say something wrong? It feels like I did—and I swear I didn't mean to."

She turned toward her room, trying to find anything to trigger a subject change. And that was when she noticed the crushed parts in her flowered carpet.

"Are those . . . ," Fitz asked.

"Footprints," she whispered.

Coming from her open window.

Sophie ducked away from the door, pressing her back against the wall to stay out of sight and wishing Sandor was there to charge in with his deadly sword.

Since he wasn't, she stretched out her mind to search for nearby thoughts. "I don't sense anyone else here, do you?"

"No, it's pretty quiet," Fitz whispered.

Almost too quiet—but that could be her paranoia getting the best of her. She could feel her fear straining against the knot under her ribs, and she slowed her breathing to keep control.

"Wait—where are you going?" Fitz asked as she squared her shoulders and turned to march through her doorway.

"How else are we going to find out why they were here?" she asked, proud of how steady her voice sounded.

Nothing looked out of place—her desk drawers were still closed tight. Her clothes neatly hung in her closet. She followed the trail of footsteps to her bed, sucking in a breath when she took a longer look at her pillow.

"I'm guessing Keefe made that," Fitz said as she reached for the midnight blue bead that had been left in the center.

She nodded, tracing her finger over the silver moonlark rendered in perfect detail.

No one else could've painted it so intricately.

And the eye shimmered with a temporary leaping crystal.

If Sophie had any doubt about Keefe's intentions, it was erased when she noticed two tiny words painted on the silver bird's wings.

Meet now.

THIRTY-EIGHT

I'M GOING," SOPHIE SAID IN THE SAME
breath that Fitz asked, "What if it's a trap?"

"It's not a trap—Keefe had to take a huge risk to come
here and leave this." She rolled the bead in her hand,
feeling the cool weight of it.

"The Neverseen could've made him do it," Fitz argued.
"We're supposed to be finding out how far they're pushing
him. Pretty sure that means we shouldn't be going along with
a super-dangerous—and kinda creepy—command. I mean,
who breaks into someone's room and leaves a bead on their
pillow, telling them to meet up without even explaining what's
going on?"

"Someone who didn't have a lot of time," Sophie said—though

secretly she did admit the whole thing had an evil-tooth-fairy vibe going on.

"He couldn't have left a note?" Fitz asked.

"A note's a lot harder to explain if anyone found him sneaking out with it. And maybe he didn't want to waste time rummaging around my room for paper and a pen. All that matters is, he wouldn't have gone to this kind of trouble if he didn't have something important to tell me. *Or* he's in danger and needs my help. Either way, I know it's risky. I know I won't find anyone who'll tell me this is a good decision. But I'm going. And I understand if you don't want—"

"No *way* am I letting you go by yourself," Fitz interrupted.

"*Letting* me?"

"Whoa—easy on the glaring. All I meant is, if you're doing this, so am I. I'll cling to your ankle as you leap away if I have to. But you realize we *will* get caught this time, right? Your parents know we're here."

"Yeah . . . I should probably leave a note, that way they won't freak out."

"I'm pretty sure the freak-out will be epic no matter what," Fitz told her. "But I guess it's still better to give some explanation."

Sophie dug a notebook and a pen from her Foxfire satchel and stared at the blank paper.

What was she supposed to say?

Found a leaping crystal from the Neverseen and decided to use it—don't know where I'm going or when I'll be back!

That should go over *really* well.

She brainstormed for another second, then went for short and sweet.

> Found a message from Keefe.
> Don't worry—we're being careful.

"I guess that covers it," Fitz said. "Though you should probably add, '*Please don't ground me for the rest of eternity.*'"

"Last chance to change your mind. I can handle myself."

"Oh, I know. I'm planning on hiding behind you if we end up facing anything scary. But we're Cognates. We're stronger *together*."

He flashed the initials side of his rings as he offered her his hand.

She took it, leaving the note on her bed as she held Keefe's bead up to the light and formed a wispy ghost of a path. "Any guesses where we're going?"

"My money's on somewhere stinky."

The joke made it easier.

So did reminding herself that they were going to see a friend.

But Sophie's knees still shook as she took the crucial step into the light, leaving their lives in Keefe's hands.

"I knew it," Fitz said, plugging his nose and glaring at his feet, which had re-formed in a puddle of oily black swirled with iridescent blue. "Selkie skin. It liquefies as they shed it."

Sophie gagged.

The sour-cheese smell coated her tongue, and the salty ocean air made it ten times worse. The whole beach was covered in the gunk—a maze of sludgy pools and slimy black rivulets trickling toward the white-capped waves. Jagged rocks jutted out of the frothy water, blanketed with sleek black creatures that looked part seal and part snake, with whiskered faces and long, coiled bodies.

"I take it those are selkies?" Sophie asked as one of the bigger beasts raised its head and let out a barklike grunt.

"Yep. I'm betting we're in Blackwater Bay," Fitz said. "Though I don't remember the cliffs being this tall when my tutor brought me here. Or this green."

"That's because this is Inktide Island," a voice behind them corrected. "Which is much more private. Or it's supposed to be. I didn't realize I'd be getting Foster-plus-one."

They spun around to find Keefe wearing another long black cloak, leaning against a clump of weathered rocks in the middle of the beach. The white eye symbol on his sleeves was almost as troubling as his casual smirk.

"So does this mean you guys are a *thing* now?" Keefe asked. "The inseparable Sophitz? Or did you decide to go with Fitzphie?"

"Dude, this is so not the time for jokes," Fitz said.

"Huh, that's pretty much what Foster told me when she first saw me at Foxfire. Do you finish each other's sentences now too?"

"Keefe—we're serious," Sophie said.

"Oh, I know. Fitz is giving me his 'I'm so serious' scowl. And you're hitting me with a whole mess of emotions." He waved his hands through the air and his smile faded. "You're back to not trusting me again? I know I was wrong about my warning—but wasn't that a good thing?"

"You think it's *good* that someone got tortured?" Fitz snapped.

All the color drained from Keefe's face. "Wait . . . what?"

"You don't know?" Sophie asked.

"No—I swear. Was it Dex? Please tell me it wasn't Dex. Or Biana? Or Linh?"

His voice cracked with each name.

"They're all fine," Sophie said. "It was—"

"We're not telling you anything until we search your memories," Fitz interrupted. "We need to make sure you weren't involved."

Keefe rolled his eyes. "Would I be here if I was?"

"Yeah, if this is a trap," Fitz said.

"Right, I forgot." Keefe turned to shout at the empty beach. "They're on to us, guys. Go ahead and attack."

Silence—aside from barking selkies.

"Oh, that's right—there's no one here except me! And do you have any idea how hard it was to get away?"

"How'd you do it?" Sophie asked.

"Don't let him sidetrack you," Fitz jumped in. "We need to stick to the plan. Like Tam said—"

"Ugh, I should've *known* Bangs Boy was part of this," Keefe interrupted. "Let me guess, he's still bitter because I wouldn't let him take that stupid reading?"

"Uh, have you seen what you're wearing?" Fitz asked.

Keefe gripped his sleeves, trying to cover the Neverseen symbols. "It's. A. *Costume.*"

"Prove it," Fitz said.

"And what happens if I say no? Are you planning to go all *Cognate power* on me?"

"Just give us five minutes," Sophie begged. "Five minutes to make sure we know what's really going on. If you'd seen what they did to Wylie . . ."

Keefe fell back a step. "They hurt *Wylie?*"

"'Hurt' is putting it nicely," Fitz said. "They drugged him, dragged him out of his room, and burned him over and over."

Gulls circled high above as Keefe watched the sky. "He'll be okay, right?"

"Physic is working on him now," Sophie whispered. "She can heal all of his wounds. Not so sure about the mental trauma."

Keefe looked green as he turned to pace. "Did they let him go? Or did he get away?"

"He got away," Sophie said.

"Wow—someone's going to be in *big* trouble."

"*That's* what you care about?" Fitz asked, shaking sludge off his shoes as he stalked closer.

"Hey—I have to think about what it's going to be like

when I go back there. You would too, if you were in my position."

"I would never be in your position," Fitz argued.

"Yeah, you're better at taking the easy way."

"What does *that* mean?"

"Nothing. It's . . . whatever." Keefe's eyes made their way back to the sky. "Did Wylie see who grabbed him?"

"Sorta," Sophie said. "He felt an invisible hand tear off his pendant, and he got trapped in a force field, so that has to be Alvar and Ruy. But he also suspected there were two others."

"I'm assuming you thought one of them was me?"

"Can you blame us?" Fitz asked.

"You? No." Keefe's eyes focused on Sophie. "But I told you, I won't cross the hard lines."

"You never said what the lines are, though," she whispered. "And I know how desperate you are to make this work."

"So you thought . . ." He choked back the rest of the words.

"If you'd known they were going after Wylie," Fitz said, his voice barely audible over the rolling waves, "would you have stopped them?"

"I would've told you guys, so the Black Swan could handle it. Just like I did with Grady and Edaline."

"But what if we couldn't get to him?" Fitz pressed. "Would you have blown your cover?"

Keefe hesitated—only a second, but it was enough.

"You don't get it," he argued. "These are people who torture someone just because they want something! People who infect an entire species with a disease just to get their way! They have a network that stretches way farther than you could ever imagine. I've only seen a tiny piece of it, and it's seriously terrifying. I can't fight it without making some hard calls!"

"Well, I hope it's worth it," Fitz snapped.

"So do I." Keefe's shoulders slumped with the confession, like his body wanted to retreat.

Salty wind whipped around them, and Sophie choked down the selkie stink. "Do you have any idea who the other two kidnappers would've been? Wylie thought one was a Guster. And he heard them say the other was keeping the path open."

Keefe brushed sand out of his hair. "The Guster would be Trix. So that probably means the other was Umber, since I got the impression that she and Trix work together a lot. Those aren't their real names. I met some of the members a few days ago, but no one would tell me who they really are—and they all kept their hoods up so I couldn't see them."

"So they still don't trust you," Sophie noted.

"Not completely. But Fintan doesn't trust anyone completely. Everyone only gets to know a tiny piece of his plans, and he only gives each person a single task for every mission. That way, everyone's expendable."

"That's pretty terrifying," Sophie mumbled, "considering what he did to your mom."

Keefe shrugged.

"Are they making any progress on their promise to rescue her?" she asked.

"Don't know, don't care. I assumed they were lying when they offered that. Look at how they've abandoned Gethen. He's been a prisoner for how many months now? And do you see them trying to get him back?"

"They tried at first," Sophie reminded him. "Until Squall froze off his fingernails. And now he's in Lumenaria, which is apparently impossible to break into."

"Maybe, but I've never once heard them talk about getting him back. And when I asked Alvar about it, he said, 'Gethen is where he belongs.'"

Fitz and Sophie shared a look.

"What? Are you guys planning to visit him again?"

"We're working on it," Sophie said.

"Well . . . I wouldn't get my hopes up. They want him locked away. I'm guessing that means he's useless."

"I hope you're wrong," Sophie said quietly. "He's pretty much the only plan we have."

"Uh, hello—you have me. I know I got a few details wrong yesterday—but I'm still working on getting Fintan's cache. I *will* get him to trust me."

"That's what I'm worried about," Sophie mumbled. "Trust never comes free."

"Maybe not. But I know what I'm willing to pay. I have my limits. I won't push them."

"That'd be a lot easier to believe if you'd show us what you're doing with them every day," Fitz said.

Keefe opened his mouth to argue, then focused on Sophie. "You really need to know, don't you?"

She nodded.

A wave crashed against the rocks, making the selkies bark so loudly it nearly drowned out Keefe's next words. "I'll give you five minutes to look around my memories—but Wonder-boy has to sit this one out."

"Since when do you only trust her?" Fitz asked.

"Since she doesn't look ready to punch me. So that's the deal." He offered his hand for a handshake.

Sophie stepped forward to take it, scowling when her shoe splashed in one of the inky puddles. "Lovely place you picked, by the way."

"Hey, I told you my next plan for sneaking away involved lots of selkie skin."

"You did. I just didn't realize you were serious."

"I'm always serious, Foster. Especially when you think I'm teasing." He cleared his throat, not quite holding her stare. "Remember—five minutes. Then we drop this."

She reached for his temples and he flinched at her touch.

"Dude, are you blushing?" Fitz asked.

"Only because I can feel what Foster's feeling," Keefe snapped back.

Sophie rolled her eyes. "I'm not feeling *anything*."

Or maybe she was feeling too much.

Fear and dread and doubt and worry. But also hope.

She gave herself three seconds to steady her nerves and let the sounds of the waves wash away the other distractions. Then she closed her eyes and took a cold, salty breath before she pushed her consciousness into Keefe's mind.

THIRTY-NINE

KEEFE'S HEAD WAS FULL OF CITIES.

Places Sophie recognized.

Some she didn't.

But they all had one thing in common.

Why are you visiting humans? she transmitted.

Not for the reason you're thinking.

You don't know what I'm thinking.

Actually, I do. Your emotions are so intense, you might as well hold up a sign saying, "I'm worried about THIS." But I'm just there to study people. It's part of my empathy training—and yep, working with the Neverseen is just as annoying as it is with the Black Swan. It's either this, chores, or hardcore skill lessons that make the stuff we did at Exillium look easy.

The scene shifted again, and for a second Sophie thought she was looking at Paris, until she realized the Eiffel Tower–esque structure was white and orange.

When did you go to Tokyo?

Yesterday. If you look at the signs, you can probably find the date somewhere. Now do you believe me when I say I had nothing to do with what happened to Wylie?

You get why we had to make sure, right?

It's still not awesome knowing you guys sat around talking about how you don't trust me.

You don't make it easy.

In his memory, she could see Keefe standing on a rooftop next to Fintan. She wasn't sure she could do that without shoving Fintan off the edge.

Hey, I'm just as disgusted with him as you are.

Quit reading my emotions!

Can't help it. You're impossible to ignore. And believe me, I get the same nauseating fury every time I look at him. He doesn't deserve to be alive after what he did to Kenric.

No, he doesn't.

If it helps, I'm not around him that much. Alvar supervises me during chores. And Ruy's the one in charge of the skill lessons. All Fintan does is take me to crowded places and make me isolate each person's feelings.

Why humans? she asked as the city scene shifted again, showing a street full of life and movement and color—and people. *So* many people. Rich and poor. Young and old. Locals and tourists. Talking, laughing, shouting—selling food and trinkets. Some wore saris and turbans, which meant Keefe was probably in some part of India—but Sophie couldn't tell which city.

Well, for one thing, the Neverseen can't exactly go hopping around the Lost Cities, Keefe reminded her. *But I can also feel most human emotions through the air without needing contact. Plus, humans fascinate Fintan. He hates them, but he's also obsessed with knowing everything about them.*

The next city was London, right in the heart of Piccadilly Circus, where people seemed to be gathering around a weird statue and watching a bunch of ads on the giant screens.

So this is all you do? she asked. *What about during the skill lessons?*

Those are just Ruy showing off. He must've been Exillium's star student, and I'm pretty stinktastic at everything, so the lessons usually end with him calling me useless.

Sophie could feel the sting the word triggered, after all the times his dad had hurled the same accusation. But she was glad he wasn't excelling at the Neverseen's training.

And that's it? she asked. *You don't do anything else?*

Pretty much. There are lots of nasty chores. And there's been the occasional mission, like the day they stormed the Sanctuary—but I had NOTHING to do with Wylie. I swear I didn't even know it was happening. I'm actually glad you guys told me, so I can prepare before I head back.

Will you be safe?

Sure—why not? I wasn't part of the botched mission. In fact, some people might get demoted.

You say that like it's a good thing.

It is *a good thing. It'll make Fintan use me more.*

But for what?

I can't worry about that, Foster. I can't think about what-ifs or maybes. I can only take it one day at a time—one assignment at a time—and fight my way through.

In the memory, Fintan smiled at something Keefe said, and Sophie's insides twisted.

I hate that he's the one training you. He's not even an Empath.

I know. But all the one-on-one time I'm getting with him is crucial if I'm going to steal his cache. Plus, there aren't any other Empaths to train me. I asked him why, and he said, "It's rare to find those who are open to new sensations."

He made his mental voice sound like Fintan, and the knot of emotions under Sophie's ribs pulled so tight, it hurt to breathe.

Sorry. I guess it's probably pretty hard to hear that after the awful times you've been in his head, Keefe mumbled.

I don't know how you stand it. It makes me want to claw my ears off—or claw his lips off, or I don't know—I just want to claw something.

I know. I'm super glad you're not clawing me. And fortunately, he doesn't talk much. Mostly he says, "Tell me what they're feeling" and points to some random person in the crowd. It only gets weird at the end. Before he brings me back to the hideout, he always asks, "If you could only save one of these people, who would you save?"

That's . . . terrifying.

I know. I totally thought he was going to burn down the city, and I had no idea what I'd do if he did. But he just scratched his chin and asked why I chose the person. He always writes down my answer in this little notebook he keeps in his pocket. Most of the time he tilts it up so I can't see what he's writing. But a couple of days ago it was windy and the pages kept flipping, so he held it at a different angle and it looked like he's making a list—but I have no idea of what. The label at the top said: "CRITERION."

FORTY

I'M GUESSING THERE'S A REASON YOU JUST *gasped*, Keefe said as the city in his memories shifted again, to a colorful barrio filled with music and dancing.

Sophie bit her lip. *Biana overheard Alvar talking to someone on his Imparter at Everglen a few months back. And he used the word "criterion." He also talked about "test subjects."*

She let that sink in before she asked, *Do you think that means they've been planning to train you like this for a while?*

Probably, Keefe said, disgust laced through every syllable. *I keep trying to tell you—I'm not the guy you want me to be.*

I don't want you to be anyone except you. Whatever the Lodestar Initiative is—it doesn't define you any more than Project Moonlark defines me. Especially since I'm starting to think their plans aren't even working. I can't remember the last time the Black Swan were ahead of all the crazy stuff going on—and it seems like the Neverseen are scrambling too. These groups may have created the game. But that doesn't mean we have to play by their rules. And if there's one thing you and I are both good at, it's making things up as we go along.

I guess I can live with that, Keefe thought as his memory changed to a quaint village-style city, with a long wooden bridge spanning the peaceful river in the center. Enormous snowcapped mountains loomed in the distance, and Sophie assumed that meant they were somewhere like Austria or Switzerland.

So . . . what are your criteria for deciding which person you would save? she asked.

It depends. I mostly look for whoever feels the happiest, since I figure they'd appreciate getting to live. Or I pick one of the kids. They're so cute and small and innocent—and wow, that's a huge wave of sappy mushiness you're hitting me with.

What do you expect? You're talking about saving kids!

And ten minutes ago you thought I was Wylie's fourth kidnapper. Remind me to thank Bangs Boy for that the next time I see him. And the Fitzster.

If you could've seen Wylie's injuries, you'd understand why we had to be sure. She had to clamp down on her memories to stop herself from picturing it. *Besides, seeing you in that robe . . .*

Yeah, I can feel how much you hate it.

"Hate" isn't a strong enough word. I want to rip it to shreds.

Well, don't. I'm not wearing anything underneath.

He snort-laughed when she scrambled back a step.

I'm kidding—though your gross-out is noted. And FYI, the reason I'm still wearing it is because I can't risk losing another one. Fintan flipped out when I came back from Foxfire without it, probably because he couldn't track me or something.

That's not the only reason.

Oh?

Yeah.

Seconds passed.

Aw, come on, Foster. I'm the cute guy who chooses to save the kids, remember? How can you resist me?

Who said anything about cute?

It totally goes without saying. Don't even try to deny it.

She couldn't.

And he knew it.

And she hated it.

If I tell you, I want something in return, she decided.

Isn't my eternal devotion enough?

Not even close.

That hurts, Foster.

That's the game. If I tell you what we found in your cloak, I want a secret in return. I want to see whatever memory you got back that freaked you out and made you run away.

His mind seemed to squirm.

Come on, Keefe. Sooner or later you're going to have to tell me anyway.

See, but "later" sounds way better than "sooner."

You think it does, because hiding stuff always sounds easier. But all it really means is that you're stuck carrying the burden all alone.

That's better than dumping it on you.

But I'm asking you to—and I promise, it's not going to change anything.

Oh, it changes everything. You'll see.

Does that mean we have a deal?

She heard him sigh. *Fine. But you go first.*

Fair enough.

She explained about the disk in his cloak, and how Prentice's memory of the symbol seemed to be connected to him calling swan song, and how they found the shadowprint of the symbol on the floor of the abandoned hideout in Paris. And while she was at it, she told him about the listening device in his old Imparter.

Your turn! she finished.

Whoa, hang on—you can't just dump all of that on me and not give me a second to process. There was a listening device in my old Imparter? How did you even have it?

Yours accidentally got switched with mine the day we searched your room and found your mom's note. Dex couldn't track the signal, but we're assuming it went to the Neverseen, and that's how they knew about our ambush on Everest and had time to prepare.

Mom of the year strikes again. His mind seemed to darken as thick clouds of anger swirled through his consciousness. *I don't know why I even get surprised anymore.*

Because you haven't let her break you—and I hope you never do.

She watched him gather the words, tucking them away somewhere safe before he asked, *So the disk you found in my cloak—was it a kind of tracker?*

Sandor and Mr. Forkle didn't think so. It wasn't covered in any enzymes, and it's made of something called duskitine, which is apparently a type of stone that reacts to starlight. We have no idea why it has a piece of the symbol carved on it, but it can't be a coincidence. And you haven't seen the symbol anywhere?

Nope. But I'm still at their stupid "new recruit" house. I bet I'll find it once I get to a real hideout. And in the meantime, maybe I need to lose this cloak and see what happens. . . .

Bad idea—especially after you took such a risk to meet with us today.

There you go again with your logic. It's really cramping my style.

Well then, why don't you stop me by showing me that memory?

Are you sure you wouldn't rather lecture me a little longer?

Tempting, but no.

When he still hesitated, she added, *Come on, Keefe, haven't you stood by me through all the weird things in my past? Let's not forget I'm the girl with the alicorn-inspired DNA.*

Yeah, but that lets you teleport—and communicate with Silveny—so it's a total win. How are she and Greyfell doing, by the way?

They're good. If they were here, Silveny would tell you to stop stalling.

Pretty sure she'd be chanting KEEFE! KEEFE! KEEFE! As everyone should be when they see me.

There you go, changing the subject again.

Caught that, huh? You're a quick one, Miss F. And I'm pretty sure I've given you way more than five minutes, so—

Nope. You're not getting out of this. We made a deal, and I'm holding you to it.

See, and I'd kinda like to find out how you'll punish me if I don't.

She was tempted to snap back with a long list of incredibly creative forms of Keefe torture. But then she'd be giving him the distraction he wanted.

Please? she tried. *I'm tired of wondering about that memory. I'm tired of worrying what side of the line you're on every time things get weird. I'm tired of having Dex tell me he thinks you're my nemesis and—*

Whoa—back up. Dizznee thinks I'm your what?

Well, he didn't actually say "nemesis"—but he implied it. We were trying to guess what the Lodestar Initiative is, and he wondered if it's the Neverseen's version of Project Moonlark, which would basically mean they made you to stop me.

Wow. That's just . . .

He burst into a fit of snorty giggles.

I'm glad you find this so amusing.

You don't? Don't tell me you actually believe him.

I don't want to. But what else am I supposed to think? You told me when you ran off that you were meant to be something other than the hero. And just a few minutes ago, you told me you're not the guy I want you to be.

Ugh. I guess you do need to see that memory, don't you?

Yeah, I really do.

Okay. The word felt sluggish, like his mind was dragging its feet. But after several seconds, a new flashback began.

FORTY-ONE

I T WAS DARK IN KEEFE'S BEDROOM. SO black he could barely make out the silhouette of his mother leaning over his bed, as her arms shook him from his dreamless sleep.

"Mom?" he asked. "Is something wrong?"

His voice was squeakier than Sophie was used to hearing it. She guessed that meant he was more like nine or ten years old.

"Everything's fine," Lady Gisela told him as she yanked back his covers.

A whoosh of cold air rushed around him and he curled up tighter, shivering in his overstarched pajamas.

"None of that," she said, grabbing his wrist to stop him from reaching for his blanket. "Put this on. It's even colder where we're going."

She tossed a thick black cloak at him as he slowly sat up.

Sophie squinted through the dim memory, half expecting to find the white eye symbol staring back at her from the sleeves. But the cloak was plain, and the coarse fabric seemed to swallow Keefe's skinny frame as he stumbled to his feet, his knees still shaky with sleep.

His eyes slowly adjusted to being awake, letting him see more of his mom, who looked as immaculate as ever. Despite the middle-of-the-night time, her lips were glossed, her heavy black cape glittered with flecks of onyx, and her shiny blond hair was twisted into an intricate updo.

She clicked her tongue as he stood there gaping at her.

"Honestly, Keefe. You can't figure out that you need to put on your shoes?"

Keefe stared at his bare feet.

Lady Gisela rolled her eyes and dropped to her knees, grabbing a pair of soft black boots from the foot of the bed.

"No socks?" Keefe asked, clinging to her shoulders as she ordered him to step into the left shoe. "And shouldn't I change first?"

"We won't be gone that long." She pulled the other boot on and adjusted the collar of his cloak, securing the fabric higher up on his neck. "There. Good enough."

"Where are we going?" Keefe asked as she strode across the

room and pulled back the curtains covering his windows. Only a sliver of moon lit the lonely night sky. "Why isn't Dad coming with us?"

"Because. This is our special secret. You like secrets, right?"

She offered half a smile as he gave an enthusiastic "Yes!"

"Good. Then let's get going." She reached for the back of her head and pulled a long silver hairpin out of her twisted style. Her hair fell around her face in silky waves, softening her features. But the look in her eyes was hard as iron as she held the pin up to the window, letting the pale silver light illuminate the smooth stone set among the swirled pieces of metal.

"Is that crystal glowing?" Keefe asked, pointing to the pin's white-blue aura.

"It's not a crystal. It's a rare starstone—which is important. Someday I'll need you to remember that. But not tonight. Tonight I just need you to take my hand."

He did, his fingers looking so much smaller than hers as they twined together. A wide golden nexus covered his left wrist, glittering with dozens of diamonds.

"Concentrate," Lady Gisela said as they stepped into the starstone's glow and let the cold rush sweep them away.

The memory shifted then—picking up after the leap, at a gleaming silver door surrounded by shadows and snow. Elvin runes had been carved into the metal, forming words that looked like gibberish to Sophie.

"Where are we?" Keefe asked as an icy breeze prickled

his ears. He dropped his mom's hand and pulled his arms against his chest, trying to preserve what little warmth he could.

"It doesn't matter yet," Lady Gisela told him. "Someday this place will be the solution our world needs. But for the moment, we're just here for security. Better keep your hands out of those sleeves. It'll be easier if your fingers go numb."

"Why?"

"You'll see. And relax," she added, tapping the frown on his lips. "It'll be over fast."

"What will?"

"So many questions. Don't you trust me?"

Keefe nodded, but his eyes were focused on the way she was holding her hairpin—more like a dagger than a fashion accessory. It drew his attention to the fact that the pin had a long, twisted stem with a needle-sharp point.

"Oh please," she said as Keefe flinched back a step. "Did I raise you to be a coward?"

"No," Keefe mumbled.

"Then give me your hand."

"What are you going to do?"

"I'm going to ensure your legacy. And that kind of gift comes with a price. Now. Give. Me. Your. Hand."

"What if I don't want a legacy?"

"Everyone wants a legacy. Or would you rather prove that your father's right about you?"

The words lit a fire inside him, a burning need to meet the challenge.

"Good boy," she said as Keefe held out his shaky left hand. "Though clearly we're going to have to work on toughening you up."

"I'm tough."

"I'll believe it when I see it."

The words echoed around Keefe's mind as his mom uncurled his fingers. Sophie could see how much he wanted to pull away. But his mom's insults had done their job. He wanted to please her more than he wanted to stop her. So he held perfectly still as she pressed the point of the hairpin against the soft pad of his thumb, lingering only a second before she sliced a thick cut from the joint to the tip.

Keefe gritted his teeth through the pain as warm red pooled from the gash.

"Let it bleed for a second," she told him. "I want a pure sample."

All Keefe could do was nod. Wooziness was setting in—he'd never seen so much blood before. And the nerves around the cut stung like he'd touched acid.

"I know what you're thinking," his mom said. "You're wondering why I can't just use your DNA, like we do for everything else."

The elves normally found anything that drew blood to be barbaric.

"Blood is our life force," Lady Gisela told him. "The deep-est essence of our being. Without it, our bodies would grow still and cold. And therein lies the power. Anyone can offer up their DNA—it doesn't take guts to lick a sensor. But to paint it with blood? Now *that's* something special. Don't you feel powerful?"

All Keefe felt was hurt. And confused. And he couldn't put a finger on the other emotion, but Sophie could.

He felt betrayed.

He didn't say that, though. He nodded like the brave, obedi-ent son he knew his mom wanted him to be, letting her pull him closer to the door.

"Last step," Lady Gisela said, stretching his hand toward a clear rectangle set into the metal, right next to the handle.

Sophie expected the door to swing open as Keefe smeared his blood across the smooth panel. But a metallic click echoed through the dark instead.

A lock clicking into place.

Lady Gisela stepped back, shaking her hair out of her eyes. "Finally done."

The blood on the panel steamed, filling the air with the unsettling scent of barbeque as the red turned to ash and then crumbled away, leaving no trace.

"This is your future, Keefe," his mother told him, stretching her arms wide and gazing at the door with obvious awe. "Your legacy. Safe and secure. Until our world is ready to change."

"Change to what?" Keefe asked, cradling his wounded thumb, which was still streaming red down his wrist.

Of course his mother hadn't thought to bring him a bandage.

She didn't answer him either.

She just grabbed his elbow and held her hairpin up to the midnight sky, leaping them both back to Keefe's room.

"Starstones," she told him, twisting her hair back into its sleek style and pinning it in place, "always remember the path back to where they've been. You'll need to know that someday."

Keefe didn't care about someday.

He cared about *now*.

And now . . . his hand really hurt.

And his limbs ached from the cold. And his stomach was queasy with fear and pain.

All he wanted to do was curl up under the covers in a little ball and cry.

"So ungrateful," his mom said as she watched him stumble toward his bed. "And so melodramatic. But I suppose that's to be expected, given your age. Give me that cloak before you sit."

Keefe tossed it to her, kicking off his boots, too. He left a bloody handprint on his blanket as he pulled the covers tightly around his neck.

Lady Gisela crinkled her nose. "I'll have to find an ointment to stop that—and something to clean up that stain before your father notices."

"Whatever," Keefe mumbled, keeping his wounded hand tight to his chest.

He squeezed his eyes shut as his mom pulled out a silver Imparter.

The last thing he remembered was her brushing his hair off his forehead and whispering, "Don't worry, Keefe. The Washer will be here soon."

FORTY-TWO

SOPHIE DROPPED HER HANDS FROM Keefe's temples, severing their mental connection. But the horrible scenes kept replaying in her mind.

"Keefe, I . . ."

There were no words.

She threw her arms around his shoulders, hugging him as tight as she could. Maybe if she never let go, she could hold the broken pieces together.

"I'm pretty sure you just ruined your shoes in a huge puddle of selkie skin," Keefe told her.

"I don't care. And you don't have to do that. You don't have to make this into a joke."

"Yes, I do."

The crack in his voice splintered through her heart, and she buried her face against his shoulder, feeling tears leak onto his cloak.

"Sorry," she mumbled. "I'm not supposed to be the one crying."

"Neither of us should. It was just a stupid cut. It didn't even leave a scar."

She leaned back to look at him. "We both know it did."

Keefe turned away, watching the waves crash onto the beach. "I don't want you feeling sorry for me."

"I can't help it. But it's not pity. It's . . . I don't know what the word for it is. I'm too conflicted."

Keefe sighed. "You always are when it comes to me."

"Well, right now I mostly want to blast my way into that ogre prison and punch your mom as hard as I can in her snobby face. And then, when the blood's streaming from her nose, I want to give her some stupid speech about our life force and ask her if she feels powerful."

"Wow, who knew you had such a dark side?"

"Certain things bring it out. And this?" Her whole body trembled as her knotted emotions stirred—a monster ready to burst from her chest.

Keefe held her steady. "I appreciate the fury, Foster. But seriously. It's not worth it."

She knew he really meant *I'm not worth it.*

She hated that most of all.

"Someday I'm going to make you see how wrong you are," she promised.

"I'm just glad you're not shoving me away."

"You really thought I would?"

"Sometimes I think you'd be better off."

He tried to pull back but she refused to let go.

"I'll only be better off when you come home and I know you're safe," she whispered.

He didn't agree. But he didn't argue, either, both of them deciding to leave it at that.

"What made you remember this?" she asked.

"I didn't find her hairpin, if that's what you're thinking— and believe me, I *tried*. The memory flashed back while I was looking for that beaded necklace I gave you. She had a bunch of hairpins in her jewelry box, and one of them pricked my finger and the whole thing rushed back. After that I searched everywhere I could think of, but she either hid the pin really well, or got rid of it—or took it with her. I even endured a conversation with my dad to ask if he remembered it, but he called starstones 'plain' and said he'd never give my mom something so drab. I'm guessing that means she bought it herself."

"She probably had it custom-made. In the memory she called it a 'rare starstone.' And I'm guessing you don't know where that door she brought you to is, or what's behind it?"

"Nope. The weird thing is, I don't think the Neverseen do either. I'd figured they'd drag me there the second I joined and make me open that door. But they've never even asked me about it. So either my mom didn't tell them, or they don't realize my blood is the key."

"Or they're waiting for the right time," Sophie said.

"Why do you think I'm still with them? You get that now, right? Whatever's on the other side of that door—whatever my mom planned—she made me a part of it. And I have to believe that means I can stop it."

"What do you think is in there?"

"No idea. But nothing good ever comes from my mom."

"One thing did," she said. "One of my favorite things."

The cold, stinky wind rushed between them as he pulled away. "I hate to break it to you, Foster, but you have terrible taste in friends. You saw how I acted in that memory. What kind of loser goes along with something like that without demanding answers?"

"A boy who's been bullied and manipulated his entire life. That's how verbal abuse works. It drains you bit by bit, until there's not enough energy left to keep fighting."

"Yeah, well, I also knew she was erasing the memory—did you catch that at the end? I was nine when that happened. I definitely knew what Washers were by then. I knew what was going to happen. And I didn't stop it because I wanted to forget. I *chose* to be oblivious."

"I would've done the same thing," a crisp, accented voice said behind them.

Sophie's cheeks burned. She'd gotten so lost in the memories, she'd forgotten Fitz was watching them.

"Sorry," he mumbled. "I didn't mean to butt in. But seriously, Keefe. You make it sound like nine years old is so grown up. You were just a kid. And you know what kids do? They trust their parents—even when part of them knows that something feels off—because our parents are our world. And what do you think would've happened if you'd told your mom no? Do you think you would've gotten out of there without giving up some of your blood?"

"I take it this means you were eavesdropping on Foster's thoughts this whole time?" Keefe asked.

"Not at first. But then Sophie gasped—and when I asked if you guys were okay, you didn't respond. So I slipped past her blocking just to make sure nothing weird was happening, and . . . I couldn't stop watching. The whole time I kept asking myself how I'd feel if I'd remembered something like that—what I'd do if I knew I was part of something that feels so ominous. And I'm pretty sure the answer is, *I'd do whatever I had to do to stop it.*"

Keefe blinked hard, and Sophie didn't think it was from the sandy wind.

"Joining the Neverseen was the only thing I could think of that might help," he whispered. "I know I've made some mistakes—and I know it's going to get messier and messier. But this *is* working. I *am* learning things. That's why I had you meet me here. I won't be able to talk tonight, and I didn't want to lose a whole day. Your parents are still in danger—don't let them drop their guard. I don't know when Fintan will make his move, but I know he still has plans for them. And I found out something else this morning—something *big*. Fintan's been trying for weeks to get the ogres to meet with him to reconcile. And last night, King Dimitar finally agreed."

FORTY-THREE

ARE YOU SURE DIMITAR'S NOT agreeing to the meeting so he'll have the perfect chance to slice off Fintan's head with his extra-scary, extra-spikey sword?" Fitz asked. "Because if I were him, that's what *I'd* want to do after the way the Neverseen's plague plan backfired on him. And I'd be good with that. They're welcome to take out Alvar, too."

"I wouldn't mind if the ogres finished off Brant, either," Sophie added, trying to scrape the selkie slime off her shoe. "Same goes for anyone else that helped attack Wylie."

"Don't worry, they'll be in huge trouble for letting him get away," Keefe promised.

"Do you know how they'll be punished?" Fitz asked.

"I know it won't be fun. Alvar told me that when Brant real-ized Sophie actually *was* the girl they'd been looking for—and that Alvar messed up the day she saw him disappear—he locked Alvar in a room and set everything on fire except one square of floor in the middle. He left him roasting in there for a whole day."

"Good," Fitz said. "I hope they do even worse for this."

"That's . . . pretty dark, dude."

"So is what he let them do to Wylie."

Sophie reached for Fitz's shaky hand, wishing she knew how to peel back some of his building anger. Fury was always his mask, but if he hid too far behind it, he might lose himself.

She also couldn't stop imagining Keefe trapped in a room, surrounded by smoke and flames. "If they find out you came here . . ."

"They *know* I'm here," Keefe told her. "There's an ogre enzyme that stinks like the entire world is rotting, and I may have *accidentally* knocked a vial of it into the laundry basin while I was washing Fintan's favorite cloaks. It can only be removed with selkie skin, so they sent me to get what I need to clean up my mess."

"He's making you do his laundry?" Sophie asked.

"It's one of my chores. That's what happens when you join an organization that attacks the gnomes. We're stuck doing everything ourselves."

"And he won't be able to tell you went to Havenfield before you came here?" Fitz asked.

"Nope. I found a way to hide five seconds from my tracker. I'm pretty sure Dex would think it's the stupidest trick ever. But it works. And I used those five seconds to drop off the bead before I headed here. It was perfect."

"But all it takes is one mistake," Sophie told him. "Especially now that the ogres are back in the picture. King Dimitar will remember you from Ravagog, and I'm sure he'll try to convince Fintan that you're a traitor."

Keefe had been their distraction during the mission in the ogres' capital, pestering the king with questions and misleading information while Sophie and Fitz searched his memories.

Keefe shrugged. "I won't be getting anywhere near King Dimitar—and not just because I sometimes have nightmares about that metal underwear he walks around in. He demanded to meet with Fintan alone."

"That sounds like a really good way for Fintan to get killed by an angry ogre," Fitz noted.

"I dunno. If the meeting unravels, I think we'd have fire-roasted ogre long before we'd have a headless Fintan," Keefe told him. "*But*, I also think this is one of those 'the enemy of my enemy is my friend' kind of deals. Or is it 'my enemy isn't my enemy if they're also my enemy's enemy'?"

"You lost me," Sophie admitted.

"Yeah, the logic's kinda wonky. What I mean is, the Neverseen and the ogres both want the Council gone. And now that King Dimitar's being forced into treaty negotiations, he must be feeling pretty desperate. He *has* to know his only chance of beating the Council is with help from the Neverseen. I'm sure the Councillors have all kinds of secret defenses that Fintan knows about, since he used to be one. And Fintan has also realized that he needs the ogres' help to pull off his plans. So my guess is, he's going to offer to share his secrets with the ogres—and provide elvin backup—*if* King Dimitar works with him to overthrow the Council. I'm sure they'll turn on each other afterward, and there's no telling who would win. But it won't matter because by then everything would already be ruined."

"But didn't the ogres and the Neverseen already try teaming up for the plague?" Fitz asked. "It didn't go well."

"Right, but they didn't really *commit*, either," Keefe reminded him. "The Neverseen sat back and let the ogres do all the dirty work, and the ogres thought the plague would be enough. If they teamed up for a *real* attack, I think it would be a whole other story."

"You really think the Council could fall?" Sophie whispered.

"Yeah, I do," Keefe said. "Don't get me wrong—the Councillors are freakishly powerful. I was a little stunned at how prepared they were to stomp us when we broke in to Exile. But they're also too slow. Too blind to a lot of our problems. Too reluctant to make the hard choices. Look at how they handled the plague. They investigated a bit, called a few assemblies, and . . . that was it. *We* had to stop it—and Calla had to give up her life."

Sophie locked her arms at her sides so she wouldn't pull on her eyelashes as the Councillors' faces filled her mind. Some good. Some cruel. Some annoying. Some she didn't even know.

None of them deserved to die.

And Oralie . . .

Imagining the ethereal Councillor in the hands of the ogres—or the Neverseen—made her want to leap back to Eternalia and beg the Council to go into hiding.

But would that really keep them safe?

And what message would that send the rest of the world?

Then again, what would happen if the Council fell?

"We have to stop it," Sophie said.

She didn't know *how.* But . . . they never knew what they were doing, and somehow they always made it work.

"There's the confident Foster we all know and love!" Keefe cheered. "I bet your head is already filling up with brilliant plans."

"Not yet," she admitted. "Warning the Council seems pointless. They'll just tell us they can handle themselves."

Or worse—they'd use it as an excuse to enact some of those restrictions that Oralie had been worried about.

"Maybe the Black Swan will have some ideas," Fitz said.

"Because they had so many awesome ideas for what to do about Wylie?" Sophie countered.

"Any chance you've manifested some new abilities that could solve all of our problems in one fell swoop?" Keefe asked Sophie.

"No—and I don't know why you keep thinking I'm going to. Wouldn't the Black Swan have triggered it when they triggered my other ones?"

"Uh, this is the Black Swan we're talking about," Keefe argued. "They take a million years to do anything—and just so you know, I'm rooting for Phaser. Think of how much havoc you could cause if you could walk through walls."

"Shouldn't we be trying to come up with an actual plan?" Fitz asked. "Instead of putting all the pressure on Sophie?"

"But Foster's always the one who figures it out. You just gotta give that fancy brain of hers a second to work."

"That's not true. I . . ." Sophie's words trailed off as an idea started to take shape.

Keefe grinned. "Go ahead, Foster. Amaze us."

She stared at the black sludge trickling across the sand. "It's not a full plan yet. But the ogres and the Neverseen already have a precarious relationship, right? So what if we do something to push it over the edge, and make sure they never trust each other again?"

"See?" Keefe said. "Told you she'd solve it. Maybe we'll get our wish and they'll destroy each other in the process. So what are you thinking? Convince Dimitar that Fintan told everyone Dimitar's butt looks dimply in those metal undies? Or maybe we fill Fintan's bedroom with those nasty ogre plants Lady Cadence used to make us peel in detention—what were they called? Curdleroots?—and he'll be like, 'Oh no Dimitar didn't—it's *on!*'"

"Do you even know where any of the Neverseen's other hideouts are?" Sophie asked.

"Wait," Fitz said. "Are you actually considering those plans?"

"No, they're totally insane. But if we're going to come up with something better, we need to know what we have to work with, like who we have access to, and how much time we have. Do you think you can find out when and where King Dimitar and Fintan are going to meet?" she asked Keefe. "Because if we can cause something to go wrong during that meeting, they'll each think the other set a trap."

"I . . . don't know. One thing I've learned as New Kid in the Evil Rebellion—it's not a good idea to ask too many questions. And I've been trying to save them to find out how to steal the caches."

"The caches *are* important," Sophie said. "But this has a bigger time crunch. It sounded like the Peace Summit is coming up quick, and I'm assuming they'll be meeting before then."

"Yeah, I guess that makes sense," Keefe said, shaking the sand off his cloak. "I'll see if I can find a way to bring the ogres up during my next empathy lesson. Maybe the fact that Fintan's going to be angry at everyone for botching the Wylie thing will make him a little more willing to open up to me."

"Be careful," Sophie begged, still imagining fiery punishments. "None of this is worth what they'll do to you if they figure out you're helping us."

"I got this," Keefe said, ducking behind the rocks he'd been leaning on when they arrived. He returned carrying a sludgy, stinky bucket. "I'd better get back. I'm sure the person meeting me at the rendezvous point is there by now."

"I think we should check in more than once a day from now on," Sophie told him as he fished out a simple blue crystal. "That way you won't have to try to slip away again. Is there another time that's safe to talk?"

"I get a breakfast break around sunrise, and a dinner break around sunset, so we could go with either of those times. Or both. But no check-ins tonight. I'm supposed to have a special skill lesson with Ruy—and even if that's changed, I should probably lie low."

"Tomorrow morning, then," Sophie said, trying not to think about how early she'd be waking up from now on.

"Woo-hoo for bonus Keefoster time! Try not to get jealous, Fitzy. She still likes you better than me—but someday I *will* wear her down. I'm sneaky like that."

"Not sneaky enough!" a voice growled behind them.

Sophie's panic mixed with dread when she realized the voice was high-pitched and squeaky.

Sure enough, when she turned around, she found Sandor, Grizel, Alden, and Grady glaring at them.

"Uh-oh—that's my cue," Keefe said, his eyes on his feet as he moved his crystal to the light and disappeared through the path.

Grady's lips pressed into a rigid line, parting enough to only release one word.

"Grounded."

Alden added, "For the rest of eternity."

FORTY-FOUR

GRADY MADE GOOD ON HIS THREAT, sending Sophie to her room the second they got back to Havenfield and informing her that she wouldn't be leaving the house again until her ears turned pointy.

Even after she'd warned him about the alliance between the Neverseen and ogres.

Even after she'd explained the plan they were working on to prevent it.

Even after she'd shared Keefe's darkest memory to help prove he was trustworthy.

Reasoning with Grady was sometimes like giving Verdi something new to eat.

And from the look in Alden's eyes as he dragged Fitz back to Everglen, she had no doubt Fitz was meeting the same fate—though Grizel's lecture would surely be less brutal than Sandor's. Sandor's stretched on for an hour and seventeen minutes—and yes, Sophie counted. He ranted for so long, her butt went numb—and she was sitting on her very soft, very comfortable bed.

Apparently Alden had come to Havenfield after Grady told him about Cyrah, and they'd gone upstairs to ask Sophie a few follow-up questions. Cue massive chaos when they found her note on the bed. They'd hailed Sandor to have him find her through the emergency trackers hidden in her clothes, and Grizel had insisted on coming along, since Fitz was her charge.

"Don't tell me you were careful," Sandor ordered when his speech finally wound down. "If you were careful, you would've waited for me. After what just happened to Wylie—"

"Keefe wasn't a part of that," she interrupted. "And they needed you at Foxfire, trying to figure out how the Neverseen got into the Silver Tower—not wasting time on me."

"Protecting you will *never* be a waste of time. You've also proven that you can't be left without supervision, so Lur and Mitya are taking over the search at the tower. Gnomish senses aren't quite as keen, but they'll be able to work much faster. And you will not leave my side from this moment forward—I don't care what any cute boys leave on your pillow."

Sophie's cheeks burned. "It wasn't about *that*. He—"

Sandor held up his hands. "Whatever your reasons, the answer will forever remain, *I go where you go.*"

"Which means you'll be seeing a lot of these walls," Grady said as he stalked into the room with Edaline. Sophie opened her mouth to argue, but he held up his hand. "We'll discuss it in the morning. Right now, I want you to eat some dinner and go to sleep."

Edaline snapped her fingers, conjuring up a tray of something neon orange and gloopy. Fortunately, elvin food always tasted better than it looked.

Sophie sighed as they each kissed her on the cheek and closed her in her room with Sandor guarding the door. If they were freaking out this much about her sneaking off to meet with Keefe, she couldn't imagine what they'd do if they found out she'd *also* visited Eternalia. . . .

You okay? she transmitted, stretching out her mind to Fitz after she'd eaten and showered and climbed into bed.

Yeah. I'm good. Though Grizel says I'm now required to participate in Sandor's dancing humiliation. There was lots of talk of matching silver pants.

Sophie giggled. *Maybe you and Sandor can work out some choreography.*

Hey—if I have to dance, you are SO dancing with me. In the frilliest, sparkliest gown Biana can find in her closet. And heels.

She knew Fitz was only teasing—but the idea sounded . . . interesting. Well, the dancing part—not the stupid dress.

What about you? he asked. *How bad is the punishment?*

I'm still awaiting sentencing.

Yikes. Waiting's the worst. Sorry.

No—I'm sorry. I'm the one who got you into this.

Nah, I chose to go. And I'm glad I did. I think I finally get where Keefe's coming from. That memory . . .

I know. I'm pretty sure I'll be having nightmares about it for a while. Though that's still less terrifying than imagining what'll happen to him if he gets caught.

Seriously, I think you were right when you told me that we're probably going to have to figure out a way to save him by the end of this. I mean, this isn't the kind of thing he can just walk away from. If he tries to leave, they will *come after him—and that's assuming he gets out before they figure out what he's doing.*

Sophie reached for Ella. *How do we save him when we don't even know where he is?*

No idea, Fitz admitted. *But . . . Keefe is dead-on about one thing. You do always find the solution.*

Gee—no pressure there.

I know. I promise, I'll do everything I can to help. I just meant . . . try not to stress about it too much. If we really need to help him, you'll figure it out.

How can you be so sure?

She could almost feel the warmth of his smile radiating through the connection between them as he told her, *Because you're Sophie Foster. That's what you do.*

. . .

"Well, at least you obeyed one thing I told you," Grady said, startling Sophie awake. "I think this is the latest you've slept as long as you've lived here—without sedatives, at least."

Sophie rubbed her eyes. "What time is it?"

"Lunchtime."

"LUNCHTIME?" Sophie groaned as he opened her shades, flooding the room with sunlight. "Ugh—I slept through my check-in with Keefe."

"Good," Grady said.

"No—not good. Now I can't make sure he's okay until dinnertime."

"You should be more worried about *you*. We need to discuss your punishment."

Sophie sighed and sat up, twisting her Sucker Punch bracelet. "I'm sorry I worried you. But . . . Fitz and I weren't actually *in* danger."

"Every minute you spend with That Boy is dangerous," Grady insisted. "If he wants to risk his own life—that's his choice. But I'm not letting him drag you—or Fitz—down with him."

"He's not dragging us down—he gave us crucial information. Why can't you see that?"

"Actually, I can. I was up late giving Mr. Forkle a thorough update on everything you told me. He's asked you to record all of your memories—especially the one about that door. And the whole Collective will be brainstorming ways to prevent this new alliance from forming. They think your plan to sabotage Dimitar and Fintan's meeting is very clever. But none of that changes the fact that you met up with a member of the Neverseen without permission and without protection—that's never going to be okay."

"Neither is grounding me for meeting with a *friend*," Sophie argued. "Especially since I left a note!"

"Yeah, let's talk about that." Grady scooted her lunch tray closer. "Your mom and I were right downstairs. You could've told us what you were doing. But you chose to scribble a hasty message and sneak away. Why do you think that is?"

Sophie hated when he made good points.

"I didn't have time to deal with anyone trying to stop me," she mumbled. "I know you guys want to keep me safe—but Keefe is putting his life on the line to help us. So . . . if he gives me instructions, I'm going to follow them—grounding or no. Same goes for whatever plan we come up with to ruin the ogre–Neverseen meeting—and if the Black Swan need me to search more of Wylie's memories, or to check on Prentice, or meet with Gethen, or—"

"I'm aware that you might find some extenuating circumstances," Grady interrupted. "In fact, I've already assured Mr. Forkle that if something urgent comes up, all he has to do is hail me. I'd prefer he bring the problem here, but if he can't, I'll allow you to go *with Sandor*."

"And I will ensure that you come home immediately after," Sandor said from the doorway.

"I'm also still going to let you have *this*"—Grady handed her a wrapped parcel—"so that you'll have a way to stay connected to your friends and the Black Swan."

Sophie peeled back the thick paper and found a new Imparter along with the black case Mr. Forkle had put Keefe's Imparter in.

"It's still in there," Grady explained. "The Black Swan's Technopath couldn't trace the signal either."

Her shoulders slumped.

"Yeah, I know. I was hoping we'd learn something from it too. But try to remember that a dead end is better than any of the awful things that could've happened if that listening device had still been active. The Black Swan locked the case so you can't open it. You're welcome to throw it away, or smash the whole thing into itty-bitty pieces—"

"I'd be *happy* to crush it for you," Sandor offered. "But Mr. Forkle suspected you'd want to hang on to it."

She did—even though she knew it was silly. Somehow knowing the Imparter still existed made it feel like she might someday discover a secret from it.

"I'm not going to put any restrictions on who you're allowed to contact," Grady added. "And I'm willing to let you have your friends visit to work on projects. Despite what you may be thinking, I'm not grounding you because I'm angry. I'm just trying to protect you—even if it means being annoying. I know you're the moonlark. I'd like to think I've been pretty support-ive. Didn't I let you fly off with Silveny to get your abilities fixed? And didn't I let you run away to join the Black Swan? If you think any of that was easy for me, you overestimate my inner calm. Most days, I want to grab you and Edaline and find somewhere safe to hide until all of this is over. But I know that's not what you want—and I'm proud of you for being so ready to accept your responsibilities. I just need you to remember that you're also my daughter, and I'd like to keep you alive."

"Okay, but . . ."

"But what?" Grady asked, when she didn't finish.

Sophie stared at the crystal stars that dangled over her bed. "If I hadn't gone to meet with Keefe, would you have gotten so angry?"

"I'm not sure what you're getting at, kiddo."

"I *mean*, if I'd snuck out with Dex or Biana to do something for the Black Swan—or if Fitz and I had left to do some Cog-nate training—would you have grounded me like this?"

"Of course," Sandor said.

Grady didn't look as sure. "That's not a fair question. None of them are actively involved with our enemies. And none of them have ever sent you home in a panicked, sobbing heap after betraying you."

"Uh, Biana and I had that huge fight at Foxfire a few months back, remember? I ran home crying and went to the cave to be alone and ended up getting kidnapped—not that Biana had anything to do with *that*. And Fitz blamed me for what happened to Alden and said all kinds of mean things that made me cry. And that ability restrictor Dex made for the Council was one of the most painful, humiliating things I've ever been through."

"So you want me to be mad at all of your friends?" Grady asked.

"No—I want to know why you're so much harder on Keefe. Now that you know what he's been through . . . why won't you cut him some slack?"

Grady let out a sigh that seemed to drain all the air from his body. "Okay, if you want to have this conversation, I guess we can."

"What conversation?" Sophie asked.

Grady raised an eyebrow. "About boys."

FORTY-FIVE

BOYS?" SOPHIE REPEATED, TRYING TO come up with any other meaning for the word besides the one Grady's raised eyebrow implied.

"Yeah, it's always awkward to talk about this stuff with your parents," he told her. "But remember, I went through this with Jolie. I know it's not easy dealing with . . . feelings."

"He means crushes," Sandor clarified, just to add the final nail to her coffin of misery.

"Ugggggggggggggghhhhhhh—seriously, *why* are we talking about this?" Sophie asked, wondering if she could slip past Sandor if she sprinted for the door.

Sandor and Grady shared a look.

"We're talking about it because you asked why I'm harder on That B—on *Keefe*," Grady said.

"He seems to be *special* to you," Sandor added. "And he also happens to be a very good-looking boy—for an elf."

"THIS IS THE WORST EVER!" Sophie shouted, flopping back on her bed and pulling her hair over her face to hide.

"I'm right there with you, kiddo. If I had my way, you wouldn't get your match lists until you're at least a hundred. *But* even if I got my wish on that, I also know that feelings . . . happen."

"Well, they're not happening here. He's. My. *Friend*."

"That's often how it starts," Sandor said. "And then the friendship turns to teasing and the teasing turns to flirting and—"

"Yeah, but this is Keefe," Sophie interrupted. "In case you haven't noticed, he teases *everyone*. It doesn't mean anything. Especially with me."

"You really believe that, don't you?" Grady asked, glancing at Sandor when she nodded.

"If you guys look at each other like that again I'm going to punch you," Sophie warned. "And I'm still wearing my Sucker Punch!"

"Look at each other like what?" Sandor asked.

"Like . . . *Isn't she cute?*"

"You *are* cute." Grady took both of her hands and pulled her back to a sitting position. "And you're sure there's nothing you want to tell me? I promise I won't freak out."

"Kinda sounds like you would. *Not* that it matters, but aren't you basically telling me that you don't approve of Keefe? Isn't that why I'm grounded?"

"You're grounded because you nearly gave me a panic melt-down," Grady told her. "And it's not about *approval*. This is your life. You'll get to choose who you share it with. But I will say this: *Anyone* who wants to be special to you should have to prove that they deserve you. Not just Keefe—though he'll definitely have more of an uphill battle. I'd be saying the same thing if we were talking about someone else. Like . . . oh . . . I don't know. Dex? Or Fitz?"

Sophie buried her face in her hands. "Someone please kill me now."

"Uh-oh, that doesn't sound good," Edaline said as she crossed the bedroom to join them. "Do I want to know what you guys are talking about?"

"Boys," Sandor and Grady said at the same time.

"That's what I was afraid of." Edaline sat on Sophie's other side and patted her knee. "If it helps, he drove Jolie just as crazy. You should ask Vertina to share some of the horror stories."

"There's nothing wrong with making sure Sophie knows that we have high expectations for anyone she chooses," Grady said. "Another thing to keep in mind, kiddo: Whenever you start to narrow it down, I *will* be having a looooooooooooooooong conversation with him."

"Please tell me he's joking," Sophie whined to Edaline.

"Don't worry, we'll come up with a plan of attack before your first Winnowing Gala," Edaline promised.

"I have a feeling I'm *really* going to regret this question," Sophie mumbled. "But . . . what's a Winnowing Gala?"

Edaline smiled. "Whenever you pick up a new match list, it's customary to hold a party and invite everyone on the list to come, so you can start narrowing down who you might actually be interested in. We never held one for Jolie, because her mind was already made up. But if you're less decided, the gala can be a fun way to start figuring it out. I know all of this probably feels huge and embarrassing, and I promise we don't have to talk about it any more for now. But I do want to make sure you know that Grady and I will support whoever you choose."

She glared at Grady until he agreed.

"And now, we'll change the subject to something that won't make you want to tug out all of your eyelashes," Edaline said, handing Sophie a thin curled-up scroll. "This is your schedule for the Council's new skill training program. Looks like you're part of the Wednesday morning group, so you'll get a break from your grounding at least once a week. And my sister told me that Magnate Leto made sure all of your friends are in the same group."

"What group are you guys in?" Sophie asked.

"None for the moment. Our house arrest continues." She kissed Sophie's cheek before she stood and straightened the fabric of her simple blue-and-white gown.

"Are you heading out?" Grady asked.

Edaline nodded. "The gnomes told me they'd have dinner waiting for you in the kitchen, since I'll probably be home late."

"Wait, you're leaving?" Sophie asked. "I thought you just said you're on house arrest."

"I am. But I'm sneaking out to Alluveterre, where there's plenty of security to protect me. Juline made the arrangements. She didn't want to at first, but she's feeling very guilty for all the things she's hidden from me over the years."

"As she should," Grady grumbled.

Edaline took his hand. "We both know we spent the majority of that time misunderstanding the Black Swan and their role in what happened to our daughter."

Grady had once believed that the Black Swan killed Jolie to punish him for resisting their efforts to recruit him.

"Why are you going to Alluveterre?" Sophie asked.

"I need to visit Wylie. I owe it to Cyrah to try to help her son. I owed her that years ago and wasn't strong enough to fulfill it. But I'm hoping it's better late than never."

"If there's anything I can do . . . ," Sophie said.

"I promise I'll let you know." She kissed Sophie's cheek before she left with Grady, the two of them heading upstairs to the Leapmaster.

"And where do you think you're going?" Sandor asked as Sophie made her way across the room.

She pointed to her bathroom. "Am I supposed to stay in my pajamas forever?"

"I suppose not. I'll give you privacy to use the bathroom and get changed. But otherwise, consider us joined at the hip."

"Well," Sophie said, flashing her most mocking smile, "at least that means I'll get to be there for all the dancing."

Sandor grumbled under his breath as she swung her hips like Grizel.

"I think she likes you," she called through the door after she'd closed it in his face. She'd expected Sandor to deny it, but he let out a squeaky sigh.

"Grizel has gone to dramatic lengths to make that abundantly clear. She and I grew up together, and everyone assumed we'd someday settle. I'm fairly certain I'm the reason Grizel joined the elvin regiments, even though she'd been offered a position in our queen's royal guard."

The idea of a goblin queen was *almost* enough to distract Sophie—but not quite.

She finished changing and left the bathroom. "So . . . I take it that means you're not interested?"

"Interest has nothing to do with it."

"Does that mean you are? Because I actually think you two could be super cute together!"

"I can assure you, we wouldn't be," Sandor said, shadowing her as she retrieved her memory log from her desk and headed for her bed. "And I love how you're suddenly the expert on all things romantic. Moments ago you proved yourself exceptionally clueless."

"I'm not clueless. I'm . . . realistic."

"As am I. The reality is that I have no time for a companion, nor do I have need of one. I'm far better suited as a warrior than a husband. I've told Grizel as much—several times. And *that* is the end of any discussion of my love life."

"I can't believe you *have* a love life," Sophie admitted. "Talk about a mind blow."

"And why is that?" Sandor huffed. "I'll have you know that among my species I am *quite* the specimen."

Sophie giggled. "Man, I wish Keefe had been here to hear you say that."

"Interesting that he was the first boy you thought of."

"Only because he'd start calling you Specimen Sandor. I'll be sure to tell him during our next check-in."

"I'm sure you will," Sandor said. "And on that note, I'll leave you to record your memories. But I'm *right* outside should you have the slightest notion of leaving."

He marched to his usual post, and Sophie slipped under the blankets and opened her memory log. Alden had given her the familiar teal book with the silver moonlark on the cover after she'd discovered that the Black Swan had hidden secrets in her brain, so she'd have a way to keep track of any that triggered. And as she flipped through the pages, it was crazy to see how long it'd been since she'd recorded any of those kinds of discoveries. For months, everything she'd projected were clues and secrets she'd found on her own.

She closed her eyes and slowly projected everything Keefe had shown her, zooming in on the details that seemed most important, like Lady Gisela's hairpin. The silver-white stone was smooth and oval, but when the light hit it, thin veins of blue shot through in an asterisk pattern.

"Dinnertime!" Grady said, making her jump as he crossed her room carrying a tray with a bottle of lushberry juice and a bowl of what looked like pink spaghetti.

"Already?" Sophie glanced out her windows and sure enough, the sun was setting. "Ugh—I almost missed my check-in with Keefe. These are going to be hard to remember."

"I think I'll sit right here, in case you learn anything important from him," Grady told her, plopping down next to her on the bed and setting the tray in her lap.

Sophie was positive his real motive involved a whole lot of spying. But she closed her eyes and pretended he wasn't there as she stretched out her mind.

Really bad time right now, Keefe told her.

You're okay, though, right?

Yeah, I just need to pay attention.

She could feel his mind trying to close down and concentrate, so she didn't ask any more questions. But a sour taste coated her tongue.

"He can't talk right now," she told Grady as she pushed the tray of food away.

"If he was in danger, I'm sure he would've told you," Grady

said, nudging her dinner back into her lap. "At least try a few bites. Flori told me it's a rare fruit called threadleens, and she grew them especially for you. When did you guys start talking?"

Sophie stirred her dinner, hoping Grady wouldn't notice that she didn't answer. "Did you know she's Calla's niece?"

Grady nodded. "I swear the Panakes sprouts twice as many blossoms every time Flori sings."

Sophie smiled as she pictured that, and she took a small bite of the pink strings—and while it definitely wasn't as delicious as starkflower stew, it tasted spicy and tangy and made her want to keep eating.

Grady scooped up her memory log as she took another forkful. "Is this the pin Keefe's mom cut him with?"

"Yeah—any idea where Lady Gisela would've bought it?"

"Not really. Lots of places make hairpins with starstones—though I'm pretty sure the stones usually flash with green veins."

"She told Keefe it was rare."

"Well, I'll ask some of the jewelers I know in Atlantis, but I'm betting whoever made it won't admit it. See how there aren't any etchings on the metal? Most artists leave a craftsman mark, like a signature."

He flipped to the next page, which showed a wide view of the door—the cold metal surrounded by snow and shadows.

"The star only rises at Nightfall," he mumbled, pointing to the runes carved into the doorframe. "That's what these say."

Sophie repeated the phrase. "Do you think it's a riddle?"

"Riddles usually lead to a *What am I?* But I'm sure the word 'star' isn't a coincidence."

"Could it be a quote from something, then? Like how the Black Swan used 'follow the pretty bird across the sky' from that old dwarven poem?"

"If it is, I've never heard it before. But I'm definitely not an expert on those kinds of things. Maybe the Collective can show it to their dwarves to see if it sounds familiar."

Sophie hoped they would—though she was pretty sure she could guess at least part of the meaning.

Whatever Lady Gisela had built.

Whatever she'd locked away with Keefe's blood.

It was going to make the world a much darker place.

FORTY-SIX

PLEASE TELL ME YOU'VE LEARNED *something we can use*, Sophie transmitted as soon as the first rays of dawn sliced through her bedroom.

Well, good morning to you too, Keefe thought. *Is this how these extra check-ins are going to be? No 'hello'? No 'I missed you'? No 'I can't stop thinking about you'?—and don't even* try *denying that last one.*

Sadly, she couldn't—but not for the reason he was teasing. He'd told her during their final check-in the night before that he'd heard Fintan get an urgent hail on his Imparter and use the word "escaped" during the conversation. But when she'd asked if that meant they were planning something for Wylie, Keefe had to go because Alvar and Ruy were fighting.

You're so cute when you worry, he told her.

Sophie grit her teeth. *Be very glad I haven't figured out how to mentally smack you. It's on my list of goals.*

Fine. Forgive me for trying to have a little fun after yesterday's drama. I guess Fintan's blaming Ruy and Brant for Wylie's escape, since Brant burned one of Wylie's bonds, and Ruy was the one who was supposed to clear out all of Wylie's pockets. Brant doesn't seem to care, but Ruy's flipping out because Fintan's threatening to change their role in some big project coming up—and no, I don't know what the project is. So Ruy spent most of last night trying to convince Alvar to say that all four of them share the blame for what happened, and Alvar won't.

No honor among criminals, huh?

Nope, Alvar's all about watching his own back. So Ruy left to try to talk Trix and Umber into it. I'm assuming that means I was right and Umber was the fourth kidnapper.

Did you ever tell me what her ability is?

I probably forgot. She's a Shade. A freakishly powerful one. She puts Bangs Boy to shame—and she doesn't have stupid hair.

I thought she always hid under her cloak.

She does. But as the crowned king of good-hair land, I can tell when I'm talking to one of my rightful subjects.

That might be the most ridiculous thing you've ever said.

Doesn't mean it's not true. How else would I know that you have an adorable case of bed hair right now?

I do not!

But when she patted her hair, she was pretty sure the whole pineapple-head situation was back. She burrowed deeper under her covers. *Did you learn anything else?*

Just that it's a bad time to be asking questions. But after everyone went to sleep, I tore open the seam in my cloak and found another black disk right where you said it would be.

Did it have a different piece of the symbol on it?

Nope, it's the same marking. And I snuck out of bed and checked all the doors to see if I could figure out what the disk does. But so far no luck.

So basically . . . we lost a whole day and learned nothing.

Whoa—when did you become Little Miss Negativity?

I'm just sick of all these vague bits of information. You're sleeping under the same roof as the enemy, and we still have no idea what they're planning.

I know. I'm working on it. We just have to be—

If you say "patient," I'm ending this conversation.

Yeah, I sound like the Forklenator—and don't go into shock, but . . . I think I'm starting to understand what he means. Look at what happened with Wylie. The Neverseen made their move, and they botched it. And now the Black Swan will make sure they never get another shot at it.

Uh . . . isn't that good?

For us, yeah. But not for the Neverseen. That's the thing—if Fintan gets too suspicious of me, I'll ruin my chance and that'll be it. So I have to make sure I wait until the time is right.

Wow, who are you and what have you done with Keefe Sencen?

Is all of this wisdom killing my cool cred?

A little. But . . . wise Keefe has a way better shot of getting out of this alive.

Oh, I'm getting out of this—unless the food here kills me. These kernalfruits we just harvested taste like banshee droppings. Next time I fake-join an evil organization, remind me to choose one that hasn't angered the gnomes, okay?

She could see the shriveled green fruit in his mind, and it looked like a cross between a pomegranate and an ear of corn—which wouldn't have been *that* bad, if the grains of fruit hadn't been coated in a black powder that looked way too much like mold.

How about you go get something good from the kitchen and describe it as you eat it? he asked.

Yeah, I'm not going to do that.

Aw, come on, Foster—I'm starving here!

He spent the rest of their conversation recounting the horrible things he'd had to eat over the last few weeks.

The whining resumed that night, during their dinner check-in—though Sophie couldn't blame him. Keefe's meal consisted of slimy, withered leaves that tasted like sneeze.

I'll keep snacks in my pocket, she promised. *That way if we meet up again, I can share.*

As if I needed another reason to wish you were here.

Shouldn't you be wishing you were here—where the food is good and there aren't any crazy murderers running free?

That does sound nice. But the crazy murderers are useful. I learned something from Fintan today—not what I was hoping to find out, but it's still important. He started venting about Brant and Ruy, and how frustrating it is to work with people who disappoint him again and again. And then he said he's counting on me to live up to my potential.

Potential for what?

He didn't say. But I took a chance and asked if he wanted me to do the Empath-lie-detector thing when he meets with King Dimitar. I told him I was worried the ogres were going to double-cross us, and he seemed impressed that I was thinking about things like that. He said it's good to see that I care so strongly about his vision—and of course he didn't say what his vision is. But he draped his arm around my shoulders—

UGH!

Yeah—I wanted to shove him away, trust me. But I held still and listened while he told me he's worried about the ogres too. And then he said that he gave King Dimitar an assignment to prove they can work together—kind of like a test.

Sophie sat up straighter. *That's perfect! We need to find out what that test is and make sure the ogres fail!*

Working on it, Keefe promised. *But I'm assuming whatever the ogres are up to will involve someone getting hurt, so no ditching Gigantor, okay?*

Like I could. Did I mention you got me grounded? I've been stuck in my room all day with nothing to do except stare at my memory log. And Sandor's standing next to me right now, telling me he wants to know everything you're saying.

Aw, give him a kiss for me—and I'm not saying that to be a brat. I'm seriously glad he's there to protect you. Everyone else has a bodyguard, right? Fitz? Biana? Dex? Grady? Edaline? Alden? Della?

Everyone except Alden and Della. But they rarely leave their house, so they're safe.

I don't know. The gates at Everglen are designed to block people from light leaping in. That won't stop ogres from popping out of the ground.

She closed her eyes, trying to squeeze out the nightmare scene Keefe had just painted. *I'll ask the Collective to send some additional guards for the Vackers—maybe dwarves, so the Neverseen won't notice any changes if they're watching. I swear, at this rate, our group has more security than the Council. Seems unfair, doesn't it?*

What do you mean?

I don't know. It's just . . . we spent hours prepping Havenfield to keep my family safe—and while we were doing that, the Neverseen snatched Wylie out of his room and tortured him.

I'm so sorry I messed that up. I'd heard them talk so much about your family that when Fintan said we were ready to shift to the next phase, I thought—

The next phase of what? Sophie interrupted.

The Lodestar Initiative.

Wait. Whatever they're planning to do to my family is part of the Lodestar Initiative? I thought the Neverseen only wanted to take them so they could control me.

That's probably part of it. But it's starting to feel like they're doing some sort of . . . gathering. It's almost like Fintan has this list of people and information he needs, and he's checking them off one by one.

Sophie's mind flashed to the cell Dex had been held in at the Paris hideout.

Was this what the room had been meant for?

You okay over there? Keefe asked. *You've gone quiet on me.*

I'm just trying to think. Is Wylie's kidnapping—and maybe his mom's death—also part of the Lodestar Initiative?

That's what I'm assuming.

He made it sound so obvious—and maybe it was. But Sophie hadn't considered the connection. Her brain throbbed under the weight of a thousand new questions.

How's Wylie doing by the way? Keefe asked.

About the same. Edaline saw him yesterday and said his wounds looked healed, but his thoughts were still so dark that they're going to keep him sedated for at least another day.

And they don't want to erase his memories?

Wylie told us not to. He wants to make sure we don't get rid of anything that could help us find out what happened to his mom.

That's . . . very brave.

Keefe's mind flashed to his nine-year-old self, curled up in a ball under the covers as he waited for the Washer to come erase his memories.

You can't compare the two, Sophie told him.

He didn't agree. But Keefe stuffed the memory away, his mind practically forcing a smile as he told her, *Fintan's supposed to come to this hideout tonight for a strategy meeting, so it's probably not a good idea to do another check-in until tomorrow morning. And be prepared for some breakfast whining. We harvested something called yolksnips today—and they smelled exactly like Iggy farts.*

Apparently they tasted like them too. But Keefe barely mentioned them when Sophie connected with his mind at daybreak. He was too excited to share his news.

He still hadn't learned anything about the test for the ogres, or Wylie, or the plan for Grady and Edaline, or Brant and Ruy's punishment, or Fintan's cache, or any of the things that had kept Sophie up most of the night.

BUT, Keefe said, his mental voice so loud, it echoed around her head. *I've finally been granted clearance to move into one of their other hideouts. You're now talking to a fully initiated member of the Neverseen!*

FORTY-SEVEN

OES THAT MEAN KEEFE SWORE
an oath?" Fitz asked, careful to keep his voice
low in the crowded Foxfire field. "Like we did
when we were accepted into the Black Swan?"

"I was afraid to ask," Sophie admitted.

She glanced around, relieved to find everyone too distracted
by the proceedings to pay attention to her group of friends—
and their bodyguards. Still, she huddled closer to Fitz, Dex,
Biana, Tam, and Linh as she added, "He said he'll be settled at
the new hideout this afternoon."

The crowd surged forward as another batch of people moved
to take their test, halting their conversation. It was the first
day of their Exillium skill training, and while Sophie and her

friends already knew their Hemispheres, everyone else was being sorted by a written exam before being given a black cape marked with a colored handprint on the back.

Red for the Left Hemisphere, blue for the Right, and purple for the Ambis.

The three Exillium tents bore the same colors. And after so many years of scorn and judgment, it seemed strangely reassuring to have the vibrant canopies stationed proudly around the glass pyramid.

Still, Sophie found her eyes constantly drifting to the twisted gold and silver elite towers. The Black Swan had stuck to their plan and kept Wylie's assault a secret, so no one around them had any idea about the added danger. Even with dozens of goblins stationed among the crowd—even with a fleet of dwarves secretly positioned under their feet—Lur and Mitya had yet to figure out how the Neverseen had gotten inside the tower. So the rebels still had a secret way to invade the campus.

"Maybe the Neverseen use a vague oath," Linh whispered when the crowd settled again. "Like the one the Black Swan had us say."

"Hopefully," Biana said. "And wait—does that mean you guys swore fealty?"

Both twins revealed the swan-shaped monocle pendants they'd tucked under their tunics.

"I was sick of Linh nagging me," Tam said, earning an eye

roll from his sister, and a sudden splash of water to the face. "Oh, it is *so* on later."

"Ready any time you are," Linh told him, tossing another sphere of water back and forth from palm to palm.

"Wow," Fitz whispered, as Dex leaned closer.

"Are we sure this is a good thing?" he asked. "Not the part about you guys joining the Black Swan—that's *awesome*. But the whole 'Keefe going to one of their serious hideouts' thing. Is he sure they won't lock him away like they did to his mom?"

"I asked him the same question," Sophie said. "And he promised he's keeping a close read on everyone's emotions. He said he'll bail if he senses anything suspicious."

"But *how* does he bail?" Biana asked. "They're not going to let him walk away now."

Fitz shared a look with Sophie. "We may have to help him get out of there—but we can't come up with a plan until we know more about where he is. So right now, we're just hoping he's being careful."

Tam snorted. "Zero chance of that."

"Probably," Sophie whispered. "But he's taking this crazy risk to help us. So we need to get the most out of it that we can."

"You told him to watch for shadows on the floor of the hideout, right?" Tam asked. "To see if they use an illuminated symbol like the one in Paris?"

Sophie nodded. "Keefe has a photographic memory. So I

told him to make sure he takes a good look at *everything*. Then he'll share it with me and I'll project it all on paper so you can check the shadows. But you'll have to come to Havenfield to see it. I'm still grounded."

Biana grinned. "So is Fitz. My dad told him he's not allowed to go anywhere until he finishes his matchmaking packet."

"Too bad for him, I finished it yesterday," Fitz said smugly.

"You did?" Sophie, Biana, Dex, and Linh asked at the same time.

Fitz shrugged. "It's not like it's hard. I just had to answer some personal questions."

"A *lot* of them," Biana said. "Aren't you worried that if you rush through, you won't give very good answers?"

"Nah. I know what I like. Besides, the questions aren't what you'd think they'd be. Sure, they ask what you find attractive, and what personality traits you like and stuff. But then it gets into all kinds of things about your genetics and abilities, and finishes with a ton of questions that are just . . . *deep*. It's like they're trying to get to know you on another level—which I guess makes sense, since we fill out the packets when we're sixteen. Our likes and dislikes are probably going to change, so they're trying to figure out the *real* us."

"You're sixteen?" Linh asked.

Dex mumbled something about Fitz being super old as Biana turned to Tam. "I don't think you guys ever told us how old you are."

Both twins had to think for a second.

"Pretty sure we're fifteen," Linh said. "It's hard to remember, thanks to my father. He was always trying to convince us that we had our inception date wrong."

"Good old Dad," Tam muttered, scanning the crowd, like he was checking to make sure his parents weren't there. "Uh, do you guys know that girl off to the right? She's staring at us pretty hard."

All of their goblins reached for their swords.

"Relax—it's just Marella," Sophie told them, dropping her voice before she added, "She's the one whose mom saw Cyrah the day she faded."

"And she's not staring at *us*," Biana corrected. "She's checking out Tam."

Tam's eyebrows shot up, and he stole another glance. Marella tossed her long blond hair—which always had a few tiny braids woven in—and gave him her flirtiest smile.

"Huh," he said.

"That's all you have to say?" Biana pressed.

"I don't know." Tam blushed brighter than Sophie would've thought possible, given his general surly demeanor. "What am I supposed to say?"

"She's not his type," Linh jumped in. "He likes brunettes."

"Gross, why do you know that?" Tam asked.

Linh smirked. "Because you're not as sly as you think."

"Is anyone else wondering why Marella's not hanging out

with Stina anymore?" Sophie asked, rescuing Tam with a subject change.

"Stina's the tall girl over there," Biana explained to the twins, tilting her head to where Stina's unruly curls stuck out above the crowd. "Her dad works with the Black Swan, so you'd *think* she'd be nice. But she still thinks she's better than everybody. And ugh, looks like she's in the Left Hemisphere. Guess that means Fitz and I get to watch her try to show off all day."

"Who's the other girl she's with?" Linh asked. "She's staring at Sophie too."

"Really?" Sophie asked, waiting before she turned to see who Linh meant. It took her a second to recognize the pretty black girl beside Stina—especially with the blue streak she'd added to her straightened hair. "That's Maruca."

"There's a Marella and a Maruca?" Tam asked. "Yeah . . . I'm never going to be able to keep that straight."

"You probably won't have to," Biana said. "Marella's been avoiding us for a while. And Maruca and I haven't talked in months—ever since I told her I couldn't trust her. She blabbed a bunch of my secrets to get back at me for becoming friends with Sophie."

Tam whistled. "Girls and your drama."

"Right—because you and Keefe get along so well." Linh flicked his bangs. "And maybe I'm just imagining this but . . . doesn't Maruca look sad?"

Sophie had to agree. Maruca's turquoise eyes were glassy, and her full lips were pressed into a tight line.

And she was still staring at them.

"Think we should go over to her?" Sophie asked.

Biana shook her head. "If she needs to talk to us, she can come over here."

Maruca didn't.

But she didn't stop staring, either.

The whole thing felt very unsettling, and Sophie was relieved when a deep voice boomed above the crowd, directing everyone's attention to where Magnate Leto hovered above them. His levitation was wobblier than he probably wanted—and his feet nearly grazed the crowd's heads—but he managed to hold himself steady despite the strong breeze that kept whipping his long black cape—marked with a purple handprint—around his legs.

"Welcome to your first round of skill training!" he said. "A momentous step in our world's history! I'll be practicing along with you, so I'm turning this session over to your talented Coaches. Everyone, please show them how much we appreciate their efforts."

Scattered applause greeted three figures as they rose from the tents and floated to where Magnate Leto had just been hovering—one wearing a long red cape, another in a long blue cape, and the third in a long purple cape. The Coaches' levitation was flawless—so smooth, they might as well have been standing on solid ground.

"Those in the Left Hemisphere will be training with me," the red Coach said, her voice even raspier than Sophie remembered it. Her auburn hair was cropped into a sleek, angled bob, and she had thick black eyeliner rimming her pale blue eyes, giving her words an air of drama as she told them, "All of you are welcome to call me Coach Wilda."

"I'm Coach Bora," the blue Coach added, his high, nasal voice a strange contrast to his slicked blond hair, olive tone, and sharply angled features. "I'll be working with the Right Hemispheres over there." He pointed to the blue canopy.

"Which of course means that all of you Ambis are with me," the purple Coach said with a smile. Her long black hair was so shiny it seemed to glow against her cinnamon-toned skin. "I'm Coach Rohana. And yes, for those wondering, it *is* essential that you train with your designated Hemisphere, regardless of where your friends or family might have been sorted. All three groups will be practicing the same skills, but you've been separated by your learning style so that we'll be able to tailor your lessons for maximum efficiency."

"It's important that you not let yourselves get frustrated if you don't immediately succeed at what we're teaching," Coach Wilda added. "The Council has asked us to focus on a particular skill—one that, for most of you, will be an entirely new way of using your mind."

"The lessons will be grueling," Coach Rohana promised. "At times they may even be confounding. But this process is about stepping-stones and building blocks that piece together with time and patience to achieve a new kind of strength."

Each Coach removed a tennis-ball-size glass orb from their cloak pockets and held the clear spheres in front of them.

When they narrowed their eyes, all three orbs exploded into a million glinting fragments.

"What you've just witnessed is one manifestation of a skill we call outward channeling," Coach Wilda shouted over the gasps. "It harnesses a power limited only by our concentration and commitment. For instance . . ."

Coach Bora pulled a metal orb from his pocket and held it in front of him.

The orb exploded, sending flakes of metal raining like confetti—or maybe "shrapnel" was a better description.

"Nothing can be spared from the will of a skilled mind," Coach Bora told them. "Not crystal. Not metal. Not stone. Not even flesh and bone."

"Did . . . they just admit they're training us to kill?" Sophie whispered to her friends.

"Sure sounded like it," Fitz mumbled.

"Indeed it did," Sandor said, glancing at the other bodyguards.

Their expressions were hard to read. Nervous? Angry?

"We sense your unease," Coach Rohana told the crowd. "And applaud you for it. Fear breeds restraint and responsibility. But it will not change the fact that this is a skill we each possess naturally. Saber-toothed tigers have claws and fangs. Peluda dragons have poison quills. Even the fragile flitterwings have venom in their tiny teeth. They do not fear these gifts. Yes, some creatures use such things to hunt and others to defend themselves. But either choice doesn't change the fact that the power exists."

Sophie could see the logic behind her reasoning. But it still felt like giving everyone guns and hoping they didn't shoot each other.

And then she remembered Keefe telling her that his Neverseen training included hardcore skill lessons . . .

Were *they* mastering outward channeling?

"It's also important to note that power is not a new feature of our world," Coach Wilda reminded them. "Many of our special abilities could cause tremendous damage should we choose to use them for such. That doesn't mean we shy away from ability training, does it?"

"Our goals here are simple," Coach Bora added. "We want you to understand your strength and to be able to call on it should you need it. And together, we want to show the world that—whether they like it or not—*we* are the strongest creatures. We do not need weapons or armor. Only the strength of our mind and the discipline and determination to master it."

Murmurs rose among the crowd—most sounding like agreement. But Sophie kept remembering Lady Cadence's warnings to the Council.

Maybe the elves would be proving their strength. Or maybe they were about to throw a match in a room full of kindling.

"You look . . . concerned," she whispered to Sandor as the Coaches instructed everyone to head to their assigned tents.

"I am. I'm not sure how I'm supposed to protect you from an attack of this nature—especially one to flesh or bone. And if crystal and stone are also vulnerable, what's to stop someone from exploding the ground we're standing on, or shattering a building around us?"

"Our own natural limitations," Magnate Leto said, sneaking up beside them. "There's a reason the Coaches chose small orbs for their demonstration. The larger the object, the more energy it takes to destroy it. And while our minds can hold an incredible amount of energy, we also drain most of it through normal daily activities. There are ways to build reserves, of course, but they take a tremendous amount of time and discipline. Very few have such skill or patience. So for most, this power will be saved for an especially desperate moment. Nothing more. And now, I must mingle among the other Ambis, lest someone suspect I have favorite prodigies."

He winked as he walked away, heading for the far side of the purple tent.

Sophie followed Tam and Linh to the back, where they used to train when they all went to Exillium together.

Halfway there, Tam and Linh froze, their widened eyes fixed on two figures.

A couple with jet-black hair and silvery eyes.

Tam and Linh's parents.

FORTY-EIGHT

WELL," TAM'S FATHER SAID, fidgeting with his cloak pin—two silver-and-black dire wolves craning their necks in a graceful howl. "This is unexpected."

"It is and it isn't," Tam said, his eyes scanning the crowd until he found Magnate Leto, who looked . . . slightly guilty. "But I'll make it easy."

Tam took Linh's hand and turned to walk away.

Their mother grabbed his arm. "Please. Maybe we should—"

Tam jerked free of her hold. "No. We shouldn't."

She dropped her eyes to the ground—her slender fingers still lingering in the air as her husband reached for her. There was tenderness in the gesture. A soft gentleness in the way he cradled his wife's shaky hand, tracing his thumb across her palm.

The love between them was obvious. Even a little sweet.

But it made the tight fist of his other hand so much more heartbreaking as he glared at his children.

"Apologize to your mother. And stop making a scene!" He glanced nervously over his shoulder at the other Ambis watching.

Tam shook his head. "It's always about appearances with you."

"Please," their mother begged as they turned away again. "I never asked for the situation that was handed to me. I've never claimed I handled it well."

"That's what we are now?" Linh whispered. "A situation?"

Her mom cleared her throat. "What do you want to be?"

"Nothing," Tam said. "Absolutely nothing."

"Then you're doing a good job," his father told him, frowning at Tam's silver bangs. Both of the twins had melted their registry necklaces and dipped their hair in the molten metal as proof that they didn't need the family that left them to fend for themselves.

Tam pulled the silver over his eyes. "You like the look?"

His father shook his head. He didn't have the arrogance of Lord Cassius, or the unsettling smile or stare. All he looked was tired.

"Children are supposed to respect their parents," he said quietly.

Linh pulled Tam away. "Respect has to be earned."

"Wait," their mom begged. "Just wait."

Linh glanced over her shoulder. "We waited for more than three years."

"I know," her mother whispered. "You look so much older."

"That's what happens when you leave your kids alone with nowhere to live and nothing to eat," Sophie snapped, no longer able to bite her tongue. She knew this moment fell into the none-of-her-business category. But she'd already watched one friend unravel because of his horrible family. She wasn't going to let it happen to Tam and Linh.

"Whatever excuses you've given yourselves," she told the Songs, "whatever lies you've let yourself believe—this is the truth, right in front of you. You have two incredibly talented, smart, powerful kids who don't need you anymore. And if you ever want them in your life again, you have to earn it."

"How?" both of the Songs asked.

Sophie shrugged. "You have to figure it out for yourselves or it won't mean anything. Come on," she told Tam and Linh, taking their hands. "We have better places to be."

"I can't believe you said that," Linh whispered as they moved to a spot in the front of the tent and Sandor stood behind her, creating a wall of muscle between them and the Songs.

Sophie lowered her eyes. "Sorry if I shouldn't have interfered."

"No—you absolutely should have," Tam said.

Linh nodded. "The look on my father's face—that was the greatest gift you ever could've given me."

"I wish I could do more." It didn't seem fair that Sophie had been given *two* loving families, when so many of her friends hadn't even gotten *one*. And for all she knew, her genetic parents were also awesome—though that was a little harder to believe, given the whole never-meeting-their-daughter-and-letting-her-be-experimented-on thing.

"Dude," a voice said behind her. "Am I in the same Hemisphere as the Great Sophie Foster? Never thought that would happen!"

Sophie turned and found a familiar face grinning at her near one of the tent poles.

"Guys, this is Jensi. And Jensi, this is Tam and Linh," Sophie introduced.

"Cool!—I love your hair!" Jensi practically shouted. "Is that real silver?—And wait—are you from Exillium?—Is that where you met Sophie?—What's it like there?"

Jensi had a way of talking like he'd drunk a dozen bottles of caffeinated soda. Tam and Linh were naturally overwhelmed.

"Jensi was one of the first people to help me find my way around Foxfire," Sophie explained. "Though I haven't seen him around much lately."

Jensi's round cheeks flushed, and he ran a hand through his messy brown hair. "Sorry—you're just always so busy—and I figured I fit in better with the Drooly Boys, anyway."

"You fit in wherever you *want*," Sophie told him. "Though, for the record, I've never seen a drop of drool on your chin."

Coach Rohana strode into the tent before Jensi could respond, carrying a big bag of purple splotchers. The Ping-Pong-ball-size orbs were like squishy paintballs, and had Sophie hoping the day's exercise would give her a chance to hurl a few at Tam and Linh's parents.

"Outward channeling requires a different understanding of your power," Coach Rohana said, rolling a splotcher around the palm of her hand. "The method you've all learned for telekinesis taught you to gather energy from deep within your core and then thrust it out with your mind, controlling the force as though the energy were an extension of your existing limbs. But you need to stop thinking of the energy as *core* energy. It's simply *your* energy—and it does not need to remain connected to you in order for you to manipulate it. In fact, it's far more powerful when you bury it in other things. For instance"—her eyes narrowed at the splotcher in her hand—"you can hide it here, letting it swell and surge until . . ."

The splotcher erupted, splattering her with purple.

"It's a bizarre concept, I realize," she said, wiping the paint off her cheeks. "And it will take time for your minds to accomplish it. In fact, I'd wager that most of you will not burst any splotchers today. We're providing them mostly to give you a goal—a first stepping-stone to strive for. But there's nothing wrong with needing several baby steps before you get there. Try to trust your instincts. Also don't be surprised if you find the process exhausting. Please take breaks if you need them. Everyone ready?" She handed the bag of splotchers to Jensi.

He grabbed enough for Sophie, Tam, and Linh before he passed the bag along and plopped next to Sophie on the purple grass. "Maybe I can absorb some of your awesomeness," he said, then told Tam and Linh about Sophie's performance during the Ultimate Splotching Championship. "Flung herself and Fitz into the wall and knocked them out cold!"

Linh laughed. "Sounds like Sophie's caused almost as many disasters as I have."

"You should come to Foxfire!" Jensi said. "You two could have a Chaos Competition—it would be epic!—Or wait—*can* you come back to Foxfire?"

Linh glanced over her shoulder at her parents. "When we're ready."

"Let's get started!" Coach Rohana called. "Place your splotcher on the ground in front of you and clear your head. I won't be giving you any specific pointers, because it's far better for you to find your own natural trick. But try to understand that your body is not an impermeable vessel holding a well of energy. It's a stake in the ground, marking the epicenter of your own personal energy cloud."

"Does Exillium training always sound this loony?" Jensi asked. "Or is this extra weird?"

"It's extra weird," Tam said.

"I don't know. I kinda get it." Linh furrowed her brow as she stared at her splotcher. "It's like how water is both without and within."

"Uh, sure . . . ," Jensi said.

Tam laughed. "Don't worry. I don't understand half the stuff my sister says."

Sophie was just as confused. But she tried to imagine her energy like a seed, and pictured herself planting it in the center of the splotcher. She hummed a song in her head to make it grow, letting the energy spread through the paint like roots through soil and . . .

. . . the splotcher burst with a squish of purple.

Jensi pumped his fist. "Told you she'd kick our butts!"

"Telepaths tend to catch on faster at this," Coach Rohana said, handing Sophie a cloth to wipe the paint off her face. "Their minds naturally hold a much larger reserve of energy, which can make it easier to transfer—though this could be a new record."

Sophie glanced at Magnate Leto, and he offered an unsurprised smile.

"Normally I'd tell you to rest, since most would find their energy depleted," Coach Rohana added. "But after such an effortless display, I'm curious to see if you can continue."

She handed Sophie a new splotcher, making her promise to take a break if she got a headache. But Sophie felt fine.

And when she planted another "seed," the splotcher splattered purple everywhere.

Coach Rohana tilted her head. "I suspect you could bring down a mountain if you sat in solitude long enough."

"Why solitude?" Tam asked.

"No distractions or activities to drain her reserve." Their Coach offered Sophie a third splotcher, and—while it took significantly longer—Sophie still managed to burst it like the others.

Only two other Ambis burst their splotchers before the end of the lesson: Magnate Leto and—surprisingly—Jensi.

"I think my osmosis theory worked," Jensi said, bouncing on the balls of his feet. "Unless this means I'm going to manifest as a Telepath—which would be *awesome!*—though I'd kinda been rooting for Phaser—like my brother—or maybe a Charger—or . . ."

He continued naming abilities, but Sophie had stopped listening, too aware of everyone watching her.

"I know what you're feeling," Linh whispered. "I've often wondered if I have more power than I should. But I stopped worrying about it after I flooded Ravagog."

"Whoa—that was you?" Jensi butted in.

Linh nodded. "First time I've ever been glad to hold so much power. And you'll do far greater things with yours," she told Sophie.

Sophie thanked her, not sure why she felt so . . . ruffled. This definitely wasn't the first time she'd discovered that her mental powers were a little too close to the scary side of the line.

But something about this skill felt *wrong*—like the elves were setting aside everything they'd believed in and going darker.

And there she was: the poster child for the New Darkness.

Jensi bounded off to brag to the Drooly Boys as soon as the Coaches dismissed them, and Sandor agreed to let Sophie stay to say goodbye to her friends. Tam and Linh lingered with her—until they noticed their parents heading over. They leaped away with seconds to spare.

The Songs were too intimidated to approach Sophie, especially when Fitz and Biana—and their bodyguards—joined her. Fitz seemed especially bummed to hear about Sophie's three-splotcher session. The most he'd accomplished was making his splotcher quiver.

Sophie was giving him a few pointers when a smug voice behind them asked, "Waiting for Dizznee?"

Sophie fought off a sigh as she turned to find Stina—and Maruca. "Why do you care?"

"I don't," Stina said. "But I figured *you* might—especially since I saw him pull Marella aside after the lesson. They've been whispering ever since. Jealous, Foster?"

Sophie rolled her eyes. "Since when are you and Marella back to being friends?"

Stina's smug expression faltered. "We never stopped. She's

just . . . having a hard time now that I manifested as an Empath."

"Oh."

Sophie wasn't sure if it was her, Fitz, or Biana who'd said it—but they had to all be thinking it. Stina had a long history of Empaths on her mother's side of the family, so the news wasn't unexpected. But poor Marella had been trying for years to trigger the ability, in the hopes that she might be able to help her mom better control her emotions.

"That's rough," Sophie mumbled.

Stina nodded. "I wish she'd manifest already—even if she doesn't get the ability she wants. It's a million times harder with all the constantly wondering *What if?*, you know?"

Sophie did know. And before she could think of what to say, she realized Maruca had gone back to staring at her.

Stina elbowed her friend. "Just say it, already. That's why you made me come over here."

Maruca nodded.

She cleared her throat so many times it almost sounded painful. Then she told Sophie, "I need you to take me to see Wylie."

FORTY-NINE

NO ONE'S GOING ANYWHERE," Sandor said, placing a heavy hand on Sophie's shoulder. Grizel and Woltzer held on to Fitz and Biana as well.

Sophie dragged Sandor with her as she moved closer to Maruca, hoping her glare hid her lie as she whispered, "I don't know why you're talking to me about this."

"Yes you do." Maruca waited for a nearby group of Left Hemispheres to wander further away before she added, "Stina told me the Neverseen attacked Wylie, and that the Black Swan have him hidden away."

"Don't look at me like that," Stina told Sophie. "I overheard my dad whispering about it—and Wylie is Maruca's family. She deserved to know what was happening."

"Wylie's your family?" Biana asked.

Maruca nodded. "I never said anything because there was so much weirdness with him and your dad. But he's my second cousin—and my mom used to take me to visit him all the time. She's freaking out right now—"

"Wait, you told your *mom*?" Stina interrupted. "You promised you wouldn't tell anyone!"

"That was before I knew what the secret was," Maruca told her. "I can't hide this from my family—no matter what I said."

She had a point. Some problems were too important to worry about breaking promises.

But Sophie still couldn't help her.

"I'm not allowed to talk about this," she whispered. "Maybe you should ask Stina's dad."

"Oh please, you know my dad's not going to tell us anything," Stina argued. "He'll just ground me for eavesdropping."

"You should've thought of that before you did it," Fitz told her.

Stina snorted. "Like you've never listened to your dad's secret conversations."

"Oh, I have," Fitz said. "But I'm always prepared to be busted if I get caught."

"Who cares about getting caught?" Maruca asked—her voice more hiss than whisper. "My mom is ready to go to the Council—"

"She can't do that!" Sophie interrupted. She checked to make sure Magnate Leto was deep in conversation with the Coaches on the other side of the field before she whispered, "The Black Swan don't want the Council to know this happened."

"Then bring us to see him," Maruca said.

"Is that a threat?" Biana asked.

Maruca shrugged, tucking her blue strip of hair behind her ear. "If that's what it takes to see Wylie."

"But you're threatening the wrong person," Sophie told her. "I don't have a crystal to get to the place where they're keeping him."

"Even if that's true, if anyone can make it happen, it's *you*," Maruca insisted. "You're their suncatcher—or their boobrie—or whatever weird bird they call you."

"It's a moonlark," Fitz told her. "Though now I'm kinda wishing they'd called it Project Boobrie."

Sophie was too stressed to smile. "You're overestimating how much the Black Swan listen to me," she told Maruca. "They shoot me down *all* the time—and they've been especially difficult about Wylie."

Maruca bit her lip. "All I'm asking is for you to try. Please. I know you don't know me—and that I haven't been very nice to you. But I need to see him. I need to know for sure that he's okay—that they haven't finally broken him."

The catch in her voice crumbled Sophie's resolve.

"Fine. I'll hail the Collective when I get home and see if they'd be willing to arrange something."

"Why not hail them now?" Maruca pressed.

Sophie pointed to the groups of kids hanging out all around them. "Because we shouldn't even be talking about this at *all* right now."

"Then let me go to your house with you," Maruca begged. "I'm not saying I don't trust you. I just might be able to help you convince them."

"She is pretty pushy," Fitz said. "It might be kind of fun to sic her on the Collective."

Sophie rubbed her temples. "If they say no, you have to promise you'll leave it at that, okay? Or find someone else to hassle about it."

Maruca nodded and Sophie pulled out her home crystal.

Stina looped her arm through Sophie's. "I'm going with you guys."

"So am I," Fitz said.

"What about Dex?" Biana asked. "He'll be sad if we all go without him."

"Then why don't you stay here," Fitz suggested. "I'll meet you back at Everglen as soon as we're done and we can trade stories."

"Yeah, I want a full update," Sophie told Biana, pointing to where she'd spotted Dex and Marella talking.

Marella had her face turned away, so it was a little hard to tell.

But Sophie could've sworn she was crying.

Sophie couldn't hail Mr. Forkle, since he was still in Magnate Leto disguise at Foxfire. So she reached out to Granite.

"Whoa," Maruca whispered when Sandor and Grizel opened the door to let Granite in. "That's a *crazy* disguise."

"It is," he said, his limbs cracking as he followed them into the living room. "And I'm trusting you not to tell anyone you've seen me like this."

"Why?" Maruca asked. "It's not like I know who you are."

"We still prefer the public know as little about our organization as possible." He turned to Sophie. "Where are your parents?"

"Out with the new stegosaurus that arrived this morning. Why—did you need them?"

"Not at the moment. I'm just glad to hear they're well and safe. And I need all of you to understand that ordinarily I would never agree to a meeting like this. The only reason I did is because I know how much your family matters to Wylie," he told Maruca. "And as it happens, Physic will be easing Wylie off the sedatives tomorrow. We've sheltered him as long as we can, but it's time for him to begin returning to reality. And it might be helpful for him to have a few familiar faces there when he wakes up—if you think you and your mother would be up for it."

"We are," Maruca assured him, wiping away a few tears. "We'll do whatever he needs. What time and where should we meet and how—"

"I'll send instructions to your house as soon as I've spoken with Physic," Granite interrupted. "Keep an eye out for a scroll tomorrow morning."

"Can I go too?" Sophie asked.

"I think it's best that we not overwhelm him," Granite said. "Plus, I fear that once he sees you, he'll grow too fixated on the favor he requested."

"What favor?" Stina and Maruca asked.

"*That* is classified," Granite told them. "As is tomorrow's meeting. No one can know that it's happening, aside from your immediate families. And speaking of which"— he stalked closer to Stina— "in the future, I hope you'll pay more respect to your father's privacy. Overhearing something does not give you the right to repeat it to others."

To her credit, Stina kept her head held high as she told him. "Maruca needed to know."

"Then you should've informed your father and let him handle the matter through proper channels. We are an *order*, Miss Heks, and there are rules and protocols that must be followed."

"Is that what you say to Sophie?" Stina snapped back.

"Miss Foster has received her fair share of lectures. She's also a very special circumstance, so I would not make the mistake of putting you—or your father—in the same category. If we have reason to view your family as a security risk, we'll have no choice but to release your father from his oath. Is that what you want?"

Stina tried for a careless shrug. But Sophie could see her tremble.

Granite must've noticed too, because he nodded, promising Maruca he'd see her the next morning, before he leaped away.

"You . . . have a very weird life," Maruca told Sophie as she stared at the cloud of gravelly dust he'd left in his wake.

"Tell me something I don't know," Sophie mumbled.

And things got even weirder after Maruca and Stina left. Fitz was just getting ready to head home when they heard another knock on the front door and found Councillor Oralie standing on the porch, dressed in full regal garb.

"Is this about Gethen?" Sophie asked.

Oralie smiled. "It's nice to see you too."

"Sorry," Sophie said, realizing how rude she was being to a Councillor. She dipped one of her embarrassingly ungraceful curtsies. "How can I help you?"

"You can call for your parents," Oralie told her as Sophie stepped aside to let her in. "We have much to arrange. And yes, it's about Gethen."

FIFTY

"Y OU GOT US A MEETING?" SOPHIE asked, for what had to be the fifth time. But it was such a relief to hear it.

Oralie smiled as she smoothed her already perfect ringlets. "Yes. I've been given clearance to escort you and Mr. Forkle into the Lumenaria dungeons next week. I'm still waiting to find out the exact day, but it will most likely be Friday. And we'll only have fifteen minutes with Gethen, so you'll need to plan your time accordingly."

"What about me?" Fitz asked.

Oralie took his hand. "I realize that you're Cognates—and that you could be a valuable asset to the meeting. But the clearance is limited to Sophie, Mr. Forkle, and myself. No exceptions."

"Aside from her bodyguard," Sandor corrected.

"You'll be able to escort her to the main gates of the fortress," Oralie told him. "Lumenaria's guards will take it from there."

Sandor stalked closer. "Miss Foster was assigned to *my* charge."

"Yes, I'm aware. In fact, I'm the one who recommended you for the assignment. But no one can enter the castle and view the security measures being put into place for the summit—even someone as well respected as you. As it is, Sophie and Mr. Forkle will be blindfolded during the walk to the dungeon."

"Seriously?" Sophie asked. "Do you really think we're going to tell someone about anything we see?"

"It has less to do with actuality and more to do with potential. The thing you must understand is that the leaders of every intelligent species will be present for the summit—and we don't allow them to bring their own guards, lest any be spies or traitors. But that means we can't use our regular bodyguards, either. A wholly new set of guards has been gathered, vetted, and trained specifically for the summit—after enduring a rigid approval process through the leaders of each world. We also guarantee that no one who isn't a guard—or an attendee of the summit—will set so much as a toe inside the castle now that we've begun organizing our security, in order to ensure that no one has any opportunity to plan a raid."

"Then how can you bring Sophie and Mr. Forkle to see Gethen?" Fitz asked.

"That's why I needed to talk to you," Oralie said, turning to where Grady and Edaline stood near the staircase, each covered in purple dinosaur feathers. "Sophie's presence has been requested at the summit."

Sophie felt her jaw fall open. Grady, Edaline, and Fitz did the same—and Sophie was pretty sure every goblin in the room sucked in a sharp breath.

"I know—I was just as surprised as all of you," Oralie told them. "But Sophie's unique role in many of our world's most recent challenges has aroused a certain curiosity about her among the other leaders—King Enki of the dwarves and Queen Hylda of the goblins especially. And King Dimitar has asked that he be allowed to cross-examine her regarding the events in Ravagog."

"All the more reason I should be there," Sandor argued.

"I can assure you, Sophie will have an abundance of security," Oralie promised. "*And*, because of her age, she'll be escorted by a parent or guardian."

"And you chose Mr. Forkle over us?" Grady asked.

"No, Mr. Forkle has been invited to represent the Black Swan. The order has made a name for itself in recent months, and the world leaders have requested to hear its thoughts on the negotiations as well. Miss Foster's guardian will be Miss Ruewen, if she's willing."

"Me?" Edaline asked as Grady shook his head.

"My wife is an incredible force to be reckoned with—but

of the two of us, I'm able to offer Sophie far better protection."

"Possibly," Oralie said. "But the leaders won't tolerate a Mesmer in their presence. I'm sure you can understand their reasoning."

"So you're asking me to send my wife and daughter into fraught treaty negotiations?" Grady asked.

"Actually, I'm asking Sophie and Edaline if they'd be willing to participate in a world-changing event, which will have more security than anyone could ever imagine," Oralie corrected. "And they will be the ones deciding if they will accept."

Grady scowled but didn't argue as he turned to Edaline. "You think this is crazy, right?"

"I do," she said, nervously snapping her fingers and making a Panakes blossom appear and disappear in her palm. "But I don't think I should be the one deciding. What do you think, Sophie?"

It felt like all of Sophie's insides were crawling up her throat. But she managed to mumble, "I think we have to go."

"Doesn't this technically mean that Edaline could go with you to see Gethen, then?" Fitz asked, breaking the silence that followed.

"I suppose it does," Oralie said. "But I wouldn't recommend it. I visited Gethen yesterday as I arranged the meeting with his guards, and he's far too eager to face Sophie again. Having anyone else she cares about in the room will only give him further ammunition."

"Oh yeah, I'm feeling *really* good about this visit," Grady grumbled.

"Same here," Sandor snarled.

"I've had enough encounters with Mr. Forkle to feel confident that he can handle Gethen," Oralie told both of them. "And I will provide any help I can."

"I can also handle myself," Sophie reminded everyone.

"No one is doubting your strength," Oralie told her. "It's what makes you Gethen's target."

"And Forkle's really okay with all of this?" Grady asked.

"I'm sure he will be once I inform him," Oralie said. "I have a meeting with him later this afternoon."

"Wait—he doesn't know?" Edaline asked. "How can that be?"

Oralie stole a glance at Sophie.

Sophie sighed, realizing it was time to come clean. "I . . . went to see Oralie and asked her to set up the meeting with Gethen, because I was worried that the Black Swan were missing an important opportunity. And, um, I also told her about Wylie."

The air shifted with the confession, taking on a charge that burned Sophie's throat.

"When did you and Oralie have this little heart-to-heart?" Grady asked.

Sophie fussed with her Sucker Punch. "Right before you grounded me."

Sandor's squeaky growl made the hairs on her arms prickle.

"So that means you went with her," Edaline said, turning to Fitz, who slunk back a couple of steps when Sandor growled again—along with Grizel. "Is that why you both had dirt in your hair?"

Sophie nodded. "Flori took us. And please don't be mad at her—or Fitz. It was all my idea."

Grady pinched the bridge of his nose. "I knew going through the teenage years again was going to be tricky. But I never prepared for *this*."

"*This* is me trying to stop the Neverseen from hurting people," Sophie snapped. "It's not like I'm sneaking around just for fun."

"Well," Oralie said, standing and removing a pink-wanded pathfinder from her cape. "Family debates aren't really my area of expertise. But I do hope you won't go too hard on Sophie. She was perfectly safe in my castle. And she was wise to come to me."

Grady didn't agree. As soon as Oralie left, he sent Fitz home to confess to Alden and sentenced Sophie to a week of Verdi pedicures. Which was why Sophie was elbow deep in T. rex toe jam when Mr. Forkle leaped into the pasture.

"I'm assuming you can guess why I'm here," he said quietly.

Sophie wiped her hands on her tunic. "I know what you're going to say—"

"I'm not sure you do." He cleared his throat several times before he told her, "I came here to thank you."

"You're right. *That* wasn't what I was expecting."

Tiny smile lines crinkled around his eyes. "I'm not saying I want you kids regularly disobeying my advice or sneaking away without your bodyguards—and just because everything worked out this time doesn't mean you should feel free to act on such whims whenever you feel them. *But* . . . in this case, you made the right decision."

"That doesn't get you out of pedicure duty!" Grady called from the next pasture over.

Mr. Forkle smiled. "And thus we have the cost of rebellion. Being right doesn't spare the consequences of breaking rules. But I'm happy to know you're ready to stand up for your convictions."

He stayed a few minutes longer, giving her a long lecture on the need for them to create a clear plan for the meeting with Gethen.

"We have a week," he told her. "And I'm counting on you to figure it out. You're finally stepping into the role we imagined for you. Now let's see what you can do."

FIFTY-ONE

*G*ET READY TO WISH YOU COULD *hug me,* Keefe said as Sophie watched the first rays of dawn paint across the murky sky. *Actually, I'm pretty sure this is good enough news that you're going to want to kiss me—and I'm happy to accept an IOU, by the way.*

Just tell me what you learned, Sophie ordered, too tired to joke around.

Keefe had skipped both their dinner and before-bed check-ins the night before, because there was another huge argument going on with the Neverseen. So she'd been up most of the night worrying—and failing to come up with a plan to rescue him.

Fine—but you should at least have to write an epic poem in my honor. Here—I'll help you. "Ode to Keefe Sencen—that brave, lovable nut. He may not have teal eyes, but he has a really cute—"

KEEFE!

All right, fine. But I'm calling you Foster Grumpypants for the rest of this conversation. And brace yourself because I'm about to blow your mind. Are you ready for it?

I've been ready for the last five minutes.

You think you're ready. But there's no way you possibly can be.

JUST TELL ME.

Okay. Just don't say I didn't try to prepare you. Fintan gave me another cloak when he moved me to this new hideout. And by the way, it's WAY nicer over here. I actually have my own room—and it doesn't smell like rotting toenails!

If that's the only news you have, I'm never talking to you again.

Wow, you ARE Foster Grumpypants. Sheesh. Everything okay?

Yeah, I'm fine. I just get nervous when you tell me the Neverseen are arguing. The last time Brant lost his temper, he killed Jolie.

Jolie's name seemed to demand a moment of silence.

I'm being careful, he promised. *And Brant's actually not the one fighting. It's all Ruy, making a big fuss about his punishment for letting Wylie get away. It's been hard to get details. But Fintan's definitely changing their roles for that big project, and Ruy thinks his new assignment is unnecessary and demeaning.*

And I'm assuming you still don't have any ideas about what the project is?

Sadly, no. Just like I haven't gotten any more info about the ogres' test, or King Dimitar's meeting with Fintan, or Fintan's cache, or any of the things I can't get anyone to talk about—but before you get all Doom and Gloom, remember, I still have huge, kiss-worthy news!

If you start talking about cloaks or rotting toenails again . . .

But that's how it started! Well, not the toenails—but whatever. Fintan made a big deal about how I needed to wear my new cloak the whole time I'm here, and I figured it had to do with the black disk you found. So last night I opened the bottom seam and yep— another disk, with a different piece of the symbol.

He shared his memory of the etching, and the pattern of dashes breaking up the line matched a ray on the opposite side of the Lodestar symbol.

Is that it? Sophie asked.

Of course not—what kind of amateur do you take me for? I also found where the symbol projects on the floor, just like Bangs Boy wanted. It wasn't there when I first got here, but it popped up when Fintan was getting ready to leave. I'm guessing it's their funky version of a Leapmaster, since the projection comes from a crystal sphere mounted to the ceiling. But I couldn't figure out how it worked, and when Fintan caught me studying it, he said I'll never be able to understand the symbol—or how to use it—without knowing the key. And THAT is the mind-blowingly awesome revelation.

It is?

Think about it—what needs a key besides a lock?

Um . . .

Wow, you really must be tired.

Yeah, thanks to you.

She tried to think of any phrases that used the word "key." And then it clicked.

Is the symbol a map?

BOOM! Admit it, I just blew your mind.

He kinda had.

But a map of what? she asked, trying to picture all the circles and rays and dashes. *Their hideouts?*

That's what I'm assuming.

His mind shifted to his memory of the symbol glowing across the dark stone floor. The ray that matched the disk in his new cloak had something extra in the end circle.

It has new runes, Sophie said.

Yep. And in case you can't read them, it says Gwynaura.

Another star.

Right again, you little star-memorizing show-off.

She ignored his teasing, letting her mind sort through the star maps she'd memorized, hoping to spot anything that might make Gwynaura unique.

It wasn't a particularly bright star. But it had a pure white glow, just like Alabestrine.

Do you think the map is based off a constellation they created? she asked.

It might be. But the stars could also just be guides. That's what lodestars are, right? So maybe Gwynaura leads to the hideout I'm at. And Alabestrine leads to Paris. And each of the other hideouts has a star and a rune to guide you to them.

But I don't understand how that actually works, Sophie told him. Light needs a crystal to bend the path where we want to go. So it's not like we can just bottle the starlight and magically end up at a Neverseen hideout.

I'm guessing that's what Fintan meant about me needing the key. But remember, a gadget projects the symbol. So I'm hoping Dizznee's Technopath brain will be able to put all the pieces together—especially since Fintan gave me one more clue to play with. He seems to want to see if I'm smart enough to figure this out, so he told me, "All you need to know is that the code is simple."

FIFTY-TWO

THE CODE IS SIMPLE," DEX MUMBLED, staring at Sophie's memory log, where she'd projected everything Keefe had shown her. "What code?"

"No idea," Sophie admitted. "Keefe was hoping you'd be able to figure that out."

"Great." Dex flopped back on her bed, repeating the clue over and over.

Fitz, Biana, and Dex—and their bodyguards—had met Sophie at Havenfield that morning to brainstorm, while Tam and Linh stayed in Alluveterre to see how Maruca's visit with Wylie went.

"So there's a symbol that's also a map, projected by a

gadget," Dex said, "and we need a key that's probably related to a code that's simple."

"Wow, my brain hurts just trying to follow that sentence," Biana said, blinking in and out of sight as she paced across Sophie's flowered carpet. "*But*, if Alvar can understand this, I'm sure we can too."

"Yeah, but they probably *gave* Alvar the key," Fitz reminded her as he slumped into Sophie's desk chair and petted Iggy through the bars of his cage. "We're stuck guessing. And don't forget there are also runes and star names and black disks hidden in cloaks and—"

"Okay, so we need to work on this piece by piece," Sophie decided, trying to massage away the headache she could feel forming. "Keefe seemed to think the gadget part was crucial, that's why he wanted me to talk to Dex."

She flipped to the page in her memory log where she'd recorded Keefe's memory of the crystal sphere. "Notice anything that might help us?"

"Maybe if I had the gadget in front of me and could open it up and see all the inner workings," Dex told her. "But I can't tell much from a picture. The only thing that stands out is this line." He traced his finger over a glowing strip of purple down the center of the crystal sphere. "That *could* be some sort of scanner."

"And what would a scanner do?" Fitz asked.

"Well, the obvious answer is 'scan stuff,'" Dex said, "which might fit, since scanners usually scan *codes*. So maybe there's a code hidden in the symbol? And the gadget scans it, and that somehow tells it to make a light path—maybe using the light from the corresponding star?"

"I guess that does make sense," Fitz said. "But, dude, couldn't they just use a Leapmaster or a pathfinder?"

"Maybe they think this method is more secure," Dex said, "since crystals can get lost or stolen, and this would only work for people they train. *Or*, maybe the Technopath who designed it wasn't very good."

"I thought you said their Technopath was super talented," Biana reminded him. "When we went through Alvar's registry records you seemed super impressed."

"They did do a lot of crazy tricks I never would've thought of," Dex admitted. "So maybe this was designed by a different Technopath. Or . . ."

"Or?" Fitz prompted when Dex didn't finish.

"Hang on. I need to think for a second," Dex said, sitting up and flipping back through the memory log until he found a page showing the symbol.

One second turned into two—then three and four and five and on and on, until Sophie got tired of counting.

"While he does that"—she turned to Biana—"did Dex ever tell you what he and Marella were talking about yesterday?"

"Oh! That's right, I only told Fitz. I guess Dex decided to

ask Marella if we could talk to her mom about the day Cyrah faded—and she freaked out. Partially because he wouldn't tell her why. But mostly because her mom can't handle that kind of stress. She told him her mom's gotten so bad lately that she won't even leave the house, and Marella thinks it's because she's heard about the awful things the Neverseen have been doing. So she can't risk freaking her out more by talking about painful memories."

"That makes sense," Sophie said quietly. "And must be so hard for her."

"I know. Dex said she cried. Makes me feel super guilty for not checking on her sooner—but now if I try, she'll think I'm just trying to get information about Cyrah."

"Probably. But there has to be *something* we can do," Sophie said. "Maybe if we—"

Dex jumped to his feet. "Do you remember those number chains I uncovered in Alvar's registry records well enough to project them?" he asked Sophie.

"Of course."

She took the memory log back and recorded the four chains of ones and zeroes, plus all the extra dashes and symbols and asterisks.

0-11-<<-1-1-1-0*

*0-1->-1->-111-0

*0->-111->>>-1-0

0-<<-1-1-11-<-0*

Dex stared at the numbers for so long that Sophie was about to turn back to her Marella conversation.

But before she did, Dex laughed and pumped his fist, shouting, "I know what the clue means!"

FIFTY-THREE

THE NUMBERS AREN'T NUMBERS!" Dex said. "Well, I guess they kinda are—it's the symbol that's not really a symbol. Or maybe it's both, depending on which way you're looking at it."

He sighed when they gave him nothing but blank stares.

"Okay, let's try this another way," he said. "Can I get something to write with?"

Sophie gave him one of her school notebooks and a pencil and he flipped to a clean page.

"Biana, can you read me the first sequence of numbers we found in Alvar's records—and give me all the dashes and symbols and stuff too?"

"Sure. It's zero, hyphen, one, one, hyphen, less than, less than, hyphen, one, hyphen, one, hyphen, one, hyphen, zero, asterisk."

Dex grinned as he stared at what he'd written. "See what happens when I convert the whole thing to pure symbols?"

He held up his drawing.

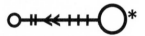

Everyone sucked in a breath.

The markings looked exactly like one of the rays in the Lodestar symbol—and not just any ray. The ray they'd connected to the Paris hideout—which happened to be where Alvar was when his registry pendant had given that code.

"And you can do the same thing with all four of the codes I found," Dex added. "The asterisk tells you which zero is the center. See?"

He drew the three remaining codes and held them up, each one matching a ray of the symbol perfectly.

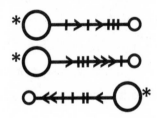

"Wow, how did you figure that out?" Fitz asked.

"It was Fintan's clue," Dex said. "I remembered whining

about how using a code made of ones and zeroes was too simple. And the really crazy part is, this isn't simple at all. It's a seriously brilliant system. The code is hidden but not hidden, still useable and scannable in both forms, *and* it keeps perfect track of their locations. See? This top one? That's the hideout that Alvar went to when he was The Boy Who Disappeared."

Sophie's stomach soured. "That's the same hideout they just moved Keefe to."

It shouldn't surprise her—and it shouldn't make her so nervous. But it really did.

"So those other two rays are hideouts Keefe hasn't seen yet, right?" Biana asked. "Does that mean we know how to find them?"

"*Technically*, yes," Dex said. "We should be able to find any of the hideouts we want, but—"

"I'd like to take this moment to make it clear that *none* of you will be leaving this house," Sandor interrupted, reminding their group that they had four goblins eavesdropping on their conversation from the hallway.

"Don't worry, we can't," Dex told him. "The only way this works is if we have one of their special gadgets to scan the code and convert it into a path for us—assuming I'm even right and that's what that gadget does."

"Can you build one?" Fitz asked.

"Not without having one to study," Dex said. "Though maybe if I play with a scanner and—"

"Again," Lovise interrupted. "No one will be building any gadgets to sneak away to see the enemy."

Dex rolled his eyes. "Just because I build it doesn't mean I'm going to use it."

All four goblins snorted a laugh.

"Yes," Sandor said, "because the four of you are known for your restraint."

"Well, you can't stop me from trying," Dex told him. "Though, honestly, I'm probably not going to be able to pull it off. The intricacy of this system is *crazy*, so the odds of me duplicating it without having something to copy are pretty much zero. Especially since I'm still not sure how the star runes fit in. The gadget could be channeling their light—but the Paris hideout was underground, so I don't know how that would work. And the stars *could* just be the names of their hideouts—but that seems too easy."

Sophie sighed. "So once again, we've learned a ton of things, but we still basically know nothing. And I don't even see a plan for what to do now."

"I guess we could tell Keefe all of this," Biana said, "and when everyone's asleep, he could sneak out of bed and—"

"Bad idea," Sophie interrupted. "I bet if he goes to another hideout without the matching black disk in his cloak, the Neverseen will know they have an intruder."

"Yeah, you're probably right," Biana mumbled. "Ugh—this whole so-close-but-so-far thing is super frustrating. Are we missing something?"

The minutes ticked by as they all stared at the symbol.

Sophie was about to give up when Biana made a weird squeaky sound.

"What if this gadget is how the Neverseen got into the Silver Tower?" she asked. "If they hid one inside somewhere, it could've let them leap in, couldn't it?"

"It depends on how the gadget works," Dex said. "The tower has tons of defenses to block people from leaping in, but maybe it uses light a different way?"

"But wouldn't someone have found the gadget during their search?" Fitz asked.

"Not if the Neverseen took the gadget with them when they left," Biana argued. "Why not have Tam search the tower to see if he can find a shadowprint, like the one in Paris?"

"That'll take *forever*," Dex warned.

"It will," Fitz agreed. "But it's better than nothing. And he could start with the Lodestar mirror, since I still think that's a weird coincidence."

"It's worth a try," Sophie decided. "And Fintan will probably be impressed when Keefe pretends he figured all of this out."

"And you can ask Gethen about it," Fitz added. "I still can't believe you're doing that without me—what's the point of being Cognates if they don't let us work together?"

"It's *almost* as ridiculous as assigning her a bodyguard and then not allowing him to accompany her on dangerous missions," Sandor shouted from the hallway.

"I'll be *fine*," Sophie told both of them. "I've handled Gethen before."

She was more worried about the fact that they were only giving her fifteen minutes. In that short time, she'd be lucky if she coaxed *one* piece of information out of him.

"What's the most important question," she said, "out of all of our questions?"

"What do you mean?" Fitz asked.

"I mean, what's the one thing we absolutely have to know—more than anything else? I'm trying to figure out what I need to focus on during the conversation."

The last time, they'd needed to learn anything they could about the gnomish plague and what might've happened to Keefe's mother. But this time the threat came in so many fragments and pieces and mysteries.

Should she ask what the Neverseen wanted with Grady and Edaline? Or about Keefe's legacy and the mysterious door into the mountain? Or should she try to get specifics about the Lodestar Initiative, and what it had to do with "test subjects" and "criterion" and Keefe's theory about a "gathering."

All of those were crucial—but were they crucial enough to be her one play in this crazy, confusing game?

The more her mind tossed the question around, the more

she realized the Neverseen had tipped their hand. It didn't matter what *she* thought was important. It mattered what they cared about—what they'd wanted so desperately that they'd taken a tremendous risk.

Which meant she needed to ask Gethen what the Neverseen wanted from Wylie.

FIFTY-FOUR

THE TRICK WITH GETHEN IS TO MAKE him think we're interested in one thing, so he doesn't have his guard up around the stuff we really need," Sophie told Fitz as they both stared at the page she'd not-so-creatively titled: *Plan for Tricking Gethen*.

The rest of the paper was blank.

And had been blank for days.

Sophie was starting to worry it would be blank for the rest of eternity.

Six days had already passed since Councillor Oralie told her they'd be visiting Lumenaria—and since the meeting was still scheduled for Friday, that meant they only had two days left to figure it out.

The most logical option—in Sophie's opinion—was for everyone to stop babying her and let her use her genetically enhanced telepathy. But the suggestion had been unanimously voted as the Worst Idea in the History of Bad Ideas. No one was willing to give the Neverseen's only Telepath a chance to mess with Sophie's head. So Mr. Forkle would be doing all the dangerous mental searching, and Sophie would once again be relegated to the role of "distractor."

"This isn't going to work," she mumbled, leaning back against the side of her bed. Her legs were going numb after so many hours of sitting on the floor, attempting to brainstorm ideas with Fitz. "Keefe and I were the distraction last time, so Gethen will be ready for that play—especially since he knows everyone's super overprotective of me."

"Then make the distraction so big he can't ignore it," Fitz said.

"Okay, but *how*?"

Annnnnnnd . . . they were back to where they'd been stuck for the last six days.

Overall, their group had made almost zero progress.

Keefe's updates had morphed into super-short answers before he'd tell her "gotta go—try not to worry" and turn his attention away. He *had* managed to tell Sophie that Fintan gave him an important assignment as a reward for solving the symbol's riddle—but everything after that had been "yes," "no," and "*relax*, Foster."

Dex, meanwhile, had made several attempts to build a version of the Neverseen's gadget. But so far, all he'd done was burn a hole in the floor of his bedroom. And Tam's search for a shadowprint of the symbol at the Silver Tower was going slooooooooooooowly. The Lodestar mirror had nothing significant, so now he was stuck going room by room by room.

Linh chose to spend her days at Alluveterre with Wylie. He'd woken up when Maruca and her mom visited, but hadn't talked to anyone since. The only things he responded to were Linh's Hydrokinetic tricks. She'd even earned half a smile when she'd shaped the water into a graceful dancer and let it splash and twirl all over the room. But it wasn't enough to stop everyone from worrying about Wylie's sanity.

And Biana might've chosen the most impossible project of all, deciding it was time to fix their friendship with Marella—even though she knew Marella would be suspicious of her motives. So far, the only words Marella had said to her were, "I liked it better when you guys had forgotten about me."

Even their latest skill lesson with the Exillium Coaches had been more exhausting than educational. They were supposed to channel their energy into the ground and cause a tremor. But Sophie was the only one in her Hemisphere who'd pulled it off—and her mighty earthquake had lasted two whole seconds. The feat seemed especially embarrassing when she compared it to the way the dwarves could crack the earth with a single stomp of their hairy feet. And it made Sophie wonder if the whole skill-training program was going to be a waste. Maybe over time the elves would learn to impress. But at the rate they were going, it would take *years*.

Even the Coaches seemed disheartened. Coach Rohana had told Sophie, "Half the battle is getting the mind to *commit*— but everyone still thinks these skills are 'common' and would rather go back to training in their abilities."

At least Grady and Edaline had found a useful way to spend their days. They'd arranged regular meetings with Lady Cadence to learn as much as they could about the ogres before the Peace Summit. Their conversations usually focused on the complicated politics between the species. But when Sophie and Fitz headed downstairs for a snack, they found the adults in an intense discussion on how best to manage King Dimitar's temper.

"You're overcomplicating it," Lady Cadence told Grady and Edaline. "All you have to do is treat him like an intelligent equal. Ogres are different from us, but they're still sophisticated, complex creatures with their own culture, their own wants and needs—"

"Who've tried to murder the entire gnomish species," Sophie interrupted. "Twice. Also stole the gnomes' homeland. And tried to cripple the Lost Cities by forcing the gnomes into slavery. And allied with the Neverseen. And—"

"I'm not saying the ogres haven't made mistakes," Lady Cadence said, earning snorts from all the goblin bodyguards.

"I'm saying that doesn't erase the good in them—especially considering that the elves are not blameless either. We've compounded the tensions between our species by refusing to take any time to understand them. Instead, we try to force them to set aside fundamental elements of their society. Who are we to decide how they should live? Who are we to micromanage other societies and species?"

"When those societies want to wage war with other species in order to steal their land, I'd say they need to be micromanaged," Sandor argued.

"No, they need to be *managed*," Lady Cadence corrected. "The fighting needs to stop—but that doesn't mean we can't find better compromises. I met with King Dimitar and—"

"*What?*" everyone simultaneously interrupted.

"Oh, don't sound so horrified. Dimitar and I have a long history, and when I heard he agreed to the summit, I asked if he'd let me visit his city."

"*You* went to Ravagog," Grady clarified.

"To what's left of it." Shadows aged Lady Cadence's prim features as she fiddled with her Markchain—a necklace King Dimitar had given her to keep her safe during her years living with the ogres. "I do not fault anyone for the destruction. But it hurts my heart that no one has taken the time to consider what the ogres have suffered. Why do you think Dimitar agreed to meet? I'm one of the few elves willing to listen, willing to open my eyes—"

"Unless you count the Neverseen," Sophie reminded her. "Did he tell you about that? How he'll be meeting with Fintan? And how Fintan assigned him a test to prove they could form another alliance?"

"Actually, he did tell me about that. And I strongly advised him against it. You have to understand—Dimitar sees no other option. Many of the restrictions the Council hopes to impose through this new treaty will force the ogres to change their very ways of being."

"And that gives him the right to form an alliance with murderers?" Fitz asked.

"Of course not, Mr. Vacker. Which is what I told Dimitar. I tried to help him find a different path. I'm still hoping the Council can create a treaty that brings peace to all of our worlds while still granting the ogres the freedom to remain who they are. But if that's not possible, I hope the king will turn to something other than violence."

"Like that'll ever happen," Sophie snorted.

Lady Cadence clicked her tongue. "You disappoint me, Miss Foster. I'd hoped you might bring a bit of compassion to this summit. After all, you're willing to excuse humans from the many grievances held against *them*, aren't you? And when it comes to violence, the humans have no rival. Yes, the ogres must learn to share this planet peacefully. And yes, they need to face the consequences for what they did with the plague, and any other species they've harmed. But if we insist on restricting them to a set of laws that would disrupt their very ways of being, we're sealing our own fate. King Dimitar values elvin guidance—but only from those who treat him as a friend."

"Yeah, well, I don't want to be King Dimitar's friend," Sophie told her.

Lady Cadence let out a slow sigh. "And that is a mistake. One I very much hope you'll reconsider, before it's too late."

"I wouldn't hold my breath," Sophie said, stalking back upstairs. "Can you believe her?" she asked Fitz as soon as they were back in her room. "She wants me to be friends with someone who's tried to kill me at least two different times—someone who's the reason Calla had to sacrifice herself!"

Fitz let out a long sigh as he sank back to the floor. "If it helps, I doubt she meant you should invite him to your Winnowing Gala."

"Ugh, now *there's* a mental picture I didn't need," Sophie grumbled, imagining King Dimitar standing among her long line of matches.

Then again, the idea of a long line of matches felt equally terrifying.

"I think her point," Fitz said quietly, "is that the ogres would cooperate more if we didn't treat them like they're our enemy. And that *does* make sense. If the Council walks into the Peace Summit planning to boss the ogres around and put them in their place, it's only going to make King Dimitar dig in his heels that much more."

"Don't ruin my pouting with your logic," Sophie mumbled.

Fitz laughed. "That sounds like something Keefe would say."

"Does it? Ugh, he must be getting in my head."

"Not too much, I hope." Fitz's tone was teasing. But there was a heat in his eyes that made her cheeks feel warm, even when he added, "I'm not sure the world can handle more than one Keefe Sencen."

Sophie's heart was pounding so loudly, she only caught the last word of his next question.

"What did you say?" she asked.

He picked up their still-blank plan for tricking Gethen. "I said, what if friendship is the answer? Instead of treating Gethen as your adversary when you meet with him, what if you made him think you came there because you want to be friends?"

"I'd never be able to pull that off," Sophie told him. "Remember, this is the guy I Sucker Punched in the face."

"Oh, believe me, I'm never going to forget that. But I'm not talking about becoming BFFs. What if you asked Gethen to be our ally? Reminded him that the Neverseen have left him rotting in that cell for months and have no plans of rescuing him? And then offer a trade?"

"The Council will never cut a deal—and I wouldn't want them to."

"I know," Fitz said. "But we're only aiming for a distraction, remember? And what could be more distracting than getting offered a chance at freedom? Tell him about Wylie. Tell him we're ready to do *anything* to stop something like that from happening again. If he makes other demands, pretend to consider them. You'll have a Councillor with you—get Oralie to back you up. It doesn't have to be real. Just convincing enough to make him think. Because the more he thinks, the more he'll let his guard down, and Mr. Forkle will be able to sneak in and learn what you need. Think it'll work?"

"I think . . . you're a genius."

Fitz's grin curled wider at that, and his eyes sparked with that same hint of heat, making Sophie's cheeks blush again.

"Not a genius," he said, tracing his fingers over his Cognate rings. "But we make a great team. Don't we?"

Sophie nodded. "The best."

FIFTY-FIVE

I CAN'T BELIEVE YOU GUYS WERE SERIOUS about the blindfold," Sophie grumbled as she clung to the rough hands of the goblins guiding her through Lumenaria. Descending a stone spiral staircase without falling to her death was hard enough when she could see where she was going.

She'd already tripped so many times, there'd been serious discussion about carrying her piggyback. And they'd barely begun their journey to the dungeon.

Sandor had escorted Sophie to the island at dawn, per the instructions Oralie had sent them, and they'd found Mr. Forkle and the golden-haired Councillor waiting on the rocky shore. Dark waves crashed in the distance, and the glowing castle sat silhouetted against the gray-pink sky as a dozen heavily armed goblins had marched out to greet them.

The guards had patted everyone down, taking any weapons, gadgets—even jewelry—before leading Sophie, Oralie, and Mr. Forkle into the main courtyard. The gates clanged closed behind them, sealing them in the fortress, and the last thing Sophie saw was Sandor's I'll-be-waiting-right-here stare before the guards covered her eyes with the starched blindfold.

Two sets of hands had pulled her forward then, one stumbling footstep after another. The air shifted as they walked. Sometimes hot, sometimes cold, sometimes sweet or salty scented, depending on the room. The staircase they were currently tackling was damp and sour. The only sound was the echoey thud of footsteps, which swelled louder in the tighter spaces.

Sophie counted every step, trying to create a mental map of the mazelike fortress. It seemed like the kind of information she might be glad to have someday—though with so many twists and turns, she hardly got an accurate picture.

"You'll be able to see again once we reach the main dungeon," the goblin holding her left hand told Sophie. She wasn't allowed to know any of the goblins' names, so she'd decided to call her guards Lefty and Righty.

Lefty caught her as she tripped again, and Sophie used the opportunity to steady herself against the wall. The surface felt wooden this time, and creaked with the impact.

Another door.

The fourth door she'd felt in the last few minutes—though there could've been others in the interim.

"We're almost there," Righty promised, her voice hoarse and wheezy. "Just a few more hallways and a final descent."

"That doesn't sound like 'almost,'" Sophie noted. "I knew this place was huge, but it didn't look *this* massive."

"Another part of the security," Oralie explained. "Lumenaria's dungeon was designed to house diplomatic prisoners—those who hold too much value to be stashed in the center of the earth in Exile. But it had to be just as unreachable."

"How many prisoners are there?" Sophie asked.

Oralie seemed to hesitate before she admitted, "I'm not certain."

"There are two," Righty told them.

"I assume your ignorance means the other prisoner belongs to a Forgotten Secret?" Mr. Forkle asked.

"It must be," Oralie said quietly.

"If it's a Forgotten Secret," Sophie asked, "how do the guards know?"

"Because we have to care for the prisoner," Lefty told her. "And because we need to know all possible threats and dangers. But we are under strict orders not to divulge any specific details, even to the Council. This way."

He pulled Sophie into a hallway that felt wider than the others. The darkness seemed thinner, fuzzing with gray.

Sweat trickled down Sophie's spine as they navigated

several more twists and turns before her guards pulled her to a stop.

"I'm going to carry you for the last part," Lefty said as he lifted her by the waist and draped her over his shoulder like a sack of potatoes. Sophie could feel her feet brushing against cold metal, and Lefty's shoulder muscles straining under her stomach as they dropped slowly down. The air smelled damp and rusty, so she assumed they were descending a ladder.

"We can take the blindfolds off now," Righty said when Lefty set her back on the ground, "but I'd recommend opening your eyes slowly."

Sophie took her advice—but the vivid white glow still sliced across her corneas like a hot blade. She'd been expecting a shadowy stone room with iron bars and other dungeony clichés. Instead, the room they stood in was round, clean, and every silvery-white stone glowed like it had been carved from the sun.

The only thing her eyes could focus on were six arched silver doors lining the room, none of which had any visible locks or handles.

Three of the goblins who'd escorted them placed both of their palms against one of the metal doors, making some sort of combination panel appear.

"Do you know the code they're entering?" Sophie asked Oralie.

"Not at the moment. The codes change three times a day,

and are passed along to the Councillors in a random order to make it impossible for anyone to predict who will have access at any given moment."

"Clever," Mr. Forkle said.

"You have no idea," Righty told him.

"Your fifteen minutes will begin as soon as they open the door," Lefty said. "And there will be no extensions."

"Don't worry," Righty added. "He won't be able to get near you. You'll have a force field that will shift as you move."

"I still want you to stay by my side," Oralie told Sophie, taking her hand. "I'd like to keep contact so I can monitor your emotions."

"And remember," Mr. Forkle added, "do not, under *any* circumstances, attempt to read his mind. No matter how much he may goad you."

"I know the plan," Sophie told him.

And it was a good one. She just had to commit.

Please let it work.

She squared her shoulders, counting to three for courage before she tightened her hold on Oralie and said, "Let's do this!"

FIFTY-SIX

SOPHIE HAD REHEARSED WHAT SHE'D say to Gethen at least a hundred times. And yet, when she stepped into his too-bright, freezing cell, the first words that came out of her mouth were, "Is that the sword in the stone?"

"Glad to hear we haven't crushed that earnest curiosity—yet," Gethen purred from the center of the floor. He sat with his head bowed and legs crossed, as if he'd been meditating—but his wrinkled gray clothes and greasy blond hair betrayed his peaceful composure. And while his bruise had healed, his nose looked permanently crooked from Sophie's punch.

He seemed thinner, too.

Paler.

Wilder.

Behind him, a waist-high stone pillar provided the round room's only ornamentation, with a gleaming silver sword jutting from the center.

"I'm not sure what you mean by *the* sword," Oralie told Sophie, "but each cell has a blade trapped permanently in stone."

"It's my entertainment," Gethen said, his piercing blue eyes studying them one by one. "Though I suspect it's mostly for the guard's enjoyment. I'm sure they've placed bets to see how long I'll keep trying. I always thought I'd be able to resist, but . . ." He held out his right hand, revealing blisters in the same pattern as the diamonds on the sword's hilt. "Sometimes I can't resist a challenge."

"It's not a challenge," Oralie told him. "It's an ever-present reminder that any power you once had is now as useless as that blade."

"So you say. But wouldn't it be ironic if someday I used that blade to chop off your pretty head?"

He jumped to his feet and grabbed the sword, sending Sophie stumbling back.

Oralie didn't blink. "The blade isn't going anywhere."

"Are you sure?" Sophie whispered. Humans had a legend about a sword in a stone, and the sword totally ended up killing people. She wondered if this was where the story came from. Lumenaria did have a Camelot-esque feel.

Gethen gave the hilt a halfhearted tug before brushing one finger down the inch of exposed blade, slicing a thin line of red into his pale skin. "Better hope I never find a way to crack this stone."

"I won't be losing any sleep over it," Oralie told him.

"No, you Councillors never do. Tell me—how'd that work out for Kenric?"

Oralie's grip tightened on Sophie's hand, stopping her from lunging for Gethen's throat. "He's not worth it."

"How can you say that?" Sophie asked, desperate to see if her inflicting was strong enough to batter Gethen through the force field.

But her fury faded when Oralie whispered, "Because Kenric would've wanted me to."

Gethen smiled. "Clearly this meeting is going to be worth the energy I'm using—though if you think I don't feel you in my head, you're a bigger idiot than I thought," he told Mr. Forkle. "If you truly want to learn something, you should let the moonlark give it a go."

The hunger in his eyes was enough to convince Sophie that everyone had been right when they told her not to search his mind.

"I only came here to talk," she said, trying to get back to the script.

"Well, then I assume this is the part where you try to distract me?"

"Actually, it's the part where I ask you for help," Sophie corrected.

One of Gethen's eyebrows shot up, and he leaned casually against the curved wall. "Something big must've happened, then—not sure I can guess what. The timeline's been reset so many times, it could be nearly anything."

Sophie bit her lip, steeling her nerves before delivering the next line. "They took Wylie."

"My goodness—they're *full* of surprises lately" was all Gethen had to say. "And a little bit desperate, if they're back to Cyrah."

"Desperate for what?" Sophie asked.

Gethen tapped his chin with his bleeding finger, stippling it with red. "Same thing we all are. Fintan just has a different approach. Gisela was all about cause and effect. Strategy and patience. Fintan's driven by impulse—not that either affects me way down here."

"Doesn't that bother you?" Sophie asked. "Don't you hate that they're carrying on with their plans while they leave you rotting in this cell?"

"Oh, I'd hardly say I'm rotting. The food is far tastier than anything the Neverseen grew, and the guards bring me a squishy pillow every night to sleep on. And who would complain about having so much time to rest and recharge?"

"You really expect us to believe you don't mind being here?" Sophie asked.

"Why not? You expect *me* to believe the offer you're about to make is real."

"I don't have an offer," Sophie said. "I came here hoping I'd find a shred of decency left."

He sucked his bleeding finger. "Sorry to disappoint. And nice trick, Forkle. You might've had me there a few weeks ago, but all this rest made me so much stronger. Good to know that's the information you're interested in, by the way. I assume that means they snatched Wylie from the Silver Tower? What's the matter—can't figure out how they got in?"

"We're working on it," Sophie snapped.

"I'm sure you are. But if you haven't figured it out already, I don't imagine you will. And even if you did, you'd need an ability you don't have to make it work. Seems shortsighted of you," he told Mr. Forkle. "If you gave her extra powers, why not give her one of everything?"

"More isn't always better," Mr. Forkle told him. "Sometimes it's simply *more*. But I wouldn't expect you to understand."

"I might, if you take the time to enlighten me." Gethen sank to the floor again, staring up at the curved ceiling. "Go ahead. Tell me a story."

"Never mind," Sophie said, turning to Mr. Forkle. "Save your energy. He's never going to help us rescue Wylie."

This was the turning point in their plan.

Gethen could either let them walk away, or . . .

"Are they holding the boy hostage?"

Sophie nodded, letting the memory of Wylie's wounds turn her eyes teary—selling the lie. "He's been missing for over a week."

"You don't approve," Mr. Forkle noted when Gethen cursed.

"Not that it matters, but no, I don't. I think it's a horrible play—sloppy and reckless and will surely end as well as Sophie's kidnapping. But that doesn't mean I'm going to help you."

"Why not?" Sophie asked.

"The Council would be prepared to show their gratitude," Oralie added.

"Yes, I'm sure they'd be happy to unlock this cage and let me go free. Maybe they'd pull that sword from the stone and give it to me as a souvenir."

"They'd be willing to offer you an *improved* situation," Oralie corrected. "There are other places you could be held. Places where it's possible to feel the passing of time." She tapped her toe against the glowing stone floor. "The lumenite keeps your world an endless day."

"Really? I hadn't noticed."

"Yes you have," Mr. Forkle said. "I can see the twitch in your eye. I bet you have no idea how long you've been in here. Maybe you should've thought to count the seconds."

"Well, Miss Foster still has that fresh-faced bloom of youth about her, so I'm guessing it hasn't been *that* long. Besides, each time they bring me a pillow it's a dead giveaway."

Oralie smiled. "They never bring the pillow at the same time. It's part of their instructions. Sometimes they go days before they cue you to sleep again. Sometimes only hours. Meals are just as scattered. Haven't you noticed how sometimes the hunger pains feel like they might tear you apart, or morning comes only minutes after you close your eyes?"

"Our bodies run on rhythm and routine," Mr. Forkle added. "Without it, we deteriorate."

"Lovely picture you both paint." Gethen cleared a catch from his voice. "But I'm still quite happy where I am."

"Then why is your mind frantically trying to guess the date?" Mr. Forkle asked. "Perhaps you're starting to realize just how long you've been abandoned?"

"They're not going to rescue you," Sophie pressed. "Oralie's offer is the best chance you have. And all you have to do is tell us where you think they would've brought Wylie."

"It won't do you any good. You'll never be able to find the hideout."

"Actually, we will." Sophie glanced at Mr. Forkle, needing his reassuring nod before she rattled off everything they'd pieced together about the Lodestar symbol. It was a risk, giving away how much they'd learned. But they needed to make an impression.

Gethen rubbed his temples. "This is what happens when you capture people. It lights a fire in their loved ones that burns wilder than Everblaze. Always a losing game."

"So take the win for yourself," Oralie told him. "One piece of information in exchange for a much more comfortable life."

Gethen stood to pace. He'd made several circles around the room before his eyes locked with Mr. Forkle's. "*Very* clever. You almost had me there—but I'm onto you now, so you can get out of my head." He turned to Sophie. "And I'll take my chances here, thank you very much. They're better than you think."

Mr. Forkle's fisted hands made it clear that Gethen wasn't lying about blocking him. And they were out of games. Out of options. Out of time.

Sophie couldn't decide if she wanted to cry or kick something.

"You honestly thought you'd beat me, didn't you?" Gethen asked as their group turned to leave. "Sorry, Miss Foster—I've been playing this game far too long. *But* you raised an interesting question. So I'm willing to make you an offer. Truth for truth. One from me. One from you."

"It's a trick," Oralie said.

"I can assure you it's not."

"How will I know you're not lying?" Sophie asked.

"You won't. But I won't know if you're lying to me, either. That's the game."

"Do I get to choose my own question?"

"Yes—but I get to go first."

Sophie glanced at Mr. Forkle. "Deal."

"Good decision. And here's my question. Has the Peace Summit already occurred?"

Sophie considered lying—but he'd probably be able to tell. And that would guarantee he'd lie with his answer.

"No," she said. "It hasn't happened."

"But it will soon?"

"That's a separate question. Now it's my turn. What was Cyrah's connection to the Neverseen?"

Gethen's eyebrows shot up. "I thought you wanted to know where they're keeping Wylie."

"I did," Sophie said. "But now I want to know this more."

"Interesting."

"That's not an answer."

"It is, actually. Her connection was interesting. You never specified that I had to give details. Just like I didn't specify a better idea on timing. We both chose our questions poorly."

Sophie sighed. "Fine. The Peace Summit will be happening soon. Now tell me what made Cyrah's connection to the Neverseen so interesting."

He sat quiet long enough to convince her he wouldn't answer. Then he told her, "Starstones."

FIFTY-SEVEN

D**O YOU THINK HE WAS LYING?** Sophie transmitted to Mr. Forkle as their group of goblins led them—blindfolded again—back up the winding staircase. The journey felt twice as endless as it had the first time, and her muscles burned from the incline.

It would be a strange lie to tell, Mr. Forkle said. *Nowhere in the conversation did we mention Lady Gisela's hairpin. Cyrah also worked with many different gems. She specialized in ribbons, but she did sell other hair accessories. And she was a Flasher, so it's possible she did some sort of light treatment to make Lady Gisela's stone flash blue.*

But why would she help the Neverseen? Sophie asked. *She knew her husband sacrificed himself for the Black Swan.*

I honestly have no idea. It's possible she was angry with us for not protecting Prentice. Or Lady Gisela could've ordered the pin without telling Cyrah its purpose. Or she could've been coerced. The Neverseen certainly aren't above blackmail, and a single mother facing the scorn of our world would be especially vulnerable. I'll have to see if Wylie knows anything that could help us narrow down the possibilities. And I'll need to do more research on starstones.

Unless this whole thing is a lie to waste our time, Sophie thought quietly.

Also a possibility. But there's too much potential to ignore it.

What about all that stuff he said about getting into the Silver Tower? Sophie asked. *Do you think the ability he hinted at was a Shade?*

That would be nice, since we're already having Mr. Tam search the tower. But Wylie's assaulters included a Shade, a Vanisher, a Guster, and a Psionipath—all abilities you do not possess. And Gethen did a brilliant job of blocking me from his memories. The energy in his mind felt different. So much stronger and purer. All this idleness must be building his reserves.

"I'm assuming the anxiety I'm feeling from both of you is related to whatever secret conversation you're having?" Oralie asked, reminding them they weren't alone. "And I'm not foolish enough to expect you to tell me what you're discussing. But I'm hoping you might be willing to answer a few simple yes-or-no questions."

"We'll do our best," Mr. Forkle promised.

"Thank you. So first, I'm guessing you've uncovered some sort of clue with starstones, and that's why the word triggered such a strong reaction?"

"Yes," Mr. Forkle said. "We recovered a memory."

"From whom?" Oralie asked.

"That's not a yes-or-no question," Sophie pointed out.

"I suppose it's not. This is going to be harder than I thought," Oralie admitted. "Okay. Do I know the person?"

"Yes," Mr. Forkle said. "But the rememberer is less important than the remembered. In the memory, Lady Gisela used a hairpin set with what she called 'a rare starstone' to light leap to a Neverseen hideout we've currently been unable to locate. And she implied that the stone would be able to guide any user to the same location. But as of this moment, the hairpin is missing."

"Thank you for not making me pry that out of you through yes-or-no questions," Oralie told him. "Does this mean you might be open to answering a few others?"

"I'll answer anything you ask," Mr. Forkle said. "But know that I'm speaking to you as my ally, not as a Councillor."

"I assume that means you don't want me to share the information with the rest of the Council?"

"My instinct is to say yes—but I might be willing to be persuaded if you gave me good reasons why they can be trusted. Our order is not secretive because we enjoy shadows and games. Merely because it was necessary to avoid certain hindrances."

"Fair enough," Oralie said. "It's definitely my hope for our groups to work freely together. But until we reach that point, I accept the need for discretion. And so you know, every guard here is well aware that anything they've seen and heard today can never be shared."

"We swore an oath," Righty chimed in, and the other goblins murmured their agreement.

"Thank you," Mr. Forkle told them.

"Back to questions, then," Oralie said, letting several seconds slip away before she spoke. "Do you believe Lady Gisela killed Cyrah?"

It was the question Sophie had been trying not to ask, and she stopped breathing as she waited for Mr. Forkle's answer.

"If Gethen wasn't lying, it *is* a possibility," Mr. Forkle said quietly. "*But* . . . if starstones are important to the Neverseen, it's also logical that Lady Gisela wasn't the only member who utilized them. And it's important to note that Gethen said 'starstones,' plural, and the memory we recovered only displayed one. So for the moment, we have no proof of anything."

"And all those things that Sophie told Gethen during their conversation," Oralie said, "about a symbol that's also a map of the Neverseen's hideouts, as well as some sort of secret code. I'm assuming that was true?"

"Mostly," Sophie mumbled. "I exaggerated how much we understand. Dex thinks he knows how the system works, but we won't be able to tell for sure until we find one of the gadgets and test it out. Tam is looking to see if there's one hidden in the Silver Tower—or at least proof that the Neverseen used one—so we'll know how they got in."

"I'd like to see the symbol," Oralie said. "And I'd like to show it to Councillor Velia. She's an expert on maps and may notice something important. She's also not the type to ask questions, and will keep everything between us. Would you be okay with that?"

"If you believe Velia would be useful in this regard, I'm willing to take you at your word," Mr. Forkle told her. "I'll send a record of the symbol as soon as I return to my office."

"And which office is that?" Oralie asked. "In one of your hideouts? Or maybe somewhere closer to home?"

"Am I to infer that you have a theory as to my identity?" Mr. Forkle asked.

"I've had *many* theories," Oralie said as they reached the top of the stairs. "But this one feels right."

"This is a trap, isn't it?" Mr. Forkle asked. "Pique my curiosity so that I'll be tempted to slip into your head to check your theory, and if I do, my emotions would give you your answer."

"I suppose that would work out rather well," Oralie told him. "But I'd prefer to wait until you're ready to tell me. And don't think I haven't noticed how quiet you're being, Sophie. I'm assuming that means you're already in on the secret."

"*Secrets,*" Sophie corrected. "I know two of his identities. Still trying to figure out the others."

"And *that* is enough about me," Mr. Forkle told them. "Did anyone else find Gethen's interest in the Peace Summit to be concerning?"

"Yes," Oralie admitted. "Even without physical contact, I could feel how desperate he was for information."

"Any idea why?" Sophie asked.

"From the glimmers I caught in his mind," Mr. Forkle said, "I suspect the Neverseen once had a plan in the event of an ogre summit, and he believes it will allow him a chance to escape."

All of the goblins laughed.

"Don't underestimate the Neverseen," Sophie warned them.

"Don't underestimate *us*," Lefty told her. "We have security beyond anything anyone could prepare for."

"But perhaps it might be wise to add a few additional measures," Oralie decided.

"Are you allowed to tell us when the summit is?" Sophie asked.

"No—but I suppose it would be wise for you to prepare. The summit is scheduled for two weeks from tomorrow. You'll receive official notice a week prior."

The goblins spent the rest of their trek discussing ways to reorganize their patrols. And soon enough, they'd reached the main courtyard.

"I expect a *thorough* update," Sandor told Sophie after her blindfold had been removed, her belongings returned, and they'd regrouped outside the castle's gates.

"I will," she promised. "But let's wait until we're back at Havenfield. That way I can explain it to everyone at the same time."

"I'll update the Collective," Mr. Forkle told her. "And perhaps we should regroup tomorrow to discuss the best course of action from here?"

"Please keep me in the loop," Oralie told them. "And I'll be sure to do the same. This is a time when working together is in all of our best interests."

"Indeed," Mr. Forkle said, offering a quick bow before raising his pathfinder to the sunlight and leaping away.

"Thank you again for arranging this meeting," Sophie told Oralie.

Oralie gave her a weak smile. "I only hope it was worth it."

Sophie made the same wish as she took Sandor's hand and leaped them both back to Havenfield.

"So should we—"

"STOP!" Sandor snapped, pulling her behind him. He unsheathed his sword and spun around, sniffing the air. "Something's wrong. *Very* wrong."

Sophie had no idea what could have him so freaked out.

And then she saw it.

Streaks of red in one of the pastures. Splashes of it in another.

Fresh blood.

FIFTY-EIGHT

SANDOR COVERED SOPHIE'S MOUTH and hefted her over his shoulder to prevent her from running away.

But she *had* to find Grady and Edaline. What if they—

"You must stop struggling and do *exactly* as I say," Sandor ordered, charging toward the grove where the gnomes lived. "I need to get you somewhere safe so I can search the grounds for your family. And I need you to be quiet, because I can't tell what we're dealing with."

He kept his sword raised, moving so fast the scenery blurred. Sophie tried to keep calm, telling herself the blood belonged to one of the animals—until Sandor slowed and uttered a string of goblin curse words.

She strained to follow his gaze and found a bloody ogre sprawled across the grass.

Dead.

She screamed and twisted in Sandor's arms.

He was no match for her adrenaline-fueled panic, and she took off into the pastures shouting her parents' names as red rimmed her vision while she ran. Her thudding heart pounded almost as hard as the rage pulsing inside her, straining against the tangled threads she'd knotted around it. She pressed her hands against her ribs, willing the emotions to hold steady. She needed to save them for whatever was coming.

She passed another dead ogre in the next clearing. Then two more.

The next body she found was a goblin with long curly hair.

Grady's bodyguard.

Sophie's voice turned into a ragged wail as she collapsed to her knees, unable to get back up—until someone grabbed her shoulder and instincts took over.

Her knotted emotions ripped free, and she shoved the darkness out of her in sickening waves, pummeling her attacker over and over. She could've raged forever, but strained, squeaky words brought her out of the frenzy.

When her vision cleared, she found Sandor collapsed on his side, teeth gritted, his body shaking from her inflicting.

"It's okay," a soft voice said behind her. "The ogres are gone."

Sophie spun around and found Flori standing with a sack of Panakes blossoms.

"I'm so sorry," she whispered. "They told me to wait for you to make sure you didn't panic. But I thought I'd have time to gather more medicine."

Sophie couldn't get her brain to form words as Flori moved to Sandor's side, placing a blossom on his chest and humming a soothing melody while she mopped the sweat off his brow with the edges of her long hair.

Sandor's features relaxed as Flori worked, the pain fading from his eyes.

"Where are they?" Sophie managed to whisper.

Flori knew who she meant. "They're safe. I'll bring you to see them as soon as Sandor's ready."

She said other things, but Sophie's brain was on never-ending repeat.

Safe. Safe. Safe. Safe. Safe.

Seconds crawled by—or maybe it was minutes. Eventually Sandor raised his shaky head.

"At least I know you *can* protect yourself," he told Sophie, offering a weak smile.

Sophie struggled to apologize, but Sandor waved the words away. "My only concern is your safety," he promised, his watery eyes focused on something in the distance.

Sophie didn't have to turn to know he was looking at Brielle's broken body.

"Come on," Flori said, taking Sophie's hand. "I'll bring you to the others."

She sang an entrance into the ground, and Sandor and Sophie followed her into the earth. The tunnel was damp and dark and pleasantly warm as Flori tangled their feet in the roots.

"Brace yourselves," she warned, shifting the cadence of her melody.

The roots obeyed her command, carrying them faster, faster, faster—far away. Into the darkness. Flori filled their journey with soothing songs, trying to keep Sophie calm and steady. But the icy terror didn't thaw until they emerged in a small hollow surrounded by towering red-barked trees.

Grady and Edaline were there—dirty and bloody, but strong enough to throw their arms around Sophie as she crashed into them, holding on with all the strength she had left.

The sobs hit then, wringing out the rest of the fear clouding her mind and unleashing a tidal wave of questions: "What happened? Are you hurt? Has someone called Elwin? Where are we? How did you get away? What's going on? WHY WERE THERE OGRES?"

"We're going to be fine," Grady promised as she reached up to wipe a scratch on his cheek. "Edaline and I were very lucky."

He glanced at something behind her, and Sophie whipped

around to find a dozen gnomes crouched around two more bodies. Flori was busy working with them, smearing their wounds with crushed Panakes petals.

"They're going to be okay," Edaline whispered, holding Sophie tighter as they studied the unconscious, blood-streaked faces of Cadoc and Lady Cadence. "Lur and Mitya went to get Elwin. They should be back any minute."

"Did you sedate them?" Sandor asked, crouching next to Cadoc and checking the pulse point at the goblin's bruised throat.

"No, that's from the shock and the blood loss," Edaline told him. "But their breathing is strong. And their hearts are holding steady. They just need medicine. And lots of rest."

Sophie nodded blankly, trying not to look at all the red. "I saw Brielle."

Grady turned away to wipe his eyes. "She saved me. Took on four ogres at once so I could get to Edaline. Three of them fell by her sword, but the fourth was faster."

Something cracked behind them.

Sophie turned and found Sandor clutching his bleeding fist, and a giant dent punched into one of the trees.

"Keefe was right about his warnings," Edaline mumbled. "The Neverseen finally came after us."

"You saw them?" Sophie asked.

She'd never forgive Keefe if he'd been there. Ever. Not even if he'd stood on the sidelines.

"No," Grady said. "But one of the ogres shouted, 'The Pyro-kinetic is waiting.' I don't know if they meant Brant or Fintan, but it doesn't matter. What matters is, their plan failed."

Sophie repeated his last words, trying to find comfort in them.

But all she could think was, *This isn't over.*

FIFTY-NINE

THE OGRES HAD *ALMOST* WON.

Somehow they'd seemed to know that Sandor wouldn't be there. They'd also positioned themselves throughout the pastures to make sure no one had anywhere to run. And they'd known to wait for the afternoon feeding, when everyone would be carrying buckets instead of weapons. They'd even prepared for Grady's ability, blocking his mesmerizing with special ogre-size versions of the thinking caps they used at Foxfire during exams. And when Edaline tried to conjure up weapons from their stockpile, the ogres had been ready to disarm her, as if they'd known exactly what she would do during the battle.

Brielle and Cadoc had fought bravely and ferociously. But there had been *ten* ogres.

Within minutes Brielle was dead, Cadoc and Lady Cadence seriously injured, and Grady and Edaline were preparing themselves to be taken.

"Verdi's the one who saved us," Grady said, his lips twitching with a dark smile. "She charged though her pasture's fence, grabbed one of the ogres with her teeth, and trampled another. The remaining ogres rushed to help and . . . I'll spare you those details, but let's say Verdi got herself a nice taste of ogre meat. And she didn't enjoy it."

"And she's okay?" Sophie asked. "They didn't . . ."

"She took some hard blows," Grady admitted. "She'll probably limp from now on. She also lost a few teeth. But several gnomes stayed at Havenfield to care for her, and I was able to get pressure on her wounds as soon as the final ogre fled."

"Coward," Sandor spit, squeezing the handle of his sword so hard, the skin on his fingers looked ready to rip.

"I know," Grady said. "And it was the ogre who murdered Brielle. He'll have a scar across his chest from her final attack. If I ever see him again . . ."

"You won't," Sandor promised. "We have hunters who will find him and shred him."

Sophie tried not to picture it—but her imagination ran wild.

Elwin saved her from the nightmares when he crawled out of the earth carrying two overfilled satchels. His tousled hair and crazy glasses gave him a bit of a mad-scientist air, but within minutes, his remedies had color flooding back into Lady Cadence's cheeks and Cadoc's eyes fluttering awake.

"I'll need to move them to the Healing Center at Foxfire to clean them up and set a few broken bones," he told Lur and Mitya. "Can you guys rig something to help us transport them through the earth? I'm afraid they might be too weak for a light leap."

The gnomes got to work, weaving fallen branches into nest-like cots. While they built, Elwin turned his attention to Grady and Edaline. They each needed a dozen elixirs—and Grady had two cracked ribs—but Elwin promised Sophie they'd make a full recovery.

"I'm fine," she told him as he snapped his fingers and flashed a blue orb around her face. "I wasn't here."

"I'm checking for signs of shock. You're borderline, so I want you to take these." He handed her two vials filled with a thick lime green syrup. "Not sedatives, I promise."

"And not that weird happy elixir you gave me after Alden's mind broke?" she checked.

"Nope. Think of these as a security blanket for your nerves. They'll take away some of that chill"—he traced a finger down the goose bumps on her arms—"and slow your heart to its normal rate. That's it."

Sophie chugged them, barely registering the honeylike taste as warmth rippled through her.

"Want me to check on Verdi?" Elwin offered.

"If it won't affect Cadoc and Lady Cadence's treatment," Edaline told him.

"And only if you can handle being around a few dead bodies," Grady added.

Elwin cringed. "How many are there?"

"Nine ogres," Edaline whispered. "And Brielle."

Everyone bowed their heads at the name, and Sandor punched the tree again.

"Here," Elwin said, reaching for Sandor's bleeding knuckles.

"Do you have an Imparter with you?" Grady asked him. "I need to hail the Council and let them know what happened."

"I can't believe they had thinking caps," Elwin mumbled. "And that the caps blocked mesmerizing."

"The Neverseen must have designed them," Edaline whispered.

Elwin nodded. "No one knows how to take down an elf better than another elf."

"Which is why you're no longer safe in the Lost Cities," Sandor announced, clenching his newly bandaged hand. "Dimitar won't accept failure—especially for this. This had to be his test to secure his new alliance."

"I wouldn't be so sure," Lady Cadence rasped from her newly made stretcher. "None of these were members of his personal guard—and none of them wore Markchains."

"So he distanced himself from the attack," Sandor snarled.

"That's not proof of innocence, only foresight. His next attack will come swiftly. Ogres are expert trackers. We need to move you somewhere even Dimitar would never dare go."

"Where are you suggesting?" Edaline asked.

Sandor's voice seemed to deepen as he said, "The best option is Gildingham. The ogres know that entering our capital city would be a declaration of war."

"Would Hylda approve our visit?" Grady asked as he rejoined them. "I thought she preferred to keep outsiders to a minimum."

"She would never turn away an elvin family in need—especially one as important as yours. I'll contact her now and make the arrangements." Sandor pulled a triangular gadget from his pocket and moved to the edge of the clearing to speak with his queen.

Sophie, meanwhile, was wondering why no one seemed to be addressing the much scarier question.

Now that the ogres had sent ten soldiers to directly attack an elvin family within the boundaries of the Lost Cities—did that mean the ogres and the elves were at war?

SIXTY

EAVE THE DIPLOMACY TO THE COUN-
cil," Mr. Forkle ordered when Sophie hailed him
on her Imparter and explained the afternoon's
tragedies.

"I think we're well beyond diplomacy," she mumbled.

"I wouldn't be so sure. Given what Lady Cadence noted
about her attackers, I have no doubt King Dimitar will claim
that anyone involved acted without his permission—which
may even be true."

"You're serious?"

"Are the Neverseen acting with the Council's permission?"
he countered. "I know you're angry and afraid—and justifiably
so. But we cannot let ourselves be controlled by fear or fury,

or rush into any actions that will only cause further death and destruction. Not without gathering evidence. So let the Councillors investigate. And try not to be surprised if they opt to proceed with the Peace Summit."

Sophie's grip on her Imparter tightened. "You really think a treaty is going to stop the ogres from killing innocent people? Or coming after my family again?"

"It depends on who's giving the orders. It's also important to keep in mind that if Dimitar was behind this incident, in some ways that's an advantage. We've been working to prevent the ogres and Neverseen from aligning, and this guarantees it. Fintan will be livid that the ogres failed. And King Dimitar will be furious over losing so many warriors."

The words would've been much more comforting if Sophie weren't picturing Brielle's bloody, broken body.

"Right now, the most important thing is to get you and your family to safety," Mr. Forkle added gently. "I agree with Sandor that Gildingham is the wisest option. Do you need me to bring you a crystal to leap there?"

"Queen Hylda has already sent her chariot," Sandor said over Sophie's shoulder. She'd forgotten he was eavesdropping. "The drivers will be here as soon as they retrieve Brielle."

His voice faltered on the name.

"My deepest sympathies," Mr. Forkle told him. "Brielle was an incredible warrior."

"One of the best," Sandor agreed, looking desperate to punch something again.

"When will she be presented in the Hall of Heroes?" Mr. Forkle asked.

"Aurification will begin as soon as she's brought to Gildingham. The presentation should be tomorrow."

"I'll let the Council know to release their goblin regiments for the ceremony," Mr. Forkle promised.

"Actually, Queen Hylda will be ordering them to remain with their assignments," Sandor told him. "She believes it would be unwise to leave the Lost Cities vulnerable. Dimitar could take advantage."

Mr. Forkle blinked. "That's incredibly generous of her."

"It is," Sandor said. "But now more than ever, we must work as allies."

Sophie wasn't familiar with some of the terms they'd been using, but she assumed they'd been talking about the goblin's version of a funeral.

"Can I go to the presentation?" she asked. "Or is it a goblins-only thing?"

"Presentations are generally only attended by our people," Sandor told her. "But Brielle is the first in the elvin regiments to be lost in a battle, so it might be good to show the public that the elves do not take her sacrifice for granted. I'll raise the matter with the queen."

"We'd like to go as well," Grady called from across the clearing, where he sat with Edaline, both of them so weary they could barely move.

"I'll ask Della to include something gold for each of you to wear when she packs up the satchels we'll be sending," Mr. Forkle told them. "Would you like us to send your imp to keep you company, Miss Foster?"

"No, I think it'd be easier for Iggy to stay with Biana."

Sophie doubted the goblins wanted a tiny purple poof causing havoc in their city.

"Please let me know once you're settled in Gildingham," Mr. Forkle told her. "And I'll keep you updated on any developments. And Miss Foster?" He touched the screen of his Imparter, like he was trying to reach across the distance between them. "I'm so relieved that you and your parents are well. Please keep it that way."

His image flashed away, and Sophie stared at the blank screen, trying to figure out what to feel—what to do.

She was on her way to sit with Grady and Edaline when the ground started to rumble.

"Don't be nervous," Sandor said as she jumped back, preparing for another ogre attack. "It's just Twinkle."

With a name like Twinkle, Sophie definitely wasn't prepared for a fifty-foot snake to burst out of the ground—especially a fifty-foot snake strapped to some sort of golden harness lined with hundreds of golden wheels. The contraption ended in a carriage that looked like a giant golden egg, covered in intricate patterns and symbols.

The snake's scales shimmered with flecks of gold, silver, and pink as it slithered into a tight coil, coming to rest with the egg carriage right in front of them.

"Twinkle is a titanoboa," Sandor explained. "And she's been trained to guide the royal chariot through the Imperial Pathways. Queen Hylda wanted to ensure that Brielle returns to Gildingham with proper honor."

In her head, Sophie's brain was screaming, *YOU CHOSE TO TAKE ME IN THE GIANT SNAKE CARRIAGE OF DOOM WHEN WE COULD'VE LIGHT LEAPED?!*

But she'd caught what he said about Brielle arriving with proper honor. If a monster-size snake offered any sort of tribute for Brielle's sacrifice, she would ride in the carriage all day, every day, without complaint.

A small whimper *did* slip through her lips, though, when Sandor led them past Twinkle's enormous head. The massive snake could've swallowed her whole without needing to unhinge her jaw, and her forked tongue kept flicking around Sophie, like she was trying to take a taste.

A seamless door in the carriage slid open, and two goblins greeted Sandor with a solemn nod as Sophie and her parents climbed in. There were no seats inside. Just a massive golden coffin and narrow spaces to stand on either side.

"Hold on to this," Sandor said, grabbing one of the golden ropes tied to the top of the carriage and handing it to Sophie. Grady and Edaline copied him, coiling the rope around one of their wrists and clinging to Sophie with their other hands as the two new goblins shouted a command to get Twinkle moving.

The carriage had no windows—the only light came from a glowing golden orb set into the ceiling—and the ride was so smooth and steady, it almost felt like they were floating. A low rumble reverberated through the silence, and Sophie counted the passing seconds, surprised when they came to a stop after only five hundred and thirty-nine.

"I didn't realize we were so close to Gildingham," Sophie said.

"We weren't. A team of Technopaths helped engineer Twinkle's chariot to allow her to move at supersonic speeds. We'll disembark after they carry out Brielle."

One of the goblins they'd traveled with slid open the door, flooding the carriage with buttery sunlight as he and the other goblin lifted the coffin.

Sophie focused on the view—her first glimpse of the goblin city, where intricate gilded buildings had been built across the rolling green foothills. The architecture had an almost fragile feel, with so many arches and pillars and windows and balconies that they looked ready to float away on a breeze. A golden lake shimmered in the distance, flowing into a river that shone like the sun. And at the top of the highest peak, a golden step pyramid loomed against the horizon.

"That's Queen Hylda's palace," Sandor said, following Sophie's gaze. "And once we're out of the carriage you'll see the Hall of Heroes, where we'll be going for Brielle's presentation tomorrow. The queen invited you to have dinner with her tonight, but I asked her to give you the night to settle in before facing any formalities."

"She wasn't offended, was she?" Grady asked.

"If anything, she was relieved. Generally the night a soldier is lost is a night of reflection for our queen. She only offered because she didn't want to seem an unfriendly hostess."

Edaline smiled sadly. "Then thanks for declining. We're going to have to rely on you for proper goblin diplomacy."

"I'll do my best. For instance, as we step out of this carriage and you see the crowd gathered below, it would be considered proper to offer a solemn wave."

"Crowd?" Sophie asked as Sandor slowly exited. Sure enough, when she followed, she could see that Twinkle had brought them to a level of the city halfway up one of the rolling hills, and the golden streets below were lined with goblin warriors who'd gathered to see them. Some were shirtless with black pants and weapons, like Sandor always wore, but most were adorned in gleaming golden armor.

"This way," Sandor said after Sophie gave the crowd what she hoped counted as a "solemn wave." He pressed his palm against a flat panel in the center of golden door set into the mountain. "Don't worry, my house is much bigger on the inside."

He wasn't wrong.

Not only was the house at least ten bedrooms—but everything was designed for someone seven feet tall. All the doorknobs were closer to Sophie's shoulder height, and she had to stand on her tiptoes in order to climb onto any of the chairs. And it was so *fancy*. Shimmering rugs. Tasseled curtains. Intricately carved furniture, all in the same warm yellow tone.

"I'm assuming there's a reason everything's gold," Sophie said.

Sandor nodded. "Gold is a weak metal. But *we* are strong. We don't build houses or walls for protection. We build them to have a place that inspires awe—a place *worth* defending."

"Well, it's incredible," Edaline told him. "I'd heard stories of the golden city, but I'd never pictured it quite this spectacular."

Sandor wandered to one of the windows. "I wish you could be here under better circumstances. But I suppose it's nice to be home. Della should be here with your clothes and things soon. In the meantime, I'll show you to your rooms."

Grady and Edaline were given their own suite at the end of the longest hall, and Sophie grabbed one more hug before following Sandor to where she'd be staying, in a room with a gilded four-poster bed covered in golden linens. She knew she should probably rest. But as soon as she was alone, she did something much more important.

I don't care if this is a bad time, she transmitted. *We need to talk. NOW.*

She repeated the call at least a dozen times before Keefe's voice rushed into her head.

Are Grady and Edaline okay?

Fury churned as fast as the queasiness in her stomach. *I take it that means you knew?*

Not until a couple of hours ago, when Fintan got a hail from King Dimitar.

So the king is behind this? She rubbed the spot under her ribs, where her tangled emotions used to be. She'd released them when she inflicted, leaving her chest cold and empty.

I don't know, Keefe said. *All Fintan told us is that Dimitar will not be our ally. I've been trying to find a way to reach you ever since. I'm so sor—*

Don't! Sophie interrupted. *Brielle's dead. Sorry isn't going to change that.*

Okay, I don't know who Brielle is, but—

She was Grady's bodyguard. THAT'S how close the ogres came to catching him. And you were supposed to warn us!

I did warn you. I just didn't know the specifics.

I know. But that's the thing neither of us have wanted to admit. If you can't give the specifics, everything you're doing is worthless.

The words hit him harder than she'd expected. But she wasn't taking them back.

I'm doing the best I can, he told her.

Maybe. But it's not enough. Half the time you can't even talk during our check-ins. This isn't working.

I know it feels like that—but I'm seriously SO CLOSE.

Even if that's true—you know what? We're getting close too. We've already figured out what the symbol means, and Gethen gave us a big clue on how to use it.

What are you saying?

I'm saying, we're coming after the Neverseen with everything we have.

Bad idea, Foster. Seriously, so bad.

I don't care. They tried to take my family from me, and I'm not going to sit back anymore. So you better find a way to get out now, Keefe. Before you get caught in the cross fire.

SIXTY-ONE

KEEFE WASN'T GOING TO LISTEN.

Sophie could tell.

He thought she didn't have a plan, and that everything she'd said was just an angry rant.

And a small part of her worried that he was right.

The other part knew they *had* to find a way to fight harder, before she lost anyone else she cared about.

But that included Keefe.

So if he wasn't ready to leave on his own, they'd have to plan a rescue—for real. No more waiting for inspiration and hoping a plan would come together. They needed to sit down and figure it out and make it happen, just like when they'd snuck into Ravagog.

Between their abilities and their skills and the information they'd gathered, there had to be a way to—

A knock at Sandor's front door interrupted her scheming.

Sophie crept to her doorway, relieved when she recognized Grizel's voice. It sounded like Grizel had brought their clothes from the Lost Cities, and Sophie made her way down the hall to pick up her satchel.

But when she turned the corner, she caught a quick glimpse of Grizel clinging to Sandor and sobbing against his shoulder as he wrapped his arms gently around her.

Sophie ducked back, not wanting to interrupt such a private moment.

"I'm sorry," Grizel whispered, her voice thick. "When the news first came through, all anyone could tell me was that a soldier was down at Havenfield. And I thought . . ."

"I don't deserve your worry." Sandor's voice was choked with fury. "I wasn't there when Brielle and Cadoc needed me. I was pacing in front of Lumenaria like a fool."

"Staying with your charge doesn't make you foolish," Grizel told him. "I would've done the same thing."

"Which proves we're both blindly stubborn beyond all reason, not that it was the right decision."

Grizel laughed softly. "The *stubborn* I'll agree to. But the *blind* part might fall squarely on you."

"I'm . . . not as blind as you think."

The shift in his tone made Sophie wonder if she should stop

listening and give them some privacy. But she couldn't seem to make her legs carry her away.

"I couldn't stop you from being assigned to Fitz," Sandor whispered. "But have you ever wondered why I assigned Brielle to watch over Grady?"

"I . . . figured it was because she was an incredible soldier," Grizel said carefully.

"She was. But we both know that charge should've gone to you. Given the rarity of Grady's talent, he needed our strongest warrior. I should've assigned you to protect him and moved Brielle to Everglen. But"—he cleared the catch from his throat—"I worried what would happen if we lived in such close quarters."

"Afraid I'd play too many games?"

"Afraid you'd win."

The confession was so soft, Sophie almost wondered if she'd imagined it.

"Is that really so frightening?" Grizel whispered.

Sandor cleared his throat again, drawing out the moment. "I chose the life of a soldier. And soldiers are strongest when they have nothing distracting them—nothing slowing their hand or forcing caution when the battle calls for risk."

"See, and I always thought the strongest soldiers were those with something worth fighting for. Something to come home to. Something they can't bear to lose that makes them refuse to surrender."

"I don't know," Sandor whispered. "But I can't stop imagining what I'd do if it were you in that coffin. How lost I'd feel."

The silence that followed was so charged, it had Sophie mentally chanting, *Kiss, kiss, kiss!* But real life never seemed to be as romantic as it was in human movies, and the moment slipped away.

"Well," Grizel said. "I suppose I should be getting back to Everglen. Queen Hylda gave me a long list of preparations to make for tomorrow."

The door had started to creak closed when Sandor said, "I haven't forgotten that I owe you a dance."

"Neither have I," Grizel whispered. "But I won't force you."

"You aren't," Sandor breathed. "I can't promise much. But I might be able to handle . . . slow."

"Slow," Grizel repeated, and the hope in her voice made Sophie steal a peek around the corner. She watched Grizel take Sandor's hands and whisper, "I'd be good with slow."

Sandor reached up to brush Grizel's cheek, and she leaned into his palm, closing her eyes and taking a deep breath. Endless seconds slipped by, neither of them seeming to mind. And when she pulled away, a shy smile curled her lips.

"Be safe," Sandor whispered.

"Always," she told him.

She was halfway through the doorway when she turned back with a teasing wink. "This won't get you out of wearing those silver pants."

Sandor sighed. "I suppose that's the least of my worries."

She left without another word, and Sandor waited for the lock to click before he turned to Sophie and said, "I knew you were listening."

"I figured," Sophie told him, too giddy to feel guilty. "And just so you know, I think you made the right decision. You guys are so—"

"Keep in mind that any comments you make about my love life give me permission to talk to you about boys," Sandor interrupted. "I'd also appreciate your discretion. Now is not the time for such things to become known."

"Done," Sophie said, dropping the conversation. "I just want to see you happy. Especially after all the sacrifices you make for me. I'm sorry again for inflicting on you. Next time I'll keep a tighter hold until I'm sure I'm fighting a threat."

Sandor shook his head as he brought over her purple backpack. "How about instead we focus on making sure there isn't a next time?"

Sophie had planned to cry at Brielle's funeral—or presentation—or whatever the goblins called it. She'd even stuffed several handkerchiefs into the pockets of her long golden gown. But sadness wasn't the theme of the ceremony. It was about bestowing honor and celebrating Brielle's accomplishments.

The Hall of Heroes itself was a massive acropolis-style structure lined with twisted golden columns and filled with golden statues that reminded Sophie of the terra-cotta warriors she'd seen in human encyclopedias—row upon row of gleaming goblins in heroic battle poses.

It seemed like a beautiful tribute, until they unveiled Brielle's statue and Sophie realized the figure was a little *too* lifelike—every detail perfect, down to the very last curl.

"Is that *her*?" she whispered, fighting off a gag when Sandor nodded. Grady and Edaline didn't look *as* horrified—but they'd definitely gone pale.

"Her body's been aurified," Sandor explained. "It's a process the elves helped us perfect. It transmutes every cell to gold, leaving no flesh or blood behind. Only a powerful likeness to remember our soldiers by." He frowned when he noticed Sophie was cringing. "Honestly, how is it that different from wrapping your DNA around a seed and letting the tree grow with some of your characteristics?"

When he put it like that, it didn't sound *as* creepy. And it wasn't Sophie's place to judge another species' culture anyway.

But she still wouldn't have wanted to be alone in the Hall of Heroes at night—and she was pretty sure she was going to have more than a few golden mummy nightmares.

She fought hard not to let any of her discomfort show on her face, since the queen had given their group seats on an elevated platform, in plain view of the entire audience.

"It was wise for you to attend," Sandor told them when everyone stood to leave. "I can tell it meant a lot to my people to see that the elves care about the soldiers who protect them."

"It did indeed," a deep, throaty voice said behind them, and Sandor immediately dropped to one knee.

"Your Highness," he mumbled. "I didn't see you there."

"That's because I snuck up on you," Queen Hylda said, tossing her intricately plaited hair. She smoothed the golden lapels of her military-style jacket as her gray eyes focused on Sophie, Grady, and Edaline. "Please, no need for such formalities," she told them as they hurried to bow as well. "You are not my subjects."

"We still owe you our respect," Grady said as he straightened. "You and your warriors have been invaluable allies."

"Well, the elves' knowledge and innovation have been equally precious for our world," Queen Hylda said. "I consider the whole arrangement to be a crucial partnership. Which is why I was hoping I might borrow young Miss Foster for a few minutes. The Council has informed me that she'll be attending the Peace Summit. And if that's the case, I have a favor to ask."

SIXTY-TWO

YOU HAD A PRIVATE AUDIENCE with the goblin queen?" Biana asked, sharing a look with Dex that seemed to say, *Why are we even surprised anymore?*

"We didn't talk for long," Sophie mumbled, checking to make sure no one around them was eavesdropping. "Queen Hylda just wanted to ask me for a favor."

Biana grinned. "Of course she did."

Despite the attack on Sophie's parents—which the Council had revealed to the public to honor Brielle's sacrifice—Mr. Forkle had managed to convince Sandor to bring Sophie to her weekly skill lesson at Foxfire. The Coaches were ramping up the training now that people finally seemed scared enough to commit to it. And it made a difference—by the end of the lesson, almost half of Sophie's Hemisphere had achieved the day's skill and cracked small stress fissures in their stones.

Sophie had shattered hers completely.

The process had left her drained—but it was a good kind of exhaustion. Far better than the five restless days she'd spent pacing around Sandor's house, brainstorming elaborate Rescue Keefe plans and then rejecting them for having too many Things That Would Get Everyone Killed. And her check-ins with Keefe now followed a repetitive pattern of her begging him to leave the Neverseen and him promising, "Soon."

Hopefully, if her group of friends worked together, they'd be able to come up with something that had a chance of success. But getting them all in the same place was proving challenging—especially Tam and Linh. The twins had even skipped the skill lesson that day. Tam was using every spare second to search the Silver Tower, desperate to find whatever last piece they needed to make everything they'd learned about the symbol come together. And Linh had been nervous to leave Wylie alone.

Mr. Forkle had felt obligated to tell Wylie what they'd learned from Gethen about his mother's death and starstones—though he left out any mention of Lady Gisela, deciding to wait until they had a better idea of precisely how she'd been involved. But hearing that his mom had likely helped the Neverseen had knocked Wylie to a new low. Granite had even brought Maruca and her mom back to see him, and all Wylie said during the visit was, "Is anyone who they say they are?"

"What kind of favor are you supposed to do for a goblin queen?" Fitz asked, dragging Sophie out of her dreary thoughts.

She waited for a group of nearby Right Hemispheres to wander away before she whispered, "She wants my support during the summit. She gave me a list of all the things she wants added to the new treaty, and asked me to decide which ones I'll vote in favor of."

"Isn't that cheating?" Biana asked. "Colluding before the summit?"

"Why would it be?" Fitz asked. "It's not a test."

"Your brother is correct," Sandor told her. "The summit is a negotiation. And the best negotiators do their homework ahead of time. I'm sure everyone is determining their allies."

"Anyone else stunned the ogres are still going through with the summit?" Dex asked. "I mean . . . they have to know everyone is going to side against them."

"King Dimitar has no choice," Grizel said, and Sophie noticed she was standing a little closer to Sandor than she truly needed to. "He's claiming innocence in the attack, insisting it was done by a band of rebels. He even sent Queen Hylda a letter offering his condolences. But he knows no one will believe him if he's not also working closely with the Council toward 'achieving a peaceful resolution.'"

She put the last words in air quotes, almost like she no

longer believed they were a possibility. But Sophie was cling-ing hard to the last shreds of her hope.

Sure, part of her wanted to march into Ravagog and stomp the ogres into the ground for what they'd done to her family. But another part kept thinking about the eerie golden bodies in the Hall of Heroes.

How many more goblins would have to be aurified if the elves and ogres went to war?

How many new trees would be added to the Wanderling Woods?

If there was any chance they could solve this without further violence, they had to try for it.

"So what kinds of things are on Queen Hylda's list?" Dex asked.

"Exactly what you'd expect," Sophie whispered. "She wants the ogres to turn over all their weapons and agree to stop any sort of offensive—or defensive—training, wants them to sur-render the borderlands they share with the goblins, and wants King Dimitar to turn over the ogre who killed Brielle. There were a bunch of things that had to do with the previous treaty too. But I didn't understand a lot of that, so I gave copies to Mr. Forkle and Oralie to see if they can help me."

"Are you going to support her list?" Biana asked.

Sophie shrugged.

She understood why Queen Hylda was drawing such a hard line. But she kept thinking about what Lady Cadence had tried to tell her, about how the new treaty would destroy fundamental aspects of the ogres' culture. She had zero sympathy for King Dimitar, but she knew thousands and thousands of innocent ogres would be affected—including the children she'd seen running around during her time in Ravagog.

"Let's just say I'm glad I still have some time to decide," she mumbled, wishing it were longer. The Council was sticking with their scheduled date, so she only had about a week and a half left. "I swear, this whole thing is way more involved than I realized. Did you guys know that summits last multiple days? I got this, like, *packet* saying Edaline and I will have our own room in the castle, and luggage isn't allowed, so we both had to send the Council our measurements and they'll provide several changes of clothes."

"Ohhhh," Biana breathed. "I bet they'll make you the most gorgeous dresses! Will you get to keep them?"

"If I do, they're yours," Sophie promised.

"And here I thought you guys would be discussing *important* stuff," Marella said, rolling her bright blue eyes as she shoved her petite frame into the center of their group. "But apparently we're standing in a suspicious-looking circle surrounded by goblins so we can discuss *clothes*?"

"Does this mean you're talking to us again?" Biana asked.

"It means I'm talking to you *today*," Marella corrected. "And only because I realized you guys were never going to leave me alone until you got what you wanted. So"—she checked over her shoulder and lowered her voice—"since my mom was actually having a pretty good day yesterday, I thought, *Fine, I'll ask her about Cyrah and prove she doesn't know anything.* Only . . ." Her eyes dropped to her feet, kicking at her scuffed shoes. "I guess she does remember something."

"And that something is?" Dex prompted.

Marella twisted one of her braids around her finger. "I'll tell you what I know *if* you do something for me."

"You know that's blackmail, right?" Fitz asked. "Or maybe it's extortion? Either way, it's super shady."

Marella shrugged, unconcerned.

"Why don't we find out what she wants before we get mad?" Biana suggested.

"Clearly you're the smart Vacker," Marella said. "And what I want shouldn't be a big deal. I just want to meet with this mysterious Mr. Forkle guy you're always talking about."

"Why?" Sophie asked.

"That's between him and me."

"Not if you want me to set up a meeting," Sophie argued. "He'll never agree without knowing the reason."

Marella sighed, twisting her braid tighter. "He's the one who triggered all of your abilities, right?"

"Most of them," Sophie corrected—and she had a sinking suspicion she knew where Marella was going with this.

Marella confirmed it a second later when she crossed her arms and arched an eyebrow. "Then I want him to trigger mine."

SIXTY-THREE

THIS IS NOT HOW THIS PROCESS WORKS," Mr. Forkle told Marella as he closed the door to Alden's circular office. He'd chosen Everglen as a meeting point, since Havenfield felt too vulnerable, and the Vackers had been generous enough to offer their home.

He'd also made Marella wait a day for the meeting, since he'd had a number of appointments forcing him to stay in Magnate Leto mode the day before. And the delay seemed to have made Marella fidgety.

Or maybe it was the hard look in Mr. Forkle's eyes as he told her, "And I don't simply mean that triggering abilities this way is unnatural. Important information about a possible murder should *never* be a bargaining chip."

"I know," Marella mumbled, sinking into one of the plush armchairs that faced the room's floor-to-ceiling aquarium. Dex, Fitz, Biana, and Sophie leaned against the windowed wall behind her, while Sandor, Woltzer, Grizel, and Lovise waited outside to give them more space. "But I've tried *everything* else," she whispered. "And I knew you'd triggered Sophie's abilities—"

"Miss Foster is a very special case," Mr. Forkle interrupted.

"Yeah, I'm aware. But I figured . . . if it doesn't work, at least I'll know I did everything I possibly could. And here, you can see I'm good for the information part." She pulled a thick, sealed envelope from the pocket of her wrinkled cape and set it on the edge of Alden's massive desk. "The secret my mom gave me is in there. If you want to open it first, that's cool."

"That won't be necessary," Mr. Forkle said, even though Sophie was ready to snatch it and tear it open. "Perhaps this will prove that you need not resort to such drastic measures, should you ever seek my help in the future."

He stepped closer, and Marella flinched. "Have you changed your mind?"

"No!" Marella straightened in her chair. "I was just wondering if it will . . . um . . . hurt?"

"Having an ability triggered can be a strange sensation— but not an unpleasant one. It's also important to keep in mind that hardly anyone manifests immediately. It will only take me a few moments to send mental energy into the portions of your brain where abilities develop—but you might not notice a change for several hours or days. Or your mind may still not be ready."

"Is there a way to specifically trigger empathy?" Marella asked.

"No. Our abilities stem from our genetics. Whatever you will or won't be has already been decided—and might I add that oftentimes nature is far smarter than we are. We may want a certain ability, only to discover that what we manifest is far better suited."

"That'd be easier to believe if it weren't coming from the guy who handpicked a billion abilities for Sophie," Marella mumbled.

"As I said, Miss Foster is a special case—though for the record, I did let her genetics guide me. Not every ability she has is one I would've chosen."

"Which ones aren't?" Sophie asked. "Besides teleporting?"

"That's irrelevant information," Mr. Forkle told her. "They're a part of you either way."

"Does she have abilities she hasn't manifested?" Dex asked.

"Let's not get sidetracked," Mr. Forkle said. "Are you ready now, Miss Redek?"

Marella took a deep breath before she nodded.

"Very well. Hold still." Mr. Forkle reached for her face, pressing two fingers against each of her temples as he closed his eyes. "I'll start in three . . . two . . . one."

"Whoa—you were right about it being strange," Marella said, scratching the top of her head. "It's super tingly—and it keeps getting warmer."

"Try to clear your mind," Mr. Forkle told her. "It's best not to focus on the process. I'm trying to trigger your instinct, not your active mind."

"Right," Marella said. "Sorry."

The seconds ticked by and Sophie found herself holding her breath, wishing with everything she had for Marella to manifest. Like Stina had said, even if Marella didn't get the ability she wanted, it would help her *so* much just knowing the issue was settled.

"One last push," Mr. Forkle said, scrunching his brow.

Marella gripped the arms of her chair and let out a tiny squeak before Mr. Forkle stumbled back and leaned against the desk. A sheen of sweat glistened across his face, and his breathing sounded like he'd just run up ten flights of stairs.

"Whoa, it's all spinny and flippy in my head right now," Marella mumbled.

"I'm not surprised. I gave you every bit of mental energy I could spare," Mr. Forkle told her. "I'll leap you home as soon as your head clears—and then you need to rest. Let me know when you feel ready."

"I might need a few minutes," Marella warned, waving her fingers in front of her eyes like her vision had blurred.

"So can we open the envelope now?" Fitz asked, already reaching for it.

"Up to you," Marella said. "Oh, but I should probably explain." She swallowed hard, rubbing her temples as she said, "I asked my mom why she'd told Cyrah she needed to be more careful, and she told me it was because Cyrah was messing with things she didn't understand. So I asked her what *that* meant and she got up and walked away. I figured she was done with the conversation, but—whoa, it's really spinny right now. Hang on."

Marella leaned her head between her knees. "Think this is a sign that it's working?"

"We'll know soon enough," Mr. Forkle told her.

She nodded carefully. "Anyway, my mom came back down and gave me the thing I put in that envelope—but only after I promised her I'd never try to use it. She told me she found it in Cyrah's stall. It doesn't look dangerous to me, but maybe I just don't know what it is."

The four friends huddled close as Fitz tore open the envelope and poured the single item into his clammy palm.

A smooth, oval starstone.

And when Fitz held it up to the light, it flashed blue.

SIXTY-FOUR

WE NEED TO FIND OUT WHERE it takes us," Sophie said, pointing to the blue beam of light that the starstone cast on the floor.

Right on cue, the door burst open and all four bodyguards rushed in, shouting the many reasons none of them would be going anywhere.

"Wow, is this how it always is for you guys?" Marella asked, rubbing her forehead.

"Pretty much." Sophie raised her hands to get everyone's attention. "I know you don't want us to do this. But starstones remember the last place they've been, so we *have* to find out where this one goes. And since goblins can't light leap without elves, some of us are going to have to go. So how about we pick a small group—two elves, two goblins—and make a quick leap? We can keep our crystals right in our hands, that way we're ready to leap away the second we re-form if there's any trouble. And I'm sure Alden and Della have some crystals we can use to make sure we end up back here and everyone knows we're safe."

"Of course," Della said, blinking into sight on the far side of the room—making Sophie wonder how long she'd been eavesdropping.

The goblins debated a couple of minutes more, and eventually admitted that Sophie's argument was solid. Which brought them to the bigger question.

"How do we decide who goes?" Fitz asked.

Of course everyone nominated themselves—and the adults did their usual adult thing and tried to claim it should be them instead of "children." Round and round it went until Grizel slipped her fingers in the corners of her mouth and destroyed everyone's eardrums with a high-pitched whistle.

"If anyone tries to start another shouting match, I will do that again," she warned. "And I won't stop until everyone has a migraine. So let's try logic instead, shall we? We already agreed that two goblins will be part of the mission—and of the four of us, those ranked the highest are Sandor and myself. And since neither of us can separate from our charges—and we all know there's no way Sophie's not going to be a part of this—that means we'll be bringing Sophie and Fitz, and they will stand behind us and do *exactly* what we say. We go. We look. We leave. It'll be five minutes, tops."

"Works for me," Fitz said, grinning at Biana when she pouted.

"Wow," Marella said. "I've never seen people fight because they all *want* to do the crazy, dangerous thing."

"Welcome to my world," Sophie told her. "Still mad at me for not dragging you into it?"

Marella shook her head. "Starting to think I'm not cut out. You're really going to blindly follow a random beam of light, knowing full well it could leap you into a room full of killers?"

"It's not even the scariest thing we've done," Fitz told her.

Mr. Forkle sighed. "I should go with you. There can just as easily be five to the group, instead of four."

"If we go with that slippery reasoning, there can just as easily be six or seven or eight," Grizel argued. "But the smaller the group, the faster and more discreet we'll be. Besides, you're looking a little wobbly."

She was right—the color still hadn't returned to Mr. Forkle's features.

"And you're supposed to be helping Marella home," Sophie reminded him. "And maybe—if Caprise is up to it—you could ask her some follow-up questions."

"My mom *is* having another kinda-okay day," Marella admitted. "She might be up to talking for a few minutes."

Mr. Forkle looked anything but thrilled with this plan, but seemed to swallow back his protests. "Very well. Make sure you leave the starstone here." He held out his hand, waiting for Sophie to pass it over. "You can just as easily step in to a path created by someone staying here, and that way we have a way to find you if we need to."

"They also have their panic switches," Dex reminded everyone.

Sandor unsheathed his sword. "We won't need them."

Grizel drew her weapon as well, with an especially impressive flourish.

Della gathered Fitz and Sophie into a hug, promising that she and Alden would be waiting for them at Everglen's gates. Biana joined in the embrace, pulling Dex along with her.

"Wow," Marella mumbled. "You guys are huggers."

"We'll be fine," Sophie said as she pulled away—though her voice was slightly scratchier than she wanted it to be.

Fitz reached for her hand, and Sandor and Grizel completed the circle as Mr. Forkle created the starstone's dim path. They each took a second to steady their nerves before together, they let the starstone's blue glow carry them away.

It wasn't the coldest leap Sophie had ever experienced. But it felt strangely turbulent, like the light was part of a windstorm whipping them around, trying to send them scattering. She rallied her concentration and wrapped it tighter around

Sandor and Grizel, refusing to lose a single particle as the world rushed back and they reformed in . . .

. . . a bedroom.

A very fancy bedroom.

Everything was velvet and silk in shades of red and black, with a bed big enough to sleep ten people.

"This isn't what I was expecting," Fitz whispered as Sandor and Grizel sniffed the air.

"Think it's Fintan's room?" Sophie asked, staring at the twinkling balefire chandelier that cascaded from the ceiling. "It wouldn't be Brant's—he can't stand to be around kindling."

"No idea," Fitz said. "I'm just glad it's empty."

The bed wasn't made, and a lump under the blankets caught Sophie's attention. She tiptoed over and peeled back the covers and found . . .

"Mrs. Stinkbottom?"

The fluffy stuffed gulon stared back at her with its glassy eyes.

"So is this Keefe's room?" Fitz asked. "I thought he didn't take Mrs. Stinkbottom with him."

"He didn't," Sophie mumbled. "So maybe . . ."

She wandered to the wall of windows and peeled back one of the curtains. Far below she could see a stark courtyard with an iron arch over the main pathway.

"We're not in a Neverseen hideout," she whispered. "We're in . . . Candleshade."

Her brain was still figuring out what to do with the idea of Lord Cassius cuddling with Keefe's favorite stuffed animal, when Fitz connected all the dots to the much more disturbing implication.

"This proves Cyrah made the starstone in Lady Gisela's hairpin, doesn't it?" he asked.

"It's worse than that," Sophie said, taking a moment to add her dread to the knot of emotions she'd been rebuilding.

She glanced around the room, making sure Lord Cassius wasn't around to hear her before she whispered, "I think it proves for sure that Lady Gisela killed her."

SIXTY-FIVE

I *HAVE TO TELL YOU SOMETHING,* SOPHIE transmitted, rubbing the growing tangle under her ribs as she pushed the call out into the night.

Fitz tightened his hold on her hand, snapping their thumb rings together.

Once she'd realized they *had* to tell Keefe about his mom, she'd asked if she could stay the night at Everglen so she wouldn't be alone. Fitz would be eavesdropping on the conversation, helping her gauge Keefe's reaction—that way she wouldn't be the only one deciding if he'd reached a danger zone of guilt and recklessness.

Sandor hadn't been thrilled with the sleepover arrangement, since he needed to return to Grady and Edaline in Gildingham.

But Grizel had teased him into trusting her to protect both of their charges. If Sophie had known a girlfriend was all it took to get Sandor to relax a little, she would've tried fixing him up months ago.

"Has he said anything yet?" Biana asked, blinking in and out of sight as she wandered Everglen's upstairs guest bedroom.

Sophie had stayed in the cozy-yet-elegant room several times since she'd moved to the Lost Cities, and it always seemed to happen when things got hard.

"What do we do if he doesn't respond?" Dex asked.

"Wait until morning and try again," Sophie mumbled, knowing it would mean a long, sleepless night—though sleep was a lost cause anyway. She hadn't realized how many hopes she'd rested on the slim excuses Mr. Forkle had given for why Lady Gisela might not be Cyrah's murderer, until they'd been ripped away.

Is this going to be another one of those nights where you spend the whole time yelling at me to come home? Keefe asked, making her sit up straighter as his thoughts filled her head. *Because as much as I love it when you get all feisty on me, now's really not a good time.*

Why? Are you with other people? Sophie asked.

Nope. But I'm working on something that's kinda time-pressed. And no, I can't tell you what it is. I don't want to get your hopes up until I know for sure if this is going to work. So let's save the lecture for tomorrow.

It's not a lecture, she transmitted. *It's . . .*

Her hands shook, and Biana and Dex scooted closer, offering support.

Hmm, Keefe said. *This sounds serious.*

It is. I'm really scared it's going to be too much. But I don't think you'd want me to keep it secret, so I don't know what to do.

I take it this means you know about my mom, Keefe thought quietly.

Sophie's and Fitz's eyebrows shot up. *You know?* she asked.

His thoughts felt a little fidgety as he told her, *Yeah. Fintan told me a couple of days ago. I didn't mention it because you've been so mad at me. Plus, I was still trying to figure out how I feel about it.*

How do you feel about it? Sophie asked.

I still don't really know. I smashed a few things—and that felt good. And I did a little sulking. But the thing is, it doesn't actually change anything. I was already done with her long before this.

I guess . . . , Sophie thought, studying Fitz's expression.

He looked as wary as she felt.

Could Keefe truly be this calm? Or was he a ticking time bomb?

So, she said, scooting away from Dex and Biana, who were elbowing her and Fitz, wanting updates on what was happening. *Are you okay with me telling Wylie about this? I promised I'd keep him updated, but I'll wait if you aren't ready to have him know.*

Why did Wylie ask for updates about my mom?

He didn't. He asked for updates about his mom.

So what does my mom have to do with his mom?

Sophie frowned. *Isn't that what we've been talking about?*

I . . . don't know anymore.

Sourness pooled in her stomach. *What exactly did Fintan tell you about your mom?*

Why don't you tell me what you were going to say first?

Fitz squeezed her hand for support as Sophie told Keefe everything they knew about the starstone Marella gave them, and where her mother had found it, and how it had leaped straight into his parents' bedroom. She even told him about his dad sleeping with Mrs. Stinkbottom at night. And each new fact rumbled around his brain like a thunderstorm.

So she killed her, Keefe said. His mental voice was flat. His mind gray, like the storm was taking over.

It looks that way, Sophie admitted. *But technically we still don't—*

Forget it, Foster. You don't have to make pretend excuses. We both know there's no way it's a coincidence that someone found a super-rare starstone leaping straight to my parents' bedroom at the place where someone died—especially since Gethen knew something about it. And it's fine. I'm fine. It's . . . whatever. I'm over it.

No you're not, she pressed.

No. But I can't deal with it right now. I'd rather focus on destroying everything she's built, piece by piece.

An understandable goal. Also a super-reckless one. And proof that the only way they'd ever get Keefe to come home would be to drag him there, kicking and screaming.

So, was that it? he asked. *Because I really do need to concentrate.*

Sophie was about to let him go when she realized he'd yet to clear up the misunderstanding. *What did you think I was going to tell you about your mom?*

His mind thundered again, darkening the space between them. *I thought you were going to tell me that no one knows where she is anymore. Dimitar went to check on her at the prison, and she'd escaped.*

SIXTY-SIX

I'M ASSUMING NO ONE KNOWS HOW SHE escaped, or if someone helped her," Mr. Forkle said, watching a stringy-looking creature floating in the dimly lit aquarium. Alden had been kind enough to loan them his office again to talk privately.

Mr. Forkle had been at the Redeks' house when Sophie hailed him with the latest news—resting after giving Marella a second burst of mental energy, since she still hadn't manifested.

"Who would help her?" Sophie asked.

The Neverseen were the ones who'd locked Lady Gisela away, and there weren't exactly a lot of other people in the Lost Cities who knew how to pull off an ogre-prison break.

"Has anyone been keeping an eye on Keefe's dad these last few weeks?" Fitz asked.

"You think *Lord Cassius* pulled this off?" Biana countered.

"I don't know. He's not really a get-his-hands-dirty kind of guy," Fitz said, which was a *tremendous* understatement, "but he did suggest a prison break when we talked to him. Plus . . . she's his wife. Is it so hard to believe he might try to save her?"

"*Trying* isn't the same as succeeding," Biana argued. "Am I really the only one who thinks it sounds impossible?"

"The implausibility of a theory rarely negates its possibility," Mr. Forkle told her. "Especially since Lord Cassius is quite capable of securing allies. I'll have our Technopath dig into his registry records and see if he can shake out anything interesting."

"I can help," Dex offered.

"Only if it becomes necessary. I don't want any of us giving this too much of our energy. It's an unexpected turn of events— even an intriguing one. But not particularly urgent, either."

"Are you sure?" Sophie asked. "Now we're not just fighting the Neverseen and the ogres, we're fighting Lady Gisela and her mysterious supporters too."

"We don't even know that she *has* supporters," Mr. Forkle reminded her. "For all we know, she slipped out of that prison by her own accord. And if she is part of some new, rising order, for the moment, they share our enemies."

"It still feels like this whole mess just got a whole lot more complicated," Sophie mumbled, sinking into one of the office's overstuffed armchairs.

Mr. Forkle took the chair across from her. "You may be right, Miss Foster. These challenges have turned out to be far more intricate than anything I'd originally imagined. And I'll confess that ever since Miss Redek's request earlier today, I've been wondering if I've prepared the four of you as fully as I should have."

"What do you mean?" Sophie asked.

He steepled his fingers and gazed through the wall of windows. Outside, a pair of moonlarks drifted across a small shimmering lake, their long silvery tails rippling the glassy water. "I mean perhaps it's time to stop holding back. I've hinted before that you might have another ability waiting to manifest—"

"I knew it!" Fitz interrupted, sporting a superbly smug grin.

"Is it cool?" Dex asked as Biana said, "Are you going to trigger it?"

"That is a decision I leave up to Miss Foster."

Sophie gripped the arms of her chair—realizing it was the same chair she'd sat on for so many other huge revelations.

Good news. Bad news. Weird news.

She couldn't tell which category this would fall into.

"All abilities come with responsibility," he said quietly. "But some are heavier than others. I told you earlier that your abilities were not all hand selected. Some were a natural result of the various tweaks I made to your genes. And this one gave me a serious amount of pause when I realized it would be part of your makeup—not because there's anything wrong with the ability. It's an incredibly valuable asset. But it's also one that could be taken advantage of."

He reached into his cloak pocket and pulled out a thin package wrapped in velvet. "I've been carrying these since the day I triggered your other abilities. I wanted to be ready in case this talent also broke through. But so far, it's remained dormant—which could mean the talent will never manifest on its own. So keep that in mind when you make this decision. You're fourteen now, growing increasingly close to the time when the manifesting window closes, so it's very possible that if we leave you be, you may never face this responsibility. And no one—including myself—will judge you for whatever you choose. It's entirely your decision."

He handed the parcel to Sophie, and she unwrapped the soft fabric, revealing two wrist-length black silken gloves.

"Am I supposed to know what these mean?" she asked, glad to see Fitz, Biana, and Dex looking just as confused. "Wait— I'm not going to be like Rogue, right?"

"I'm assuming that's a human?" Mr. Forkle asked.

"Sort of. She's a character in these comics my sister loved, where some people have genetic mutations that give them superpowers. Hers makes it so she can't ever touch anyone without absorbing their power—and if she touches them too long, she'll kill them."

"Humans and their wild imaginations," Mr. Forkle said with a small smile. "No, you'll be nothing like this *Rogue*. In fact, it's quite the opposite. Nothing will affect *you*. But you'll be able to empower others with the touch of your hands. It's a rare ability called an Enhancer."

Dex's eyes widened. "I've heard of that! Won't it mean that even being around her will make all of us more powerful?"

"To a very small extent, yes," Mr. Forkle said. "But it's something most won't ever notice. The true boost comes from the touch of your fingertips," he told Sophie. "Your body will store energy there, ready to transfer on contact. Hence the gloves— though they're not a full solution. More a temporary buffer, to ensure you don't accidentally enhance someone, and to buy a few precious seconds for you to break away should anyone try to take unwanted advantage. Still, I'm sure you can imagine how Fintan or Brant might abuse this ability should they discover it."

She definitely could. "And there's no way to turn it off? Like how I shield my mind from people's thoughts?"

Mr. Forkle shook his head. "This ability is more like being a Polyglot. You don't tell your mind to translate the other languages. It just *does*. The energy will gather in your fingertips the same way. Covering your hands or avoiding contact are the only ways to prevent it."

Sophie traced a finger across the silky gloves, trying to imagine wearing them all the time. It made her hands feel hot and itchy and—

"If it helps," Fitz said, squatting next to her chair, "the gloves won't feel like what you're thinking. I wore human gloves once—they were awful. I felt like my hands couldn't touch or grab anything. Our gloves are like a second skin. Try them on, you'll see."

After a slight hesitation, Sophie slipped her fingers into the cool, thin fabric. It seemed to suction against her skin, feather-light and almost undetectable as she flexed her grip a few times.

Fitz reached for her hand, and she still felt the heat of his palm and the smoothness of his skin and the stupid flutter in her heart.

"I'm sure you could wear your Cognate rings on top if you want," he told her.

"Same goes for your panic switch," Dex added helpfully.

"Actually, that will make removing the gloves far trickier when she wants to enhance someone," Mr. Forkle reminded them. "Better to wear as she is, with accessories underneath."

"And I'll really have to wear them all the time?" Sophie asked.

"It will depend on the situation," Mr. Forkle said. "When you're home, or safe among friends, the gloves will not be necessary. But at school or running errands—or certainly whenever you take any risks—you will want to ensure that you're protected."

"And does the ability do anything to benefit *me*?"

"Yes and no. Your own abilities will remain unaffected. But

those around you will become stronger, which *is* an advantage—especially since you've chosen to surround herself with a group of incredibly talented friends. Imagine how much more they could accomplish if you enhanced their power. The downside is, you could do the same for your enemies."

Sophie rubbed her head, trying to build a mental pros-and-cons list. "What would you do?" she asked Fitz. "If you were the one having to make this choice?"

He brushed his hand through his hair and stared out the window. "Honestly? I don't know. I'm sure it would take our Cognate powers to a whole other level—but I would never want to put you in more danger just for that."

"I feel like there has to be a gadget I could make that would give you more control than a pair of gloves," Dex mumbled. "I wonder what would happen if I made some tweaks to two nexuses—one for each wrist."

He started mumbling to himself, switching to a techie language no one else understood as Sophie focused on Biana. "What about you?"

"I think . . . if you do it, that means it's on us to step up," she said quietly. "We're the ones who get stronger, so we need to work harder to protect you."

"And I know I speak for your currently absent bodyguard," Grizel said, slinking out of the shadows, "when I say that—should you choose to take on this ability—you must make every effort to keep it secret."

"I agree," Mr. Forkle said. "But the decision is still yours, Miss Foster. And we will support whatever you decide."

Sophie stared at her hands, trying to imagine all the crazy ways being an Enhancer would change everything.

Then she thought about Wylie.

And Brielle.

And Kenric.

And Jolie.

And all the nights she'd lost sleep, worrying about her friends and family. All she'd wanted was to keep them safe—and here was a new, important way.

"Trigger the ability," she whispered. "I can handle it."

SIXTY-SEVEN

LAST CHANCE TO CHANGE YOUR mind," Mr. Forkle told Sophie as he held his fingers a hairsbreadth from her temples.

She took a deep, calming breath as her friends squeezed her hands.

"Do it."

The second his fingers pressed down, warmth flooded into Sophie's head. The sensation felt strange—like sunshine tickling her brain—but also soothingly familiar, taking Sophie back to the other times she'd had her abilities triggered. She'd barely been conscious during those moments, so she'd never experienced the moment when the talent *clicked*—like someone flipped a switch, sending new currents of energy pulsing from head to toe. Her heart raced just as fast, her breaths shallow and frenetic—until the rush settled into her hands and turned warmer. Threads of heat seemed to weave together under the skin of her fingers, forming a thin layer that felt inherently *right*. She hadn't realized how empty her hands had been without it. But now she was exactly as her body meant her to be.

"Feels like it already worked," Mr. Forkle said as he backed away, sinking into the chair and rubbing his sweaty temples. "But perhaps we should test it to be sure?"

Sophie offered Fitz a hand. "Care to try it out, Captain Cognate?"

Fitz beamed his movie-worthy smile. "I'd be honored—though I'm not sold on that nickname."

He reached for her hand, his touch as warm and gentle as ever. Their fingers twined together and . . .

"Whoa. It's like . . . having all the fog shoved out of my mind—which is extra weird because I never thought my concentration was cloudy." He let go of Sophie's hand and creases settled across his brow. "Ugh. And now it's all fuzzy again." He took her hand and his face relaxed. "Wow, this is going to make me want to hold your hand all the time."

Biana rolled her eyes. "Easy now, big brother. Let go of my friend or I will drop you like we're playing bramble."

Fitz blushed and did as Biana ordered.

Sophie was sure her cheeks couldn't get any redder as Biana grabbed her hand and instantly turned invisible.

"This is *so* crazy," Biana's disembodied voice whispered. "I don't even have to *try* to keep the light away. It just glides through me like I'm made of glass."

"My turn!" Dex said, rushing closer as Biana reappeared.

"Perhaps we shouldn't treat Miss Foster like she's our shiny new toy," Mr. Forkle warned.

"Right," Dex mumbled. "Sorry."

"Don't be," Sophie said. "I'm curious too. And who knows, maybe you'll suddenly know how to build one of those Lodestar symbol gadgets. Or those special nexuses to replace the gloves like you'd been talking about."

"Oh, that's true!" Dex's palm felt a little sweaty as he wrapped his fingers around hers and closed his eyes. "Wow, my brain feels like it's working on a hundred things at once. It's . . . I can't keep up with it all—owww."

"Are you okay?" Sophie asked as he stumbled back, rubbing his head.

"Yeah, just info overload. I bet it would've been different if I'd been holding whatever gadget I wanted to work on, since my ability always focuses on something specific. Instead I got this random mix of, like, memories and blueprints and . . . I don't even know. *So* many good ideas—I'm afraid I'm going to forget them all."

"Here," Biana said, handing him a notebook and pen from one of Alden's desk drawers. "Maybe make some notes?"

"Good idea!" Dex dropped into a chair and scribbled furiously.

"It doesn't hurt when you're passing the power to us, right?" Fitz asked Sophie.

"No. All I get is a tingle in my fingers. And it doesn't feel like it drains me either—but that might change if you hold on for a long time."

"Your body will give you cues to let you know if you're pushing yourself too hard," Mr. Forkle assured her. "Though I do think you should try to rest now. Triggering an ability is an exhausting process—and you've had a very long, very challenging day."

Sophie wanted to protest, but as soon as she stood, her head felt twirly. And by the time she'd made it back to the guest room, she barely managed to change into her pajamas and grab Ella before she collapsed into the giant bed.

It was a dreamless, dead-to-the-world kind of sleep, and she might've kept it up forever if someone hadn't shaken her awake.

When she opened her eyes, she was staring into the face of a stuffed sparkly red dragon.

"Mr. Snuggles is always the best thing to see when you first wake up," Fitz told her—and Sophie almost blurted that his glittering teal eyes were even better, but managed to spare herself the humiliation.

Biana laughed from the doorway. "You two are ridiculous—has anyone told you that? Now get dressed." She tossed a very long, very fitted, very red tunic onto Sophie's bed.

"Don't scowl at me like that—it's camouflage," Biana told her. "The fancier your clothes are, the more people won't wonder about your new gloves. *And* you look awesome in red. All you need is a white blouse and some black leggings—you have those, right? Oh—and a killer pair of boots. In fact, I have the perfect ones!"

Sophie sighed as Biana raced off. "She's going to turn me into her little doll."

"Probably," Fitz agreed. "But at least she's right." Sophie figured he was referring to Biana's camouflage-the-gloves strategy—which *was* pretty brilliant, despite how annoying Sophie was sure it was going to be.

But Fitz gave her his most charming smile and added, "Red is definitely your color."

If she were a cartoon character, Sophie's eyes would've turned into little hearts.

"Hurry up and get dressed," Biana shouted from down the hall, saving Sophie from having to come up with a coherent response.

"Why, are we going somewhere?" Sophie called after her.

"Yep." Biana rushed back into the room, proudly holding up a pair of boots with alarmingly tall wedge heels. "While *someone* was getting their beauty sleep, I went to the Silver Tower with Tam to see if having a Vanisher with him made a difference. And we finally figured out how the Neverseen got in!"

SIXTY-EIGHT

I THOUGHT WE'D RULED OUT THE LODE-star mirror," Sophie said as she stood in the center of the Hall of Illumination, surrounded by a circle of twenty mirrors reflecting their group from every angle.

Dex, Fitz, Linh, Alden, Della, Mr. Forkle, *and* Sandor, Grizel, Lovise, and Woltzer had all come with them to see what Biana and Tam had discovered.

"We *have* ruled it out," Tam told Sophie. "Believe me, I've stared at that thing so long, I've gone cross-eyed. All it does is reflect pure light and make me tear up from the glare."

"Then, um . . . why are we here?" Dex asked.

"Because I'm a genius," Biana informed him. "I knew the Neverseen wouldn't be obvious enough to have the actual mirror be the answer. But I kept thinking the name couldn't totally be a coincidence. So I spent way too long staring at my reflection." She ignored Fitz when he coughed, *"What else is new?"* and several in their group laughed. "And that's when I thought to ask: What do lodestars do?"

"Guide people?" Sophie guessed.

Biana nodded. "They show you the way. So what do you see when you look in the mirror—besides your really bright reflection?"

Mr. Forkle sucked in a breath. "You see the mirror directly across from it!"

Everyone rushed to the other mirror, stepping on toes and knocking elbows as they crushed closer.

"It's the Cimmerian," Alden said, tracing a hand down the smooth glass. "One of the hardest mirrors to understand the meaning of."

"It really is," Mr. Forkle said, "I've always suspected it's because many are too distracted by the disruption to their appearance."

"Can't say I blame them," Della mumbled, glaring at the heavy shadows in her reflection. "This mirror is the only thing that ever makes me feel haggard."

"But I still don't understand," Grizel said. "How does it give the Neverseen access to the tower?"

"Because they brought a Shade," Biana said, nudging Tam forward. "Go on. Show them how cool you are."

Tam flushed, squaring his shoulders as he approached the glass. "This is hard to explain. But the mirror multiplies shadows, so I decided to see what'd happen if I messed with them."

He stretched his hand toward the glass and pulled his fingers into a fist, dragging every shadow from their reflections into the center of the mirror like a big black hole.

"And don't ask me why," Tam said, "but my instincts told me to do this."

He spun his wrist in a tight circle, and the shadows followed—curling into a spiral that seemed to sink in on itself as the pattern spun round and round and round.

"What exactly are we looking at?" Mr. Forkle asked.

"I'm not totally sure," Tam admitted. "At first I thought it was just an optical illusion. But then I did *this*"—he shoved his hand through the center of the spiral, making his arm disappear up to the elbow and earning a chorus of gasps—"and I realized it's a gateway. Something about the shadowvapor moving through the glass changes its density."

He pulled his arm back and wiggled his perfectly healthy, normal fingers.

"Just don't ask me to explain the crazy science behind it, okay?" Tam said, "But this is how the Neverseen got into the tower. Maybe they levitated once they were inside so they wouldn't leave a scent trail. But they came from here."

He pushed his whole body through the mirror, disappearing

into the glass. Everyone yelped when he peeked his head back from the other side—and all four goblins drew their swords.

"It's a pretty tight space, so if you want to check it out, you'll have to take turns," he told them. "Probably no more than two or three at a time. But basically, I'm in a secret room hidden somewhere between the towers."

"Someone needs to make sure the space is truly secure before any more of us go through," Sandor decided, blocking Sophie as he pushed forward.

Grizel jumped in front of him, placing a hand in the center of his chest. "I'm smaller *and* my senses are sharper."

Sandor's jaw twitched—ready to argue—but when Grizel leaned in and whispered something, he nodded and took a slow step back.

Tam disappeared through the mirror to clear the path as Grizel tapped Sandor's nose and turned to study the glass. She skimmed her fingers across the swirling shadows before she shrugged and leaped through like a gazelle.

"Do you think they have security telling them we found the hidden room?" Fitz asked.

Dex frowned. "I don't feel any tech or signals."

"And wouldn't someone have come to check it by now?" Biana asked. "Tam and I found this over an hour ago, before we came back to wake up Sophie and get you guys."

Sophie's cheeks flushed. "Sorry I overslept."

"Yes, how dare you take a few hours to recover after manifesting a new ability?" Biana scolded.

"What new ability?" Linh and Sandor asked at the same time.

Sophie held up her gloved hands. "Enhancer."

Linh nearly knocked Della over as she scrambled back. "Sorry." She hugged her arms around herself. "It's not you. It's just still such a struggle for me to maintain control. I can't imagine what kind of flood I'd cause if someone enhanced my ability."

"Yeah, that would *not* be a good idea," Tam said, peeking his head through the glass again. "Not unless we want to wipe out a couple of cities."

"Why does this sound like an ability that's going to increase the challenge of protecting you?" Sandor asked Sophie.

"Because it will." Mr. Forkle explained about the gloves, and how they'd do everything they could to keep the ability secret. But how it was a part of Sophie now. Always.

Grizel peeked her head through the mirror, locking eyes with Sandor. "Don't blame me. We all know Sophie would've triggered the ability even if you'd been there."

"Still, I leave you my charge for *one* night," he grumbled.

"So what's it like on the other side of the mirror?" Sophie asked, eager for a subject change.

She'd expected Tam to answer, but Biana jumped in. "It wasn't at all what I'd imagined. I was rooting for creepy furniture and crazy gadgets and all kinds of cool villainy things. But it's just a cramped, empty stone room that looks like it's been there since they built the tower."

"Does that mean the Neverseen have been around for thousands of years?" Linh asked.

"I suppose it's possible," Mr. Forkle said. "But most likely the room once served some other long-forgotten purpose, and Fintan or Brant—or maybe their Shade—stumbled across it and made it their own."

"Either way, it's definitely how they got in," Grizel said, climbing back out through the mirror. "Their scent is everywhere—but it's also stale, so I don't think they've been back since they took Wylie."

"Am I the only one who still doesn't understand how they actually get into the tower?" Dex asked. "So . . . they get *here*"—he pointed to the floor in the Hall of Illumination—"by coming through *there*"—he pointed to the swirling Cimmerian mirror—"where there's another secret room. But how do they get in *that* room?"

Biana grinned. "Go see for yourself."

Dex didn't need to be told twice, practically sprinting through the mirror.

"*Ohhhhh, it has one of the Lodestar symbol gadgets!*" he breathed.

That was all the invitation Sophie needed to go charging after him, shivering from the waves of cold that rippled across her skin as she passed through the glass. Fitz was right on her heels, and they nearly tripped over each other in the claustrophobic space.

"I'm fine," she told Sandor as his head peeked through the mirror, which looked like a swirling black square on the other side. "Better wait for me out there—we can barely move."

She couldn't imagine how the Neverseen managed to fit Alvar, Ruy, Trix, Umber, *and* Wylie's unconscious body within the narrow, musty walls. But they must have. The Lodestar symbol glowing across the floor proved it.

"It has runes," Fitz said, stepping back to uncover the letters in another circle at the end of one of the rays. "Looks like it says Pallidrose. I'm guessing that's another star."

"Another solo star," Sophie agreed as her mind connected with the memory. "It also glows with pure white light, so those definitely seem to be their criteria. But how does this thing work? I'm assuming we have to *do* something?"

"We're hoping Dex can figure it out," Biana called through the mirror.

"I'll have to get a closer look at the gadget." Dex levitated up to the ceiling and traced his finger along the curved edge. "Weird—I don't feel a lot of mechanisms in this thing. I can't even figure out where it opens."

"I wonder if Tam has to do something," Sophie said. "Or maybe Biana. Gethen made it sound like it relied on someone using their abilities, and they're the only ones that match."

"We already thought about that earlier," Biana said. "I tried everything I could think of."

"So did I," Tam admitted.

"Do you think it would help if you enhanced them?" Fitz asked Sophie.

"I . . . don't know." The ability was so new, she hadn't even thought of it. But she peeled off her right glove and offered Tam her hand, wondering if her stomach would always feel this churny whenever she went to touch anyone now.

Tam looked just as nervous as he curled his fingers around hers and the shadows sprang to life on the floor, creating a thick black outline around the glow of the Lodestar symbol.

"That's so crazy," he mumbled. "I couldn't feel that darkness before."

He tightened his grip on Sophie, pulling her with him a few steps as he followed the shadows to one of the rays they had yet to discover the rune for.

"I think this is how they left," he whispered. "See how the shadows are gathering?"

The bits of darkness were puddling together, like rivers of selkie skin flowing into the empty circle.

The darkness rippled like water, parts of it rising up with a rune.

"I think maybe . . ."

"Wait," Fitz said, lunging to grab Sophie's arm as Tam stepped down on the pool of shadows. His fingers connected with her skin right as an arctic rush blasted up and tangled around the three of them, dragging them into the darkness and blasting them away.

SIXTY-NINE

O KAY, *WHAT* JUST HAPPENED?"
Fitz asked, still clinging to Sophie as she
and Tam fought to regain their balance on
the mossy, uneven floor.

The symbol glowed under their feet—the only light in the
damp, murky room they'd somehow been transported to.
Something dripped in the distance, and their breaths clouded
the air. The bitter cold clawed through Sophie's clothes, and
she silently thanked Biana for insisting she add a thick black
cape to her outfit to match her gloves.

"I . . . think I just leaped us using starlight absorbed by a
shadow," Tam whispered. "I didn't even know I could do that.
But when I touched Sophie's hand, my instincts took over."

"So this is another hideout?" Sophie asked, slipping her glove back on. She pointed to the new rune illuminating the ray of the symbol under Tam's shoes.

"Valkonian," Fitz whispered. "I'm assuming that's another white-light star?"

Sophie nodded.

Her eyes were adjusting to the murk, letting her pick out more details as she crept forward to get a better view. The moss made the stones slippery, and uneven cracks tried to trip her stupid heeled boots. But she could see brighter light ahead, and carefully tiptoed over.

"It looks like we're in some sort of human ruin," she whispered, brushing a hand across one of the damp, crumbling walls.

She'd never been to Scotland, but something about this place reminded her of it—an old, decaying castle, complete with cracked, cut-glass windows leaking rays of gray-blue light. Thick vines covered the ancient stones, and the air smelled of earth and sea. "I don't hear any thoughts around here, do you?"

Fitz shook his head. "How much do you think they're freaking out back at Foxfire?"

"Sandor's probably tracking me as we speak—actually, wait." Sophie ran her hands down her red tunic. "These are Biana's clothes. I doubt they have trackers."

"Dex could hack into our registry feeds," Fitz said. "Or maybe our panic switches."

"We might need them to," Sophie realized. "I'm not wearing my home crystal, since I'm not supposed to go back to Havenfield until the gnomes finish installing the extra security."

Fitz patted his pockets and cursed under his breath. "I didn't bring my pathfinder, either."

"Good thing you have me." Tam pulled a purple-tinted pendant out from under his cape. "It only goes to Alluveterre, but the gnomes can take us from there."

"Wait," Sophie said as he held the crystal up to catch the faint rays of light. "Shouldn't we look around before we go? Isn't this where they brought Wylie?"

"It's where they went when they left the Silver Tower," Tam said. "I know that's why the shadows called to me. But I can't imagine this is where they held him hostage. There's no cell— not even any totally solid walls. And I don't see any rope."

"Can you do that shadow trick again to the symbol here, and see if they went somewhere else?" Fitz asked.

"But why would they bother coming here in the first place?" Sophie asked. "The symbol in the Silver Tower could've taken them to any of their hideouts, right?"

"It felt like it," Tam agreed.

"So then there has to be a reason they chose *here*," Sophie said. "Maybe this part is just the facade to disguise the real hideout, and the shelter's underground? We should fan out and see if we can find a hidden staircase or door or something."

"I'm with you on everything except the fanning-out part,"

Fitz told her. "I think we should stay close so we don't get separated."

"But that's going to make the search take way longer," Sophie argued. "If I'm right about why Keefe's cloak had those disks hidden in it, we've probably triggered some sort of alarm already."

"All the more reason to stay together," Tam said. "I'll keep my crystal in my hand, and we should all hang on to each other—that way if we need to leap away fast, we can."

Sophie couldn't argue with that logic, and did her best to keep a hold on Fitz. But a strange pattern in the cut-glass windows caught her attention.

She let go to take a closer look—just for the briefest second.

And the distance saved her from being caught by the first burst of blinding white light.

The beam of searing energy curled into a wall around Fitz and Tam, trapping them in a narrow force field that shocked them as they pressed against the inner side, fighting to escape.

"It's about time you decided to come and play," Ruy shouted from somewhere in the shadows as he launched another force field toward Sophie. She dove and rolled to avoid it, the edge of the energy clipping her shoulder and stinging with tingles that burned like acid-coated needles.

She gritted her teeth through the pain and crawled behind a crumbling pillar, tucking herself into the darkness to wait him out. She couldn't strike until she had a clear lock on his location.

In the meantime, she let the fury build, stewing with her unraveling emotions, rimming her vision with red. She'd only have one chance at this—one moment to drop Ruy before he caged her in his trap.

A scrape of shoe on stone gave her the direction she needed, and she leaped from the shadows, arms raised, ready to blast Ruy with the full force of her wrath.

But there were four black-cloaked figures waiting for her— and even with their hoods raised, she could see enough of their faces to recognize them.

Ruy.

Brant.

Alvar.

And Keefe.

SEVENTY

YOU?" SOPHIE BREATHED, FEELING the fight whoosh out of her as the reality of fighting Keefe kicked her in the stomach.

The panic in his eyes made it clear he was just as horrified to see her.

"Don't!" Brant shouted, his scarred features twisting as he grabbed Ruy's arms with his only hand. "If you shield her, she can't burn."

A thread of white flame sparked to life at the stumpy end of Brant's other arm, twisting into fingerlike tendrils.

"She can *inflict*," Ruy reminded him.

"But she won't." Brant released his hold on Ruy and pulled Keefe close, waving the flames under Keefe's chin. "She still cares about this one. And she knows I'll melt his face off if she misbehaves."

"He's one of us!" Alvar shouted.

"*That's* still up for debate. But he can prove it now." Brant's scarred lips curled into what little smile they were able to form as he moved his flame-fingers closer to Keefe's throat. With his real hand, he reached into his cape and withdrew the Ruewen crest pin he'd stolen from Sophie months and months ago. "I think I've held on to the past long enough, don't you?"

Sophie knew what was coming, even before Brant shoved Keefe toward her and held the small eagle pin in the searing white flame. The jewels crusting it sparked and crackled, and the pin turned into a red-hot brand.

But he pressed it into Keefe's palm, instead of hers.

Keefe thrashed and screamed, eyes watering, teeth gritted in agony.

"Now," Brant told Keefe, pulling the pin away. "Show her that same pain. And in case you're having trouble following along, Sophie, here's how this is going to work. You tell us where you're keeping Wylie, and I'll have lover boy here put the scars somewhere only you can see them. Try to resist, and he'll give you the same makeover you gave me. And if you fight me," he told Keefe, "I'll melt off parts of your body one by one. Starting with your fingers."

Desperation screamed through Sophie's head as her brain scrambled for a plan.

Somewhere through the chaos she realized there was another voice in the mix.

Sophie, can you hear me?

Fitz?

His thoughts were muffled and staticky, but she was stunned he could reach her at all.

Tam's breaking down the force field with darkness, he explained, *and he says he'll be able to slip his shadow through the cracks and cloud Brant's mind. It'll blind him for a few seconds. Will that be long enough for you to drop him with your inflicting before he burns Keefe?*

It probably would—but only if she was willing to drop *all* of them.

Keefe's too close to Brant, she warned. *I'll have to take out everyone.*

I don't see any other option, do you?

She glanced at the flames under Keefe's nose, and the oozing blister on his hand.

Tell Tam to do it! she transmitted as she reached deep inside, gathering every last emotion and fueling them with any dark thoughts she'd ever had.

Brant flinched, dropping his flames, and Sophie took Tam's cue, letting the cold waves pour out of her, their jagged edges tearing across everything within reach.

Seconds stretched into eternity and reality vanished into pure, pulsing power—and rage.

So.

Much.

Rage.

She wanted to bathe in it, drown in it, let the anger take control until she'd punished anyone and everyone who'd ever hurt her. But she'd held on to one thread of good through the barrage—one wisp of a thought that tethered her to who she needed to be.

Keefe.

The name peeled back the dark curtain and let in a blistering, blinding rush as she dropped to her knees, her hands feeling for shaking limbs across the cold stones. She found him right as her eyes shifted back into focus, and she pulled him into her lap.

If you can hear me, Keefe, try to fight through the darkness, she transmitted. *The pain's not real. Shove it aside and come back to the surface.*

"Tam broke the force field," Fitz said behind her, making her jump. "And he's stamping out Brant's flames. The stones are damp, so the only thing that caught was his cloak. How can I help?"

"Find something to restrain the Neverseen. When this wears off . . ."

"On it," Fitz said.

He turned to leave—then pivoted back. "Stop looking so guilty, Sophie. You did this to save him. Like he said, sometimes things have to get worse before they get better."

She focused on a happier promise. "It's almost over."

And it was, wasn't it?

This was a *huge* victory.

In one afternoon, they'd caught Alvar, Ruy, and Brant—three of the most prominent players in the Neverseen. And now that they knew how to use the gadget and the symbol, they had a way to track down sixteen hideouts.

And they had Keefe.

She craned her neck to watch Tam and Fitz work—stripping each shaking figure of their cloak and shredding the fabric into makeshift rope to bind their hands and feet and cover their mouths and eyes.

"We need to get out of here," Tam said. "Some of their buddies will probably wonder what's taking so long. And these guys could wake up any minute."

Fitz punched his brother in the face. "That should keep him knocked out longer."

"He's not the one I'm worried about," Tam told him. "If that Psionipath wakes up, he'll trap us in two seconds."

Fitz sighed and left Alvar in a bound heap so he could pull Ruy into a choke hold.

Tam held Brant the same way. "I'm keeping his mind clouded with shadow so he can't start any more fires. But I'll feel a lot better when he's locked up in a fireproof cell."

"Me too," Sophie said. "But I don't think it's safe to leap Keefe until he's out of the daze."

"Leap . . . where?" Keefe grunted between labored breaths.

Sophie hugged him tighter. "I'm so sorry—I couldn't take them down without hurting you."

He grit his teeth into a pained smile. "Admit it . . . Foster . . . you're enjoying this . . . a little."

"Never." She rubbed her eyes with her gloved fingers, trying to fight back sobs.

"It's not that bad," he promised, and when she met his eyes, she could see the haze of pain slowly fading.

It crashed right back when he tried to uncurl his blistered, blackened hand. The metal pin seemed to have fused with his skin. "Remind me to kick Brant in the junk a few times once he's awake."

"Only if I get a turn," she said. "Physic has lots of burn salve at Alluveterre. I'm sure she'll get you fixed up."

"Physic?" Keefe asked. "Why not Elwin?"

"Tam's the only one who has a leaping crystal with him, and he's been living at the hideout. We kinda came here by accident—it's a long story. I'll tell you once we're back in the Lost Cities."

"He has a crystal to Alluveterre?"

"Yeah. Why?"

Keefe closed his eyes.

"What's wrong?" she asked. "Is it hurting?"

"No, it's . . ." He took a slow breath and pulled himself up, cradling his singed hand. "I *can't* go with you guys. I know you think this fixes everything—but Fintan's vision is *huge*. And all of this will only be a small setback. We still need someone on the inside—"

"Do you really think Fintan will trust you after you let everyone else get captured?" Sophie interrupted. "Think of what he did to your mom, and she only cost him one prisoner. Look at what Brant just did to you!" She grabbed his wrist, forcing him to see his oozing wound. "Would they do that if they trusted you?"

Keefe turned away, not quite fighting off his shudder. "That's why you have to let me take Alvar."

"Yeah, that's never happening," Fitz practically growled.

"It has to. I know it's brutal—but think of the bigger picture. If I bring Alvar back, I'm the hero who saved one of the team. And Alvar's the safest one for me to take. He's always believed in me—you heard him defend me when Brant sparked the flames! And he's never killed anyone—"

"No, he just kidnaps people and watches them be tortured," Sophie snapped.

"Believe me, I'll make him pay for that—but right now we have to play this smart. Ruy and Brant are part of Fintan's big plan, so take them, lock them up, and have Forkle interrogate the crud out of them until we find out what they know. But they'll only know a piece, so I'll use Alvar to keep my 'in' and learn the rest. I'll be safe. Fintan . . . likes me."

"Dude, save your daddy issues for another time," Tam

ordered. "Fintan doesn't care about you. He doesn't trust you. And if you go back to him, he'll destroy you."

Keefe's eye roll was epic. "Don't you need to go fix your bangs or something?"

"You can hate me all you want," Tam told him. "It won't mean I'm not right. Admit that now, and you might still have a chance to fix what really matters. Or you can wait until you've lost her. It's your call."

"Lost who?" Fitz asked.

Tam shook his head. "We need to go."

"Tam's right," Sophie said, her legs shaking as she stood. "Come on, Keefe. You're never going to get another chance like this. I've tried for weeks to figure out how to get you away from them, and this is it. You're safe. You'll be long gone before they realize what happened. And we'll hide you somewhere until we shut down every single one of their hideouts connected to the symbol. And that'll be the end of it."

"But it won't be," he mumbled. "That's what I'm trying to tell you. There's still so much more to do."

"Then do it *with* us."

She offered him her gloved hand, and her eyes pleaded with him to take it this time.

After a breathless second, he did.

He let her pull him to his feet, leaning on her to stay steady. "I know what matters, Foster," he whispered. "And it's *all* that matters."

The intensity of his stare turned everything floaty and fluttery. But it all crashed back down when he lunged for Tam and snatched the Alluveterre crystal from his hand.

"What are you doing?" Fitz shouted as Keefe bolted to Alvar and hefted him over his shoulder.

"I bet I can trade this for the information I need to steal the caches. And I'd stay back if I were you," he told Fitz and Tam. "You don't want those guys waking up if you jostle them around too much, do you?"

"Then drop him with your inflicting," Tam shouted at Sophie.

But Sophie had drained all her pent-up emotions when she took down the others. All she had left was shock, and a sickening sadness.

"Please don't do this," she begged. "If you leave here with that crystal, you'll trap us—and you'll compromise Alluveterre."

"The Black Swan can sacrifice one hideout for what this will get me," Keefe said. "And you can teleport. There has to be a cliff around here you can jump off to get the momentum."

"Are we supposed to haul two bodies with us as we try to find it?" Sophie argued.

"Use your telekinesis. You're the amazing Sophie Foster. You'll figure it out."

"And you're making a seriously huge mistake," Tam warned.

"Maybe. I'm pretty good at that—but I'm even better at fixing things. That's still what I'm trying to do here. Trust me."

"How?" Sophie's voice cracked along the edges. "After all the times you've lied or ignored us or betrayed us? How do we ever trust you again?"

"I don't know," he whispered.

"And I don't know if I can forgive this one," she whispered back.

Keefe swallowed hard, eyes focused on his feet as he nodded. "Yeah . . . I can feel that. And if you needed proof that I'm not doing this for me—that's it, okay?"

It definitely was not okay.

Nothing about this was okay.

"I'm sorry," Keefe whispered. "You have no idea how much. I'm also guessing this means no more check-ins. So please, please, *please* be careful. Keep your bodyguards close and know that I *will* end this."

It did feel like an end as he stepped onto the glowing Lodestar symbol. She just didn't know what it was the end of.

"Oh—I forgot to tell you," he mumbled. "I finally know how the black disks work. If you have the one you need, and you give the right command . . ."

He moved to a circle at the end of one of the rays and whispered, "Gwynaura."

The ray flashed so bright, Sophie had to look away.

By the time the glow faded, Keefe and Alvar were gone.

SEVENTY-ONE

S O . . . THAT HAPPENED," TAM MUMBLED. "You guys okay?"

Fitz looked like he wanted to stab *many* things.

"Fine," Sophie said, pressing her shaky hand against the glass to steady it. She'd moved to the cracked window, staring at the long grassy field swaying in the wind. "Just trying to figure out how to get out of here. We could be wandering a long time trying to find a cliff."

"And my levitation's not strong enough to lift a whole other person," Tam said. "Especially since it sounds like we need to be pretty high up if we're going to teleport. So weird that you need to free-fall."

"I guess we could press our panic switches," Fitz suggested.

"I thought of that," Sophie said, "but it seems like something about this place must be interfering with the signal—otherwise wouldn't Dex have already brought in the cavalry? He said the stronger trackers could be traced anytime, remember?"

"So what does that leave?" Tam asked. "A telepathic call to Forkle?"

That could work. But the suggestion gave her a better idea. She wasn't ready for another big dramatic scene. And Silveny had made her promise to call for help if she ever needed her.

She only sent the transmission twice before a giddy *SOPHIE! SOPHIE! SOPHIE!* blasted into her brain.

But Silveny picked up on her mood almost immediately. *SOPHIE NEED HELP?*

Yeah, Sophie told her. *I don't know where I am, but—*

FIND! FIND! FIND!

The alicorn's voice flashed away and Sophie barely had time to race outside before thunder cracked the sky and two shimmering alicorns—both gleaming silver, but one bigger, with blue-tipped wings—soared out of the void and circled around the gray, restless clouds.

SOPHIE! FRIEND! HELP!

Both alicorns tucked their wings and dove, slowing their fall at the last second and touching down in the long grass. Clearly Sophie's ability to track thoughts to their locations came from her alicorn-inspired DNA.

"Thank you," Sophie whispered, taking a cautious step forward. She knew Silveny trusted her—but Greyfell was always warier, especially now that he was going to be a daddy.

His deep brown eyes flickered to hers, and then to the empty field, his fur bristling, hooves stamping.

I don't like it here either, Sophie told him. *We'll be quick. We just need to load up.*

"Leave it to you to have our world's most valuable creatures at your beck and call," Tam said behind her as he dragged Brant over.

"And I'm risking their lives by doing it—if the Neverseen show up . . ."

She socked Brant in the face to make sure he stayed unconscious.

Fitz did the same to Ruy.

BAD PEOPLE? Silveny asked.

The worst, Sophie transmitted.

Silveny's thoughts darkened. *BITE THEM?*

Maybe once we get back. Right now, can you and Greyfell lean down so it's easier to load them?

"I'm staying with Brant," Tam said as Sophie and Fitz helped him hoist the limp body onto Greyfell's back. "Can you two both fit on the other alicorn, *and* hold Ruy?"

"We'll make it work," Fitz said, "But I want you to sit behind me," he told Sophie. "That way I can be a buffer between you and Ruy."

"I don't need you to protect me," she argued.

"I know. But *I'd* prefer knowing you're safe. Please? You have no idea how hard it was standing in that force field, watching them attack you. Just thinking about it . . . " He flung Ruy over Silveny's neck and climbed on before offering Sophie a hand. She let him pull her up, blushing when she wrapped her arms around his waist. They had to sit so close, she doubted a piece of paper could've been squeezed in between them.

READY? Silveny asked.

FLY! Sophie told her, and with a majestic flap, both alicorns launched into the sky.

The cold wind whipped her hair and cheeks, turning everything numb—and numb was good. Sophie could use a lot more numb in her life.

Silveny tried to distract her with a quick update on Operation Alicorn Baby—which was thankfully all good news. Then they reached a high enough altitude to dive.

"Hold on tight!" Sophie warned Tam. "And it's okay to scream during this next part."

"I'll be fine," Tam promised—but Sophie heard a fair amount of squealing and yelping as the alicorns zipped toward the ground.

Right when it looked like they'd be splattering all over the grass, thunder cracked and the void split the space in front of them, swallowing them in black.

"Remind me never to lose my leaping crystal again!" Tam

groaned as they drifted through the dark nothingness. "You know how to get us out of here, right?"

Sophie nodded.

She just wasn't quite ready to head back to reality—especially a reality where Keefe had betrayed them *again*.

Fitz must've noticed her hesitation, because he leaned back and whispered, "Whatever happens next, I'm right here with you. You know that, right?"

"I do."

The best part was, she actually believed him.

"Ready?" she asked.

"Sorta. I have to keep reminding myself we're bringing home prisoners."

So did Sophie.

They'd landed a huge win.

But she had a feeling they were both thinking about what they'd lost.

"Okay," she said, tightening her hold. "Here goes nothing."

Her head filled with a clear image of the Silver Tower as white light cracked through the void, blasting them back to Foxfire.

SEVENTY-TWO

SOPHIE HAD BRACED FOR TEARS AND screaming and lectures—and her friends and family definitely delivered the second they arrived. Silveny and Greyfell were kind enough to circle over the campus a few times to let everyone get the brunt of it out of their systems, before they swooped in for a gentle landing in the lush purple grass.

Everyone sprinted to meet them, and Sophie realized their welcome party had grown, now including Elwin, all twelve Councillors, Grady and Edaline, Kesler and Juline, Granite, Wraith, and Blur, and—maddeningly—Tam and Linh's parents, all surrounding them in a massive circle.

Questions were shouted. Explanations were demanded. But

it all screeched to a halt when everyone spotted the Neverseen prisoners draped across the alicorns' backs.

Sandor took charge then, ordering everyone to stay back as Woltzer and Lovise hauled Brant and Ruy to the ground and stood guard over their unconscious forms. Edaline conjured up the thickest rope from their supply shed at Havenfield, and Sandor and Grizel bound the prisoners more securely before Elwin poured his strongest sedative down their throats.

"What are you going to do with them?" Grady asked, the words as shaky as his hands. His eyes stayed locked on Brant, and he positioned himself in front of Edaline and Sophie.

"Let us handle it," Mr. Forkle told him.

"*We'll* handle it," Councillor Emery corrected, his deep voice triggering a silence that seemed to still even the wind. The other Councillors gathered around him, their gleaming circlets testifying to their authority as they focused on the members of the Collective. "The Neverseen's crimes stretch well beyond your order."

"Very well," Mr. Forkle said. "What is *your* plan for the prisoners?"

"*That* is to be determined." Emery closed his eyes and turned away to moderate a telepathic debate with the other Councillors.

Everyone else swarmed closer to Sophie, Tam, and Fitz.

"You smell like smoke," Elwin noted, trying to flash an orb of red light around Sophie—even though Edaline was busy strangle-hugging her.

"I'm fine," Sophie promised, not letting her eyes stray to the glass pyramid in the distance. "Tam and Fitz helped me take them down before things got out of control."

"We're fine too," Fitz said as his parents and Biana practically crushed him. "Thank goodness Tam's shadows could break us out of Ruy's force field."

"Is that true?" Tam's mother asked. "You're a hero?"

"Still not ready," Tam said, raising a hand to halt his parents as they approached. Instead, he wrapped his arm around Linh, and she buried her face in his shoulder.

"You guys have a *lot* of explaining to do," Dex told them. "Do you know you trapped me in that room? The mirror sealed shut the second Tam vanished. Sandor had to smash the glass."

Biana begged for the whole story, and Sophie was grateful Fitz had the energy to tell it. He kept it short and sweet, focusing on their victories.

There's clearly more you're not saying, Mr. Forkle transmitted.

See for yourself. Sophie's nails dug into her palms as her mind replayed the whole showdown, from the moment the Neverseen arrived, to Keefe's latest betrayal. *You need to move Wylie out of Alluveterre—now. And Tam and Linh can't go back.*

No, they can't.

Mr. Forkle's eyes flicked to Granite, and Granite scrambled for his pathfinder.

"Excuse me," he told the Councillors. "I must check on my son."

"Your son?" Councillor Terik asked, catching Granite's slip.

"Yes, I have a son, and another life behind this disguise. Surely that doesn't come as a surprise. And hopefully someday you'll learn to cooperate with us and I won't have to hide. But until then . . ."

Granite leaped away, and Blur and Wraith followed.

"One of our hideouts has been compromised," Mr. Forkle explained. "Fortunately, it sounds like the Neverseen are facing the same dilemma."

"On a *way* larger scale, right?" Biana asked. "If Tam does that shadow trick again, won't that take you to all of their hideouts?"

"Any that are connected to the symbol," Tam said. "Not sure if that's all of them."

"Then shouldn't we get moving on that?" Alden asked. "We don't want to give them a chance to clear out."

"We also don't want to be hasty," Councillor Emery said. "First let's handle the prisoners in our custody. We've voted to move them to Lumenaria, where we're already holding their co-conspirator. We'd been hoping to send a message during the summit that this worthless rebellion will soon be a thing of the past. And what better way to do so than to present them with three defeated prisoners? We'll arrange a viewing on the first night."

"I'm assuming you'll also be performing a memory break?" Mr. Forkle asked.

"Not until after the summit."

"That might be too late." Sophie squared her shoulders as all eyes focused on her. "We have reason to believe the Neverseen have a larger plan in the works—a plan that both Ruy and Brant were involved with. Interrogating them is our only chance to learn how to stop it."

"And what is your reason for believing this?" Councillor Emery asked.

Sophie thought she was ready to throw Keefe to the wolves. But . . . her voice wouldn't cooperate.

When Tam and Fitz didn't chime in either, she went with a different tactic.

"You're really going to doubt us—after everything we've uncovered? You don't think this proves we might know a little more than you?"

"When it comes to the dirty schemes of this refuse," Councillor Emery said, sneering at Brant and Ruy, "perhaps you are ahead of us. But *we* must think beyond this simple rebellion. We're trying to send a message to the other species of this world that they should fear and respect our power—and showing them a group of drooling, mindless wastes is not an image we're willing to present. We must *always* appear strong—always superior—even when it comes to our prisoners. Let them see we faced and stopped a worthy foe. And when the Summit is over, we will shatter and squeeze every shred of truth out of these disgraces. But only after we ensure they do not diminish the respect for our kind."

"That doesn't mean we can't interrogate them," Mr. Forkle reminded the Council. "With cleverness, we might be able to glean a few crucial truths."

"Perhaps," Councillor Emery said. "The matter will be taken under consideration *after* the prisoners are properly secured, and *after* we've searched every last one of these hideouts you claim to be able to lead us to. It's about knowing what deserves priority."

Please don't argue any further, Mr. Forkle transmitted as Sophie opened her mouth. *I'll raise the issue again tomorrow, once a few more things are settled. For the moment, it is wise to focus on storming the hideouts.*

Fine, Sophie told him. Out loud, she asked the Council, "Are you going to let us help with the raids on the hideouts?"

"It sounds like we'll require young Mr. Song's assistance," Councillor Emery said, ignoring Tam's scowl at the use of his family name. "The remainder of you should return to your homes."

"It's not that we don't value your assistance," Oralie jumped in. "It's that you've risked your lives enough. I wish we could spare Tam the responsibility as well, but his talent—and the nature of this gadget—make him crucial. I have no doubt we'll need your assistance for many things in the days ahead. So please, take this time to rest."

"I'm not opposed to keeping you safe," Edaline told Sophie gently, wrapping an arm around her shoulders.

The other parents agreed, and that seemed to settle it—except Linh, who insisted on staying with her brother.

"I think it would be wise if you all stayed together," Mr. Forkle told Sophie and her friends. "That way it's easier to reach you with updates and questions."

Alden and Della offered up Everglen, and that became the plan.

"Oh, and Miss Foster?" Councillor Terik said as the Councillors prepared to leap away. "Thank you for bringing the alicorns for a visit. It's good to see they're both healthy and thriving. Let's hope it remains that way."

The last words reminded her that Silveny and Greyfell probably shouldn't linger.

She made her way over and stroked Silveny's velvety nose.

SOPHIE OKAY?

Thanks to you, Sophie told her.

Silveny's deep brown eyes seemed to peer right through her, and the motherly alicorn searched Sophie's emotions until she landed on the one subject Sophie had been hoping to avoid.

KEEFE?

He . . . isn't here.

Silveny nuzzled Sophie's side. *GOOD,* she said. *KEEFE! FRIEND! GOOD!*

I hope so, Sophie told her, breaking eye contact before she ended up a sobbing mess.

She'd cry for Keefe later. Right now, she had to focus.

You and Greyfell should get somewhere safe—and get some snacks. Remember, you're eating for two.

Silveny nudged Sophie's hand. She trotted closer to Greyfell and both alicorns dipped their heads, almost in a bow as Sophie told them she'd check on them soon.

SOON! Silveny agreed as she and Greyfell floated into the sky.

Right before they teleported away, Silveny sent one final transmission.

KEEFE GOOD SOON!

"Wylie has been moved. As has Prentice—to be safe," Mr. Forkle told them after he'd arrived at Everglen that night. Despite the late hour, everyone was still wide awake, gathered in Everglen's glittering dining room—a room Sophie hadn't been in since the day Oralie, Bronte, and Kenric had tested her for Foxfire. The thronelike chairs, sweeping chandelier, and silk-draped windows looked far too grand for such an exhausted group, and no one had touched the platters of food Della had set out—even the mallowmelt. "They've been set up in a secure cabin high in the mountains, where they'll be able to recover together," he added. "Neither seemed strained at all by the sudden move. If anything, they seemed more relaxed than ever."

"What about Tam and Linh?" Biana asked. "Where will they live now?"

"We're setting up a secure residence for them here in the

Lost Cities. That way they'll no longer feel so isolated. Blur has offered to serve as their guardian, and the Council will be assigning them goblin bodyguards. And they've been granted permission to attend Foxfire, once the term resumes again."

Sophie tried to focus on the good news, and the hopeful hints in his tone. But . . . "You'll never be able to use Alluveterre as a hideout again, will you?"

Fitz had spent the last few hours sharing the heartbreaking details about Keefe stealing Tam's crystal and helping Alvar escape. No one except Grady—who'd had quite a few choice comments about *That Boy*—had known what to say. Especially Alden and Della.

"Never is a long time," Mr. Forkle told Sophie. "Most things tend to be much more temporary. And while it's a regrettable setback, it's nothing compared to what the Neverseen have lost this evening. That's another thing I'm happy to report. With the help of Mr. Tam—and a loyal contingent of goblins and dwarves—the Council has now raided all sixteen of the hideouts connected by the Lodestar symbol. Some had long been abandoned, but the others had very recently been sacked."

"So they were empty?" Fitz asked.

"Stripped and scorched, yes," Mr. Forkle admitted. "I'll give them credit for speed and efficiency—it must've been a mad, destructive scramble. And please try not to look so distressed by this news. Gathering more prisoners and evidence would've been nice—but either way, this is a significant victory in our favor. We've now shut down the majority of their network."

"But you don't think we got it all?" Biana asked.

"I think that Fintan's too clever to not have a few emergency evacuation areas. Plus, none of the hideouts had a silver door marked 'The star only rises at Nightfall.'"

Sophie rubbed the new knot forming under her ribs.

So Keefe's legacy was still out there, waiting for him.

She wondered what his mom would say if she'd seen what her son had done that day. Would she have been proud he'd chosen the Neverseen over his friends? Or furious he'd remained with the people who'd imprisoned her?

"I think that's all we can do for tonight," Mr. Forkle said, standing and reaching into his cloak for a pathfinder. "Blur will be bringing Tam and Linh here soon—and then I hope you'll all go to bed and *try* to sleep."

"Wait!" Dex said. "I almost forgot—do you still have Keefe's old Imparter?"

"I returned it to Miss Foster, to do with as she wished," Mr. Forkle told him. "Why?"

"I can't stop thinking about it, ever since Sophie did that enhancing thing to me. I think there's something we missed. Do you have it, Sophie?"

"It should still be at Havenfield," she said.

"I'll retrieve it for you tomorrow," Sandor promised as he stood to bring Grady and Edaline back to the safety of

Gildingham. Before he left, he gave Sophie a *long* lecture on how she was not to leave Grizel's sight even for a second—or trigger any more abilities.

And true to his word, Sandor returned to Everglen the next day, holding the black case he'd collected from her room.

"Is it okay for us to talk around the Imparter?" Biana asked as Dex popped open the case and slid his finger across the silver screen.

"Yeah it's a different kind of signal than I realized." He tapped the screen in each of the corners. "Hmm, it's being fussy again." He glanced at Sophie. "Would it be weird if I asked to hold your hand?"

Tam smirked. "Smoooooooth."

Sophie rolled her eyes. "I know what he meant."

She pulled off her glove, and the second their fingers touched . . .

"Whoa," Dex breathed. "That is such a rush!"

The seconds slipped by, and he tapped the screen a few more places before telling the Imparter, "Bypass."

The gadget beeped and went dark.

"Was that supposed to happen?" Linh asked.

"I don't know." Dex flipped the Imparter over, tapping a few more places.

The silence shifted from tense to restless to *endless*. Then a voice blared from the screen.

"Password?"

SEVENTY-THREE

WHAT'S THE PASSWORD?" Biana whispered.

"No idea," Dex admitted. "And I don't feel a way to hack it. That same crazy-smart Technopath who built all the stuff with the Lodestar symbol must've been the one who designed this."

"Okay," Linh said. "Anyone have any guesses?"

"With Keefe it could seriously be anything," Fitz reminded them.

Tam smirked at Sophie. "I have a theory."

"So do I," she said. "His mom's the one who rigged the gadget, right? So what would *her* password be?"

"But she didn't make it for herself—she wanted Keefe to

find this, didn't she?" Fitz asked. "Didn't the note she left for him kinda hint at it? So she would've picked something she hoped Keefe would guess."

He made a good point. Sophie reread the note in her mind.

"What about 'legacy'?" she asked.

"Access granted," the Imparter chirped, and Sophie felt ice ripple across her nerves.

"Access to what?" Biana whispered.

The screen stayed blank.

"Shouldn't it be doing something?" Fitz asked.

"It is," Dex said. "It opened a private line."

"So it's hailing somebody right now?" Sophie asked.

Dex nodded and they all leaned closer, watching the ominously silent screen.

"Are we sure this is a good idea?" Fitz asked after what felt like an eternity but was probably less than thirty seconds.

"Better to know than wonder, right?" Biana said. "But here's what I don't get. It took Dex's Technopath skills—*enhanced* Technopath skills—to get to the place where you entered the password, right? Wouldn't that mean Keefe never could've gotten there on his own?"

"It's only that difficult for *us*," Dex said, "because I had to bypass the primary sensor, which is what Keefe could've used to gain access. I'd actually noticed that there was a weird, two-tone gear the last time I took the Imparter apart. But I didn't realize it meant the sensor read different things on different sides until I got the boost from Sophie."

"So what else does it read?" Sophie asked.

"Blood."

Everyone squirmed.

"Is it still hailing?" Tam asked.

Dex nodded. "But I doubt anyone's going to answer. His mom probably set this up before they imprisoned her, so I'm sure her Imparter got taken or destroyed."

"How much longer should we wait?" Biana asked.

"Maybe give it another minute?" Sophie said. "Just in case."

She counted the passing seconds, and at around seventy-five Dex told everyone, "I guess that's it."

He swiped a finger across the screen, frowning when the Imparter flashed pale blue. "Wait—was it not actually hailing yet?"

"How would we know?" Fitz asked.

"Ugh, this thing makes no sense! It's like—"

"Hello?" a crackly, garbled voice blared from the Imparter. Even with the distortion, the sound was unmistakable.

Lady Gisela.

They all leaned back in case she could somehow see them. But the Imparter's screen stayed silver, keeping the conversation limited to their voices.

"Keefe?" Lady Gisela asked. "Is someone there?"

Fuzzy static.

"It's you, isn't it, Sophie?"

"Yes." The word slipped out before Sophie could think it through.

"Where's my son?" Lady Gisela demanded.

Sophie glanced at her friends for help, but they only offered blank stares.

"He's . . . where you planned for him to be," she mumbled.

Lots of crackles and static flooded the connection, and when Lady Gisela's voice came back it sounded like the end of a sentence. All Sophie caught was "run things."

"Can you repeat that?" Sophie asked.

"I said it was never my plan to let that idiot run things."

"You mean Fintan?"

Static was her only answer.

"Are you still there?" Sophie asked.

More crackles. Then Lady Gisela said, "I asked if anyone else has been captured."

"Why would I tell you that?"

"Because you have no idea what you're dealing with. And I do."

"And I'm supposed to believe you're going to help me?"

"Exactly," Lady Gisela said. "Because you care about my son. And I don't have a lot of options. So we're both going to suffer through this miserable truce."

Sophie glanced at her friends for guidance, and their expressions all seemed to be unanimously screaming *DON'T YOU DARE TRUST KEEFE'S MOM*. And Sophie had no intention of doing so. But that didn't mean she couldn't try to learn something from her.

"I'll ask you again," Lady Gisela said. "Where's my son? Is he with Brant and Fintan?"

Sophie bit her lip, deciding one tiny piece of information was worth the risk. "He's with Fintan."

"Does that mean Brant's been captured?"

"Tell me why it matters."

"You don't need to know. Who else was taken? Ruy?" When Sophie didn't respond, Lady Gisela said, "I'll take that as a yes. And I need you to listen very carefully. You have to do exactly as I say, or you'll regret it."

"Is that a threat?"

"It's a warning—based on truths and hard realities I don't expect you to understand."

"You know what I don't understand?" Sophie asked. "What you did to Cyrah Endal."

Lady Gisela's voice darkened. "Whatever you think you know is one small, twisted piece of a much larger, much grander whole."

"That sounds like a fancy way of trying to justify a murder."

"Murder," Lady Gisela repeated. "Believe what you want. You may not trust me, Sophie. And you may not like me. But right now, we both care about the same thing. Which means you need to listen to me. Get my son far away from the Neverseen."

The demand was so ironic, Sophie couldn't quite choke back her laugh.

"I take it that means you've tried?" Lady Gisela asked.

"Yeah, and there's pretty much no reasoning with him. He has this desperate need to try to make up for all the creepy things you've done."

"Don't blame this on me. This is what they want. *Their* vision."

"That would mean a lot more if you'd tell me what you're talking about."

"But it would also distract you from what matters. You can't stop this, Sophie. Don't try. It's been in place for too long. So get my son back before it all comes crashing down, and contact me when it's done. And next time, make sure you hail me using his blood."

SEVENTY-FOUR

I'M ASSUMING MR. DIZZNEE TRIED TRACK-
ing the signal," Mr. Forkle said as he studied the now
silent Imparter sitting on Everglen's dining room table.
His eyes were red rimmed and shadowed, and he wore
the same clothes from the day before—and Sophie couldn't
decide if it was the thronelike chair, or if his ruckleberries were
wearing off, but he looked smaller.

"I tried everything," Dex said, "Even with Sophie enhancing
my ability, I got nowhere."

Mr. Forkle nodded. "And I'm *also* assuming that you're not
going to tell Mr. Sencen about this?"

"Doesn't seem like a good idea," Sophie said. "If we couldn't
get him to leave the Neverseen when he had the perfect chance

and the perfect reason, how is telling him that his mom *wants* him to leave going to help? Besides, for all we know Lady Gisela's using us to get Keefe back so she can grab him and force him into his *legacy*."

"Oh, I'm certain her motives are selfish," Mr. Forkle said. "If I'm understanding this correctly, it sounds like this 'vision' Fintan has may be separate from the Lodestar Initiative that Lady Gisela created, and she fears it will wreck her own plans."

"Shouldn't we let it, then?" Dex asked.

"Ah, but that's a risky game. Blindly choosing between two evils could backfire far too easily. For all we know, Lady Gisela could truly be the safer path."

"But she probably killed Wylie's mom," Linh argued.

"And Fintan definitely killed Kenric," Sophie reminded her.

"Yeah . . . they're both horrible options," Biana said. "I want to take them both down."

"Hard to do when we don't actually know what either of them are planning," Fitz mumbled. "After all our investigations into Lodestar, we *still* don't know what the Initiative actually entails. And Fintan's *vision* is even more vague."

"I feel like Keefe is the key," Sophie said quietly.

"Ugh, if he heard you say that, there'd be no living with him," Tam grumbled.

Sophie smiled. It was strange that she could miss Keefe *and* want to bash his face in. "I just meant that there has to be a reason both Fintan and Lady Gisela want him on their side.

It might be because they need him to open that door in the mountain. But then why wouldn't Fintan have made Keefe do that right away?"

"It feels like we're missing something," Biana said. "Doesn't it?"

"When aren't we?" Sophie mumbled, replaying the conversation with Lady Gisela in her mind. There had to be deeper meanings to her vague warnings and advice.

"I guess all we really need to know," she said quietly, "for the moment, at least, is whether Keefe is safer where his mom wants him to be, or safer where he's at?"

"He's safest when he's not in the dark about that decision," Mr. Forkle told her. "And can choose based on knowledge, and not his own misguided reasoning."

The logic hit home.

"I guess I'll tell him what his mom said and see what he does," Sophie decided. "The rest is up to him."

"Try to make it quick," Mr. Forkle told her. "We have lots of other things to discuss when you're done."

"You want me to tell him now?" Sophie asked

"Why put off the inevitable?"

"Uh, who are you and what have you done with the guy who's always telling us to be patient?" Tam asked.

A sad smile curled Mr. Forkle's lips. "Perhaps I'm learning to see the folly in delay. Haste can be dangerous too, of course. But there's a difference between caution and hesitation. Plus, I need Miss Foster's mind free of distraction for what's coming next."

"What's coming next?" Sophie asked.

"One thing at a time, Miss Foster. First settle things with Mr. Sencen."

Sophie sighed, not sure she was ready to have this conversation—especially in front of an audience. But she closed her eyes and transmitted Keefe's name.

Foster? He responded immediately. *What's wrong? I thought you weren't talking to me.*

I wasn't, she admitted. *Is this a bad time?*

Um . . . give me a second.

His mind went silent for a beat—long enough for Sophie to tug out an itchy eyelash.

Okay—I told everyone I had to poop, he said a little too proudly. *That should keep them away for a few minutes.*

Ugh, TMI.

You realize I'm not actually pooping, right? I mean, I know we've shared a lot of things, but I don't think poop should be one of them—unless it's sparkly and from an alicorn. Or blasting like a geyser out of a gulon.

Stop talking about poop!

She shook her head, trying to knock those lovely mental images away and regain her focus. *I have to show you something, and you might want to sit down for it.*

The only way to do that involves a less-than-awesome-smelling toilet—this new hideout is miserable. *Everything is sweaty and sticky—and we're all crammed into this tiny room.*

How many of you are there?

Just me, Trix, Alvar, and Umber. Fintan moved everyone else to a different place. And it's starting to feel like they're my babysitters— they never let me out of their sight.

That . . . doesn't sound like a good sign.

She'd expected him to deny it. But his mind dimmed a little, before he changed the subject. *So what did you need to tell me?*

Right. Brace yourself. This is going to be tough to see. She gathered her concentration and replayed what Lady Gisela had told her word for word.

That . . . complicates things, he mumbled. *And it could all be a trick.*

It definitely could.

But you think I should do what she said and get out?

It doesn't matter what I think. It's not like you listen to me.

The thought had a snap to it, and Sophie could see Keefe's mind sting. But she wasn't going to apologize.

I think a better question is, CAN you get out? she asked.

It'll be rough, he admitted. *But my escape plan will still work. If I use it, though, it'll destroy every single thing I've been working toward.*

I guess you'll have to decide what's most important, then.

His mind seemed to ripple with a sigh. *What happens if I leave?*

What do you mean?

I mean . . . doesn't everyone hate me?

Sophie glanced at her friends, each watching her silently from their fancy chairs. *You have some serious apologizing to do,* she said. *But I don't think any of us can actually hate you—even when we really, really, really want to.*

I could've done without that third "really."

Maybe. But you deserve it.

I do. He replayed his mom's words again before he told her, *I'd better get back—but that's not my decision. I need more time to think.*

Think away, Sophie told him. *You know where to find me.*

"Actually, you won't be here if Mr. Sencen decides to come home in the next few days," Mr. Forkle warned after she'd closed down the mental conversation. "That's why I needed you to focus. I received a scroll this morning—as I'm sure your mother did as well—informing me that the envoy will be retrieving me at five o'clock this evening to bring me to Lumenaria. The Councillors finally agreed that it's imperative we interrogate Ruy and Brant as soon as possible. So they're moving up the Peace Summit, starting tonight."

SEVENTY-FIVE

SOPHIE AND EDALINE'S ENVOYS ARRIVED at Sandor's house at five o'clock sharp, and Sophie was relieved one of them was a familiar face— Righty, the goblin who'd helped guide her when she'd visited Lumenaria. Apparently, Righty had been assigned as Sophie's personal guard for the course of the summit, and the other envoy would be guarding Edaline.

Sandor gave both goblins a long list of procedures and instructions—along with a few threats of violence and dismemberment if anything went wrong.

"We've been well trained," Edaline's guard assured him.

Sophie decided to call her Bunhead. It matched her hairstyle, and her graceful movements as she crossed the room, handing them black tunics, pants, slipperlike shoes, and gloves to change into.

"The simple garb is just until you clear security," Righty explained. "Once you're settled into your rooms you'll find more proper attire for the summit."

"Will our rooms be near each other?" Edaline asked.

"You'll have your own double suite," Bunhead told her.

That was, unfortunately, the only good news. The rest was a whole lot of yuck, starting with the fact that Sophie wasn't allowed to bring Ella. No jewelry was allowed either, except their registry pendants, so Sophie had to leave behind her Cognate rings, panic switch, and Sucker Punch.

"Be safe," Grady whispered as he strangle-hugged his wife and daughter. "And here's hoping this will be a quick summit."

"What's the longest one has ever gone?" Sophie asked, regretting the question when Edaline told her, "A little over three months."

The words kept repeating in Sophie's mind as she endured the security searches at Lumenaria's gates—and the dread grew much louder during the lecture on castle rules. The basic gist was: *If you aren't in an assigned meeting or gala, you'll be locked in your room for your own safety.* It was hard to decide what sounded scarier—the locked-in-her-room part, or the *gala*.

And it could stretch on for *months*.

Even the walk to her room felt endless. No blindfolds that

time, not that it made the journey any clearer, considering how twisty the halls were, and all the identical staircases and doors.

"Your rooms will not have a view," Bunhead warned. "The Council wanted you in the underground quarters, where the security is easier for us to control."

"So basically, they're locking us in the dungeon," Sophie said.

Righty smiled. "I'm sure you'll find the accommodations much more pleasant."

Their rooms *were* beautiful—marble floors, and walls broken up with intricate tapestries and paintings. Ornate chandeliers cast a warm pink light, and all the furniture was overstuffed and draped in luxurious fabrics. The décor was elegant and tasteful—the colors lush and regal. But the lack of windows still made it feel like a cell.

Their door also had two locks—one to keep anyone from getting in. The other to prevent them from leaving.

"We'll let you get changed for the introductory dinner," Bunhead told them. "Knock four quick times when you're ready to go and we'll open the door."

The lock clicked, and Sophie's misery was sealed when she checked her new wardrobe. Her "day gowns" had so many ruffles and gathers they made Cotillion dresses look plain. And her "evening gowns" had just as many frills—with fun bonuses like sweeping trains and corseted bodices and all kinds of other things that were clearly meant to destroy her.

"Remind me what any of this has to do with negotiating a peace treaty?" Sophie asked as Edaline helped her fasten the hundreds of tiny buttons that secured the silky teal gown she'd chosen. The color was her favorite, and the skirt wasn't *as* puffy as a lot of the others. But the drop-waist bodice was so fitted, she wondered how she would sit. And the neckline scooped and squeezed in ways that made her cheeks blush.

"This summit is about more than making King Dimitar sign his name on a piece of paper," Edaline told her. "It's about reminding the world of the sheer magnificence of our culture. Displaying our wealth, beauty, and confidence all work to create the ideal impression."

"Yeah, well, if they wanted me to be confident, they should let me wear shoes I can actually walk in," Sophie grumbled, holding up her impossibly slender heels.

"I guess you'll have to settle for looking beautiful—and so grown up! If any of your boys were here . . ."

Edaline didn't finish the sentence—or name the boys—and for that, Sophie gave her a hug.

"And you understand what's going to happen at the dinner?" Edaline asked as she knocked to let their guards know they were ready.

Sophie fussed with her teal gloves. "I'm going to try not to cause an interspecies incident when I'm introduced to the other leaders. Then we're all supposed to eat fancy food in a stuffy room while everyone pretends they're not secretly wishing they could kill each other."

Edaline smiled, looping her arm through Sophie's as they started the long trek to where dinner would be held. "Not *everyone* hates each other. The animosity exists mostly between the goblins, ogres, and trolls. The dwarves and gnomes are generally content to live and let live, so long as everyone extends that courtesy to them."

"Then let's hope we're seated next to them," Sophie mumbled. "And that none of the food requires knives."

"I'm sure it won't. Did you notice they didn't even give us any hairpins?"

After seeing the damage Lady Gisela had done with one, Sophie wasn't surprised.

"Are we going a different direction than the way we came?" Sophie asked as they started up a winding staircase. "I can't get my bearings."

"And you won't," Bunhead explained. "The paths are intentionally ambiguous to ensure that no one will ever find their way through unless they've been trained."

"Or get really lucky," Righty added.

"Don't be nervous," Edaline told her when they finally reached a set of embossed golden doors. "All you have to do is smile and act natural."

Sophie felt anything but natural as she took in the splendor of the room. The elves were never shy with their displays of wealth, but this? This was something else entirely. The space had the feel of a moonlit terrace garden, but they were still very much indoors, and every fragile flower, every graceful tree, every cascading vine, and every sweeping balustrade—even the stars winking across the swirled black ceiling—had been intricately carved from jewels or cast from precious metals. It was the perfect marriage of nature and craft—a new level of mastery—and everyone in the room could only stare in wonder.

Well, everyone save for one.

King Dimitar couldn't have looked more bored as he leaned his gorilla-size body against the trunk of a tree—a Panakes tree, Sophie realized, which made her wish she still wore her Sucker Punch. He wore his usual metal diaper—though the waistline had been rimmed with glittering black jewels, which matched the stones set into his earlobes—and idly traced a clawed finger along the tattoos crowning his bald head.

"A child in a Peace Summit," he said as Sophie tried to hurry past him. "And yet they criticize my people for training our children to defend themselves."

"If it were only for defense," Councillor Alina said, swishing over in an iridescent gown that shifted from green to purple with every motion, "I doubt anyone would have a problem."

"And yet the greatest defense is a strong offense, isn't it?" Dimitar countered, smiling to show his pointed teeth.

"Is that what you'd call the warriors you sent to capture my family?" Sophie asked, ignoring the warning squeeze Edaline gave her arm.

King Dimitar straightened, his bulging muscles flexing with the motion. "If *I'd* planned that mission, your mother would not be standing at your side—though I'm not convinced your family was even the target. Not everything revolves around you, Miss Foster."

He stalked away, leaving Sophie to drown in the fresh wave of questions.

If Dimitar wasn't lying about the attackers being unsanctioned rebels—which she was far from ready to believe—who else would they have been after?

Lady Cadence? She was one of the ogres' most loyal supporters.

"There you are, Miss Foster," Councillor Bronte said behind her, drawing her back to the present. Sophie turned to find him standing with Councillor Oralie and Councillor Terik, all looking resplendent in their suits, gowns, and capes in the same jeweled tones as their circlets.

Edaline had been right about the elves screaming wealth, power, and confidence. It was like having the prom kings and queens milling around the room.

"Empress Pernille was just telling me she hadn't had the privilege of meeting you," Bronte told Sophie. "Perhaps you'd be willing to let us make the introduction?"

Sophie nodded, letting the Councillors lead her away. But

her mind was still so stuck on the idea of Lady Cadence being the target that she nearly trampled a small, strange creature that looked like a cross between a sloth, a pot-bellied pig, and a small child, with fuzzy skin, an upturned nose, and a short chubby body dressed in a purple tutu.

"Empress Pernille," Councillor Oralie said, dipping a graceful curtsy. "Forgive us for not seeing you."

The creature chirped a reply, and it took Sophie's Polyglot skills a moment to realize she was listening to the ruler of the trolls.

"I'm so sorry," Sophie said, fumbling through a curtsy. "I should never be allowed to wear something this huge—it will only end in disaster."

Empress Pernille blinked her round, yellow eyes. "Rarely do I ever hear an elf address me in my own language—and with such a precise accent."

Sophie stared at her gloves. "I wish I could take credit. But my ability made the shift unconsciously."

"Intelligent, talented, and humble—I see why I hear often of your influence," the Empress said, before turning to Oralie. "Perhaps we could have a word?"

Oralie motioned for the Empress to follow her through an arch lined with cut amethyst flowers, to a more secluded corner of the room.

As soon as Bronte and Terik had wandered away, Sophie whispered to Edaline, "*That's* what trolls look like?" She'd seen images of them as fierce beasts with lots of claws and muscles—meanwhile Empress Pernille could've easily been mistaken for a Muppet.

"The trolls age in reverse," Edaline whispered. "Their bodies shrink with time, rather than growing. And their features soften."

"Does that mean the ancient trolls look like babies?" Sophie asked.

"Not quite that extreme. Sorry, I suppose I should've warned you."

"Anything else I should be prepared for?" Sophie asked.

"I can't think of anything. Actually, yes I can. King Enki is bald."

She pointed across the room, and Sophie did a double take.

Dwarves normally had long, scraggly fur and squinty, pointed facial features that reminded Sophie of oversize talking moles. But the king looked like a plucked chicken, his textured skin a mottled pattern of peach, brown, and black—which looked extra strange considering his pants were made of soft white fur.

"Is that what happens when dwarves age?" Sophie asked.

"No, it's a statement," Edaline said. "The dwarves view it a sign of power and strength for their king to wax himself bare. I've never really wanted to know why."

Sophie did her best not to stare, focusing instead on the king's heavy crown—a thick ring of carved, opalescent shell.

She'd gotten up close and personal once with the giant-sand-crab-like creatures the shell had come from, and still found it strange the king would want any part of its body curled around his head.

He caught her looking and tapped his feet as he offered a bow.

The rest of the introductions were more what Sophie had prepared for. Queen Hylda looked fierce and statuesque in her gleaming golden armor. And a gnome Sophie had seen around Havenfield—now wearing a suit woven from Panakes petals—had been selected to represent his kind, which had no ultimate leader.

"You're handling yourself very well," Mr. Forkle told her, emerging from the shadows he'd been lurking in. "Far better than I could've ever planned."

"Is this what you designed me for?" she asked, raising an eyebrow.

Mr. Forkle smiled. "I designed you to be something new, Miss Foster. Something to get people's attention. And above all else, to be *you*."

The compliments weren't particularly sappy—but the way he said them turned her throat thick.

"Thank you," she whispered.

"For what?"

"For giving me this life—crazy and confusing as it always is."

It was Mr. Forkle's turn to look away, swiping at his eyes.

When he turned back to say something else, the words were drowned out by loud fanfare.

All twelve Councillors gathered in the center of the room to announce that it was time for dinner, and Councillor Liora snapped her fingers and made a U-shaped table appear before them, covered in flowers and candles and dome-covered plates at every place setting. The Councillors took the seats in the center, while the other leaders were stationed along the sides. Sophie was relieved to be seated between her mom and Mr. Forkle.

They feasted on several kinds of gnomish fruit, thinly sliced and artfully arranged. Some tasted like steak and lobster and other fancy things. Others were richer and earthier. No one cleared their plate, but everyone found their favorites and seemed happy when Liora conjured the dishes away.

"It's always refreshing to see our worlds gather in the pursuit of peace," Councillor Emery said as he stood to address his guests. "And to have this rare opportunity for enlightened interchange and mutual benefit. The real work begins tomorrow, but we wanted to end this first night with something we hope you'll find heartening. As many of you know, the complex problems of our modern world have led to the rise of certain groups within the Lost Cities. And while the Black Swan have proven themselves to be both resourceful and reasonable—which is why they're represented here at this Summit—the Neverseen have unfortunately caused incredible chaos. Halting their efforts has proven a challenge, but we finally have proof of our inevitable victory."

Three holograms flashed to the center of the U shape: Brant, Ruy, and Gethen—live projections of each of the prisoners in their blindingly bright cells. They sat in nearly identical poses—backs straight, legs crossed, eyes closed—looking more like meditating monks than warmongering villains.

And yet, as Sophie watched, the faintest whiff of a smile curled Gethen's lips, reminding her how desperate he'd seemed for information about the summit.

They're up to something, she thought, right as a pair of goblins burst into the room and whispered a breathless message to Councillor Emery.

"Is something wrong?" King Dimitar asked.

"'Wrong' is not the word I would use." Councillor Emery glanced at the other Councillors, waiting for each to nod. "I've just received word that the current leader of the Neverseen— an elf named Fintan Pyren—is outside the gates of this castle demanding to be admitted to the proceedings."

SEVENTY-SIX

WHY AREN'T THEY ARREST-*ing him?* Sophie transmitted to Mr. Forkle as the various leaders shouted questions at the Council. *They should be dragging Fintan to one of those cells to join his co-conspirators!*

Diplomacy is rarely as straightforward as it may seem, Mr. Forkle told her. *Both Queen Hylda and Empress Pernille are requesting that Fintan be allowed to participate in the Summit's proceedings. Haven't you been listening?*

She hadn't. Her mind had been too busy piecing scarier things together.

Fintan's arrival.

The fact that none of the prisoners had looked particularly upset about being in their cells.

Lady Gisela telling her "this is what they want."

Even the plan Keefe had mentioned—the one he'd said Brant and Ruy were ordered to take part in, which Ruy had considered unnecessary and demeaning.

Could it have involved letting themselves get captured?

They're up to something, she transmitted. *Probably a jailbreak. It's perfect. They'd get to humiliate the Council, impress or scare the world leaders,* and *get Gethen back, all in one go.*

You may be right, Mr. Forkle said. *And in case you are, I think it would be quite unwise to allow Fintan anywhere near those cells, don't you?*

He stood, clearing his throat as he waited for the room's attention. "For the record, I think Fintan should be heard during the proceedings as well."

At least half the room gasped—Sophie included—even though she knew what Mr. Forkle was trying to do.

"You honestly want to jeopardize the security of these proceedings?" Oralie asked, ignoring the protocol of letting Councillor Emery do the speaking.

"No. I want him to be placed under heavy guard in the small storage outbuilding in the main courtyard," Mr. Forkle said calmly. "And he can remain there until the morning negotiations, in which case he'd be brought into the meeting. Keep as many guards on him as you like—and lock him back in the outbuilding when the proceedings are over. There's no reason for him to attend the galas or dinners."

"There's no reason for him to attend anything at all!" Alina argued. "He's a Pyrokinetic."

"Yes, and lumenite doesn't burn," Mr. Forkle reminded her. "Isn't that why the Ancient Councillors chose it when they built this fortress?"

Oralie stood, her fragile hands gripping the end of the table. "I can't believe anyone is considering this. That lunatic is bent on destroying everything we hold precious. What can we possibly gain from allowing his voice to be heard?"

"Perspective," Empress Pernille told her. "For millennia we've been told there's one way—the elvin way. And now, it appears the elvin way is divided. I find it hard to believe I'm the only one who'd like to know what these other elves have to say—especially since one alternate elvin perspective is already being presented by the Black Swan. Why not hear the other?"

"Because he's a murderer!" Oralie shouted.

"So am I, by elvin standards," Queen Hylda said. "So are most of us. Death goes hand in hand with war."

"*You're* in favor of Fintan joining us?" Councillor Bronte asked the goblin queen. "After his involvement in what happened with Brielle?"

"It's *because* of his involvement in Brielle's death that I would like to hear him out. I'd like to understand what her life was taken for."

"None of us are saying we'll agree with his logic," King Enki added. "We'd simply like to hear what that logic *is*. Isn't it our responsibility to consider the issues from every possible side before we render a decision?"

Sophie was surprised to realize King Dimitar was staying silent during the debate. And he glared at those supporting Fintan's admission with a murderous sort of rage.

The Councillors looked just as disgusted. But—ever the diplomats—they put it to a poll, making it clear that the Council's vote would only count for one. Mr. Forkle was given a vote, since he was a leader of his order. Sophie and Edaline were excluded as observers. The final verdict: four to three in favor of letting Fintan attend.

"Well," Councillor Emery said, massaging his temples. "It appears we have some adjustments to make. So we ask that you please return to your rooms—and understand that you will not be able to leave them for the rest of the night. We need to ensure everyone's safety as we drastically amend our protocols."

Righty and Bunhead shuffled Sophie and Edaline away from the crowd, leading them through a set of balefire-lit halls into the bowels of the fortress.

As soon as the door closed to their suite, Edaline pulled Sophie close. "It looked like you and Mr. Forkle were having a telepathic conversation while everyone argued. Please tell me what's going on. I promise I'm strong enough to handle it."

For most of the time Sophie had spent with her adoptive

family, Edaline had been the fragile one, broken by her grief over losing Jolie. But there was no weakness in Edaline's voice or any tremors in her hands as she rubbed Sophie's back.

So Sophie leaned closer and whispered, "We think the Neverseen are going to attempt a prison break, and we're trying to figure out how to stop them."

Edaline nodded slowly. "And I'm assuming Mr. Forkle didn't ask the Councillors to move the prisoners, because you're worried that's what the Neverseen want?"

"Actually, I think he just knew the Council would never go along with it," Sophie admitted. "But your reason is important too."

"So what does Mr. Forkle want us to do?"

"No idea," Sophie admitted, not missing the way Edaline had included herself in their planning. "It's so hard to strategize when we don't have any idea what they're thinking. Everything we do could play right into their hands."

"Do you think Keefe will have any insights?"

"If he does, they'll probably be super vague and warn us about the wrong thing," Sophie grumbled. But on the off chance, she decided to reach out to him.

Just the girl I wanted to talk to, Keefe told her.

No time for banter, Keefe—Fintan just talked his way into the Peace Summit. I'm pretty sure he's planning to break Ruy, Gethen, and Brant out of the dungeon. In fact, I'm betting Brant and Ruy are a part of it.

Keefe's mind unleashed a bunch of words she'd get in trouble for using.

I take it that means we're guessing right? she asked.

You might be. I know Fintan's off on a mission right now—and Alvar told me they've been building toward it for a while. He said it would make the world lose all faith in the Council.

Sophie's stomach did a twist-flip move that made her really wish she hadn't eaten so much dinner.

Ugh, I'm the biggest idiot on the planet if that nightmare at the Pallidrose hideout was a ploy to get them captured, Keefe mentally grumbled. His thoughts strayed to his burned hand, and Sophie could tell the nerves still hurt him, even though the skin had healed.

It was probably her cue to tell him he wasn't an idiot—but he *had* done some pretty idiotic things.

Then again, so had she.

If getting arrested was part of their plan, we all played right into it. All we can do is hope we've caught our mistake with enough time to stop them.

And I'm assuming you're at the summit? he asked. *Never mind, of course you are. You're probably right where it's most dangerous.*

I am, Sophie said. *And so is Edaline.*

More inappropriate words pounded through his head. *Why would the Council let Fintan in? Didn't they learn after what happened to Kenric?*

It wasn't their decision. Some of the other leaders wanted to hear what he had to say. And Mr. Forkle figured it was safer than letting Fintan anywhere near the cells.

I guess I can see that. But I have a bad feeling about this, Foster.

So do I. Is there anything else you can think of that will tell us what we're dealing with?

Not much. I heard Alvar and Fintan debating about whether or not someone was going to "deliver." So that might mean there's another person who needs to bring them something. Maybe King Dimitar?

Maybe. But he looked pretty furious when Fintan showed up.

Edaline was still rubbing Sophie's back, and Sophie tried to focus on the feeling—tried to keep her head clear so she could think instead of panicking.

It's not too late to beat this, Keefe thought, his mind humming with a new sort of momentum. *Keep your head down and your eyes open, and don't go anywhere without Sandor.*

Sandor's not here. Lumenaria has its own security force.

Can you trust them?

I don't know. My guard seems nice.

Nice isn't good enough. If there is another person helping Fintan, it would make sense that they'd be part of the security. So don't hesitate to unleash that Foster rage on anyone who feels like a threat, okay? I'll be there as soon as I can.

You will? How?

Still figuring that out. I don't know if I'll be able to get inside the castle, but I'm sure there's somewhere on the island I can hide.

Sophie doubted that, but she had a more pressing question. *What about your babysitters?*

Already working on it. That's what I was trying to tell you when you first reached out to me. I decided I'm leaving the Neverseen. Tonight.

SEVENTY-SEVEN

SOPHIE PULLED AWAY FROM EDALINE as the crush of emotions hit her. She couldn't decide if she wanted to laugh or cry or shred a few of her bed's fancy tasseled pillows.

On the one hand—Keefe was leaving the Neverseen!

On the other: WHY COULDN'T HE HAVE FIGURED IT OUT BEFORE HE FREED ALVAR, AND STOLE THE CACHE, AND THE ALLUVETERRE CRYSTAL, AND WHEN IT WASN'T SUPER DANGEROUS FOR HIM TO ESCAPE, AND ARRRRGGGGGHHHHH!

Hey, Keefe said, reminding her that their thoughts were still connected. *I don't blame you for the rage-fest, Foster—but I promise I'm going to make it up to you. All of it. Starting tonight.*

She sank onto her bed, deciding sitting was a good idea. *I know you want to help—but coming to Lumenaria is a bad idea. The island is nothing but a cold, rocky beach, and I'm sure there are goblins patrolling it. And Alvar and the others might expect you to go there. I think you should head to Sandor's house in Gildingham. That's where Grady is. They'll keep you safe.*

Uh, I'm pretty sure the most dangerous place I could be right now is alone in a room with your dad and Gigantor.

Flashes of the torturous "boys" conversation raced through Sophie's mind. *Hmm, you might have a point there.*

So it's settled, then, Keefe said. *I'll be outside Lumenaria as soon as I bust out of here. I don't care if there are patrols, I'll find a way to evade them. I want to be close—that way if you need me, I can help.*

Sophie could think of a thousand reasons why that was a horrible plan. But there were other things to worry about.

How are you going to get away from everyone at the hideout? she asked. *You said it was going to be rough.*

It probably will be. And I know everything I've done lately has been made of epic fail. But this is different. I'm back to playing my own games. And Team Foster-Keefe is going to win!

"You both look tired," Mr. Forkle noted as Sophie and Edaline took their seats at the formal summit breakfast.

Tired was an understatement. They'd stayed up late discussing Keefe—and then Sophie's brain had spent the rest of the night churning out nightmares.

But she could tell King Dimitar was listening to their conversation, so she told Mr. Forkle, "They wouldn't let me bring Ella. How do people sleep without stuffed animals? I didn't know where to put my arms."

Queen Hylda and Empress Pernille laughed at her joke, and Sophie was glad she'd made it. She hadn't noticed they were also eavesdropping.

Now is not a wise moment for secrets, Mr. Forkle transmitted as Sophie picked halfheartedly at one of the pastries, getting chocolate on her silky gloves.

She told him what Keefe had decided and added, *I've tried checking on him a few times and he hasn't responded.*

There's nothing the Neverseen can do to stop you from communicating with him. If he's ignoring you, it's only because he needs to concentrate.

Technically, there was *one* way the Neverseen could silence Keefe forever—but she was *not* letting her mind go there. Nope. Nope. Nope.

I wish he wasn't coming here, she told Mr. Forkle. *It's way too risky, and he's only doing it because he feels like he needs to make everything up to me.*

He does *need to make it up to you. Haven't you realized that yet? That's why you and Mr. Sencen work so well together. You both push each other to believe in yourselves. Don't go easy on him now because you're afraid he's too fragile. The more you let him prove himself, the more he'll realize he's still worthy.*

Their conversation ended when a fleet of goblins marched into the room and announced that they'd be escorting everyone to a room called The Circle. It was a long trek, and Sophie cursed her stupid heels—and her much-too-poofy silver-blue gown—as they trudged through a dozen different halls and then up an endless winding staircase.

The Council was waiting for them in the highest room in the tower, at a glowing round table that Sophie was sure had been the inspiration for King Arthur's legend. Twenty-one chairs circled the table at evenly spaced intervals—twelve for the Councillors, three for Sophie and Edaline and Mr. Forkle, one for each of the other intelligent species' leaders, and one that remained empty—until the entire circular wall had been lined shoulder to shoulder with goblin soldiers. Then four additional guards marched into the room, surrounding a figure who rattled with every step.

"Sorry I'm late," Fintan said, waving a chained hand as he clanked into his seat. "The security here is *murder*."

Oralie's cheeks turned as green as the simple gown she wore. Sophie wondered if the outfit was a tribute to Kenric. The elves always wore green to plantings—the color of life.

Councillor Emery cleared his throat as he stood. "As some of you know, this room is designed to remind us that we're all equals. Debate is expected. Emotions will surely run high. But that doesn't mean we can't listen to and respect each other. We all share the same goal: a united world where our people can coexist peacefully, with a proper balance of freedom and structure to maintain order—"

"And there we have the greatest lie of the elves," Fintan interrupted, struggling to stand with his clunky chains. "We talk of freedom and equality—but demand authority and superiority. And why shouldn't we? Simply put: We're better, on every level. Smarter. More powerful. With talents and skills none of you can even comprehend."

Angry shouts erupted from the other rulers, and Sophie slouched in her chair.

She'd heard the elves refer to themselves as superior many times—and it had always made her uncomfortable. But to broadcast it so boldly in front of the other species was both uncalled-for and insulting.

"There's no need to be offended," Fintan called over them, resting his chained hands on the glowing table. "Being superior isn't all it's cracked up to be. We're stuck solving all of *your* problems, trying to keep millions of people with different wants and needs and challenges satisfied with their lives. Why do you think we're here?"

"Before you start shouting again," Councillor Bronte interrupted, "remember that you're the ones who voted that Fintan be allowed to attend. Perhaps now you see why we've been working so hard to silence him."

"But I *won't* be silenced!" Fintan shouted. "Because the old ways are failing—and have been failing for centuries. This world doesn't need diplomacy. It needs quick, decisive leadership from someone who offers actual solutions. Someone not afraid of making the hard choices. Someone willing to make changes. Let's be honest—how many of you fully expect to have most of your demands ignored during these negotiations?"

"And how many would prefer to suffer the consequences of ill-conceived plans?" Councillor Emery countered.

"You look confused," Mr. Forkle whispered to Sophie.

"I don't understand why they're letting Fintan go on like this," she whispered back.

"Because they take the 'equals at the round table' concept very seriously. And they're probably also hoping he'll wear himself out."

"But shouldn't they at least insist he talk about the ogre treaty?" Sophie asked. "Isn't that why we're here?"

"We are indeed," Mr. Forkle said, rising from his seat and addressing the other leaders. "What you're witnessing is the folly of the Neverseen. They don't offer solutions. They shout and wail and stir up unrest, and make everyone lose focus on what actually matters. Let's not forget that we're here today because one leader"—he pointed to King Dimitar—"decided to violate the treaty his people signed, in large part because he was listening to the advice of the Neverseen. Surely you've heard of the disgusting plague they unleashed on the gnomes in a pitiful attempt to force the species into slavery. And the betrayals sadly haven't ended there. Only a handful of days ago, a small band of ogres attacked an innocent elvin family, killing one of the loyal goblins who was there to protect them."

"The latter incident was done without my permission," King Dimitar argued, turning to address Sophie and Edaline. "I cannot force you to believe me—nor will I apologize for something I'm not responsible for. But I will offer you what little I know. The Neverseen proposed an alliance, and spoke of a different test to verify my commitment."

"Which was?" Sophie asked.

Dimitar glared at Fintan. "That is irrelevant. What matters is I decided not to participate—and I did so after receiving sound advice from one of your own. The same someone who happened to be present during the attack at Havenfield."

"Lady Cadence?" Sophie confirmed.

"Seems rather coincidental, don't you think, that a group of ogres rebelling against *my* resolve to separate from the Neverseen would involve themselves in an assault that includes the very person who encouraged me to reject Fintan's offer?"

"My goodness," Fintan said. "Who knew the ogres were such excellent story spinners?"

He was the picture of nonchalance, except for the subtle twitching of his jaw.

Meanwhile Dimitar's expression was hard as iron—no sign of doubt or remorse. Sophie would never be foolish enough to trust the ogre king. But that didn't mean he never spoke the truth.

And the idea of two ogre threats—one from the King and one from this emerging rebellion—opened a whole new realm of horrors.

"Either way," Mr. Forkle said, taking back command of the floor. "Rebels or not, it does not change the fact that the ogres have turned violent, unruly, and willfully disobedient. And if they want the freedom of sharing this planet, they must agree to behave. *That's* what we're here to discuss—not whatever madness this fool is trying to distract everyone with. He's here only to stir up trouble and flatter himself." He flicked an arm at Fintan in a dismissive wave.

"Isn't it ironic to hear such speech coming from someone who is himself the leader of a rebellion?" Fintan asked. "Someone who trusts the Council so little he won't stand in front of them under his true identity. Someone who relies on fake names and false appearances and works on his projects in the shadows. He may like to believe he's better than me, but in all the ways that matter, we are very much the same. And we've both earned the power we've acquired because the people of this planet—regardless of their species—are desperate for the guidance and direction needed to survive the coming crisis. Our world has far greater issues than rebellious ogres—in fact, I happen to know that a primary reason King Dimitar was initially open to my suggestions is something you all grow more frustrated with every day. And if you think this Council is ever going to offer you a solution, get ready to be severely disappointed. They'll hem and haw and return to their glittering castles—maybe even erase the problem from their minds and pretend it no longer exists."

"And what exactly is this problem you speak of?" King Enki asked.

Fintan's eyes focused on Sophie, his lips curling into a smile that gave her prickles. "The problem is humans."

SEVENTY-EIGHT

WHAT DO WE DO," FINTAN asked, "with a species that's clever enough to build and create, and yet foolish enough to design its own ruin? Creatures so violent, they're always at war—but with others of their own kind? Creatures that destroy everything they touch, including this planet we're all forced to share? Creatures so prolific, they've consumed the majority of the productive lands, and yet even the Councillors themselves refuse to classify them as intelligent? Creatures we hold to no treaties—no codes of honor—and no laws except their own flawed logic? Creatures that don't even know we exist?" His eyes roved around the table, before coming to rest again on

Sophie. "To them, we're nothing more than silly stories and legends. We're magical. Mythical. Credited to their own fanciful imaginations. And should they discover our existence, their only response would be violence. And yet what has our Council done about it?"

"Another clever way of distracting us from the actual issues at hand," Councillor Emery said. "At this rate, the summit will stretch on indefinitely."

"We can't have that," Fintan told him. "I have a timeline to stick to."

"A timeline for what?" Queen Hylda asked.

"The realization of my vision."

Laughter shattered the silence, mixed with slow, mocking applause. Sophie was surprised to realize it was coming from King Dimitar as he stood to address the table.

"I must say, that was a far more impassioned performance than he gave me when he first mentioned his vision—which at the time, he was calling his Lodestar Initiative."

"Yes, I had to streamline things after you failed so spectacularly," Fintan informed him.

"I suppose I did." King Dimitar turned to the representative of the gnomes. "We all know I let myself be coerced into unleashing the plague. Call it cruel if you like, but I was assured it would be in the best interests of everyone in the long run. I have since come to realize that the Neverseen's promises are no more useful than the Council's blatant refusal to acknowledge anyone's concerns. Don't make my mistake and be fooled by his pretty lies. He'll offer the sun and the moon—so long as you do his bidding. In the end, you'll have nothing to show except grief and ruin. And the same applies to the things you'll hear from all of the elves at this table. Any of these new elvin orders only benefit themselves. Why else would they be focusing their talents and skills on deadly actions and altering their children to make them into weapons?"

"I'm not a weapon!" Sophie snapped when he shot her a glare.

"I don't know what you are, Miss Foster. But I no longer care. You and your friends destroyed half my city and received full pardons instead of punishment. You invaded my mind—twice—and suffered no lasting consequences. Isn't your very existence a violation of the most fundamental elvin laws? And yet here you are, in top-level treaty negotiations, with an equal seat among the leaders of entire worlds. I don't fear the Council—I fear what they'll let you grow to become. And more than that, I fear what lengths he'll go to"—he pointed to Fintan—"in order to stop you. And I want no part of it."

"So what are you saying?" Councillor Emery asked him.

"I'm saying I've looked long and hard for the so-called benefits I've gained from the leadership of the elves. And I can't find any. But I'm also not naïve enough to believe I can stand against you—nor will I align myself any longer with self-serving rebellions. I've spent weeks watching my people suffer the consequences of the trust I put in lunatics. I won't let them suffer any further. All I want—all I came to this summit to achieve—is a treaty that allows my people to remain separate. Leave us our lands and let us be, and I guarantee you'll never see or hear from us again. Draft a treaty that specifies that and I'll sign in a heartbeat."

The discussion that followed seemed even more circular than the table, and after a dozen times around, King Dimitar laughed. "I offer to disappear—and essentially give you everything you want in the process—and still you argue and hesitate?"

"I think," Councillor Emery said carefully, "that things are moving quite quickly in a rather unexpected direction. So I propose we take a brief recess to allow a moment to process."

Righty and Bunhead rushed Sophie and Edaline back to their locked rooms, and Mr. Forkle convinced the goblins to let him tag along.

"I don't understand what's happening in there," Edaline said, collapsing onto a settee in their sitting room.

Mr. Forkle took one of the armchairs. "I think . . . Dimitar spent much of his life believing ogres were actually the superior species, and planning to someday use the plague to take power. It's why he fell for Fintan's lies—and now that he's been properly humbled, he's trying to cut his losses and protect his people. Which has nothing to do with you, Miss Foster. Everything you brought upon Ravagog was provoked and necessary."

"I know," Sophie mumbled.

But it still didn't feel good being called a monster—especially by one of the creepiest people she'd ever met.

Then again, the Dimitar speaking in the Circle wasn't the bloodthirsty beast she'd come to expect. He was articulate. Logical. Clearly concerned for his people. Much more like the king Lady Cadence had described. And the thought that Sophie had played any role in convincing him the best course of action was total isolation made her glad she hadn't eaten any breakfast.

"Did either of you notice how many of the leaders nodded along when Fintan went into his tangent about humans?" Edaline asked quietly.

"Everyone but King Dimitar," Mr. Forkle said. "And I suspect that's simply a refusal to agree with Fintan. Humans truly are quite the conundrum—creatures we're forbidden to help, with weapons powerful enough to destroy the whole planet."

"But what's the solution to that?" Sophie asked.

"Ours is a work in progress," Mr. Forkle admitted.

"And Sophie plays a part in it?" Edaline pressed.

"*That* will be up to her. She's running her own life now. Has been for quite some time."

"Unless Fintan pulls off his 'vision,'" Sophie mumbled, her nerves knotting up just thinking about it.

This is what they want.

Had Lady Gisela meant those words for this potential prison

break—assuming they were right about that threat? Or for some much grander, much darker scheme?

"Perhaps you should use these moments to check on Mr. Sencen," Mr. Forkle suggested. "Rather than worrying yourself sick with unanswerable questions."

He made a good point—though Sophie's heart seemed to lodge in her throat as she transmitted her call with Keefe's name.

If he didn't answer . . .

'Bout time you reached out, Foster.

Tears burned Sophie's eyes and she had to blink them back. Edaline pulled her into a hug to keep her from wobbling.

You're safe? she asked.

I'm better than safe. I'm free! And FREEZING. I had to ditch all my cloaks—and this cave is not blocking the wind like it's supposed to. I mean, it's an ocean cave—it has one job to do!

Does that mean you're here?

Yep. The security patrols don't seem to know this cave exists. So if you need me, I'm close. Call me and I'll find a way to reach you. In the meantime, I'll be practicing my body temperature regulation and hoping nothing with lots of teeth and fangs also calls this cave home.

How did you escape? Was it as rough as you thought it would be?

A little better. A little worse. But I made it. What about you— how's it going at the summit?

Super weird.

She'd just started to tell him about the strange speeches by both Fintan and King Dimitar when Righty and Bunhead knocked to notify them the recess had ended.

King Dimitar was the last to return to the Circle, and refused to take his seat. "I've said my piece," he told everyone. "And have no further reason for debate. I've named the terms I'll agree to for this treaty. You should all find them more than reasonable."

"And you truly wish to withdraw your people from the rest of the intelligent species?" Councillor Emery asked.

Dimitar nodded. "So long as you will leave my people in peace."

"And how do we know this isn't a ploy to remain unsupervised, so you can build your weapons and train for a large-scale invasion?" Queen Hylda asked.

"If the lack of supervision is the issue, I'm happy to grant access to Lady Cadence whenever she wants. Will that satisfy your concerns?"

"It does for me," King Enki voted first.

"And me," Empress Pernille agreed.

Queen Hylda acquiesced next, followed by the gnomish leader whose official name seemed to be Thales the Sower.

"I suppose it works for us as well," Councillor Emery said. "What about you?" he asked Mr. Forkle.

"I believe it's a strange decision," he said. "But I see no objection. And I'd suggest adding language that makes for a simple process to renegotiate should the ogres someday change their minds."

"What about me?" Fintan asked, "I get an equal vote in these proceedings. And this is madness. Sheer, hasty madness. Surely we should take the night to sleep on it."

"My people need me," King Dimitar argued. "And honestly, if I have to suffer through another day of this nonsense I'll be tearing out my teeth just so I have something sharp to throw at you. As I understand it, this does not call for a unanimous vote, only a majority, which I clearly have. Draft the treaty."

"As you wish," Councillor Emery said, rolling up the sleeves of his silver tunic and taking the clean scroll Councillor Liora conjured. "Looks like we're in for a late night."

"Not if you write fast," Dimitar told him. "I'll make this simple. No confusing legalese. No loopholes and amendments. All we need are simple lists of 'I will' and 'I won't.' For example, I *won't* act against any other intelligent species if you *will* allow my people to keep ourselves separate."

And so it went, with King Dimitar mapping out simple, clear demands that none of the other leaders had issue with, and Councillor Emery furiously scribbling it all down. It would've been a relief—if Fintan hadn't looked so stressed. Even Mr. Forkle seemed to notice.

The third time Fintan requested the time, Mr. Forkle asked, "In a hurry?"

"Quite the opposite," Fintan assured him. But he noticeably

paled when Councillor Emery marked the end of the treaty lists with an intricate flourish.

"Would you like to check it over before you sign?" he asked Dimitar.

"No." King Dimitar took the pen and scratched his name. "Done."

One by one, the other leaders added their signatures, and Sophie watched Fintan the whole time. He kept his features composed—and didn't ask for the time again. But tiny beads of sweat trickled down his brow.

"Take this to the records room and have it sealed," Councillor Emery told one of the goblins, handing him the signed scroll. "And ring the bells to mark the official end."

"And take Fintan to the dungeon," Oralie added, sending ten guards swarming around him. "Having a seat at this table does not excuse you of your crimes. You will be held here until a tribunal can determine your final sentencing."

Fintan rolled his eyes. "How predictable of you."

Earth-shaking bells rang through the castle, vibrating the walls.

"Does that mean we're free to leave?" Edaline asked as Sophie tried to keep up with how fast everything was moving.

Could they really have arrested the leader of the Neverseen *and* secured an ogre peace treaty in less than five minutes?

Apparently they had, because Councillor Emery nodded. "Though I hope you'll stay to celebrate at the gala."

"The *gala*," Fintan whispered, so softly he probably thought no one could hear him.

Sophie did. She was watching him so intently, she missed the part where Edaline agreed they'd stay. But she didn't miss the relief in his eyes.

Or the way he smiled at her and said, "Sounds like you'll be celebrating all night," as the goblins dragged him away.

"I think you should leave," Sophie said, as soon as she and Edaline were back in their rooms. "Fintan looked way too happy. And he's down in the prison, where he wanted to be. And he's no longer worried about time. I bet he needed to keep the leaders here up until the hour they'd arranged. And that's why he seemed so stressed when King Dimitar rushed the process—but now he knows everyone will be staying for the gala."

This is what they want.

"And how does getting rid of me change any of that?" Edaline asked.

"Because I'll know you're safe while I figure out what to do."

Edaline took Sophie's gloved hands. "I'm not leaving without you, so let's not waste time debating that. Do you think we should tell the Council what you're thinking?"

"I doubt they'll listen. They'll go on and on about all the security and how impossible it would be for anyone to breach it."

"The security here *is* amazing," Edaline noted. "But I know how sharp your instincts are. If you think there's a problem, we can't ignore it. I just wish I were as good at planning things as you are. The best I can come up with is to go to the gala and talk to Oralie. She made the meeting with Gethen happen—she might be able to sway the Council again."

"I guess that's true," Sophie said, heading for the door.

Edaline grabbed her hand and pulled her back. "Actually, I'd prefer you wait here. If Fintan's planning something, there's a good chance it includes *you*. I saw the way he watched you during the negotiations—like a prize he'd so desperately love to collect. Which means you should stay behind a locked door, where he can't get anywhere near you. Please, Sophie. Use the time to brainstorm backup plans. Or chat with Keefe. Or both."

"Fine," Sophie reluctantly agreed. "But if you're not back in fifteen minutes, I'm coming after you."

She kissed Sophie's cheek and tucked a strand of hair behind Sophie's ear. "I love you so much, sweetheart. Thank you for trusting me."

SEVENTY-NINE

EVERY SECOND FELT LIKE AN HOUR—
and by the time eight minutes had passed,
Sophie was ready to bang her head against the
marble walls.

She'd used two of those minutes to ditch her stupid dress
and change into the simple black clothes she'd been wearing
when she arrived. The rest she'd spent pacing and thinking.

Whenever there were this many unanswered questions, it
always meant they were missing something. And the one that
bothered her the most was: *How were the Neverseen planning to
get out of their cells?*

She'd seen the sturdy locks.

The heavy metal doors.

And lumenite didn't burn, so Fintan's power was useless.

She tried to figure out what she would do if she were trapped, and her mind kept circling back to her recent skill training.

The splotchers she'd exploded.

The stone she'd shattered.

She traced her hand across the cold stones around her door.

Coach Rohana had told her, *I suspect you could bring down a mountain if you sat in solitude long enough.* Was *that* why Gethen had seemed so content in his cell? Had he been taking the time to rest and build his reserves to break through the doors?

A faint tremor shook the floor, and Sophie tried to tell herself her mind was playing tricks on her. But then she realized the crystals on the chandeliers were swaying.

The motion was so subtle, she wouldn't have noticed it if she hadn't been paying attention.

But she *was* paying attention.

And as she watched, a tiny rustle made the crystals quiver again.

Someone could be walking on the floor above her. Or the wind could be strong enough to shake the castle. Or . . .

Four dangerous prisoners could be breaking out of their dungeon cells.

But why now?

If this was just about embarrassing the Council in front of the other leaders, why not escape the second the summit began?

This is what they want, Lady Gisela had told her—but she'd also told her something else. Something Sophie had thought was just metaphor or hyperbole. But maybe it had been another warning.

Get my son back before it all comes crashing down.

Keefe had told her that Fintan wanted to take out the Council. And here they were all under one roof—the same roof as Gethen. And Gethen had had *months* to build his reserves.

Gethen is where he belongs.

The perfect inside man, hidden in the one place they wouldn't have been able to access any other way. Maybe the person they'd been counting on to *deliver.*

But . . . if Gethen brought down the castle—wouldn't they all be crushed in the rubble?

Fintan had known the Council would arrest him—he'd said as much to Oralie. He'd also stalled the proceedings, making sure it all happened on his timeline. And he wasn't suicidal, so why would he want to be down in the dungeon when it happened? Why would he order Brant and Ruy to get themselves captured?

Ruy.

A powerful Psionipath could shield them under a force field. Keep them alive. Make sure they survived.

It was sickening how perfectly they'd planned everything—and even worse how many clues she'd missed. The warning signs had been there all along, and she hadn't paid close enough attention.

The floor shook again, telling her the time to wonder was over.

This was happening.

And the tremors were only beginning.

KEEFE! she transmitted. *If you can hear me, make sure you stay away from the castle. Gethen is going to knock it down. THAT's Fintan's vision.*

She sent the same transmission to Mr. Forkle, begging him to start evacuating. Then she pounded on her door, demanding her guards let her out.

When no one answered, she gathered her mental strength and imagined singing the energy into the lock and the stones around it. Deeper and deeper the power sank, coiling so tight it felt like a wound-up spring. All she had to do was let go.

The explosion knocked her back, but she caught herself on a nearby table, her whole body shaking as she stared at the rubble around her now-open door.

If she could cause that much destruction with so little practice or energy . . .

This is what they want.

She bolted down the hallway as the floor rumbled again, trying to figure out the best plan. She could fight her way to the dungeon—but it would be four against one. And she might not get there in time.

The next tremor was sharper, sending dust swirling through the air. Too strong to be ignored, but too weak to be felt by anyone else—especially a bunch of people higher up at a party, nibbling treats and admiring the splendor and congratulating themselves on the day's victory.

And somewhere among them was Edaline.

Sophie changed direction, her goal clear as she doubled her speed, ducking down halls at random. The maze felt alive, stretching and spreading and shifting, anything to prevent her from getting where she needed to be.

A staircase looked familiar, but most of the doors it led to were locked. She finally chose a path through a hall lined with blue flames, hoping the light was a good sign.

The longer she ran, the more the tremors grew, until she could see cracks fissuring through the stones. The dust made her chest throb and her eyes water—or maybe that was the panic—as she started screaming Edaline's name.

More doorways. More stairs. More halls. More quakes gaining momentum—like distant thunder rolling in with the storm.

She tried to track Edaline with her mind, but her fear shattered her concentration. She'd nearly broken down when she recognized a new sound.

Footsteps.

"EDALINE?"

"SOPHIE?" Mr. Forkle shouted.

She sprinted toward the sound, taking a flight of stairs three at a time before she crashed hard into his bloated belly.

"Is Edaline with you?" she gasped.

"No—she went looking for you. Oralie ordered all the goblins to the dungeon after she talked to your mother. But none of them have made it back, and then the shaking started."

That explained why there'd been no guard outside her door. She couldn't think about what that might mean for poor Righty and Bunhead.

"The Councillors are trying to clear the castle," Mr. Forkle said, grabbing her arm and spinning her around. "I'll show you the fastest way to the exit."

Sophie jerked out of his grip. "Not until I find Edaline."

"Hopefully that's where she's waiting for you. I'd told her that if I found you, I'd send you there."

But there was no sign of Edaline at the exit.

"I'll find her," Mr. Forkle promised. "Get to the beach and go as far as you can. It's hard to know where the rubble will fall."

"I'm not leaving without my mom!"

He blocked her from charging past him. "We both know that's not what she would want. Go somewhere safe. I'll find her and get her out."

"How can you be so sure?"

"I found you, didn't I?"

Technically, *she'd* found *him*—but this wasn't a time for technicalities. It was a time for action. And hope. And trust.

So she did as he asked, and made her way to the courtyard. But when she looked at the once-gleaming castle—now dulled, with wavering walls and light leaking through the cracks—she couldn't walk away.

She couldn't risk a lifetime of wondering *What if I'd stayed?*

She turned and raced back in, keeping her left hand on the wall, hoping it'd help her find her way out when she needed the exit. Faster and faster she ran as the dust and pebbles pelted her, the ground splitting beneath her feet.

Her balance mostly held, but one particularly hard jolt knocked her over and she cried out as her knees crashed into the sharp ground.

"Sophie?" Edaline shouted. "Is that you?"

Just like that, she was on her feet again, coughing as she ran, lungs burning, hair flying—and then there was Edaline. Dusty and panting, her once-lovely gown now filthy and shredded.

She threw her arms around Sophie, hugging her even as she dragged her back the way she'd come. "We have to go."

They ran as fast as they could.

But it wasn't fast enough.

They'd just reached one of the widest halls when the floor collapsed beneath them, whipping their hearts into their throats as they plummeted.

They crashed into the next level down, stones raining all around them—one piece big enough to crush and kill.

Sophie watched it fall, trying to knock it back with her telekinesis. But it had too much momentum. It would've landed right on top of them if Edaline hadn't snapped her fingers, conjuring it away.

"Whoa, that's intense," Edaline said, shaking from the effort. "I've never dumped something that big in the void. But it worked. Come on—this place is coming down fast."

They'd only gone a few steps when a tremor split the wall, sending more stones hurtling toward them.

Edaline snapped her fingers and conjured them each away. But the effort took a huge toll.

"Here," Sophie said, ripping off her gloves. "It'll make you stronger."

Edaline pulled her close. "We'll get through this. I promise."

"Together," Sophie told her as she led Edaline forward.

Step by fumbling step, they made their way through the maze, and Edaline used her enhanced strength to conjure away anything that tried to crush them. Eventually, they spotted a crack that offered a teasing glint of the ocean. It wasn't wide enough to fit through, but Sophie sang the last of her energy into the stones, blasting their way outside to the cold, misty air.

With the final dregs of their energy, they scrambled over the glowing destruction and kept crawling and clawing until they reached a sandy clearing where the waves drowned out most of the noise.

"I think we'll be safe here," Sophie whispered, curling closer to Edaline to keep warm.

Edaline tangled her arms around her, quietly sobbing onto Sophie's shoulder. Sophie held her tight, promising it was almost over as she watched the dark waves roll across the shore.

She was about to close her eyes when she spotted four figures crossing the beach in long black cloaks.

When she blinked, they were gone.

EIGHTY

THERE YOU ARE," A CHOKED VOICE said, and Sophie slowly forced herself back to consciousness.

It hurt to focus through all the grit and dust crudding up her poor, dry eyes. But after a few seconds the world sharpened and she found a beautiful blond boy leaning over her.

Keefe's smile was somehow both breathtaking and heart-breaking, but it faded as he stroked her cheek and whispered, "When you and Edaline weren't with the survivors . . ."

"Edaline!" Sophie gasped, and blood flooded her brain as she sat up too quickly. She breathed through the head rush, searching the clearing until . . .

"She looks okay," Keefe said, squatting beside Edaline and using his dirty tunic to wipe some red off her bruised cheek. Edaline stirred at the touch, but not enough to wake up, and Sophie decided to let her sleep.

"Did everyone else make it out?" she whispered.

"Um . . . I know Councillor Terik's hurt pretty bad. I guess he might lose part of his leg—or maybe he lost it already? I couldn't tell. I saw the blood and I bolted so I wouldn't hurl all over everybody. But Elwin was working on him, so hopefully he'll be okay. Physic's here too. Most of the injuries looked pretty minor—just cuts and scratches. Broken bones. Nothing life threatening. Though I heard a lot of the goblins were down in the dungeon when it happened, and so far none of them have come back out."

Sophie shuddered.

The motion made her cough—she was pretty sure she'd be coughing up lumenite forever—and Keefe scooted closer, patting her back until the fit calmed.

She leaned against him, soaking up his warmth. "How bad do I look?"

"You could never look bad. But, um . . ." He brushed a finger across her forehead and showed her the red. "Want me to take you to Elwin?"

"No, he should work on the urgent cases first. Is Grady here? Or Fitz and Biana?"

"The island's on lockdown, even for friends and family,

until the dwarves stabilize the ruins—though Biana managed to sneak over for a couple of minutes. *Vanishers*. She was looking for you guys and totally tackled me when she saw me. I guess she didn't realize I'd already left the Neverseen, so there was a lot of threatening and punching. But I deserved it. I deserve so much worse." His throat closed off, and it took several tries to clear it. "All those months with them, thinking I was playing everything perfectly. I bet they were onto me the whole time. Just like my mom said. And they were planning this."

He punched the sand, sending it spraying around them.

Sophie held him tighter. "This is *not* your fault, Keefe. None of us realized what they were up to."

"Yeah, but I was *living* with them. Helping them. And all I have to show for it is this."

He reached into his pocket and pulled out two clear glass marbles. One with seven colorful tiny crystals set inside. The other with nine.

"You stole the caches?" Sophie whispered, watching them roll around his palm.

Together, the two gadgets contained sixteen Forgotten Secrets.

"It was the only thing that went right with my escape. And I was so smug about it. But who cares? I mean, seriously—who cares about a bunch of dusty old secrets when people can do *that*?" He gestured behind her, to the ruined castle.

"It's still huge," Sophie promised. "I know it doesn't feel like it—but the secrets in those caches have to be important. That's a victory!"

"A pretty weak one," he grumbled, trying to look away.

She reached up and turned his chin back, waiting for him to meet her eyes. "You have to let this go. Don't let this ruin what we have here."

"What do we have?"

She ignored the darkness shredding his tone. "We have a new start. A new lead. A new weapon in this fight."

Also a new world.

At the thought, Sophie forced herself to finally look back at the destruction. The majestic castle was nothing more than a few jagged pieces. When she squinted at it, she could almost imagine it was a giant gnarled hand, reaching out of the ground as the beast it belonged to tried to claw its way to freedom.

It also looked like a message. The Neverseen had just told the whole world that they were the ones to be feared.

"You should probably transmit to Fitz that you're okay," Keefe said quietly. "I hadn't found you when I saw Biana." He looked away again, swiping at his eyes. "If you hadn't been okay—"

"But I *am*," she assured him.

She closed her eyes, picturing Fitz's handsome face as she transmitted, *I'm okay, and so is Edaline. Please tell Grady for me. I promise I'll let you know more soon.*

"Okay, I let Fitz know," she told Keefe. "Have you seen Mr. Forkle?"

Keefe flinched at the name.

"What?" she asked.

The anguish on his face told her everything she needed to know.

"Hey," Keefe said holding her steady as she struggled to stand. "He's not dead, okay? He's just . . . missing."

"But he's missing because of me! I made him go back to find Edaline—and then I went back and found her anyway!"

"Deep breaths, Foster. Try to remember that you were 'missing' a few minutes ago, and yet you're fine. There's a lot of beach to search. A lot of debris to sort through."

She tried to see it like that, but the nausea wouldn't fade.

"Is anyone else missing?" she asked, trying to prepare herself for the worst.

But she definitely wasn't ready for him to whisper, "Oralie."

The world spun upside down and inside out. "We have to find them."

She was half crying, half hyperventilating as she stumbled forward—and immediately collapsed.

"Okay, how about you lean on me and we'll start searching the beach?" Keefe offered.

She shook her head. "We can't afford to waste time. If they're hurt . . ."

She closed her eyes, letting her concentration brew and

bubble before she stretched her mind across the space of the island. She could feel a ton of people on the beach—but no one she was looking for, so she fanned her thoughts toward the ruins and . . .

"I think I feel something! It's weak, but it's *there*."

"Can you isolate it? We can tell the dwarves and as soon as they've secured the structure they'll go in—"

"What do you mean 'as soon as they've secured the structure'?"

"King Enki said it's not safe for anyone to go in right now. All the parts that are still standing have big cracks compromising their integrity, so there's no way to know if the whole thing is going to come down—especially in this wind. He said he'd have it secured by sunset."

"That's too long," Sophie said. "They have to be hurt. Otherwise why aren't they here?"

Keefe tore his hand through his hair, shaking loose dust and sand. "What are the odds of me talking you out of this?"

"Definitely none."

"Then I guess I'm coming with you." He glanced at Edaline, who was still sleeping restlessly. "She's going to freak when she wakes up alone."

Sophie nodded and wrote, *I'm okay—went to find Forkle* in the sand, hoping this note would cause less trouble than her last one.

Then she headed for the rubble.

"Not that way," Keefe said, grabbing her hand and dragging

her into the shadows. "The dwarves are working just around that bend. If they spot us, they'll make sure we don't get anywhere near the castle. We'll have to sneak around the back and find another way in."

They didn't talk as they walked; Sophie was too busy trying to hold on to whatever weak connection she'd found to guide them.

"That looks pretty sturdy," Keefe said, pointing to an arched doorway half blocked by a fallen pillar. "Think you can run for it? We'll want to make sure we're not seen."

"Yeah, just give me a second." She took a couple of breaths and channeled some extra energy to her legs. "Okay."

Keefe nodded, peeking around the corner. "I think we're clear. Ready, go!"

The ground seemed to shift under their feet, but the entrance held steady as they ducked inside, into a dark, dusty hallway.

"We need to find a way up," Sophie whispered, trying not to think about the tightness in her chest. Seeing the cracked walls and floor dredged up flashbacks of the collapse. "It feels like they're above us."

Keefe squeezed her hand. "You okay?"

"Yeah." But she was glad he didn't let go as he took the lead, carving out a precarious path through the maze.

The staircase they found was too crumbling to trust.

"What if we levitate?" Keefe asked, pointing to where the center of the stairs had caved in. "It might be our best shot—but only if you're up for it."

"I'm up for it," Sophie said, rallying her concentration again.

Keefe held tight as they floated, and she had a feeling he was carrying her more than she was lifting herself, but she still fought to push against gravity as hard as she could.

"We need to stop here," she whispered. "It's this level."

She pointed left and Keefe took the lead again.

"So, quick question," he said as they picked their way through an especially dark hallway. "Is there a reason I keep getting this crazy rush every time I touch your hand?" He cleared his throat when he realized how that sounded, "What I mean is, your emotions always feel strong. But now they're on another level."

"It's because I manifested as an Enhancer. I'm supposed to wear gloves, but I took them off to help Edaline."

She figured he'd pick his most creative *I told you so* and gloat about knowing she'd manifest another ability. Instead, all he said was, "So that rush was an even clearer reading of your emotions?"

"Probably. Why?"

"No reason." But when she stole a glance from the side of her eye, she could see a glint of a grin in the dim light.

She was deciding whether to ask him about it, when a strained voice called, "Is someone there?"

"Oralie?" Sophie shouted, racing toward the sound. She hurdled bits of wall and furniture until she reached a crushed golden doorway. Inside was a disaster zone of toppled tables and cracked jeweled trees and twisted balustrades and fallen chunks of starry sky. The air was heavy with the scent of dusty stone and spoiling food and something decidedly iron.

"Over here," Oralie called, and they found her in the clearest corner leaning over a dark shape. Her hands looked glossy and red and they were pressing on . . .

"NO!" Sophie shouted, wobbling so hard, Keefe had to keep her from collapsing.

The shape beside Oralie moved, lifting its head and confirming Sophie's horrible suspicion.

"You kids really shouldn't have come," Mr. Forkle wheezed.

EIGHTY-ONE

WE HAVE TO GET YOU TO Elwin," Sophie said, dropping to her knees and trying to make sense of what she was seeing.

There was so much red—dripping from his mouth, streaming down his arms and forehead. But the real problem was his abdomen.

Oralie was doing her best to keep pressure on the wound, but the gash was so wide and so deep—and near so many important organs.

"Elwin can't help," Mr. Forkle said. "Trust me, I know enough about these things. Sometimes there is no fix. Even for elves. This is my swan song."

Sophie shook her head, grabbing a tablecloth off one of the fallen tables. "Help me lift him, Keefe, and then go get Elwin. If I tie this around his waist, it should hold enough pressure on the wound to give you guys time to get here. Bring Physic too. And a couple of goblins to carry him. And—"

"Miss Foster, this is one time when your stubbornness isn't going to make a difference," Mr. Forkle interrupted. "I've had this same conversation with Oralie. You have to let me go."

"NO!" Tears leaked down Sophie's cheeks. "No—they don't get to do this. They don't get to take you."

"It won't be as bad as you think." His voice had a horrible gurgle to it, but Sophie ordered herself not to think about it.

"I don't understand his wound," she told Oralie. "It almost looks like he's been stabbed."

Oralie looked away.

"It's okay, I'll tell her," Mr. Forkle said, reaching for Sophie's hands. They were so cold and slick—and red—it made it hard to listen as he said, "This is mostly my fault. You kept trying to tell me Gethen was important. And I kept stalling. Focusing on the wrong things. I should've been at his cell every day, fighting my way into his mind."

"I don't understand—did Gethen . . ."

Oralie nodded. "The sword."

That was all she could get out. But it was enough.

As Gethen broke the castle apart, he must've freed the sword in his cell.

But wouldn't it be ironic if someday I used that blade to chop off your pretty head?

"He came to make good on his threat," Mr. Forkle wheezed. "But I blocked him with a clever mind trick—the same one, incidentally, I used to make him back off that day at your human home, when he was dressed as a jogger and tried to take you away. And then I took out Brant. Gethen didn't like that. So he got me back."

"Wait—you took out Brant?" Keefe asked, his eyes widening when Oralie pointed to a cloth-wrapped lump in the corner. Definitely body-size.

"Mr. Forkle shoved him away from me right as a huge chunk of ceiling fell," Oralie whispered, pressing a fresh part of cloth over his oozing wound.

"And you're sure Brant's really . . . ," Keefe asked. "After Fintan . . ."

Oralie nodded. "His skull was crushed completely. Gray matter everywhere."

Something felt wrong with this new information—but Sophie couldn't piece it together. All she could hear were Mr. Forkle's labored breaths growing slower and wetter and heavier.

It was hard to see past the blood, but his body seemed to be in a strange in-between state. Like the ruckleberries were wearing off, but hadn't completely.

"I need the three of you to promise me something," he

rasped. "I need you to remove my body from here. Don't let anyone see it. And you must promise you won't do a planting in the Wanderling Woods. No one can know."

"Won't they have to know, though?" Sophie asked. "When the other yous disappear?"

"The Collective has always had a contingency plan. You'll see it soon enough. And don't worry—they'll make sure you still get the answers I owe you. Secrets never die." He pressed something cold and round into her palm, and Sophie realized it was the gadget where he stored the things he wanted to remember. "Give that to Granite." He turned to Councillor Oralie. "And make me a seed. Coil it with my hair, and bring it to Miss Foster to keep safe. She'll know when and where to plant it."

"How?" Sophie asked. "And why are we talking about this—you're not dying!"

"Yes, I am. But it's okay. I've done far more with this life than I ever could've imagined. I've lived five lives. I'm ready to surrender them. But before I do, I need you to promise you won't let this change you. Don't fall down the bitter, angry hole that death opens up inside of us. It's not a productive place to be. And there's no reason for it. I promise, I've made my peace. I've won more times than I've lost. I can be happy with that. Please be happy with me."

His eyes begged Sophie to assure him, but she couldn't make her mouth form the words.

It was too much.

Too hard.

Mr. Forkle grabbed Keefe's hand. "She needs you now more than ever. Don't let this break her."

"I won't," Keefe promised.

Mr. Forkle nodded, closing his eyes as he reached for Oralie. "Take care of my moonlark."

"No," Sophie said, shaking his shoulder. "Don't give up. Just hold on a little longer."

"Time is a funny thing. Once it's gone, it's gone. But then it passes to someone else. You'll do great things with it, Sophie. Wonderful, incredible things. I'm sorry I won't be there to see them. But don't let that stop you from living them. Dream. Fight. Love. Take risks. Allow yourself to be happy."

"There has to be something we can do," Sophie argued.

"You've already done it," he said. "Thank you for being brave enough to find me this one last time. You gave me the gift of goodbye."

He coughed again, a horrible rattly sound, and Sophie was crying too hard to hear him take his final breath.

But she saw his chest fall still.

Felt Keefe's arms wrap around her, letting her fall apart on his shoulder as he held on tight, keeping her together.

EIGHTY-TWO

ORALIE KEPT HER PROMISES, somehow making Mr. Forkle's body disappear from Lumenaria—and Brant's as well—before the dwarves arrived to help them out of the rubble. And a few days later she visited Sophie at Havenfield and gave her the Wanderling seed, tucked inside a golden locket for Sophie to wear.

Now that the new security measures had been completed—gates even higher than those at Everglen, plus a whole host of underground defenses—Sophie was back living at home, trying not to feel haunted by memories.

"You know what the worst part is?" she whispered as Oralie turned to leave. "I don't even know which 'him' this tree will be."

Oralie hesitated a second, then stepped close and pulled Sophie into a hug.

"I bet that's why he gave you the seed," she whispered. "When the time comes, it'll be one final secret you share together."

"Maybe," Sophie mumbled. "Most days, all I can think about is that he'll never see me heal Prentice. After all the years he waited."

Oralie cleared her throat, slowly pulling away. "Any word from the Collective on their contingency plan?"

"Not yet." She'd passed Mr. Forkle's gadget along to Granite, but as far as she knew, he hadn't tried to access it. "They're being super vague—but I guess I should be used to that."

Oralie smiled sadly. "Sometimes it's good when things don't change."

"And sometimes they have to."

Change was definitely a theme in the elvin world.

It was too early to tell if the attack at Lumenaria would bring all the leaders closer or farther apart. For the moment, they were working together to help the Council rebuild and recover. Elwin and Dex were collaborating on a prosthetic leg for Councillor Terik. And the dwarves and gnomes were still cleaning up the rubble. But nothing would ever be the same.

Sophie spent most of her time at home, hiding under the swaying branches of Calla's Panakes tree, listening to the gentle songs of the leaves and trying not to wonder if things would've been different if she'd thought to carry some of the healing blossoms with her.

Her friends visited, of course—Keefe more than any. He seemed to be taking his promise to Mr. Forkle very seriously. He wouldn't tell Sophie where he was staying—claiming it was safer if she didn't know. But he assured her that the Collective had set him up somewhere the Neverseen—and his mom—wouldn't be able to find him.

His new goal was "never ignore anything," and he'd started making long lists of things he'd remembered, either from his past or from his time with the Neverseen. It wasn't accomplishing much. But it made him feel better. And Sophie wanted to be as prepared as possible before they contacted Keefe's mom to find out what she wanted from her son.

Fitz was also a frequent visitor, and he kept his visits more casual, usually showing up to bring a thoughtful little gift to make her smile. That day he outdid himself, bringing her a sparkly red dragon charm he'd named Mini Snuggles.

"Biana thought she remembered you having a charm bracelet," he told her as he placed the tiny dragon in her gloved hand.

"I do." Grady and Edaline had bought it for her when they'd believed she was dead, as a way to commemorate their visits to her Wanderling. And Mr. Forkle had used it to sneak her secret messages a few times. But Sophie decided it was probably better not to share any of those less-than-cheerful memories and tarnish his amazing gift.

He sat down beside her, leaning against Calla's tree and studying the image she'd been staring at in her memory log.

Four black cloaked figures leaping away from the destruction of Lumenaria.

Four.

She was positive she hadn't imagined it.

Fintan.

Ruy.

Gethen.

And . . . who?

She'd assumed it was Brant, but now she knew he'd been dead by then. So who else could it have been?

It was possible that Alvar had met up with them. But Sophie had a much more terrifying theory. The goblins had told her there was another prisoner in that dungeon—connected to a Forgotten Secret.

And no other bodies had been found in the rubble.

When she'd told Oralie her theory, the pink-cheeked Councillor had blanched and made Sophie promise not to tell anyone. But Sophie would always share things with her friends.

None of them had been happy to hear they might be facing a mysterious new enemy, but Keefe had been quick to point out that the caches could hold the prisoner's identity. Dex was already working hard, trying to break through the caches' security, and Sophie had no doubt he'd figure it out.

"You know, I've been thinking," Fitz said, silencing her

thoughts as he closed the memory log and set it aside for the day. "You owe me a favor."

"I do?"

"Yep! We made a deal—remember? If you didn't call in your favor from me in one month, the favor became mine. And I hate to break it to you, but it's been way more than a month."

Sophie sighed. "I knew that deal was going to come back and haunt me. I should've just made something up and gotten the favor over with."

"You probably should have. But you didn't, so . . . I win!" He shook his hair, flashing his most adorably confident smile, "And I gotta say, I kinda get why you hesitated with this. It's a *big* decision. I mean, on the one hand, I could go for the obvious and make you share whatever secret you keep almost telling me."

Sophie's mouth turned to sandpaper.

"So that still freaks you out, huh? That might be proof that it needs to happen."

His eyes locked onto hers, refusing to let her look away. And when she swallowed, it was so loud, she was sure the entire world heard it.

"Or," he said. "We could skip the talking."

"And do what?" she asked, hating her voice for cracking.

"Any ideas?"

He was so close now, she could feel his breath warming her cheeks.

He leaned a tiny bit closer and someone cleared his throat—*very* loudly.

"Am I interrupting something?" Keefe asked. He'd raised one teasing eyebrow—but he wasn't smiling. And he was fidgeting. A *lot*.

Fitz leaned back against the tree again, his casual posture not matching his scowl. "Just finding new ways to drive Sophie crazy. I had to step up my game while you were gone. What about you?"

"Is that another list?" Sophie asked, pointing to the paper in Keefe's hands.

Somehow the question made Keefe look even more miserable, and he twisted the page so tightly, it looked ready to shred.

"Okay—this is just a theory, so . . . try not to freak out until we really think it through," he said carefully. "I almost don't want to tell you, but I don't want to find out I was right and regret it later."

"Yeah, you're definitely freaking me out," Sophie told him.

He took a deep breath. "Fine, here goes. You told me King Dimitar thinks the ogres who attacked Havenfield were actually after Lady Cadence. And I couldn't figure out why that bugged me. But I realized today that if Dimitar's right and that attack wasn't about Grady and Edaline, then that means the Neverseen never went after your family. And I *know* I heard them talk about it. A *lot*. That's what this whole list is—eleven different times where they mentioned a plan for your family."

"So what are you saying?" Fitz asked.

Keefe closed his eyes, looking a little green when he spoke again. "The thing is, when you look at this list, I wrote down verbatim what I remember them saying. And . . . they never once said 'Grady and Edaline.' They always said 'family.' I just assumed, since you live with them—and Grady's so powerful— that it had to be them. But . . . they're not your only family."

Everything turned cold as Sophie jumped to her feet. "You think they meant my human family?"

"I'm just saying it's *possible*. But you check on them pretty regularly, right? So—"

She shook her head, rubbing the knot under her chest to keep her panic at bay. "I haven't in a while. There's been so much going on, I forgot and . . ."

She ran inside, with Fitz and Keefe right behind her as she sprinted up the stairs and dug her round silver Spyball out of her desk drawer.

"Show me Connor, Kate, and Natalie Freeman," she whispered, using her family's new names.

The Spyball flashed warm in her hands, before red letters blazed across it.

Two terrifying words.

Not Found.

EIGHTY-THREE

BREATHE," KEEFE SAID, AND IT TOOK Sophie a second to realize she wasn't.

She sucked in a sharp breath, coughing as her chest tightened. "Why would the records not be found?" she whispered.

"It could mean lots of things," Fitz promised. "Maybe their names were changed. You weren't supposed to know them, right? So maybe the Councillors found out you did, and changed them. Or maybe my dad changed them after the Neverseen broke in to the registry, since it was hard to tell which files they'd accessed."

Or maybe finding out where her family had been hidden was the reason the Neverseen broke in to the registry in the first place. . . .

"I'll hail my dad to see what he knows. Hang on." Fitz ducked into the hall, and Sophie could hear him whispering into his Imparter as she clung to Keefe, staring blankly at the Spyball.

"Okay—I was kinda right," he said, stalking back into the room a couple of minutes later. "Their names weren't changed—but their registry files were deleted after the break-in, just to be extra safe. And Spyballs pick up registry feeds, so that's why it's saying 'not found.' There's no feed if there's no record to match it to. Make sense?"

Sophie nodded, taking lots of slow, deep breaths and trying to convince herself that the crisis was over.

But it didn't feel over. And it wouldn't. Not until . . .

"I need to see them," she said. "Can you get their address from your dad? I don't care if he gets mad. I *need* to see them."

"Yeah, one sec," Fitz said, slipping back into the hall again for a longer conversation.

"It's going to be okay, Foster," Keefe promised, brushing a rebellious tear off her cheek. "Whatever this is, we'll figure it out and fix it."

"My dad can't give me the address," Fitz said as he returned, "but he has a leaping crystal that goes there. And he'll take you right now for a quick check, if you're ready."

"I am," Sophie told him, already untying her cape. Her tunic, pants, and gloves still looked a little elfy, but she wasn't going to waste time changing.

"I'm coming with you," Fitz said, throwing his cape on the bed next to hers.

"Ditto," Keefe said, doing the same.

"As am I," Sandor announced as he melted out of the shadows. Now that he and Grizel were spending more time together, she'd been teaching him to improve his stealth.

"I'm in as well," Grizel said, appearing at Sandor's side.

Sophie didn't have the energy to argue. "Fine—just try not to look so gobliny."

"Gobliny?" Sandor repeated as Sophie raced downstairs to answer the door.

"Really, Miss Foster, I'm positive you have no reason to worry," Alden assured her as he pulled her in for a hug. "Ready to go?"

Sophie felt anything but ready—but she grabbed Alden's hand as the rest of them linked into a circle, and they all stepped into the beam of bluish light and zipped away.

The house was bigger than Sophie had expected. Small by elvin standards, but at least triple the size of her old house in San Diego. Tudor-style, so it looked like it belonged in a fairy tale—especially butted up against the thick evergreen forest. They weren't in a neighborhood, so there were no other houses around. But there were two cars parked in the driveway and lights on in a bedroom upstairs.

"See?" Alden said. "All is calm and peaceful."

"Maybe," Sophie said. "But I need to see them."

Alden grabbed her shoulder to stop her. "*That* would be very bad. You know how memory wipes work—the Washers can't possibly get every memory. And all it takes is the right trigger and . . ."

He snapped his fingers.

"I didn't say I'm going to let them see me," she argued. "Some of the windows have the curtains open. I just need to take a quick peek. Make sure they're really in there. I promise they'll never know I was here."

Alden sighed. "Be *careful*—and do not be seen."

Sophie nodded and sprinted across the grass, with Fitz and Keefe keeping pace beside her, and Sandor and Grizel on alert a few steps back.

Everyone almost had a heart attack when a dog started barking from the backyard—a deep, husky howl that could probably be heard for miles around.

"Think that'll make them come outside?" Fitz asked as they ducked under the front bay window and hid among the bushes.

"If they do, we'll leap away as soon as I hear the front door," Sophie promised, holding up her home crystal to prove it.

She hadn't realized how hard she was shaking—though she shouldn't have been surprised. She hadn't been this close to her family in more than a year—closer to two years, actually.

And much as she understood why she couldn't let them see her, she also had to admit she didn't want to—not because she was afraid they'd remember her.

Because she knew how much it would hurt if they *didn't*.

"Deep breaths," Keefe said, hooking his arm through hers and pulling her closer to the window.

"It sounds quiet in there," Fitz whispered. "Think it's safe to peek?"

Sophie nodded, doing a silent countdown in her head.

Three . . . two . . . one.

She popped up on her knees, careful to only raise herself up high enough to peer through the spotted glass.

"Everything okay?" Fitz asked when she didn't duck back down.

Sophie frowned. "The house is a mess. *Way* messier than my mom would ever allow it to be."

"People change," Keefe said, popping up to see for himself.

"I guess." But Sophie was starting to learn that when dread pooled up inside her, it was because her instincts were a couple of steps ahead.

Two cars in the driveway.

Dog barking early in the morning with no one shushing it.

Messy house.

Too quiet.

Not found.

This wouldn't end well.

"I have to get inside," Sophie said, ignoring Sandor's protests as she marched over to the door and tried the handle.

It was locked, but her parents still kept a spare key under the smallest flowerpot.

Before she could change her mind, she unlocked the door and slipped inside.

Her heart sank with every step, every new detail her eyes picked up. Dirty dishes in the sink that had to be at least a week old. Papers strewn all over the tables and floor.

"Seems pretty quiet," Keefe said behind her.

"Too quiet," she whispered. No human thoughts blaring into her brain—though human minds did quiet down while they were sleeping.

The stairs creaked as they climbed, but no one startled awake. And the master bedroom was empty. Bed unmade. Lights still on.

"Maybe they're on vacation," Fitz said, offering whatever weak hope he could.

It was Sandor who finally crushed it, calling from downstairs. "The yard smells like ash. As does the house."

Sophie closed her eyes and nodded, letting the tears she'd been fighting slip down her cheeks.

The Neverseen used ash to disguise their scent.

"They were here," she whispered. "They took them. Why would they take them?"

This couldn't just be about controlling her. If that were all it was, they'd have let her know the second they had her family. Instead they'd kept quiet. Letting her discover it all on her own. Maybe even hoping she wouldn't.

Keefe took her by the shoulders, his expression fierce, determined. "I don't know what's going on. But we'll find them, okay? We'll get them back. I *promise.*"

"But we don't even know where they are—where to start," Sophie reminded him. The sobs were coming fast and furious now, but she didn't fight them back.

She was so tired of fighting.

Tired of losing.

"There has to be a clue," Fitz said. "We'll take this whole place apart if we have to. Then we'll find them and we'll bring them back and we'll make sure they're happy and safe and that nothing bad ever happens to them again, okay?"

No—it wasn't okay.

It would never be okay.

The Neverseen had her family!

"Does 'Nightfall' mean anything?" a shaky female voice said behind them, eliciting quite a few gasps. "That's what they said. They didn't know I was hiding here—one of them had talked about listening for thoughts, so I let my mind go dark and silent. And I heard them say, 'Take them to Nightfall.'"

"Nightfall?" Keefe repeated as Sophie spun around, following the trail of panicked human thoughts to the voice.

There.

On the wall behind them, a door was open just a crack. Probably a closet or a bathroom.

"It's okay to come out," Fitz promised. "We're here to help."

Several seconds passed before the door swung open and a young girl stepped slowly out.

She was taller than Sophie remembered. Thinner. Her curly brown hair cut short. But even with all those changes, Sophie would've recognized her little sister anywhere.

Her sister's eyebrows pressed together, like she was straining extra hard to figure out what to say.

When their eyes met, she whispered, "Sophie?"

ACKNOWLEDGMENTS

Yay—you're still here! That means you're still speaking to me!

(Or perhaps you're still clinging to the hope that I wouldn't be cruel enough to pause the story there. But after what I did to you at the end of *Neverseen*, surely you know better. *Mwahahahahaha.*)

I know these game-changer endings are a severe test of your patience—and I promise I don't do them to torture you! (Though the torture *is* a fun bonus.) Each book in a series is really more like a chapter in a much longer story—so the good news is, this means there are more books ahead!

And you guys are the reason this series keeps growing. If you weren't reading Sophie's story and doing all of the fantastic things you do to spread the word, I would've had to cut things short long ago. So thank you, thank you, thank you!!!

I also could *not* have gotten through the rather stressful process of writing this book if it weren't for the support of an incredible group of people.

Mom and Dad, I definitely owe you a trophy for Best Promoters Ever for championing my book to basically everyone you talk to for longer than five seconds, and for baking hundreds of cupcakes for my launch parties.

Laura Rennert, you deserve the SuperAgent trophy—as does everyone at Andrea Brown Literary and the Taryn Fagerness Agency—for all of the tireless ways you keep my career on track.

Liesa Abrams Mignogna, your trophy is shaped like a Batmobile because you really are the Batgirl of all editors. Thank you for not strangling me for falling so behind schedule, and for continuing to believe in Sophie and crew. I also want to give the Most Awesome Publisher trophy to everyone at Simon & Schuster, especially Mara Anastas, Mary Marotta, Jon Anderson, Katherine Devendorf, Julie Doebler, Emma Sector, Carolyn Swerdloff, Catherine Hayden, Tara Grieco, Jennifer Romanello, Jodie Hockensmith, Faye Bi, Lucille Rettino, Michelle Fadlalla, Anthony Parisi, Candace McManus, Matt Pantoliano, Amy Bartram, Mike Rosamilia, Christina Pecorale, Gary Urda, and the entire sales team. And the Most Gorgeous Cover trophy goes to Karin Paprocki and Jason Chan. I don't know how you guys keep upping your game, but I adore you for it.

Cécile Pournin and everyone else at Lumen Editions deserve the Undeniably Awesome French Publisher trophy for their unfailing enthusiasm and care for this series. And Mathilde Tamae-bouhon earns the Translator of the Year trophy for bravely tackling my insanely long books. I also want to give the Outstanding International Fans trophy to my French readers, who wait so patiently for the translated editions.

Kari Olson, I owe you the Ultimate Brainstormer trophy for helping me puzzle out this plot and constantly talking me off the "I'll never not be writing this book" ledge. And Victoria Morris, I give you the Fabulous Beta Reader prize for reading so quickly and chiming in with encouragement right when I need it most.

And the Best Support Group trophy goes to Erin Bowman, Lisa Cannon, Christa Desir, Debra Driza, Nikki Katz, Lisa Mantchev, Sara McClung, Ellen Oh, Andrea Ortega, Cindy Pon, CJ Redwine, James Riley, J. Scott Savage, Amy Tintera, Kasie West, Natalie Whipple, and Sarah Wylie. (And to anyone I've forgotten, here's the Most Forgiving Friend trophy for understanding how deadline brain constantly fails me.)

I also have to give the Ultimate Champions trophy to all of the teachers, librarians, bloggers, and booksellers who've done so many tremendous things to keep this series growing, especially Mel Barnes, Alyson Beecher, Katie Bartow, Lynette Dodds, Maryelizabeth Hart, Faith Hochhalter, Heather Laird, Katie Laird, Kim Laird, Barbara Mena, Brandi Stewart, Kristin

Trevino, Andrea Vuleta, and so many others. If I listed you all, this book would double in thickness, which might cause serious back injury to my poor readers. So I'll just give every single one of you a round of applause.

applauds

And now, I'll stop rambling and get back to writing. On to book six!